D0865165

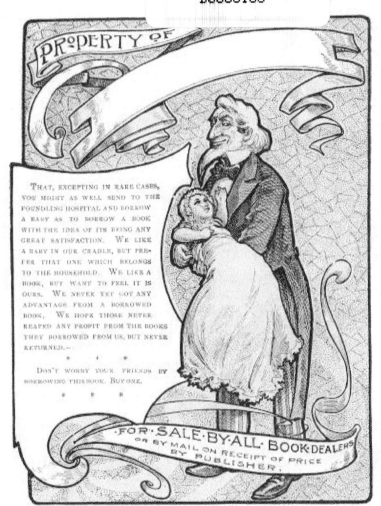

PROPERTY OF

THAT, EXCEPTING IN RARE CASES, YOU MIGHT AS WELL SEND TO THE FOUNDLING HOSPITAL AND BORROW A BABY AS TO BORROW A BOOK WITH THE IDEA OF ITS BEING ANY GREAT SATISFACTION. WE LIKE A BABY IN OUR CRADLE, BUT PREFER THAT ONE WHICH BELONGS TO THE HOUSEHOLD. WE LIKE A BOOK, BUT WANT TO FEEL IT IS OURS. WE NEVER YET GOT ANY ADVANTAGE FROM A BORROWED BOOK. WE HOPE THOSE NEVER REAPED ANY PROFIT FROM THE BOOKS THEY BORROWED FROM US, BUT NEVER RETURNED.—

* * *

DON'T WORRY YOUR FRIENDS BY BORROWING THIS BOOK. BUY ONE.

* * *

FOR · SALE · BY · ALL · BOOK · DEALERS OR BY MAIL ON RECEIPT OF PRICE BY PUBLISHER.

PESCHEL PRESS – P.O. BOX 132 – HERSHEY, PA 17033 – EMAIL: PESCHEL@PESCHELPRESS.COM – WWW.PESCHELPRESS.COM

The Complete, Annotated Mysterious Affair at Styles

The
Complete,
Annotated
Mysterious Affair
at Styles

By
Agatha Christie

With Notes, Essays and Chronologies
by

Bill Peschel

PESCHEL PRESS ~ HERSHEY, PA

Cover design by Bill Peschel.

www.peschelpress.com

ISBN-13: 978-1-950347-01-8

ISBN-10: 1-950347-01-X

Second edition: March 2019

To Teresa,

For Trusting and Believing

PREFACE

The Complete, Annotated Mysterious Affair at Styles contains an array of features.

Footnotes: There are two types: basic definitions that most readers can ignore, and deeper explanations of words, idioms, cultural references and discussions about Agatha Christie and *Styles*.

To figure out what to annotate, several people of various ages and reading levels read *Styles* and marked the words they did not understand. They noted cultural and literary references, words understandable to British readers but not Americans, such as flat, wilful murder, and wardrobe. In short, anything they didn't know. What is the purpose of a spill vase? What is a land girl? Where is Essex? Times change and so things every reader was familiar with in 1920 are often forgotten today. With the passing years, even big events such as World War I need an explanation.

Once that was finished, I went through the suggestions to define the words according to how they are used in the story and to explain the meaning and source of the idioms and phrases in *Styles*.

Interpretations: Explanations of subjects possibly unfamiliar to readers, such as the subtleties of England's social classes, the inquest system, and the current value of money.

Essays: In the appendices are stories about how *Styles* was written and Christie's development as a writer, how Poirot was created, her use of racial stereotypes, the history of strychnine, the murderous Dr. Palmer, and more. They can help deepen your understanding of the novel and explain certain events and cultural references that were important in Christie's time.

Chronology of Christie's life and works: Including significant events, moves, home purchases, publication info and lists of her novels and short-story collections, her Poirot, Miss Marple, Inspector Battle, and Tommy and Tuppence books, and the novels published under her Mary Westmacott pen-name.

Reference works: A list of books and websites consulted in the making of *Styles*. Those of special interest to Christie fans are highlighted.

The Quotable *Styles*: A collection drawn from the novel and TV show of sayings by and about Poirot, his observations on detection, and other subjects.

About this edition: The novel was copyrighted 1920 by John Lane Co. and renewed in 1948 by Agatha Christie Mallowan. The U.S. copyright expired in 1976, and will expire in Great Britain and European Union countries in 2046, 70 years after Christie's death in 1976. Yes, this book will be under copyright in these countries for 126 years.

To maintain the flavor of the original publication, no attempt has been made to modernize the spelling of words.

Now for a personal request.

If you like this book, tell your friends. Mention it on your social network or the website where you bought this book. Email me at peschel@peschelpress.com. Tell me I'm not alone in thinking annotations and extras help the reader and enhance the reading experience.

Word of mouth spurs sales, helps me support my family and encourages me to publish more annotations.

Bill Peschel
Hershey, Pa.
April 2013

Cast of Characters

Hercule Poirot. Belgium's greatest detective. After his retirement from the police force, Poirot became a private inquiry agent and worked throughout Europe. Known for his faith in order, method, and his "little grey cells" while disdaining tangible evidence such as footprints and cigarette ash. He met his friend, Capt. Arthur Hastings, during an investigation when the latter worked for Lloyd's of London. As *Styles* opens in 1917, Poirot is a refugee from the German occupation of Belgium and the guest of Emily Inglethorp, staying at Leastways Cottage near her home at Styles Court.

Captain Arthur Hastings. Poirot's friend and companion in detection. Hastings met Poirot while working for Lloyd's of London. While Poirot lamented his friend's absence of order and method and thought him possessed "of an imbecility to make one afraid," he was capable of "stumbling over the truth unawares." In 1917, Hastings was recuperating from war injuries in London.

John Cavendish. The 45-year-old husband of Mary Cavendish and stepson of Emily Inglethorp. He lives at Styles Court, the family home in Essex, where his friend Hastings had visited often as a child.

Mary Cavendish. John's wife, who gave Hastings "the impression of a wild untamed spirit in an exquisitely civilized body." Her friendship — and something more? — with Dr. Bauerstein would alienate her husband's affections.

Emily Inglethorp. The dominating owner of Styles Court and stepmother to John and Lawrence Cavendish. Despite being over 70, she was "an energetic, autocratic personality, somewhat inclined to charitable and social notoriety, with a fondness for opening bazaars and playing the Lady Bountiful." It was her energetic efforts to find housing for Belgian refugees that brought Poirot to Leastways Cottage, the lodge outside Styles Court.

Alfred Inglethorp. Emily Inglethorp's younger second husband, and "a bare-faced fortune hunter" to John Cavendish. Poirot, however, would bestow on him the ultimate compliment of being a "man of method."

Lawrence Cavendish. Emily Inglethorp's stepson. He had studied medicine and taken his degree, but did not practice. Now 40, he'd "gone through every penny he ever had publishing rotten verses in fancy bindings" and was dependent on his stepmother for financial support.

Cynthia Murdoch. Emily Inglethorp's guest at Styles. Mrs. Inglethorp went to school with Emily's mother and took Emily in after her parents died and left her penniless. She works in the dispensary at the Red Cross hospital in Tadminster, where she provides Emily with bromide powders. She likes to display her talent for impersonating male characters at parties.

Evelyn (Evie) Howard. The "excellent specimen of well-balanced English beef and brawn" and factotum at Styles. She is also Emily's friend and unhappy that she had married Alfred.

Dr. Bauerstein. A visitor taking a rest cure in Styles St. Mary for a nervous breakdown. The tall, bearded doctor is considered the greatest living expert on poisons. His friendship with Mary Cavendish will cause dissension among the inhabitants of Styles.

Dr. Wilkins. Mrs. Inglethorp's doctor who provided her tonic.

Dorcas. The parlourmaid who assists Poirot with his inquiries.

Wells. The middle-aged man with the typical lawyer's mouth who handles Mrs. Inglethorp's legal affairs.

Elizabeth Wells. The second housemaid at Styles, who testifies about the state of the front door.

Manning. Head gardener at Styles who plays a role in Emily Inglethorp's legal affairs.

William Earl. The under-gardener and one of Manning's two assistants, the other being, according to Dorcas, "a new-fashioned woman gardener in breeches and such-like."

Amy Hill. The shop assistant who testifies about a legal proceeding involving William.

Albert Mace. The chemist's assistant who testifies about who he sold strychnine to before the fatal event.

Sir Ernest Heavywether, K.C. A renowned barrister. He was "famous all over England for the unscrupulous manner in which he bullied witnesses."

Mr. Phillips, K.C. The prosecutor with the difficult task of convicting a defendant Poirot is not convinced is guilty.

Detective-Inspector James Japp. The man from Scotland Yard who appreciates Poirot's skills.

Superintendent Summerhaye. Japp's partner in the investigation. He is suspicious of Poirot's abilities.

Mrs. Raikes. Farmer Raikes' wife, a young woman of a gipsy type with "a vivid wicked little face." Her assignations with one of the residents of the Hall will raise suspicions.

TABLE OF CONTENTS

To My Mother[1]

---

[1] *Mother.* Clarissa (Clara) Miller (1854-1926) encouraged Christie's writing. When she ran into trouble finishing the first draft of *Styles*, Clara suggested that she spend two weeks alone at a Dartmoor hotel to finish it.

Chapter I

I Go to Styles

THE INTENSE INTEREST AROUSED in the public by what was known at the time as "The Styles Case" has now somewhat subsided. Nevertheless, in view of the world-wide notoriety which attended it, I have been asked, both by my friend Poirot and the family themselves, to write an account of the whole story. This, we trust, will effectually silence the sensational rumours which still persist.

I will therefore briefly set down the circumstances which led to my being connected with the affair.

I had been invalided home from the Front;[1] and, after spending some months in a rather depressing Convalescent Home,[2] was given a month's sick leave. Having no near relations or friends, I was trying to make up my mind what to do, when I ran across John Cavendish. I had seen very little of him for some years. Indeed, I had never known him particularly well. He was a good fifteen years my senior, for one thing, though he hardly looked his forty-five years. As a boy, though, I had often stayed at Styles, his mother's place in Essex.[3]

---

[1] Captain Hastings had been wounded on the Western Front. Styles is set during World War I (1914-1918) when Germany, Austria-Hungary, and the Ottoman Empire fought Russia on the Eastern Front, France and Great Britain on the Western Front, and Italy on the Southern Front.
[2] A hospital for wounded soldiers. During the war, many country homes were turned into convalescent homes where patients received medical treatment and could recuperate in pleasant surroundings.
[3] A county northeast of London.

We had a good yarn[4] about old times, and it ended in his inviting me down to Styles to spend my leave there.

"The mater[5] will be delighted to see you again—after all those years," he added.

"Your mother keeps well?" I asked.

"Oh, yes. I suppose you know that she has married again?"

I am afraid I showed my surprise rather plainly. Mrs. Cavendish, who had married John's father when he was a widower with two sons, had been a handsome woman of middle-age as I remembered her. She certainly could not be a day less than seventy now. I recalled her as an energetic, autocratic personality, somewhat inclined to charitable and social notoriety, with a fondness for opening bazaars and playing the Lady Bountiful.[6] She was a most generous woman, and possessed a considerable fortune of her own.

Their country-place, Styles Court, had been purchased by Mr. Cavendish early in their married life. He had been completely under his wife's ascendancy,[7] so much so that, on dying, he left the place to her for her lifetime, as well as the larger part of his income; an arrangement that was distinctly unfair to his two sons. Their step-mother, however, had always been most generous to them; indeed, they were so young at the time of their father's remarriage that they always thought of her as their own mother.

Lawrence, the younger, had been a delicate youth. He had qualified as a doctor but early relinquished the profession of medicine, and lived at home while pursuing literary ambitions; though his verses never had any marked success.

---

[4] Swapping stories. The word was inspired by sailors during the age of sail, who would pass the time during the tedious process of making ropes by telling tales.

[5] British schoolboy slang for mother, from the Latin word *mater*.

[6] A character from the romantic comedy *The Beaux' Stratagem* (1707) by George Farquhar. Lady Bountiful was a charitable but patronizing woman from an aristocratic family.

[7] Controlling influence.

John practiced for some time as a barrister, but had finally settled down to the more congenial life of a country squire.[8] He had married two years ago, and had taken his wife to live at Styles, though I entertained a shrewd suspicion that he would have preferred his mother to increase his allowance, which would have enabled him to have a home of his own. Mrs. Cavendish, however, was a lady who liked to make her own plans, and expected other people to fall in with them, and in this case she certainly had the whip hand,[9] namely: the purse strings.

John noticed my surprise at the news of his mother's remarriage and smiled rather ruefully.

"Rotten little bounder[10] too!" he said savagely. "I can tell you, Hastings, it's making life jolly difficult for us. As for Evie —you remember Evie?"

"No."

"Oh, I suppose she was after your time. She's the mater's factotum, companion, Jack of all trades! A great sport—old Evie! Not precisely young and beautiful, but as game as they make them."[11]

---

[8] *Barrister:* With solicitor, one of two classes of lawyers in the British legal system. The solicitor works with the client and communicates the facts of the case to the barrister, who speaks on the client's behalf in court. *Congenial:* Pleasant. *Country squire:* The word squire has changed in meaning since its origins in medieval times as a stage a boy moves through to become a knight. By the late 17th century, the squire was the head of the family that owned land around a village. Over time, it mutated into an informal title for men who were not members of the nobility but who still commanded authority or respect, then as a role (e.g., "playing the country squire").

[9] A colloquial phrase meaning to hold an advantage over another. Probably derived from the way drivers of wagons or carriages use a whip to direct their horses.

[10] A socially unacceptable or ill-mannered man, probably derived from the idea that the miscreant has stepped beyond the boundary of good behavior.

[11] *Factotum:* A general servant with wide-ranging responsibilities. From the Latin for "do everything." *Jack of all trades:* A person capable of performing many skills. The phrase appears in print as early as 1612 in a book of prison experiences that talks of "Some broken Cittizen, who hath plaid Jack of all trades." Soon afterwards, it began its path toward the derogatory variation

"You were going to say—?"

"Oh, this fellow! He turned up from nowhere, on the pretext of being a second cousin or something of Evie's, though she didn't seem particularly keen to acknowledge the relationship. The fellow is an absolute outsider, anyone can see that. He's got a great black beard, and wears patent leather boots in all weathers![12] But the mater cottoned[13] to him at once, took him on as secretary—you know how she's always running a hundred societies?"

I nodded.

"Well, of course the war has turned the hundreds into thousands. No doubt the fellow was very useful to her. But you could have knocked us all down with a feather when, three months ago, she suddenly announced that she and Alfred were engaged! The fellow must be at least twenty years younger than she is! It's simply bare-faced fortune hunting; but there you are—she is her own mistress, and she's married him."

"It must be a difficult situation for you all."

"Difficult! It's damnable!"

Thus it came about that, three days later, I descended from the train at Styles St. Mary, an absurd little station, with no apparent reason for existence, perched up in the midst of green fields and country lanes. John Cavendish was waiting on the platform, and piloted me out to the car.

"Got a drop or two of petrol still, you see," he remarked.

"Jack of all trades, master of none." The name Jack has been used to represent the common man as early as the 14th century. The name shows up in folklore — Jack Spratt, little Jack Horner, Jack Frost — and a number of trades, such as lumberjack and steeplejack. *Game:* Eager to do anything.

[12] Patent leather is a fine-grained cow hide that's been polished to a waterproof glossy finish. The locals would never think to wear such fancy shoes and would be suspicious of anyone who did.

[13] To take a fancy to or agree with. Possibly derived from the habit of cotton threads to adhere to rough or napped material.

"Mainly owing to the mater's activities."

The village of Styles St. Mary was situated about two miles from the little station, and Styles Court lay a mile the other side of it. It was a still, warm day in early July. As one looked out over the flat Essex country, lying so green and peaceful under the afternoon sun, it seemed almost impossible to believe that, not so very far away, a great war[14] was running its appointed course. I felt I had suddenly strayed into another world. As we turned in at the lodge gates,[15] John said:

"I'm afraid you'll find it very quiet down here, Hastings."

"My dear fellow, that's just what I want."

"Oh, it's pleasant enough if you want to lead the idle life. I drill with the volunteers twice a week, and lend a hand at the farms. My wife works regularly 'on the land'.[16] She is up at five every morning to milk, and keeps at it steadily until lunchtime. It's a jolly good life taking it all round—if it weren't for that fellow Alfred Inglethorp!" He checked the car suddenly, and glanced at his watch. "I wonder if we've time to pick up Cynthia. No, she'll have started from the hospital by now."

---

[14] The term was in common use before it was applied to what we now call World War I. After Germany won the Franco-Prussian War in 1870, the next "great war" was anticipated by a genre of invasion literature with England as the target. Germany played the villain in George Tomkyns Chesney's *The Battle of Dorking* (1871), but in William Le Queux's *The Great War in England in 1897* (1894), it was a coalition of French and Russian troops that attacked and Germany who came to England's rescue.

[15] A small house or cottage on the grounds of a large home reserved for the gatekeeper, gardener or other workers. Derived from the medieval Latin *lobia* or *laubia* for a hall or lobby (that is, a room near the entrance of a building).

[16] *Volunteers:* The Volunteer Training Corps was a militia formed during the war to repel a possible German invasion. The government issued uniform guidelines and regulations, but required the units to provide their own clothing and, until 1917, their own weapons. *On the land:* Mary Cavendish was working as a volunteer helping a farmer with the chores. The war caused a severe shortage of agricultural workers, and women were recruited to fill the gap. See the essay "An Army of Land Girls" in the appendix for more details.

"Cynthia! That's not your wife?"

"No, Cynthia is a protégée of my mother's, the daughter of an old schoolfellow of hers, who married a rascally solicitor. He came a cropper, and the girl was left an orphan and penniless. My mother came to the rescue, and Cynthia has been with us nearly two years now. She works in the Red Cross Hospital at Tadminster, seven miles away."[17]

As he spoke the last words, we drew up in front of the fine old house. A lady in a stout tweed skirt,[18] who was bending over a flower bed, straightened herself at our approach.

"Hullo, Evie, here's our wounded hero! Mr. Hastings—Miss Howard."

Miss Howard shook hands with a hearty, almost painful, grip. I had an impression of very blue eyes in a sunburnt face. She was a pleasant-looking woman of about forty, with a deep voice, almost manly in its stentorian[19] tones, and had a large sensible square body, with feet to match—these last encased in good thick boots. Her conversation, I soon found, was couched in the telegraphic style. [20]

---

[17] *Protégée:* The female form of protégé, meaning a person who is guided by another. From the French word *protéger* for "protected." *Solicitor:* A class of lawyer that did legal work outside of court. When an advocate was needed in the courtroom, the solicitor would call in a barrister and "instruct" him on the particulars of the case. *Cropper:* To fall. Derived from falling "neck and crop," a variation of "head over heels." The phrase eventually became applied to a major failure or a fatal injury. *Tadminster:* A fictional village. Christie rarely set her books in identifiable locations, apart from major cities such as London and her native Devon.

[18] *Stout:* Fat in this case, although the word could also mean firm, brave and sturdy. *Tweed:* A rough woolen fabric woven in a check or herringbone (V-shaped) pattern.

[19] A powerful voice. Inspired by Stentor, the herald in the *Iliad* whose voice, according to Homer, "was as powerful as fifty voices of other men." In Book 7 of *Politics*, Aristotle wrote, "For who can be the general of such a vast multitude, or who the herald, unless he have the voice of a Stentor?"

[20] Concise or terse. A telegraph is any device used to send messages through signals seen by sight. (It was U.S. inventor Samuel Morse (1791-1872) who took the word and applied it to his invention that used electricity and wires

"Weeds grow like house afire. Can't keep even with 'em. Shall press you in. Better be careful."

"I'm sure I shall be only too delighted to make myself useful," I responded.

"Don't say it. Never does. Wish you hadn't later."

"You're a cynic, Evie," said John, laughing. "Where's tea to-day—inside or out?"[21]

"Out. Too fine a day to be cooped up in the house."

"Come on then, you've done enough gardening for to-day. 'The labourer is worthy of his hire', you know.[22] Come and be refreshed."

"Well," said Miss Howard, drawing off her gardening gloves, "I'm inclined to agree with you."

She led the way round the house to where tea was spread under the shade of a large sycamore.

---

to send signals.) The need to send messages fast and accurately required boiling it down to as few words as possible.

[21] *Cynic:* Someone who believes a person is motivated solely by self-interest. Named for the Cynics, the school of philosophers in ancient Greece who believed in living a simple life free of possessions and rejecting sex, wealth, power and fame. Their habit of scorning others for not following their example probably inspired the negative attitude that we regard as cynicism. *To-day:* The word "today" was originally two words that over time was melded into one. People speaking Old English, an early form of the English language from roughly 650 to 1150, would say "to dæge" for "on (the) day." Sometime during the 16th century, the word came to be written with the hyphen and would stay that way until the early 20th century. The same process happened with "tomorrow," which you will see written as "to-morrow" (in Old English they'd say "to morgenne" for "on (the) morrow").

[22] From Luke 10:7, in which Jesus appointed 70 disciples — 72 in some versions — and told them to travel "as lambs among wolves" to spread his message: "And into whatsoever house ye enter, first say, Peace be to this house. And if the son of peace be there, your peace shall rest upon it: if not, it shall turn to you again. And in the same house remain, eating and drinking such things as they give: for the labourer is worthy of his hire." A similar phrase also appears in 1 Timothy 5:18.

A figure rose from one of the basket chairs,[23] and came a few steps to meet us.

"My wife, Hastings," said John.

I shall never forget my first sight of Mary Cavendish. Her tall, slender form, outlined against the bright light; the vivid sense of slumbering fire that seemed to find expression only in those wonderful tawny[24] eyes of hers, remarkable eyes, different from any other woman's that I have ever known; the intense power of stillness she possessed, which nevertheless conveyed the impression of a wild untamed spirit in an exquisitely civilised body—all these things are burnt into my memory. I shall never forget them.

She greeted me with a few words of pleasant welcome in a low clear voice, and I sank into a basket chair feeling distinctly glad that I had accepted John's invitation. Mrs. Cavendish gave me some tea, and her few quiet remarks heightened my first impression of her as a thoroughly fascinating woman. An appreciative listener is always stimulating, and I described, in a humorous manner, certain incidents of my Convalescent Home, in a way which, I flatter myself, greatly amused my hostess. John, of course, good fellow though he is, could hardly be called a brilliant conversationalist.

At that moment a well remembered voice floated through the open French window[25] near at hand:

"Then you'll write to the Princess after tea, Alfred? I'll write to Lady Tadminster for the second day, myself. Or shall we wait until we hear from the Princess? In case of a refusal, Lady Tadminster might open it the first day, and Mrs. Crosbie the second. Then there's the Duchess—about the school fete."[26]

---

[23] A chair for outdoor or porch use made from woven rattan or wicker.

[24] A warm, sandy color. From the Anglo-French word for "tanned."

[25] A single or matching pair of frames with panes of glass set in an outside wall that are large enough to act as either doors or windows.

[26] Here is Mrs. Inglethorp playing the Lady Bountiful as she plans a charity bazaar — a two-day affair in which donated items will be sold — and a school fête — an event featuring entertainment and activities to raise money

There was the murmur of a man's voice, and then Mrs. Inglethorp's rose in reply:

"Yes, certainly. After tea will do quite well. You are so thoughtful, Alfred dear."

The French window swung open a little wider, and a handsome white-haired old lady, with a somewhat masterful cast of features, stepped out of it on to the lawn. A man followed her, a suggestion of deference[27] in his manner.

Mrs. Inglethorp greeted me with effusion.[28]

"Why, if it isn't too delightful to see you again, Mr. Hastings, after all these years. Alfred, darling, Mr. Hastings—my husband."

I looked with some curiosity at "Alfred darling". He certainly struck a rather alien note. I did not wonder at John objecting to his beard. It was one of the longest and blackest I have ever seen. He wore gold-rimmed pince-nez,[29] and had a curious impassivity of feature. It struck me that he might look natural on a stage, but was strangely out of place in real life. His voice was rather deep and unctuous. He placed a wooden hand

---

for the school. For the bazaar, she plans to ask a princess to officially open the event the first day and Lady Tadminster, later identified as the wife of the local member of Parliament, to perform the same duty on the second. *Princess:* A title bestowed on the wife of a prince, the daughter of the sovereign or the granddaughter of the sovereign through the male line. In 1917, there were at least 20 princesses for Mrs. Inglethorp to ask, including several daughters and granddaughters of Queen Victoria. *Duchess:* The wife of a duke, the highest rank in the peerage. Even though she doesn't have a title, Mrs. Inglethorp's comfort in inviting duchesses and princesses to open her charity bazaar says something about the firmness of her character.

[27] Showing respect or esteem to a superior or elder.

[28] Unrestrained or heartfelt.

[29] A pair of glasses consisting of two lenses connected by a metal bridge, sometimes with a string attached that is looped around the neck or a vest button. They stay on the face by pinching the nose. Not surprisingly then, the word is derived from the French *pincer*, "to pinch," and *nez*, for "nose."

in mine and said:[30]

"This is a pleasure, Mr. Hastings." Then, turning to his wife: "Emily dearest, I think that cushion is a little damp."

She beamed fondly on him, as he substituted another with every demonstration of the tenderest care. Strange infatuation of an otherwise sensible woman!

With the presence of Mr. Inglethorp, a sense of constraint and veiled hostility seemed to settle down upon the company. Miss Howard, in particular, took no pains to conceal her feelings. Mrs. Inglethorp, however, seemed to notice nothing unusual. Her volubility,[31] which I remembered of old, had lost nothing in the intervening years, and she poured out a steady flood of conversation, mainly on the subject of the forthcoming bazaar which she was organizing and which was to take place shortly. Occasionally she referred to her husband over a question of days or dates. His watchful and attentive manner never varied. From the very first I took a firm and rooted dislike to him, and I flatter myself that my first judgments are usually fairly shrewd.

Presently Mrs. Inglethorp turned to give some instructions about letters to Evelyn Howard, and her husband addressed me in his painstaking voice:

"Is soldiering your regular profession, Mr. Hastings?"

"No, I was in Lloyd's."[32]

"And you will return there after it is over?"

"Perhaps. Either that or a fresh start altogether."

---

[30] *Impassivity:* No appearance of emotion. *Unctuous:* Smooth and greasy, from the Latin *unctus* for "anointing." *Wooden hand:* Not literally a hand made of wood, but a handshake given without emotion. Christie loves to emphasize unpleasant people as a red herring, and this paragraph nicely sets up Alfred Inglethorp as a villain.

[31] Capable of a rapid flow of speech.

[32] An insurance and reinsurance market. Not a company in the traditional sense, but a corporate body where its members pool their money and spread the risk of providing insurance. Founded at Edward Lloyd's coffee house about 1689, it was more formally organized in 1774 as the Society of Lloyd's and incorporated in 1871 by Parliament.

Mary Cavendish leant forward.

"What would you really choose as a profession, if you could just consult your inclination?"[33]

"Well, that depends."

"No secret hobby?" she asked. "Tell me—you're drawn to something? Every one is—usually something absurd."

"You'll laugh at me."

She smiled.

"Perhaps."

"Well, I've always had a secret hankering to be a detective!"

"The real thing—Scotland Yard?[34] Or Sherlock Holmes?"

"Oh, Sherlock Holmes by all means. But really, seriously, I am awfully drawn to it. I came across a man in Belgium once, a very famous detective, and he quite inflamed me. He was a marvellous little fellow. He used to say that all good detective work was a mere matter of method. My system is based on his—though of course I have progressed rather further. He was a funny little man, a great dandy,[35] but wonderfully clever."

"Like a good detective story myself," remarked Miss Howard. "Lots of nonsense written, though. Criminal discovered in last chapter. Every one dumbfounded. Real crime—you'd know at once."

"There have been a great number of undiscovered crimes," I argued.

"Don't mean the police, but the people that are right in it.

---

[33] Although she was in her mid-twenties when she wrote *Styles,* Christie sometimes used phrases more familiar to earlier generations. "Consult your inclination" — meaning considering what you want — was commonly in use from 1820 to 1850 but also appears in the Colonial-era papers of George Washington and Thomas Jefferson.
[34] London's Metropolitan Police. Its original HQ was at 4 Whitehall Place, where its rear entrance opened onto Great Scotland Yard, hence the name.
[35] A man who pays considerable attention to his appearance and is willing to spend money and time to always appear better dressed than you. Derived possibly from the 17th century phrase "Jack-a-dandy" for a conceited man.

The family. You couldn't really hoodwink them.[36] They'd know."

"Then," I said, much amused, "you think that if you were mixed up in a crime, say a murder, you'd be able to spot the murderer right off?"

"Of course I should. Mightn't be able to prove it to a pack of lawyers. But I'm certain I'd know. I'd feel it in my fingertips if he came near me."

"It might be a 'she,'" I suggested.

"Might. But murder's a violent crime. Associate it more with a man."

"Not in a case of poisoning." Mrs. Cavendish's clear voice startled me. "Dr. Bauerstein was saying yesterday that, owing to the general ignorance of the more uncommon poisons among the medical profession, there were probably countless cases of poisoning quite unsuspected."

"Why, Mary, what a gruesome conversation!" cried Mrs. Inglethorp. "It makes me feel as if a goose were walking over my grave.[37] Oh, there's Cynthia!"

A young girl in V. A. D. uniform[38] ran lightly across the lawn.

---

[36] To deceive. Its earliest known use from 1562 suggests blinding or obscuring a person's vision with a hood as in during a robbery. In Elizabethan times, blind man's buff (or bluff) was called the "hoodwinke game," adding groping about and deception to the definition.

[37] Mrs. Inglethorp is shivering. In medieval times, the connection between the living and the dead was closer, and it was believed that a person's final resting place was predetermined. The earliest recorded use of "somebody walking over my grave" was by Jonathan Swift in 1738. The use of a goose is a variant from America — interesting, since Christie's father was born there — to add the implication of feeling goose bumps on one's skin.

[38] Voluntary Aid Detachment. An organization founded by the Red Cross and the Order of St. John in 1909 to provide nursing services, particularly in hospitals, during wartime. Drawn from the middle and upper classes and given only a few weeks of training, volunteers worked at hospitals and convalescent homes. Their duties included changing linen, sterilizing equipment, serving meals and assisting doctors and senior nurses. These genteel women — Christie included — found that nursing was not as romantic as the prop-

"Why, Cynthia, you are late to-day. This is Mr. Hastings—Miss Murdoch."

Cynthia Murdoch was a fresh-looking young creature, full of life and vigour. She tossed off her little V. A. D. cap, and I admired the great loose waves of her auburn hair, and the smallness and whiteness of the hand she held out to claim her tea. With dark eyes and eyelashes she would have been a beauty.

She flung herself down on the ground beside John, and as I handed her a plate of sandwiches she smiled up at me.

"Sit down here on the grass, do. It's ever so much nicer."

I dropped down obediently.

"You work at Tadminster, don't you, Miss Murdoch?"

She nodded.

"For my sins."

"Do they bully you, then?" I asked, smiling.

"I should like to see them!" cried Cynthia with dignity.

"I have got a cousin who is nursing," I remarked. "And she is terrified of 'Sisters'."[39]

"I don't wonder. Sisters are, you know, Mr. Hastings. They simp—ly are! You've no idea! But I'm not a nurse, thank heaven, I work in the dispensary."[40]

"How many people do you poison?" I asked, smiling.

Cynthia smiled too.

"Oh, hundreds!" she said.

"Cynthia," called Mrs. Inglethorp, "do you think you could write a few notes for me?"

"Certainly, Aunt Emily."

She jumped up promptly, and something in her manner

---

aganda portrayed it, but a rough profession that exposed them to war's consequences.

[39] A senior nurse. The name survives from the early Christian era, when nuns took care of the sick and injured.

[40] A room where medicines are stored and prepared. From the Latin *dispensare* for "to weigh out" or "to disburse."

reminded me that her position was a dependent one,[41] and that Mrs. Inglethorp, kind as she might be in the main, did not allow her to forget it.

My hostess turned to me.

"John will show you your room. Supper is at half-past seven. We have given up late dinner for some time now. Lady Tadminster, our Member's wife[42]—she was the late Lord Abbotsbury's daughter—does the same. She agrees with me that one must set an example of economy. We are quite a war household; nothing is wasted here—every scrap of waste paper, even, is saved and sent away in sacks."[43]

I expressed my appreciation, and John took me into the house and up the broad staircase, which forked right and left half-way to different wings of the building. My room was in the left wing, and looked out over the park.[44]

John left me, and a few minutes later I saw him from my window walking slowly across the grass arm in arm with Cynthia Murdoch. I heard Mrs. Inglethorp call "Cynthia" impatiently, and the girl started[45] and ran back to the house. At the same moment, a man stepped out from the shadow of a tree and walked slowly in the same direction. He looked about forty, very dark with a melancholy[46] clean-shaven face. Some violent emotion seemed to be mastering him. He looked up at my window as he passed, and I recognized him, though he had changed much in the fifteen years that had elapsed since we last met. It was John's younger brother, Lawrence Cavendish. I wondered what it was that had brought that singular expression

---

[41] A person who needs financial support from another, especially a family member.

[42] A member of Parliament, Britain's legislative body.

[43] To help the war effort, households were encouraged to recycle as much as possible. Wastepaper was reused for various forms of packaging, including corrugated containers.

[44] A tract of land that could include lawns, woodlands and pastures used for recreation and as a game preserve.

[45] Give a sudden jerking movement out of surprise or alarm.

[46] A feeling of sadness, sometimes from no particular cause.

to his face.

Then I dismissed him from my mind, and returned to the contemplation of my own affairs.

The evening passed pleasantly enough; and I dreamed that night of that enigmatical[47] woman, Mary Cavendish.

The next morning dawned bright and sunny, and I was full of the anticipation of a delightful visit.

I did not see Mrs. Cavendish until lunch-time, when she volunteered to take me for a walk, and we spent a charming afternoon roaming in the woods, returning to the house about five.

As we entered the large hall, John beckoned us both into the smoking-room.[48] I saw at once by his face that something disturbing had occurred. We followed him in, and he shut the door after us.

"Look here, Mary, there's the deuce[49] of a mess. Evie's had a row[50] with Alfred Inglethorp, and she's off."

"Evie? Off?"

John nodded gloomily.

"Yes; you see she went to the mater, and—Oh, here's Evie herself."

Miss Howard entered. Her lips were set grimly together, and she carried a small suit-case. She looked excited and determined, and slightly on the defensive.

"At any rate," she burst out, "I've spoken my mind!"

"My dear Evelyn," cried Mrs. Cavendish, "this can't be true!"

Miss Howard nodded grimly.

"True enough! Afraid I said some things to Emily she

---

[47] Someone or something difficult to understand.

[48] A room set aside in a home or club for that purpose. Smoking rooms were generally for men only, which served the dual purpose of keeping the smell away from the rest of the place and giving men an excuse to gather away from the ladies.

[49] Devil. A way of invoking Satan without being blasphemous.

[50] Argument. Of unknown origin.

won't forget or forgive in a hurry. Don't mind if they've only sunk in a bit. Probably water off a duck's back,[51] though. I said right out: 'You're an old woman, Emily, and there's no fool like an old fool.[52] The man's twenty years younger than you, and don't you fool yourself as to what he married you for. Money! Well, don't let him have too much of it. Farmer Raikes has got a very pretty young wife. Just ask your Alfred how much time he spends over there.' She was very angry. Natural! I went on, 'I'm going to warn you, whether you like it or not. That man would as soon murder you in your bed as look at you. He's a bad lot. You can say what you like to me, but remember what I've told you. He's a bad lot!'"[53]

"What did she say?"

Miss Howard made an extremely expressive grimace.

"'Darling Alfred'—'dearest Alfred'—'wicked calumnies'[54] —'wicked lies'—'wicked woman'—to accuse her 'dear husband'! The sooner I left her house the better. So I'm off."

"But not now?"

"This minute!"

For a moment we sat and stared at her. Finally John Cavendish, finding his persuasions of no avail, went off to look up the trains.[55] His wife followed him, murmuring something about persuading Mrs. Inglethorp to think better of it.

As she left the room, Miss Howard's face changed. She leant towards me eagerly.

"Mr. Hastings, you're honest. I can trust you?"

I was a little startled. She laid her hand on my arm, and sank her voice to a whisper.

---

[51] Duck feathers are very resistant to water, so the phrase implies that the hurtful remark did not wound Mrs. Inglethorp's feelings.

[52] A very old proverb, implying that, if people gain wisdom through age, an old fool is worse than a young fool. The phrase was first recorded in 1546 as "But there is no foole to the olde foole, folke saie."

[53] A group or person of an unsavory kind.

[54] False accusations intended to damage someone's reputation.

[55] Examine the train schedule.

"Look after her, Mr. Hastings. My poor Emily. They're a lot of sharks—all of them. Oh, I know what I'm talking about. There isn't one of them that's not hard up and trying to get money out of her. I've protected her as much as I could. Now I'm out of the way, they'll impose upon her."

"Of course, Miss Howard," I said, "I'll do everything I can, but I'm sure you're excited and overwrought."[56]

She interrupted me by slowly shaking her forefinger.

"Young man, trust me. I've lived in the world rather longer than you have. All I ask you is to keep your eyes open. You'll see what I mean."

The throb of the motor came through the open window, and Miss Howard rose and moved to the door. John's voice sounded outside. With her hand on the handle, she turned her head over her shoulder, and beckoned to me.

"Above all, Mr. Hastings, watch that devil—her husband!"

There was no time for more. Miss Howard was swallowed up in an eager chorus of protests and good-byes. The Inglethorps did not appear.

As the motor drove away, Mrs. Cavendish suddenly detached herself from the group, and moved across the drive to the lawn to meet a tall bearded man who had been evidently making for the house. The colour rose in her cheeks as she held out her hand to him.

"Who is that?" I asked sharply, for instinctively I distrusted the man.

"That's Dr. Bauerstein," said John shortly.

"And who is Dr. Bauerstein?"

"He's staying in the village doing a rest cure, after a bad nervous breakdown.[57] He's a London specialist; a very clever

---

[56] Anxious or excited and nervous.

[57] Although Dr. Bauerstein doesn't seem to be following the regimen, a rest cure was a medical treatment developed during the 19th century to treat mental disorders, especially post-childbirth depression in women. Patients would be required to stay in bed and be fed, clothed, massaged and washed by a nurse. Their diet would emphasize fatty dairy products in the belief that

man—one of the greatest living experts on poisons, I believe."

"And he's a great friend of Mary's," put in Cynthia, the irrepressible.[58]

John Cavendish frowned and changed the subject.

"Come for a stroll, Hastings. This has been a most rotten business. She always had a rough tongue, but there is no stauncher friend in England than Evelyn Howard."

He took the path through the plantation,[59] and we walked down to the village through the woods which bordered one side of the estate.

As we passed through one of the gates on our way home again, a pretty young woman of gipsy type[60] coming in the opposite direction bowed and smiled.

"That's a pretty girl," I remarked appreciatively.

John's face hardened.

"That is Mrs. Raikes."

"The one that Miss Howard—"

"Exactly," said John, with rather unnecessary abruptness.

I thought of the white-haired old lady in the big house, and that vivid wicked little face that had just smiled into ours, and a vague chill of foreboding crept over me. I brushed it aside.

"Styles is really a glorious old place," I said to John.

He nodded rather gloomily.

"Yes, it's a fine property. It'll be mine some day—should be mine now by rights, if my father had only made a decent

---

it would revitalize them. It was found that the treatment did not help, and could hurt the patient by causing the muscles to atrophy through lack of exercise and creating blood clots in the legs.

[58] Unable to be controlled or restrained.

[59] An area set aside to cultivate plants, particularly trees.

[60] A European ethnic group also called the Romani or Romany, believed to originate in the Indian subcontinent from about the 11th century. Their ethnicity and apartness — traits shared with Jews — has subjected them to curiosity, suspicion and sometimes exclusion and persecution.

will. And then I shouldn't be so damned hard up as I am now."

"Hard up, are you?"

"My dear Hastings, I don't mind telling you that I'm at my wit's end for money."

"Couldn't your brother help you?"

"Lawrence? He's gone through every penny he ever had, publishing rotten verses in fancy bindings. No, we're an impe-cunious[61] lot. My mother's always been awfully good to us, I must say. That is, up to now. Since her marriage, of course—" he broke off, frowning.

For the first time I felt that, with Evelyn Howard, something indefinable had gone from the atmosphere. Her presence had spelt security. Now that security was removed—and the air seemed rife with suspicion. The sinister face of Dr. Bauerstein recurred to me unpleasantly. A vague suspicion of every one and everything filled my mind. Just for a moment I had a premonition[62] of approaching evil.

---

[61] Habitually poor. Formed by adding *in-* (meaning "not") to the Latin word *pecunia* for "wealthy." Over time, the word evolved to impecunious.

[62] A feeling, without reason, that something will happen, most likely unpleasant.

CHAPTER II

THE 16TH AND 17TH OF JULY

I HAD ARRIVED AT STYLES ON the 5th of July. I come now to the events of the 16th and 17th of that month. For the convenience of the reader I will recapitulate[1] the incidents of those days in as exact a manner as possible. They were elicited[2] subsequently at the trial by a process of long and tedious cross-examinations.

I received a letter from Evelyn Howard a couple of days after her departure, telling me she was working as a nurse at the big hospital in Middlingham,[3] a manufacturing town some fifteen miles away, and begging me to let her know if Mrs. Inglethorp should show any wish to be reconciled.

The only fly in the ointment[4] of my peaceful days was Mrs. Cavendish's extraordinary, and, for my part, unaccountable preference for the society[5] of Dr. Bauerstein. What she saw in the man I cannot imagine, but she was always asking him up to

---

[1] To recall events briefly.

[2] Revealed or called forth, in this case through questioning by the barristers.

[3] A fictional city.

[4] "I never could see why flies shouldn't be in ointment," Bertie Wooster says in P.G. Wodehouse's *The Code of the Woosters*. "What harm do they do?" Although he had won the scripture knowledge prize at preparatory school, Bertie had forgotten Ecclesiastes 10:1: "Dead flies cause the ointment of the apothecary to send forth a stinking savour: so doth a little folly, him that is in reputation for wisdom and honour."

[5] Being in the company of a person or persons.

the house, and often went off for long expeditions with him. I must confess that I was quite unable to see his attraction.

The 16th of July fell on a Monday.[6] It was a day of turmoil. The famous bazaar had taken place on Saturday, and an entertainment, in connection with the same charity, at which Mrs. Inglethorp was to recite a War poem,[7] was to be held that night. We were all busy during the morning arranging and decorating the Hall[8] in the village where it was to take place. We had a late luncheon and spent the afternoon resting in the garden. I noticed that John's manner was somewhat unusual. He seemed very excited and restless.

After tea, Mrs. Inglethorp went to lie down to rest before her efforts in the evening and I challenged Mary Cavendish to a single at tennis.

About a quarter to seven, Mrs. Inglethorp called us that we should be late as supper was early that night. We had rather a scramble to get ready in time;[9] and before the meal was over the motor was waiting at the door.

The entertainment was a great success, Mrs. Inglethorp's recitation receiving tremendous applause. There were also some

---

[6] This reference sets the story in 1917, when the war had fallen into a stalemate. In April, the British launched an offensive intended to break the German lines. Despite significant gains during the first two days, the campaign failed at the cost of 150,000 lives, most of them British.

[7] A genre of poetry popular during the war, usually written by a soldier. World War I was the first conflict in which a large number of English poets participated, many of whom perished, such as Rupert Brooke and Wilfred Owen. Among the notable literary figures who served were Siegfried Sassoon, H.H. Munroe ("Saki") and Robert Graves.

[8] A government building that can act as a community center.

[9] The dress code could be formal or informal depending on the occasion and the host's whim. At Styles Court, judging from the *Poirot* TV episode, informality ruled and men wore a suit and shirt with a rigid collar and tie and women wore dresses suitable for wearing in public but not formal evening wear. George Gowler, the butler at Greenway, Christie's home in Devon, recalled the tradition that he would decide the dress code for dinner: "If I was wearing my full Butler's uniform it meant dressing up for dinner. If I was in the white coat [and black trousers] it was casual."

tableaux[10] in which Cynthia took part. She did not return with us, having been asked to a supper party, and to remain the night with some friends who had been acting with her in the tableaux.

The following morning, Mrs. Inglethorp stayed in bed to breakfast, as she was rather overtired; but she appeared in her briskest mood about 12.30, and swept Lawrence and myself off to a luncheon party.

"Such a charming invitation from Mrs. Rolleston. Lady Tadminster's sister, you know. The Rollestons came over with the Conqueror[11]—one of our oldest families."

Mary had excused herself on the plea of an engagement with Dr. Bauerstein.

We had a pleasant luncheon, and as we drove away Lawrence suggested that we should return by Tadminster, which was barely a mile out of our way, and pay a visit to Cynthia in her dispensary. Mrs. Inglethorp replied that this was an excellent idea, but as she had several letters to write she would drop us there, and we could come back with Cynthia in the pony-trap.[12]

We were detained under suspicion by the hospital porter, until Cynthia appeared to vouch for us, looking very cool and sweet in her long white overall. She took us up to her sanctum, and introduced us to her fellow dispenser, a rather awe-inspiring individual, whom Cynthia cheerily addressed as "Nibs."[13]

---

[10] A "living picture," in which party guests are costumed and posed to enact scenes from history or literature. For example, *How to Entertain a Social Party* (1875) describes a tableaux from a French literary folktale about the murderous Bluebeard, in which his new wife, Fatima, discovers in a locked closet the heads of his previous brides. The tableaux in the Hall were probably on more patriotic subjects.

[11] William the Conqueror (c.1028-1087), the Normandy nobleman who won the battle of Hastings in 1066 and ruled England as King William I.

[12] A light, sporty two- or four-wheeled carriage.

[13] *Porter:* A hospital worker responsible for moving patients and equipment. *Vouch:* To confirm the identity or character of a person. *Overall:* A loose-

"What a lot of bottles!" I exclaimed, as my eye travelled round the small room. "Do you really know what's in them all?"

"Say something original," groaned Cynthia. "Every single person who comes up here says that. We are really thinking of bestowing a prize on the first individual who does not say: 'What a lot of bottles!' And I know the next thing you're going to say is: 'How many people have you poisoned?'"

I pleaded guilty with a laugh.

"If you people only knew how fatally easy it is to poison some one by mistake, you wouldn't joke about it. Come on, let's have tea. We've got all sorts of secret stories in that cupboard. No, Lawrence—that's the poison cupboard. The big cupboard—that's right."[14]

We had a very cheery tea, and assisted Cynthia to wash up afterwards. We had just put away the last tea-spoon when a knock came at the door. The countenances[15] of Cynthia and Nibs were suddenly petrified into a stern and forbidding expression.

"Come in," said Cynthia, in a sharp professional tone.

---

fitting one-piece garment worn over ordinary clothes to protect them from heavy wear. *Sanctum:* A sacred place. Hastings obviously does not mean this literally. *Nibs:* Generally used as a mocking title for a self-important person. Origins unknown, but there are several theories. It could have been a play on the last name of Admiral Sir William Penn (1621-1670) — the end of a fountain pen is called a nib. Or, it could be derived from the French *nebs*, for "protruding" or "prominent," such as a nose, a definition which itself might have inspired the pen/nib connection. The *American Heritage Dictionary of the English Language* suggests that it is a variation of nob, slang for a "person of wealth or social standing."

[14] In her memoirs, Christie recounts a story from her pharmaceutical training in which a pharmacist's mistake resulted in her making extremely powerful suppositories. As a student, she couldn't tell him he had made a dangerous mistake without receiving a reprimand, so she "accidentally" dropped the tray of suppositories and stepped on them.

[15] The expression on their faces.

A young and rather scared looking nurse appeared with a bottle which she proffered to Nibs, who waved her towards Cynthia with the somewhat enigmatical remark:

"I'm not really here to-day."

Cynthia took the bottle and examined it with the severity of a judge.

"This should have been sent up this morning."

"Sister is very sorry. She forgot."

"Sister should read the rules outside the door."

I gathered from the little nurse's expression that there was not the least likelihood of her having the hardihood[16] to retail this message to the dreaded "Sister".

"So now it can't be done until to-morrow," finished Cynthia.

"Don't you think you could possibly let us have it to-night?"

"Well," said Cynthia graciously, "we are very busy, but if we have time it shall be done."

The little nurse withdrew, and Cynthia promptly took a jar from the shelf, refilled the bottle, and placed it on the table outside the door.

I laughed.

"Discipline must be maintained?"

"Exactly. Come out on our little balcony. You can see all the outside wards there."[17]

I followed Cynthia and her friend and they pointed out the different wards to me. Lawrence remained behind, but after a few moments Cynthia called to him over her shoulder to come and join us. Then she looked at her watch.

"Nothing more to do, Nibs?"

"No."

"All right. Then we can lock up and go."

I had seen Lawrence in quite a different light that after-

---

[16] Courage and fortitude.

[17] Buildings away from the main building used to house patients.

noon. Compared to John, he was an astoundingly difficult person to get to know. He was the opposite of his brother in almost every respect, being unusually shy and reserved. Yet he had a certain charm of manner, and I fancied that, if one really knew him well, one could have a deep affection for him. I had always fancied that his manner to Cynthia was rather constrained,[18] and that she on her side was inclined to be shy of him. But they were both gay enough this afternoon, and chatted together like a couple of children.

As we drove through the village, I remembered that I wanted some stamps, so accordingly we pulled up at the post office.

As I came out again, I cannoned into a little man who was just entering. I drew aside and apologised, when suddenly, with a loud exclamation, he clasped me in his arms and kissed me warmly.[19]

"*Mon ami*[20] Hastings!" he cried. "It is indeed *mon ami* Hastings!"

"Poirot!" I exclaimed.

I turned to the pony-trap.

"This is a very pleasant meeting for me, Miss Cynthia. This is my old friend, Monsieur Poirot, whom I have not seen for years."

"Oh, we know Monsieur Poirot," said Cynthia gaily. "But I had no idea he was a friend of yours."

"Yes, indeed," said Poirot seriously. "I know Mademoiselle Cynthia. It is by the charity of that good Mrs. Inglethorp that I am here." Then, as I looked at him inquiringly: "Yes, my friend, she had kindly extended hospitality to seven of my country-

---

[18] Done against his will.

[19] Cheek kissing is a customary greeting in Europe and many other parts of the world. Specifics vary widely from country to country. So diverse are the rules according to the possible combinations — male to male, female to male, female to female, kissing relatives, friends or strangers, the amount of alcohol involved or the social event — that outsiders are often advised to be prepared for anything and to let the other person take the lead.

[20] My friend.

people who, alas, are refugees from their native land. We Belgians will always remember her with gratitude."[21]

Poirot was an extraordinary looking little man. He was hardly more than five feet, four inches, but carried himself with great dignity. His head was exactly the shape of an egg, and he always perched it a little on one side. His moustache was very stiff and military.[22] The neatness of his attire was almost incredible. I believe a speck of dust would have caused him more pain than a bullet wound. Yet this quaint dandyfied little man who, I was sorry to see, now limped badly,[23] had been in his time one of the most celebrated members of the Belgian police. As a detective, his flair[24] had been extraordinary, and he had achieved triumphs by unravelling some of the most baffling cases of the day.

He pointed out to me the little house inhabited by him and his fellow Belgians, and I promised to go and see him at an early date. Then he raised his hat with a flourish to Cynthia, and

---

[21] Germany launched World War I on the Western Front by invading Belgium as part of the Schlieffen Plan to conquer France. This was called the "Rape of Belgium," first as a reference to the violation of the country's neutrality, then to the German atrocities such as murder, robbery and arson committed against the civilian population. It was estimated that 1.5 million Belgians — 20 percent of the population — fled the country, many of them reaching Britain. For more details, see the essay "Brave Little Belgium" in the appendix.

[22] Many armies have regulations that ban facial hair or require it to be grown in a certain way. In Britain, for example, soldiers were forbidden to shave their upper lip beginning in the 1860s. The development of manly facial hair became a status symbol. The rule was abolished in 1916 by the adjutant-general because he wanted to shave his mustache off.

[23] Unlike Sherlock Holmes' friend Dr. Watson, whose wound traveled between his shoulder and leg depending on the story, Poirot recovered completely from his injury since it is never mentioned again. His recovery must have been miraculous, because later in *Styles* he "darted from one object to the other with the agility of a grasshopper."

[24] The French word for "to smell" morphed into English to mean skill or talent. Thanks to the movie *Office Space*, it's also come to mean the cute badges worn by the waitstaff at chain restaurants.

we drove away.

"He's a dear little man," said Cynthia. "I'd no idea you knew him."

"You've been entertaining a celebrity unawares," I replied.

And, for the rest of the way home, I recited to them the various exploits and triumphs of Hercule Poirot.

We arrived back in a very cheerful mood. As we entered the hall, Mrs. Inglethorp came out of her boudoir. She looked flushed and upset.

"Oh, it's you," she said.

"Is there anything the matter, Aunt Emily?" asked Cynthia.

"Certainly not," said Mrs. Inglethorp sharply. "What should there be?" Then catching sight of Dorcas, the parlourmaid,[25] going into the dining-room, she called to her to bring some stamps into the boudoir.[26]

"Yes, m'm." The old servant hesitated, then added diffidently:[27] "Don't you think, m'm, you'd better get to bed? You're looking very tired."

"Perhaps you're right, Dorcas—yes—no—not now. I've some letters I must finish by post-time.[28] Have you lighted the fire in my room as I told you?"[29]

---

[25] In large, upper-class households, the parlourmaid maintained the house's public rooms, such as the sitting, drawing and dining rooms. As young as 19, they ranked in the household hierarchy below the housekeeper (who supervised the maids) and above the between-maid and the scullery maid. In middle-class households such as Styles Court, however, the parlourmaid was older and assumed the butler's role. "Most high-class and wealthy families employed a butler and a parlourmaid in preference to two parlourmaids," former servant Margaret Powell noted in *Servants' Hall*. "A butler gave tone to the house. The middle-classes had parlourmaids only."

[26] A woman's private room, although it could also mean a dressing room. From the French *bouder* for "sulking place."

[27] Modestly

[28] The time when mail is picked up to be delivered.

[29] Although the concept of central heating has been known since Roman times, it was slow to come to England. Well-to-do houses installed it during the late Victorian era, when many older or poorer homes burned coal or

"Yes, m'm."

"Then I'll go to bed directly after supper."

She went into the boudoir again, and Cynthia stared after her.

"Goodness gracious! I wonder what's up?" she said to Lawrence.

He did not seem to have heard her, for without a word he turned on his heel and went out of the house.

I suggested a quick game of tennis before supper and, Cynthia agreeing, I ran upstairs to fetch my racquet.

Mrs. Cavendish was coming down the stairs. It may have been my fancy, but she, too, was looking odd and disturbed.

"Had a good walk with Dr. Bauerstein?" I asked, trying to appear as indifferent as I could.

"I didn't go," she replied abruptly. "Where is Mrs. Inglethorp?"

"In the boudoir."

Her hand clenched itself on the banisters, then she seemed to nerve herself for some encounter, and went rapidly past me down the stairs across the hall to the boudoir, the door of which she shut behind her.

As I ran out to the tennis court a few moments later, I had to pass the open boudoir window, and was unable to help overhearing the following scrap of dialogue. Mary Cavendish was saying in the voice of a woman desperately controlling herself:

"Then you won't show it to me?"

To which Mrs. Inglethorp replied:

"My dear Mary, it has nothing to do with that matter."

"Then show it to me."

"I tell you it is not what you imagine. It does not concern

wood in stoves and fireplaces. It wasn't until the 1970s that the use of central heating became widespread.

you in the least."

To which Mary Cavendish replied, with a rising bitterness:
"Of course, I might have known you would shield him."

Cynthia was waiting for me, and greeted me eagerly with:
"I say! There's been the most awful row! I've got it all out of Dorcas."

"What kind of a row?"

"Between Aunt Emily and him. I do hope she's found him out at last!"

"Was Dorcas there, then?"

"Of course not. She 'happened to be near the door'. It was a real old bust-up. I do wish I knew what it was all about."

I thought of Mrs. Raikes's gipsy face, and Evelyn Howard's warnings, but wisely decided to hold my peace, whilst Cynthia exhausted every possible hypothesis, and cheerfully hoped, "Aunt Emily will send him away, and will never speak to him again."

I was anxious to get hold of John, but he was nowhere to be seen. Evidently something very momentous had occurred that afternoon. I tried to forget the few words I had overheard; but, do what I would, I could not dismiss them altogether from my mind. What was Mary Cavendish's concern in the matter?

Mr. Inglethorp was in the drawing-room[30] when I came down to supper. His face was impassive as ever, and the strange unreality of the man struck me afresh.

Mrs. Inglethorp came down last. She still looked agitated, and during the meal there was a somewhat constrained silence. Inglethorp was unusually quiet. As a rule, he surrounded his wife with little attentions, placing a cushion at her back, and altogether playing the part of the devoted husband. Immediately after supper, Mrs. Inglethorp retired to her boudoir again.

"Send my coffee in here, Mary," she called. "I've just five minutes to catch the post."

---

[30] A room where guests can be received and entertained. Originally called in the 16th century a withdrawing room, as in "a room to withdraw to."

Cynthia and I went and sat by the open window in the drawing-room. Mary Cavendish brought our coffee to us. She seemed excited.

"Do you young people want lights, or do you enjoy the twilight?" she asked. "Will you take Mrs. Inglethorp her coffee, Cynthia? I will pour it out."

"Do not trouble, Mary," said Inglethorp. "I will take it to Emily." He poured it out, and went out of the room carrying it carefully.

Lawrence followed him, and Mrs. Cavendish sat down by us.

We three sat for some time in silence. It was a glorious night, hot and still. Mrs. Cavendish fanned herself gently with a palm leaf.[31]

"It's almost too hot," she murmured. "We shall have a thunderstorm."

Alas, that these harmonious moments can never endure! My paradise was rudely shattered by the sound of a well known, and heartily disliked, voice in the hall.

"Dr. Bauerstein!" exclaimed Cynthia. "What a funny time to come."

I glanced jealously at Mary Cavendish, but she seemed quite undisturbed, the delicate pallor[32] of her cheeks did not vary.

In a few moments, Alfred Inglethorp had ushered the doctor in, the latter laughing, and protesting that he was in no fit state for a drawing-room. In truth, he presented a sorry spectacle, being literally plastered with mud.

"What have you been doing, doctor?" cried Mrs. Cavendish.

"I must make my apologies," said the doctor. "I did not really mean to come in, but Mr. Inglethorp insisted."

"Well, Bauerstein, you are in a plight," said John, strolling in from the hall. "Have some coffee, and tell us what you have

---

[31] A hand fan woven from straw, bamboo or raffia.
[32] An unhealthy pale appearance.

been up to."

"Thank you, I will." He laughed rather ruefully, as he described how he had discovered a very rare species of fern in an inaccessible place, and in his efforts to obtain it had lost his footing, and slipped ignominiously[33] into a neighbouring pond.

"The sun soon dried me off," he added, "but I'm afraid my appearance is very disreputable."[34]

At this juncture,[35] Mrs. Inglethorp called to Cynthia from the hall, and the girl ran out.

"Just carry up my despatch-case,[36] will you, dear? I'm going to bed."

The door into the hall was a wide one. I had risen when Cynthia did, John was close by me. There were therefore three witnesses who could swear that Mrs. Inglethorp was carrying her coffee, as yet untasted, in her hand.

My evening was utterly and entirely spoilt by the presence of Dr. Bauerstein. It seemed to me the man would never go. He rose at last, however, and I breathed a sigh of relief.

"I'll walk down to the village with you," said Mr. Inglethorp. "I must see our agent over those estate accounts." He turned to John. "No one need sit up. I will take the latch-key."[37]

---

[33] An act causing disgrace or shame.

[34] Not considered respectable in appearance.

[35] At this point in time, from the Latin *jungere* for "to join."

[36] A small box, usually equipped with a lock, used to keep important papers.

[37] *Estate accounts:* Records indicating the amount and source of income and expenditures flowing through an estate. *Latch-key:* A key consisting of a rod with a notched paddle at the end used to open a door's lock. This is a forerunner of the tumbler lock used today.

CHAPTER III

THE NIGHT
OF THE TRAGEDY

TO MAKE THIS PART OF MY STORY clear, I append the following plan of the first floor[1] of Styles.

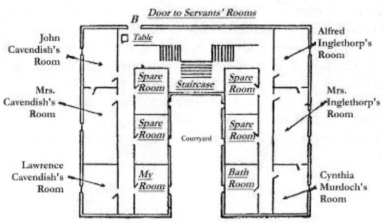

The servants' rooms are reached through the door B. They
have no communication with the right wing, where the Inglethorps' rooms were situated.

It seemed to be the middle of the night when I was awakened by Lawrence Cavendish. He had a candle in his hand, and
the agitation of his face told me at once that something was
seriously wrong.

"What's the matter?" I asked, sitting up in bed, and trying
to collect my scattered thoughts.

---

[1] The first floor in English households is called the second floor in the U.S.

"We are afraid my mother is very ill. She seems to be having some kind of fit. Unfortunately she has locked herself in."

"I'll come at once."

I sprang out of bed; and, pulling on a dressing-gown,[2] followed Lawrence along the passage and the gallery[3] to the right wing of the house.

John Cavendish joined us, and one or two of the servants were standing round in a state of awe-stricken excitement. Lawrence turned to his brother.

"What do you think we had better do?"

Never, I thought, had his indecision of character been more apparent.

John rattled the handle of Mrs. Inglethorp's door violently, but with no effect. It was obviously locked or bolted on the inside. The whole household was aroused by now. The most alarming sounds were audible from the interior of the room. Clearly something must be done.

"Try going through Mr. Inglethorp's room, sir," cried Dorcas. "Oh, the poor mistress!"

Suddenly I realized that Alfred Inglethorp was not with us—that he alone had given no sign of his presence. John opened the door of his room. It was pitch dark, but Lawrence was following with the candle, and by its feeble light we saw that the bed had not been slept in, and that there was no sign of the room having been occupied.

We went straight to the connecting door. That, too, was locked or bolted on the inside. What was to be done?

"Oh, dear, sir," cried Dorcas, wringing her hands, "whatever shall we do?"

"We must try and break the door in, I suppose. It'll be a tough job, though. Here, let one of the maids go down and wake Baily and tell him to go for Dr. Wilkins at once. Now then, we'll have a try at the door. Half a moment, though, isn't

---

[2] A robe designed to be worn over sleepwear.
[3] An open-sided passage that, in this case, runs between two staircases.

there a door into Miss Cynthia's rooms?"

"Yes, sir, but that's always bolted. It's never been undone."

"Well, we might just see."

He ran rapidly down the corridor to Cynthia's room. Mary Cavendish was there, shaking the girl—who must have been an unusually sound sleeper—and trying to wake her.

In a moment or two he was back.

"No good. That's bolted too. We must break in the door. I think this one is a shade less solid than the one in the passage."

We strained and heaved together. The framework of the door was solid, and for a long time it resisted our efforts, but at last we felt it give beneath our weight, and finally, with a re-sounding crash, it was burst open.

We stumbled in together, Lawrence still holding his candle. Mrs. Inglethorp was lying on the bed, her whole form agitated by violent convulsions,[4] in one of which she must have over-turned the table beside her. As we entered, however, her limbs relaxed, and she fell back upon the pillows.

John strode across the room, and lit the gas.[5] Turning to Annie, one of the housemaids, he sent her downstairs to the dining-room for brandy. Then he went across to his mother whilst I unbolted the door that gave on the corridor.

I turned to Lawrence, to suggest that I had better leave them now that there was no further need of my services, but the words were frozen on my lips. Never have I seen such a ghastly look on any man's face. He was white as chalk, the can-dle he held in his shaking hand was sputtering onto the carpet,[6] and his eyes, petrified with terror, or some such kindred emo-tion, stared fixedly over my head at a point on the further wall. It was as though he had seen something that turned him to stone. I instinctively followed the direction of his eyes, but I

---

[4] An uncontrollable movement of the muscles.

[5] Although electric power lines had been spreading since the 1880s, it took decades to reach every home. By the early 1920s, only 10 percent of British homes were electrified. The rest used gas lighting.

[6] Spraying melted wax.

could see nothing unusual. The still feebly flickering ashes in the grate,[7] and the row of prim ornaments on the mantelpiece, were surely harmless enough.

The violence of Mrs. Inglethorp's attack seemed to be passing. She was able to speak in short gasps.

"Better now—very sudden—stupid of me—to lock myself in."

A shadow fell on the bed and, looking up, I saw Mary Cavendish standing near the door with her arm around Cynthia. She seemed to be supporting the girl, who looked utterly dazed and unlike herself. Her face was heavily flushed, and she yawned repeatedly.

"Poor Cynthia is quite frightened," said Mrs. Cavendish in a low clear voice. She herself, I noticed, was dressed in her white land smock.[8] Then it must be later than I thought. I saw that a faint streak of daylight was showing through the curtains of the windows, and that the clock on the mantelpiece pointed to close upon five o'clock.

A strangled cry from the bed startled me. A fresh access of pain seized the unfortunate old lady. The convulsions were of a violence terrible to behold. Everything was confusion. We thronged round her, powerless to help or alleviate. A final convulsion lifted her from the bed, until she appeared to rest upon her head and her heels, with her body arched in an extraordinary manner. In vain Mary and John tried to administer more brandy.[9] The moments flew. Again the body arched itself in

---

[7] A metal framework in a fireplace used to hold wood or coals.

[8] Mary Cavendish was a land girl, a volunteer who helped with the farm chores while the men were off fighting. Her uniform included a white smock, sort of a full-body apron, to protect her clothes as she worked. In 1917, the year after Christie finished *Styles*, the land girls were organized into the Women's Land Army. For details, see "An Army of Land Girls" in the appendix.

[9] Brandy was valued as a medicine and a stimulant, although alcohol was later discovered to work as a depressive. The *British Pharmacopoeia* of 1907 said a dose of alcohol "increases the output of blood from the heart, and slightly raises blood pressure. ... Its action may be due either to a direct

that peculiar fashion.

At that moment, Dr. Bauerstein pushed his way authoritatively into the room. For one instant he stopped dead, staring at the figure on the bed, and, at the same instant, Mrs. Inglethorp cried out in a strangled voice, her eyes fixed on the doctor:

"Alfred—Alfred—" Then she fell back motionless on the pillows.

With a stride, the doctor reached the bed, and seizing her arms worked them energetically, applying what I knew to be artificial respiration.[10] He issued a few short sharp orders to the servants. An imperious wave of his hand drove us all to the door. We watched him, fascinated, though I think we all knew in our hearts that it was too late, and that nothing could be done now. I could see by the expression on his face that he himself had little hope.

Finally he abandoned his task, shaking his head gravely. At that moment, we heard footsteps outside, and Dr. Wilkins, Mrs. Inglethorp's own doctor, a portly, fussy little man, came bustling in.

In a few words Dr. Bauerstein explained how he had happened to be passing the lodge gates as the car came out, and had run up to the house as fast as he could, whilst the car went on to fetch Dr. Wilkins. With a faint gesture of the hand, he indicated the figure on the bed.

"Ve—ry sad. Ve—ry sad," murmured Dr. Wilkins. "Poor dear lady. Always did far too much—far too much—against my advice. I warned her. Her heart was far from strong. 'Take it

---

stimulant effect on cardiac muscle, or to the fact that it affords a readily assimilable source of energy." Brandy could also be given by injection, intravenously or rectally.

[10] This was the Silvester method, in which the patient is laid supine and the arms are pressed onto the chest to force air from the lungs, then pulled above the head to draw in fresh air. It is named for the English physician Henry Silvester (1828-1908) who developed the method.

easy,' I said to her, 'Take—it—easy'. But no—her zeal for good works was too great. Nature rebelled. Na—ture—re—belled."

Dr. Bauerstein, I noticed, was watching the local doctor narrowly. He still kept his eyes fixed on him as he spoke.

"The convulsions were of a peculiar violence, Dr. Wilkins. I am sorry you were not here in time to witness them. They were quite—tetanic[11] in character."

"Ah!" said Dr. Wilkins wisely.

"I should like to speak to you in private," said Dr. Bauerstein. He turned to John. "You do not object?"

"Certainly not."

We all trooped out into the corridor, leaving the two doctors alone, and I heard the key turned in the lock behind us.

We went slowly down the stairs. I was violently excited. I have a certain talent for deduction, and Dr. Bauerstein's manner had started a flock of wild surmises[12] in my mind. Mary Cavendish laid her hand upon my arm.

"What is it? Why did Dr. Bauerstein seem so—peculiar?"

I looked at her.

"Do you know what I think?"

"What?"

"Listen!" I looked round, the others were out of earshot. I lowered my voice to a whisper. "I believe she has been poisoned! I'm certain Dr. Bauerstein suspects it."

"What?" She shrank against the wall, the pupils of her eyes dilating[13] wildly. Then, with a sudden cry that startled me, she cried out: "No, no—not that—not that!" And breaking from me, fled up the stairs. I followed her, afraid that she was going to faint. I found her leaning against the bannisters,[14] deadly pale. She waved me away impatiently.

"No, no—leave me. I'd rather be alone. Let me just be quiet for a minute or two. Go down to the others."

---

[11] An involuntary contraction of the muscles.
[12] A conclusion or thought based on little evidence.
[13] Enlarging.
[14] A handrail supported by posts.

I obeyed her reluctantly. John and Lawrence were in the dining-room. I joined them. We were all silent, but I suppose I voiced the thoughts of us all when I at last broke it by saying:

"Where is Mr. Inglethorp?"

John shook his head.

"He's not in the house."

Our eyes met. Where was Alfred Inglethorp? His absence was strange and inexplicable. I remembered Mrs. Inglethorp's dying words. What lay beneath them? What more could she have told us, if she had had time?

At last we heard the doctors descending the stairs. Dr. Wilkins was looking important and excited, and trying to conceal an inward exultation[15] under a manner of decorous[16] calm. Dr. Bauerstein remained in the background, his grave bearded face unchanged. Dr. Wilkins was the spokesman for the two. He addressed himself to John:

"Mr. Cavendish, I should like your consent to a post-mortem."[17]

"Is that necessary?" asked John gravely. A spasm of pain crossed his face.

"Absolutely," said Dr. Bauerstein.

"You mean by that—?"

"That neither Dr. Wilkins nor myself could give a death certificate under the circumstances."

John bent his head.

"In that case, I have no alternative but to agree."

"Thank you," said Dr. Wilkins briskly. "We propose that it should take place to-morrow night—or rather to-night." And he glanced at the daylight. "Under the circumstances, I am

---

[15] A joyful feeling.

[16] Marked by proper behavior.

[17] An autopsy in which the corpse is examined to determine the cause of death. Depending on the circumstances surrounding the death, permission of the next of kin was sometimes sought. Today, the sudden death of a person as healthy as Mrs. Inglethorp should trigger a post-mortem.

afraid an inquest[18] can hardly be avoided—these formalities are necessary, but I beg that you won't distress yourselves."

There was a pause, and then Dr. Bauerstein drew two keys from his pocket, and handed them to John.

"These are the keys of the two rooms. I have locked them and, in my opinion, they would be better kept locked for the present."

The doctors then departed.

I had been turning over an idea in my head, and I felt that the moment had now come to broach[19] it. Yet I was a little chary[20] of doing so. John, I knew, had a horror of any kind of publicity, and was an easygoing optimist, who preferred never to meet trouble half-way. It might be difficult to convince him of the soundness of my plan. Lawrence, on the other hand, being less conventional, and having more imagination, I felt I might count upon as an ally. There was no doubt that the moment had come for me to take the lead.

"John," I said, "I am going to ask you something."

"Well?"

"You remember my speaking of my friend Poirot? The Belgian who is here? He has been a most famous detective."

"Yes."

"I want you to let me call him in—to investigate this matter."

"What—now? Before the post-mortem?"

"Yes, time is an advantage if—if—there has been foul play."

"Rubbish!" cried Lawrence angrily. "In my opinion the

---

[18] A hearing, usually led by the coroner, in which a jury examines the evidence and declares, if possible, the cause of death and who should be tried for it.

[19] To raise for discussion a difficult topic. From the Latin word meaning "to pierce."

[20] cautious or wary.

whole thing is a mare's nest[21] of Bauerstein's! Wilkins hadn't an idea of such a thing, until Bauerstein put it into his head. But, like all specialists, Bauerstein's got a bee in his bonnet.[22] Poisons are his hobby, so of course he sees them everywhere."

I confess that I was surprised by Lawrence's attitude. He was so seldom vehement[23] about anything.

John hesitated.

"I can't feel as you do, Lawrence," he said at last. "I'm inclined to give Hastings a free hand, though I should prefer to wait a bit. We don't want any unnecessary scandal."

"No, no," I cried eagerly, "you need have no fear of that. Poirot is discretion itself."

"Very well, then, have it your own way. I leave it in your hands. Though, if it is as we suspect, it seems a clear enough case. God forgive me if I am wronging him!"

I looked at my watch. It was six o'clock. I determined to lose no time.

Five minutes' delay, however, I allowed myself. I spent it in ransacking the library until I discovered a medical book which gave a description of strychnine poisoning.[24]

---

[21] An illusion. The earliest phrase is "to find a mare's nest," suggested by the fact that mares — female horses — do not make nests.

[22] To be preoccupied with an idea. The phrase "to have bees in one's head," was first recorded in 1513. The phrase morphed into its current meaning by 1790.

[23] A display of strong feeling.

[24] The standard reference works were *A Textbook of Medical Jurisprudence, Toxicology and Public Health* (1902) by John Glaister (1856-1932) and *Medicine and Toxicology* (1893) by J. Dixon Mann (1840-1912). For more information, see the "Poison Nuts and Quaker Buttons" essay in the appendix.

CHAPTER IV

POIROT INVESTIGATES

THE HOUSE WHICH THE BELGIANS occupied in the village was quite close to the park gates. One could save time by taking a narrow path through the long grass, which cut off the detours of the winding drive. So I, accordingly, went that way. I had nearly reached the lodge, when my attention was arrested by the running figure of a man approaching me. It was Mr. Inglethorp. Where had he been? How did he intend to explain his absence?

He accosted[1] me eagerly.

"My God! This is terrible! My poor wife! I have only just heard."

"Where have you been?" I asked.

"Denby kept me late last night. It was one o'clock before we'd finished. Then I found that I'd forgotten the latch-key after all. I didn't want to arouse the household, so Denby gave me a bed."

"How did you hear the news?" I asked.

"Wilkins knocked Denby up to tell him. My poor Emily! She was so self-sacrificing—such a noble character. She over-taxed her strength."

A wave of revulsion swept over me. What a consummate[2] hypocrite the man was!

"I must hurry on," I said, thankful that he did not ask me whither I was bound.

In a few minutes I was knocking at the door of Leastways Cottage.

---

[1] To approach someone boldly or aggressively.
[2] Complete in every detail. Perfect.

Getting no answer, I repeated my summons impatiently. A window above me was cautiously opened, and Poirot himself looked out.

He gave an exclamation of surprise at seeing me. In a few brief words, I explained the tragedy that had occurred, and that I wanted his help.

"Wait, my friend, I will let you in, and you shall recount to me the affair whilst I dress."

In a few moments he had unbarred the door, and I followed him up to his room. There he installed me in a chair, and I related the whole story, keeping back nothing, and omitting no circumstance, however insignificant, whilst he himself made a careful and deliberate toilet.[3]

I told him of my awakening, of Mrs. Inglethorp's dying words, of her husband's absence, of the quarrel the day before, of the scrap of conversation between Mary and her mother-in-law that I had overheard, of the former quarrel between Mrs. Inglethorp and Evelyn Howard, and of the latter's innuendoes.[4]

I was hardly as clear as I could wish. I repeated myself several times, and occasionally had to go back to some detail that I had forgotten. Poirot smiled kindly on me.

"The mind is confused? Is it not so? Take time, mon ami. You are agitated; you are excited—it is but natural. Presently, when we are calmer, we will arrange the facts, neatly, each in his proper place. We will examine—and reject. Those of importance we will put on one side; those of no importance,

---

[3] To attend to one's appearance through washing and dressing. From the mid-16th century French word *toilette* for the cloth clothes were wrapped in. It was then used for the cloth laid over the shoulders while a person's hair is being combed and powdered. Then it was applied to the cloth that covered the dressing table which held the mirror, makeup and powders, then to the act of cleaning and dressing oneself. By the 19th century, this elegant word for a civilized act became the name of a plumbing fixture and the room it occupies. Bringing this definition full circle, note that those who won't say "going to the toilet" because it's crude will say "going to the powder room" instead.

[4] An insinuation reflecting negatively on a person's character or reputation.

pouf!"—he screwed up his cherub-like face, and puffed comically enough—"blow them away!"

"That's all very well," I objected, "but how are you going to decide what is important, and what isn't? That always seems the difficulty to me."

Poirot shook his head energetically. He was now arranging his moustache with exquisite care.

"Not so. *Voyons!*[5] One fact leads to another—so we continue. Does the next fit in with that? *A merveille!*[6] Good! We can proceed. This next little fact—no! Ah, that is curious! There is something missing—a link in the chain that is not there. We examine. We search. And that little curious fact, that possibly paltry[7] little detail that will not tally, we put it here!" He made an extravagant gesture with his hand. "It is significant! It is tremendous!"

"Y—es—"

"Ah!" Poirot shook his forefinger so fiercely at me that I quailed before it.[8] "Beware! Peril to the detective who says: 'It is so small—it does not matter. It will not agree. I will forget it.' That way lies confusion! Everything matters."

"I know. You always told me that. That's why I have gone into all the details of this thing whether they seemed to me relevant or not."

"And I am pleased with you. You have a good memory, and you have given me the facts faithfully. Of the order in which you present them, I say nothing—truly, it is deplorable! But I make allowances—you are upset. To that I attribute the circumstance that you have omitted one fact of paramount importance."

"What is that?" I asked.

"You have not told me if Mrs. Inglethorp ate well last

---

[5] Let us see.
[6] Marvelous!
[7] Of little or no value.
[8] To show fear or a desire to move away. Of unknown origin.

night."

I stared at him. Surely the war had affected the little man's brain. He was carefully engaged in brushing his coat[9] before putting it on, and seemed wholly engrossed in the task.

"I don't remember," I said. "And, anyway, I don't see—"

"You do not see? But it is of the first importance."

"I can't see why," I said, rather nettled.[10] "As far as I can remember, she didn't eat much. She was obviously upset, and it had taken her appetite away. That was only natural."

"Yes," said Poirot thoughtfully, "it was only natural."

He opened a drawer, and took out a small despatch-case, then turned to me.

"Now I am ready. We will proceed to the chateau,[11] and study matters on the spot. Excuse me, mon ami, you dressed in haste, and your tie is on one side. Permit me." With a deft gesture, he rearranged it.

"*Ca y est!*[12] Now, shall we start?"

We hurried up the village, and turned in at the lodge gates. Poirot stopped for a moment, and gazed sorrowfully over the beautiful expanse of park, still glittering with morning dew.

"So beautiful, so beautiful, and yet, the poor family, plunged in sorrow, prostrated[13] with grief."

He looked at me keenly as he spoke, and I was aware that I reddened under his prolonged gaze.

Was the family prostrated by grief? Was the sorrow at Mrs. Inglethorp's death so great? I realized that there was an emotional lack in the atmosphere. The dead woman had not the gift of commanding love. Her death was a shock and a distress, but

---

[9] Poirot is using a clothes brush to remove loose dirt, debris and lint from it.

[10] Irritated or annoyed.

[11] The French word for a large country house.

[12] Done! The phrase could also mean "that's it" or "got it" depending on the context.

[13] To lie face-down. To lie face-up, by the way, is to lie supine.

she would not be passionately regretted.

Poirot seemed to follow my thoughts. He nodded his head gravely.

"No, you are right," he said, "it is not as though there was a blood tie. She has been kind and generous to these Cavendishes, but she was not their own mother. Blood tells—always remember that—blood tells."

"Poirot," I said, "I wish you would tell me why you wanted to know if Mrs. Inglethorp ate well last night? I have been turning it over in my mind, but I can't see how it has anything to do with the matter?"

He was silent for a minute or two as we walked along, but finally he said:

"I do not mind telling you—though, as you know, it is not my habit to explain until the end is reached. The present contention is that Mrs. Inglethorp died of strychnine poisoning, presumably administered in her coffee."

"Yes?"

"Well, what time was the coffee served?"

"About eight o'clock."

"Therefore she drank it between then and half-past eight—certainly not much later. Well, strychnine is a fairly rapid poison. Its effects would be felt very soon, probably in about an hour. Yet, in Mrs. Inglethorp's case, the symptoms do not manifest[14] themselves until five o'clock the next morning: nine hours! But a heavy meal, taken at about the same time as the poison, might retard its effects, though hardly to that extent. Still, it is a possibility to be taken into account. But, according to you, she ate very little for supper, and yet the symptoms do not develop until early the next morning! Now that is a curious circumstance, my friend. Something may arise at the autopsy to explain it. In the meantime, remember it."

As we neared the house, John came out and met us. His

---

[14] Appear to the naked eye.

face looked weary and haggard.[15]

"This is a very dreadful business, Monsieur Poirot," he said. "Hastings has explained to you that we are anxious for no publicity?"

"I comprehend perfectly."

"You see, it is only suspicion so far. We have nothing to go upon."

"Precisely. It is a matter of precaution only."

John turned to me, taking out his cigarette-case, and lighting a cigarette as he did so.

"You know that fellow Inglethorp is back?"

"Yes. I met him."

John flung the match into an adjacent flower bed, a proceeding which was too much for Poirot's feelings. He retrieved it, and buried it neatly.

"It's jolly difficult to know how to treat him."

"That difficulty will not exist long," pronounced Poirot quietly.

John looked puzzled, not quite understanding the portent of this cryptic saying.[16] He handed the two keys which Dr. Bauerstein had given him to me.

"Show Monsieur Poirot everything he wants to see."

"The rooms are locked?" asked Poirot.

"Dr. Bauerstein considered it advisable."

Poirot nodded thoughtfully.

"Then he is very sure. Well, that simplifies matters for us."

We went up together to the room of the tragedy. For convenience I append a plan of the room and the principal articles of furniture in it.

[15] Looking exhausted and sick, especially from worry or fatigue.
[16] *Portent:* A sign or warning that an important event is about to happen. *Cryptic:* Something that is mysterious or obscure.

46

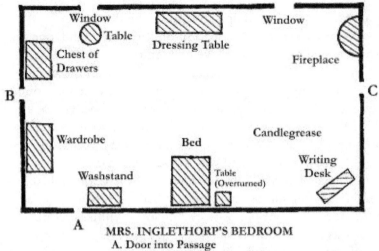

MRS. INGLETHORP'S BEDROOM
A. Door into Passage
B. Door into Mr. Inglethorp's Room
C. Door into Cynthia's Room

Poirot locked the door on the inside, and proceeded to a minute[17] inspection of the room. He darted from one object to the other with the agility of a grasshopper. I remained by the door, fearing to obliterate any clues. Poirot, however, did not seem grateful to me for my forbearance.[18]

"What have you, my friend," he cried, "that you remain there like—how do you say it?—ah, yes, the stuck pig?"[19]

I explained that I was afraid of obliterating any foot-marks.

"Foot-marks? But what an idea! There has already been practically an army in the room! What foot-marks are we likely to find? No, come here and aid me in my search. I will put down my little case until I need it."

He did so, on the round table by the window, but it was an ill-advised proceeding; for, the top of it being loose, it tilted up,

---

[17] A very short time. From the Latin *minuta* for "made small."
[18] Exhibiting restraint or self-control.
[19] Poirot is mixing his English idioms. One can bleed like a stuck pig, or stare like a stuck pig, but one does not stand like a stuck pig. Perhaps he meant stand like a stick in the mud.

and precipitated[20] the despatch-case on the floor.

"*Eh voila une table!*"[21] cried Poirot. "Ah, my friend, one may live in a big house and yet have no comfort."

After which piece of moralizing, he resumed his search.

A small purple despatch-case, with a key in the lock, on the writing-table, engaged his attention for some time. He took out the key from the lock, and passed it to me to inspect. I saw nothing peculiar, however. It was an ordinary key of the Yale type,[22] with a bit of twisted wire through the handle.

Next, he examined the framework of the door we had broken in, assuring himself that the bolt had really been shot. Then he went to the door opposite leading into Cynthia's room. That door was also bolted, as I had stated. However, he went to the length of unbolting it, and opening and shutting it several times; this he did with the utmost precaution against making any noise. Suddenly something in the bolt itself seemed to rivet his attention. He examined it carefully, and then, nimbly whipping out a pair of small forceps[23] from his case, he drew out some minute particle which he carefully sealed up in a tiny envelope.

On the chest of drawers there was a tray with a spirit lamp[24] and a small saucepan on it. A small quantity of a dark fluid remained in the saucepan, and an empty cup and saucer that had been drunk out of stood near it.

---

[20] Make something happen. In this case, the tilting table made the despatch-case fall to the floor.

[21] While *en voilà* means simply "this is," Poirot is implying that the table is inferior, such as, "*What* a table!" Christie does not specify the kind of table this is, but because it tilts so easily, it could be an occasional table, a small stand with no particular function that could be folded and put away.

[22] Linus Yale Sr. invented the pin-tumbler lock, so for a long time, keys were called Yale keys. Yale locks are more resistant to tampering than the locks that use latch keys.

[23] An instrument commonly used by surgeons and jewelers for grasping small objects.

[24] A Primus stove, a pressurized portable stove developed in 1892. It ran on kerosene with the help of methylated spirits.

I wondered how I could have been so unobservant as to overlook this. Here was a clue worth having. Poirot delicately dipped his finger into liquid, and tasted it gingerly. He made a grimace.

"Coco[25]—with—I think—rum in it."

He passed on to the debris on the floor, where the table by the bed had been overturned. A reading-lamp,[26] some books, matches, a bunch of keys, and the crushed fragments of a coffee-cup lay scattered about.

"Ah, this is curious," said Poirot.

"I must confess that I see nothing particularly curious about it."

"You do not? Observe the lamp—the chimney is broken in two places; they lie there as they fell. But see, the coffee-cup is absolutely smashed to powder."

"Well," I said wearily, "I suppose some one must have stepped on it."

"Exactly," said Poirot, in an odd voice. "Some one stepped on it."

He rose from his knees, and walked slowly across to the mantelpiece, where he stood abstractedly fingering the ornaments, and straightening them—a trick of his when he was agitated.

"Mon ami," he said, turning to me, "somebody stepped on that cup, grinding it to powder, and the reason they did so was either because it contained strychnine or—which is far more serious—because it did not contain strychnine!"

I made no reply. I was bewildered, but I knew that it was no good asking him to explain. In a moment or two he roused himself, and went on with his investigations. He picked up the

---

[25] In her memoir, Christie recalled Miss Howse, "the dragon presiding over all spelling in The Bodley Head books," who insisted that cocoa be spelled this way. "I am still not a good speller, but at any rate I could spell cocoa the proper way. What I was, though, was a weak character. It was my first book — and I thought *they* must know better than I did."

[26] An oil-fueled bedside lamp with a chimney made of glass.

bunch of keys from the floor, and twirling them round in his fingers finally selected one, very bright and shining, which he tried in the lock of the purple despatch-case. It fitted, and he opened the box, but after a moment's hesitation, closed and relocked it, and slipped the bunch of keys, as well as the key that had originally stood in the lock, into his own pocket.

"I have no authority to go through these papers. But it should be done—at once!"

He then made a very careful examination of the drawers of the wash-stand. Crossing the room to the left-hand window, a round stain, hardly visible on the dark brown carpet, seemed to interest him particularly. He went down on his knees, examining it minutely—even going so far as to smell it.

Finally, he poured a few drops of the coco into a test tube, sealing it up carefully. His next proceeding was to take out a little notebook.

"We have found in this room," he said, writing busily, "six points of interest. Shall I enumerate them, or will you?"

"Oh, yes," I replied hastily.

"Very well, then. One, a coffee-cup that has been ground into powder; two, a despatch-case with a key in the lock; three, a stain on the floor."

"That may have been done some time ago," I interrupted.

"No, for it is still perceptibly damp and smells of coffee. Four, a fragment of some dark green fabric—only a thread or two, but recognizable."

"Ah!" I cried. "That was what you sealed up in the envelope."

"Yes. It may turn out to be a piece of one of Mrs. Inglethorp's own dresses, and quite unimportant. We shall see. Five, this!" With a dramatic gesture, he pointed to a large splash of candle grease on the floor by the writing-table. "It must have been done since yesterday, otherwise a good housemaid would have at once removed it with blotting-paper and a hot iron.[27] One of my best hats once—but that is not to the point."

"It was very likely done last night. We were very agitated. Or perhaps Mrs. Inglethorp herself dropped her candle."

"You brought only one candle into the room?"

"Yes. Lawrence Cavendish was carrying it. But he was very upset. He seemed to see something over here"—I indicated the mantelpiece—"that absolutely paralysed him."

"That is interesting," said Poirot quickly. "Yes, it is suggestive"—his eye sweeping the whole length of the wall—"but it was not his candle that made this great patch, for you perceive that this is white grease; whereas Monsieur Lawrence's candle, which is still on the dressing-table, is pink. On the other hand, Mrs. Inglethorp had no candlestick in the room, only a reading-lamp."

"Then," I said, "what do you deduce?"

To which my friend only made a rather irritating reply, urging me to use my own natural faculties.

"And the sixth point?" I asked. "I suppose it is the sample of coco."

"No," said Poirot thoughtfully. "I might have included that in the six, but I did not. No, the sixth point I will keep to myself for the present."

He looked quickly round the room. "There is nothing more to be done here, I think, unless"—he stared earnestly and long at the dead ashes in the grate. "The fire burns—and it destroys. But by chance—there might be—let us see!"

Deftly, on hands and knees, he began to sort the ashes from the grate into the fender, handling them with the greatest caution. Suddenly, he gave a faint exclamation.

"The forceps, Hastings!"

---

[27] Although the electric iron was invented in 1882, the lack of electricity at Styles required the use of flatirons, made of a heavy block of metal that would be heated on a stove. A box iron, with its container into which coals could be poured, could also be used.

I quickly handed them to him, and with skill he extracted a small piece of half charred paper.

"There, mon ami!" he cried. "What do you think of that?"

I scrutinized[28] the fragment. This is an exact reproduction of it:—

I was puzzled. It was unusually thick, quite unlike ordinary notepaper. Suddenly an idea struck me.

"Poirot!" I cried. "This is a fragment of a will!"

"Exactly."

I looked up at him sharply.

"You are not surprised?"

"No," he said gravely, "I expected it."

I relinquished the piece of paper, and watched him put it away in his case, with the same methodical care that he bestowed on everything. My brain was in a whirl. What was this complication of a will? Who had destroyed it? The person who had left the candle grease on the floor? Obviously. But how had anyone gained admission? All the doors had been bolted on the inside.

"Now, my friend," said Poirot briskly, "we will go. I should like to ask a few questions of the parlourmaid—Dorcas, her name is, is it not?"

We passed through Alfred Inglethorp's room, and Poirot

---

[28] Examined carefully.

delayed long enough to make a brief but fairly comprehensive examination of it. We went out through that door, locking both it and that of Mrs. Inglethorp's room as before.

I took him down to the boudoir which he had expressed a wish to see, and went myself in search of Dorcas.

When I returned with her, however, the boudoir was empty.

"Poirot," I cried, "where are you?"

"I am here, my friend."

He had stepped outside the French window, and was standing, apparently lost in admiration, before the various shaped flower beds.

"Admirable!" he murmured. "Admirable! What symmetry! Observe that crescent; and those diamonds—their neatness rejoices the eye. The spacing of the plants, also, is perfect. It has been recently done; is it not so?"[29]

"Yes, I believe they were at it yesterday afternoon. But come in—Dorcas is here."

"Eh bien, eh bien! Do not grudge me a moment's satisfaction of the eye."

"Yes, but this affair is more important."

"And how do you know that these fine begonias[30] are not of equal importance?"

I shrugged my shoulders. There was really no arguing with him if he chose to take that line.

"You do not agree? But such things have been. Well, we will come in and interview the brave Dorcas."

Dorcas was standing in the boudoir, her hands folded in front of her, and her grey hair rose in stiff waves under her

---

[29] Poirot refers to carpet bedding, the practice of planting two or more contrasting flowers to create geometric patterns. It is designed to be enjoyed from a distance, such as from a second-story window or terrace.

[30] A perennial flowering plant distinguished by its showy flowers — in white, pink, scarlet or yellow — and its marked leaves.

white cap.[31] She was the very model and picture of a good old-fashioned servant.

In her attitude towards Poirot, she was inclined to be suspicious, but he soon broke down her defences. He drew forward a chair.

"Pray be seated, mademoiselle."[32]

"Thank you, sir."

"You have been with your mistress many years, is it not so?"

"Ten years, sir."

"That is a long time, and very faithful service. You were much attached to her, were you not?"

"She was a very good mistress to me, sir."

"Then you will not object to answering a few questions. I put them to you with Mr. Cavendish's full approval."

"Oh, certainly, sir."

"Then I will begin by asking you about the events of yesterday afternoon. Your mistress had a quarrel?"

"Yes, sir. But I don't know that I ought—" Dorcas hesitated. Poirot looked at her keenly.

"My good Dorcas, it is necessary that I should know every detail of that quarrel as fully as possible. Do not think that you are betraying your mistress's secrets. Your mistress lies dead, and it is necessary that we should know all—if we are to avenge her. Nothing can bring her back to life, but we do hope, if there has been foul play, to bring the murderer to justice."

"Amen to that," said Dorcas fiercely. "And, naming no names, there's one in this house that none of us could ever abide! And an ill day it was when first he darkened the threshold."

Poirot waited for her indignation to subside, and then, resuming his business-like tone, he asked:

---

[31] Being the model of a "good old-fashioned servant," Dorcas probably wore a cap-style hat with a black ribbon around the brim, instead of the smaller version which looks more like a band around the head.
[32] Miss

"Now, as to this quarrel? What is the first you heard of it?"

"Well, sir, I happened to be going along the hall outside yesterday—"

"What time was that?"

"I couldn't say exactly, sir, but it wasn't tea-time by a long way. Perhaps four o'clock—or it may have been a bit later.[33] Well, sir, as I said, I happened to be passing along, when I heard voices very loud and angry in here. I didn't exactly mean to listen, but—well, there it is. I stopped. The door was shut, but the mistress was speaking very sharp and clear, and I heard what she said quite plainly. 'You have lied to me, and deceived me,' she said. I didn't hear what Mr. Inglethorp replied. He spoke a good bit lower than she did—but she answered: 'How dare you? I have kept you and clothed you and fed you! You owe everything to me! And this is how you repay me! By bringing disgrace upon our name!' Again I didn't hear what he said, but she went on: 'Nothing that you can say will make any difference. I see my duty clearly. My mind is made up. You need not think that any fear of publicity, or scandal between husband and wife will deter me.' Then I thought I heard them coming out, so I went off quickly."

"You are sure it was Mr. Inglethorp's voice you heard?"

"Oh, yes, sir, whose else's could it be?"

"Well, what happened next?"

"Later, I came back to the hall; but it was all quiet. At five o'clock, Mrs. Inglethorp rang the bell and told me to bring her a cup of tea—nothing to eat—to the boudoir. She was looking dreadful—so white and upset. 'Dorcas,' she says, 'I've had a great shock.' 'I'm sorry for that, m'm,' I says. 'You'll feel better

[33] With dinner in the upper classes traditionally served at 8 p.m. or even later, the custom arose in the early Victorian era of serving tea with biscuits, scones, bread and butter, cakes, and pastries in the mid-afternoon. The time differed from house to house, but Dorcas' comment that she heard the argument about 4 p.m., long before teatime, implies a serving at 5 p.m. The tradition died out during World War I due to food rationing and was continued only at tea shops and hotels.

after a nice hot cup of tea, m'm.' She had something in her hand. I don't know if it was a letter, or just a piece of paper, but it had writing on it, and she kept staring at it, almost as if she couldn't believe what was written there. She whispered to herself, as though she had forgotten I was there: 'These few words—and everything's changed.' And then she says to me: 'Never trust a man, Dorcas, they're not worth it!' I hurried off, and got her a good strong cup of tea, and she thanked me, and said she'd feel better when she'd drunk it. 'I don't know what to do,' she says. 'Scandal between husband and wife is a dreadful thing, Dorcas. I'd rather hush it up if I could.' Mrs. Cavendish came in just then, so she didn't say any more."

"She still had the letter, or whatever it was, in her hand?"

"Yes, sir."

"What would she be likely to do with it afterwards?"

"Well, I don't know, sir, I expect she would lock it up in that purple case of hers."

"Is that where she usually kept important papers?"

"Yes, sir. She brought it down with her every morning, and took it up every night."

"When did she lose the key of it?"

"She missed it yesterday at lunch-time, sir, and told me to look carefully for it. She was very much put out about it."

"But she had a duplicate key?"

"Oh, yes, sir."

Dorcas was looking very curiously at him and, to tell the truth, so was I. What was all this about a lost key? Poirot smiled.

"Never mind, Dorcas, it is my business to know things. Is this the key that was lost?" He drew from his pocket the key that he had found in the lock of the despatch-case upstairs.

Dorcas's eyes looked as though they would pop out of her head.

"That's it, sir, right enough. But where did you find it? I looked everywhere for it."

"Ah, but you see it was not in the same place yesterday as it was to-day. Now, to pass to another subject, had your mistress a dark green dress in her wardrobe?"

Dorcas was rather startled by the unexpected question.

"No, sir."

"Are you quite sure?"

"Oh, yes, sir."

"Has anyone else in the house got a green dress?"

Dorcas reflected.

"Miss Cynthia has a green evening dress."

"Light or dark green?"

"A light green, sir; a sort of chiffon,[34] they call it."

"Ah, that is not what I want. And nobody else has anything green?"

"No, sir—not that I know of."

Poirot's face did not betray a trace of whether he was disappointed or otherwise. He merely remarked:

"Good, we will leave that and pass on. Have you any reason to believe that your mistress was likely to take a sleeping powder last night?"

"Not last night, sir, I know she didn't."

"Why do you know so positively?"

"Because the box was empty. She took the last one two days ago, and she didn't have any more made up."[35]

"You are quite sure of that?"

"Positive, sir."

"Then that is cleared up! By the way, your mistress didn't ask you to sign any paper yesterday?"

"To sign a paper? No, sir."

"When Mr. Hastings and Mr. Lawrence came in yesterday evening, they found your mistress busy writing letters. I suppose you can give me no idea to whom these letters were ad-

---

[34] A light transparent fabric woven from highly twisted yarns in a plain weave. Usually made of silk, and after 1945 of nylon, it feels soft and slippery and is used primarily in evening wear, scarves and linings.

[35] Before the rise of large pharmaceutical companies in the 1950s, most prescriptions were made up, or compounded, by the pharmacist at the retail level (called drugstores in the U.S. and chemist's in Britain).

dressed?"

"I'm afraid I couldn't, sir. I was out in the evening. Perhaps Annie could tell you, though she's a careless girl. Never cleared the coffee-cups away last night. That's what happens when I'm not here to look after things."

Poirot lifted his hand.

"Since they have been left, Dorcas, leave them a little longer, I pray you. I should like to examine them."

"Very well, sir."

"What time did you go out last evening?"

"About six o'clock, sir."

"Thank you, Dorcas, that is all I have to ask you." He rose and strolled to the window. "I have been admiring these flower beds. How many gardeners are employed here, by the way?"

"Only three now, sir. Five, we had, before the war, when it was kept as a gentleman's place should be. I wish you could have seen it then, sir. A fair sight it was. But now there's only old Manning, and young William, and a new-fashioned woman gardener in breeches and such-like. Ah, these are dreadful times!"[36]

"The good times will come again, Dorcas. At least, we hope so. Now, will you send Annie to me here?"

"Yes, sir. Thank you, sir."

"How did you know that Mrs. Inglethorp took sleeping powders?" I asked, in lively curiosity, as Dorcas left the room. "And about the lost key and the duplicate?"

"One thing at a time. As to the sleeping powders, I knew by this." He suddenly produced a small cardboard box, such as chemists use for powders.

"Where did you find it?"

"In the wash-stand drawer in Mrs. Inglethorp's bedroom. It

[36] The war's demand for manpower caused a severe servant shortage. At Goodwood House in West Sussex, the staff dropped by 1917 from 20 to 12. In one titled family, the wife wrote in a letter that her chauffeur had been drafted and her butler fell ill: "It is a gt. bore losing one's Butler, as somehow it is the last male servant one expected to be bereft of."

was Number Six of my catalogue."

"But I suppose, as the last powder was taken two days ago, it is not of much importance?"

"Probably not, but do you notice anything that strikes you as peculiar about this box?"

I examined it closely.

"No, I can't say that I do."

"Look at the label."

I read the label carefully: "'One powder to be taken at bedtime, if required. Mrs. Inglethorp.' No, I see nothing unusual."

"Not the fact that there is no chemist's name?"

"Ah!" I exclaimed. "To be sure, that is odd!"

"Have you ever known a chemist to send out a box like that, without his printed name?"

"No, I can't say that I have."

I was becoming quite excited, but Poirot damped my ardour by remarking:

"Yet the explanation is quite simple. So do not intrigue yourself, my friend."

An audible creaking proclaimed the approach of Annie, so I had no time to reply.

Annie was a fine, strapping[37] girl, and was evidently labouring under intense excitement, mingled with a certain ghoulish enjoyment of the tragedy.

Poirot came to the point at once, with a business-like briskness.

"I sent for you, Annie, because I thought you might be able to tell me something about the letters Mrs. Inglethorp wrote last night. How many were there? And can you tell me any of the names and addresses?"

Annie considered.

"There were four letters, sir. One was to Miss Howard, and one was to Mr. Wells, the lawyer, and the other two I don't think I remember, sir—oh, yes, one was to Ross's, the caterers

---

[37] Tall and strong.

59

in Tadminster. The other one, I don't remember."

"Think," urged Poirot.

Annie racked her brains in vain.

"I'm sorry, sir, but it's clean gone. I don't think I can have noticed it."

"It does not matter," said Poirot, not betraying any sign of disappointment. "Now I want to ask you about something else. There is a saucepan in Mrs. Inglethorp's room with some coco in it. Did she have that every night?"

"Yes, sir, it was put in her room every evening, and she warmed it up in the night—whenever she fancied it."

"What was it? Plain coco?"

"Yes, sir, made with milk, with a teaspoonful of sugar, and two teaspoonfuls of rum in it."

"Who took it to her room?"

"I did, sir."

"Always?"

"Yes, sir."

"At what time?"

"When I went to draw the curtains, as a rule, sir."

"Did you bring it straight up from the kitchen then?"

"No, sir, you see there's not much room on the gas stove, so Cook used to make it early, before putting the vegetables on for supper. Then I used to bring it up, and put it on the table by the swing door,[38] and take it into her room later."

"The swing door is in the left wing, is it not?"

"Yes, sir."

"And the table, is it on this side of the door, or on the far-ther—servants' side?"

"It's this side, sir."

"What time did you bring it up last night?"

"About quarter-past seven, I should say, sir."

"And when did you take it into Mrs. Inglethorp's room?"

---

[38] A door that pivots on a double-sided hinge so that it can be opened in either direction.

"When I went to shut up, sir. About eight o'clock. Mrs. Inglethorp came up to bed before I'd finished."

"Then, between 7.15 and 8 o'clock, the coco was standing on the table in the left wing?"

"Yes, sir." Annie had been growing redder and redder in the face, and now she blurted out unexpectedly:

"And if there was salt in it, sir, it wasn't me. I never took the salt near it."

"What makes you think there was salt in it?" asked Poirot.

"Seeing it on the tray, sir."

"You saw some salt on the tray?"

"Yes. Coarse kitchen salt, it looked. I never noticed it when I took the tray up, but when I came to take it into the mistress's room I saw it at once, and I suppose I ought to have taken it down again, and asked Cook to make some fresh. But I was in a hurry, because Dorcas was out, and I thought maybe the coco itself was all right, and the salt had only gone on the tray. So I dusted it off with my apron, and took it in."

I had the utmost difficulty in controlling my excitement. Unknown to herself, Annie had provided us with an important piece of evidence. How she would have gaped if she had realized that her "coarse kitchen salt" was strychnine, one of the most deadly poisons known to mankind. I marvelled at Poirot's calm. His self-control was astonishing. I awaited his next question with impatience, but it disappointed me.

"When you went into Mrs. Inglethorp's room, was the door leading into Miss Cynthia's room bolted?"

"Oh! Yes, sir; it always was. It had never been opened."

"And the door into Mr. Inglethorp's room? Did you notice if that was bolted too?"

Annie hesitated.

"I couldn't rightly say, sir; it was shut but I couldn't say whether it was bolted or not."

"When you finally left the room, did Mrs. Inglethorp bolt the door after you?"

"No, sir, not then, but I expect she did later. She usually did lock it at night. The door into the passage, that is."

"Did you notice any candle grease on the floor when you did the room yesterday?"

"Candle grease? Oh, no, sir. Mrs. Inglethorp didn't have a candle, only a reading-lamp."

"Then, if there had been a large patch of candle grease on the floor, you think you would have been sure to have seen it?"

"Yes, sir, and I would have taken it out with a piece of blotting-paper[39] and a hot iron."

Then Poirot repeated the question he had put to Dorcas:

"Did your mistress ever have a green dress?"

"No, sir."

"Nor a mantle,[40] nor a cape, nor a—how do you call it?—a sports coat?"

"Not green, sir."

"Nor anyone else in the house?"

Annie reflected.

"No, sir."

"You are sure of that?"

"Quite sure."

"Bien! That is all I want to know. Thank you very much."

With a nervous giggle, Annie took herself creakingly out of the room. My pent-up excitement burst forth.

"Poirot," I cried, "I congratulate you! This is a great discovery."

"What is a great discovery?"

"Why, that it was the coco and not the coffee that was poisoned. That explains everything! Of course it did not take effect until the early morning, since the coco was only drunk in the middle of the night."

"So you think that the coco—mark well what I say, Hastings, the coco—contained strychnine?"

---

[39] A pad of highly absorbent paper and a major trope in Golden Age mysteries. When using a fountain pen, turning the page over to write on the back risked smearing the still-wet ink. Pressing the page on the blotting paper would prevent this.

[40] A loose cloak or cape usually worn over indoor clothing.

"Of course! That salt on the tray, what else could it have been?"

"It might have been salt," replied Poirot placidly.

I shrugged my shoulders. If he was going to take the matter that way, it was no good arguing with him. The idea crossed my mind, not for the first time, that poor old Poirot was growing old. Privately I thought it lucky that he had associated with him some one of a more receptive type of mind.

Poirot was surveying me with quietly twinkling eyes.

"You are not pleased with me, mon ami?"

"My dear Poirot," I said coldly, "it is not for me to dictate to you. You have a right to your own opinion, just as I have to mine."

"A most admirable sentiment," remarked Poirot, rising briskly to his feet. "Now I have finished with this room. By the way, whose is the smaller desk in the corner?"

"Mr. Inglethorp's."

"Ah!" He tried the roll top tentatively. "Locked. But perhaps one of Mrs. Inglethorp's keys would open it." He tried several, twisting and turning them with a practiced hand, and finally uttering an ejaculation of satisfaction. "Voila! It is not the key, but it will open it at a pinch." He slid back the roll top, and ran a rapid eye over the neatly filed papers. To my surprise, he did not examine them, merely remarking approvingly as he relocked the desk: "Decidedly, he is a man of method, this Mr. Inglethorp!"

A "man of method" was, in Poirot's estimation, the highest praise that could be bestowed on any individual.

I felt that my friend was not what he had been as he rambled on disconnectedly:

"There were no stamps in his desk, but there might have been, eh, mon ami? There might have been? Yes"—his eyes wandered round the room—"this boudoir has nothing more to tell us. It did not yield much. Only this."

He pulled a crumpled envelope out of his pocket, and tossed it over to me. It was rather a curious document. A plain, dirty looking old envelope with a few words scrawled across it, apparently at random. The following is a facsimile[41] of it.

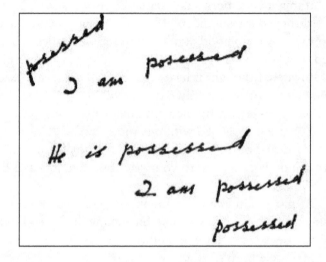

---

[41] An exact copy. From combining the Latin words *fac* for "make" and *simile* for "like."

CHAPTER V

'IT ISN'T STRYCHNINE, IS IT?'

WHERE DID YOU FIND THIS?" I asked Poirot, in lively curiosity.

"In the waste-paper basket. You recognise the handwriting?"

"Yes, it is Mrs. Inglethorp's. But what does it mean?"

Poirot shrugged his shoulders.

"I cannot say—but it is suggestive."

A wild idea flashed across me. Was it possible that Mrs. Inglethorp's mind was deranged? Had she some fantastic idea of demoniacal possession?[1] And, if that were so, was it not also possible that she might have taken her own life?

I was about to expound these theories to Poirot, when his own words distracted me.

"Come," he said, "now to examine the coffee-cups!"

"My dear Poirot! What on earth is the good of that, now that we know about the coco?"

"Oh, là là![2] That miserable coco!" cried Poirot flippantly.

He laughed with apparent enjoyment, raising his arms to heaven in mock despair, in what I could not but consider the worst possible taste.

"And, anyway," I said, with increasing coldness, "as Mrs.

[1] *Deranged:* Possessed by an evil spirit or demon. *Demonical:* Possessed by an evil spirit or demon.

[2] There, there. An exclamation expressing surprise, pleasure (especially towards a beautiful woman), distress, disappointment, or commiseration.

Inglethorp took her coffee upstairs with her, I do not see what you expect to find, unless you consider it likely that we shall discover a packet of strychnine on the coffee tray!"

Poirot was sobered at once.

"Come, come, my friend," he said, slipping his arms through mine. "*Ne vous fachez pas!*[3] Allow me to interest myself in my coffee-cups, and I will respect your coco. There! Is it a bargain?"

He was so quaintly humorous that I was forced to laugh; and we went together to the drawing-room, where the coffee-cups and tray remained undisturbed as we had left them.

Poirot made me recapitulate the scene of the night before, listening very carefully, and verifying the position of the various cups.

"So Mrs. Cavendish stood by the tray—and poured out. Yes. Then she came across to the window where you sat with Mademoiselle Cynthia. Yes. Here are the three cups. And the cup on the mantel-piece, half drunk, that would be Mr. Lawrence Cavendish's. And the one on the tray?"

"John Cavendish's. I saw him put it down there."

"Good. One, two, three, four, five—but where, then, is the cup of Mr. Inglethorp?"

"He does not take coffee."

"Then all are accounted for. One moment, my friend."

With infinite care, he took a drop or two from the grounds in each cup, sealing them up in separate test tubes, tasting each in turn as he did so. His physiognomy underwent a curious change. An expression gathered there that I can only describe as half puzzled, and half relieved.

"*Bien!*" he said at last. "It is evident! I had an idea—but clearly I was mistaken. Yes, altogether I was mistaken. Yet it is strange. But no matter!"

And, with a characteristic shrug, he dismissed whatever it was that was worrying him from his mind. I could have told

---

[3] Don't be angry with me.

him from the beginning that this obsession of his over the coffee was bound to end in a blind alley, but I restrained my tongue. After all, though he was old, Poirot had been a great man in his day.

"Breakfast is ready," said John Cavendish, coming in from the hall. "You will breakfast with us, Monsieur Poirot?"

Poirot acquiesced.[4] I observed John. Already he was almost restored to his normal self. The shock of the events of the last night had upset him temporarily, but his equable[5] poise soon swung back to the normal. He was a man of very little imagination, in sharp contrast with his brother, who had, perhaps, too much.

Ever since the early hours of the morning, John had been hard at work, sending telegrams—one of the first had gone to Evelyn Howard—writing notices for the papers, and generally occupying himself with the melancholy duties that a death entails.

"May I ask how things are proceeding?" he said. "Do your investigations point to my mother having died a natural death—or—or must we prepare ourselves for the worst?"

"I think, Mr. Cavendish," said Poirot gravely, "that you would do well not to buoy yourself up with any false hopes. Can you tell me the views of the other members of the family?"

"My brother Lawrence is convinced that we are making a fuss over nothing. He says that everything points to its being a simple case of heart failure."

"He does, does he? That is very interesting—very interesting," murmured Poirot softly. "And Mrs. Cavendish?"

A faint cloud passed over John's face.

"I have not the least idea what my wife's views on the subject are."

The answer brought a momentary stiffness in its train. John broke the rather awkward silence by saying with a slight effort:

"I told you, didn't I, that Mr. Inglethorp has returned?"

---

[4] Accept with reluctance.
[5] Marked by a steady temperament.

Poirot bent his head.

"It's an awkward position for all of us. Of course one has to treat him as usual—but, hang it all, one's gorge[6] does rise at sitting down to eat with a possible murderer!"

Poirot nodded sympathetically.

"I quite understand. It is a very difficult situation for you, Mr. Cavendish. I would like to ask you one question. Mr. Inglethorp's reason for not returning last night was, I believe, that he had forgotten the latch-key. Is not that so?"

"Yes."

"I suppose you are quite sure that the latch-key *was* forgotten—that he did not take it after all?"

"I have no idea. I never thought of looking. We always keep it in the hall drawer. I'll go and see if it's there now."

Poirot held up his hand with a faint smile.

"No, no, Mr. Cavendish, it is too late now. I am certain that you would find it. If Mr. Inglethorp did take it, he has had ample time to replace it by now."

"But do you think—"

"I think nothing. If anyone had chanced to look this morning before his return, and seen it there, it would have been a valuable point in his favour. That is all."

John looked perplexed.

"Do not worry," said Poirot smoothly. "I assure you that you need not let it trouble you. Since you are so kind, let us go and have some breakfast."

Every one was assembled in the dining-room. Under the circumstances, we were naturally not a cheerful party. The reaction after a shock is always trying, and I think we were all suffering from it. Decorum and good breeding naturally enjoined that our demeanour should be much as usual,[7] yet I could not

---

[6] A sensation of constriction in the throat to indicate revulsion at someone or something.

[7] *Decorum:* The conventions of polite behavior. *Breeding:* The idea that a person's morals and characteristics were passed down from generation to generation was strongly held in a society with rigid social classes and an agricul-

help wondering if this self-control were really a matter of great difficulty. There were no red eyes, no signs of secretly indulged grief. I felt that I was right in my opinion that Dorcas was the person most affected by the personal side of the tragedy.

I pass over Alfred Inglethorp, who acted the bereaved widower in a manner that I felt to be disgusting in its hypocrisy. Did he know that we suspected him, I wondered. Surely he could not be unaware of the fact, conceal it as we would. Did he feel some secret stirring of fear, or was he confident that his crime would go unpunished? Surely the suspicion in the atmosphere must warn him that he was already a marked man.

But did every one suspect him? What about Mrs. Cavendish? I watched her as she sat at the head of the table, graceful, composed, enigmatic. In her soft grey frock, with white ruffles at the wrists falling over her slender hands, she looked very beautiful. When she chose, however, her face could be sphinx-like in its inscrutability.[8] She was very silent, hardly opening her

---

tural tradition where traits were bred in and out of animal bloodlines. *Enjoined:* To forbid or prohibit.

[8] The sphinx is a mythical beast with the head of a human and the body of a lion. This reference is to the Great Sphinx of Giza, a huge statue 241 feet long, 63 feet wide and nearly 6 stories tall that sits on the Giza Plateau outside Cairo, Egypt. The source of its smile has been the subject of much speculation, such as this obscene ditty by that prolific poet Anonymous:

Oh, the sexual life of the camel
Is stranger than anyone thinks
In moments of amorous passion
He frequently buggers the sphinx.

But the sphinx's posterior passage
Is clogged with the sands of the Nile
Which accounts for the hump on the camel
And the Sphinx's inscrutable smile.

Inscrutability: Difficult to understand.

lips, and yet in some queer way I felt that the great strength of her personality was dominating us all.

And little Cynthia? Did she suspect? She looked very tired and ill, I thought. The heaviness and languor of her manner were very marked. I asked her if she were feeling ill, and she answered frankly:

"Yes, I've got the most beastly headache."

"Have another cup of coffee, mademoiselle?" said Poirot solicitously. "It will revive you. It is unparalleled for the *mal de tête*."[9] He jumped up and took her cup.

"No sugar," said Cynthia, watching him, as he picked up the sugar-tongs.[10]

"No sugar? You abandon it in the war-time, eh?"

"No, I never take it in coffee."

"*Sacré!*"[11] murmured Poirot to himself, as he brought back the replenished cup.

Only I heard him, and glancing up curiously at the little man I saw that his face was working with suppressed excitement, and his eyes were as green as a cat's. He had heard or seen something that had affected him strongly—but what was it? I do not usually label myself as dense, but I must confess that nothing out of the ordinary had attracted *my* attention.

---

[9] headache

[10] A utensil with two claw- or spoon-shaped ends used for serving sugar lumps. In the 1700s, Europeans bought sugar in brown loafs that had to be cut apart and ground for home use. Czech sugar refiner Jakub Rad patented a sugar cube press in 1843 after his wife complained that she cut her finger while chopping sugar. By the 1870s, sugar merchant Henry Tate was making cubes and building a fortune that would let him become a philanthropist and the founder of London's Tate Gallery.

[11] Literally "sacred" or "holy," used as an exclamation or curse. Since those words would sound odd in this context, a translator might have Poirot say "Heavens!" instead. He's reacting this way because French coffee is typically drunk with sugar.

In another moment, the door opened and Dorcas appeared. "Mr. Wells to see you, sir," she said to John.

I remembered the name as being that of the lawyer to whom Mrs. Inglethorp had written the night before.

John rose immediately.

"Show him into my study." Then he turned to us. "My mother's lawyer," he explained. And in a lower voice: "He is also Coroner—you understand.[12] Perhaps you would like to come with me?"

We acquiesced and followed him out of the room. John strode on ahead and I took the opportunity of whispering to Poirot:

"There will be an inquest then?"

Poirot nodded absently. He seemed absorbed in thought; so much so that my curiosity was aroused.

"What is it? You are not attending to what I say."

"It is true, my friend. I am much worried."

"Why?"

"Because Mademoiselle Cynthia does not take sugar in her coffee."

"What? You cannot be serious?"

"But I am most serious. Ah, there is something there that I do not understand. My instinct was right."

"What instinct?"

"The instinct that led me to insist on examining those coffee-cups. *Chut*[13] no more now!"

We followed John into his study, and he closed the door behind us.

Mr. Wells was a pleasant man of middle-age, with keen eyes, and the typical lawyer's mouth. John introduced us both, and explained the reason of our presence.

"You will understand, Wells," he added, "that this is all

---

[12] A public official charged with investigating a death when there is reason to believe it was not by natural causes.
[13] Hush!

strictly private. We are still hoping that there will turn out to be no need for investigation of any kind."

"Quite so, quite so," said Mr. Wells soothingly. "I wish we could have spared you the pain and publicity of an inquest, but of course it's quite unavoidable in the absence of a doctor's certificate."[14]

"Yes, I suppose so."

"Clever man, Bauerstein. Great authority on toxicology,[15] I believe."

"Indeed," said John with a certain stiffness in his manner. Then he added rather hesitatingly: "Shall we have to appear as witnesses—all of us, I mean?"

"You, of course—and ah—er—Mr.—er—Inglethorp."

A slight pause ensued before the lawyer went on in his soothing manner:

"Any other evidence will be simply confirmatory,[16] a mere matter of form."

"I see."

A faint expression of relief swept over John's face. It puzzled me, for I saw no occasion for it.

"If you know of nothing to the contrary," pursued Mr. Wells, "I had thought of Friday. That will give us plenty of time for the doctor's report. The post-mortem is to take place to-night, I believe?"

"Yes."

"Then that arrangement will suit you?"

"Perfectly."

"I need not tell you, my dear Cavendish, how distressed I am at this most tragic affair."

---

[14] A certificate, signed by a doctor and filed with the authorities that contains information about the decedent including the cause of death. A doctor's certificate has been required to issue a death certificate in Great Britain since 1879.

[15] The branch of science that deals with the nature, effects and detection of poisons.

[16] Used to support facts previously given during the hearing.

"Can you give us no help in solving it, monsieur?" interposed Poirot, speaking for the first time since we had entered the room.

"I?"

"Yes, we heard that Mrs. Inglethorp wrote to you last night. You should have received the letter this morning."[17]

"I did, but it contains no information. It is merely a note asking me to call upon her this morning, as she wanted my advice on a matter of great importance."

"She gave you no hint as to what that matter might be?"

"Unfortunately, no."

"That is a pity," said John.

"A great pity," agreed Poirot gravely.

There was silence. Poirot remained lost in thought for a few minutes. Finally he turned to the lawyer again.

"Mr. Wells, there is one thing I should like to ask you—that is, if it is not against professional etiquette. In the event of Mrs. Inglethorp's death, who would inherit her money?"

The lawyer hesitated a moment, and then replied:

"The knowledge will be public property very soon, so if Mr. Cavendish does not object—"

"Not at all," interpolated John.

"I do not see any reason why I should not answer your question. By her last will, dated August of last year, after various unimportant legacies to servants, etc., she gave her entire fortune to her stepson, Mr. John Cavendish."

"Was not that—pardon the question, Mr. Cavendish—rather unfair to her other stepson, Mr. Lawrence Cavendish?"

"No, I do not think so. You see, under the terms of their father's will, while John inherited the property, Lawrence, at his stepmother's death, would come into a considerable sum of money. Mrs. Inglethorp left her money to her elder stepson,

---

[17] The number of times the mail was delivered in a day depended on the location. Morning and afternoon deliveries were common, but during the Victorian era, mail was delivered hourly in London, from 7:30 a.m. to 7:30 p.m., and six times a day in other major cities.

knowing that he would have to keep up Styles. It was, to my mind, a very fair and equitable distribution."

Poirot nodded thoughtfully.

"I see. But I am right in saying, am I not, that by your English law that will was automatically revoked when Mrs. Inglethorp remarried?"

Mr. Wells bowed his head.

"As I was about to proceed, Monsieur Poirot, that document is now null and void."

"*Hein!*"[18] said Poirot. He reflected for a moment, and then asked: "Was Mrs. Inglethorp herself aware of that fact?"

"I do not know. She may have been."

"She was," said John unexpectedly. "We were discussing the matter of wills being revoked by marriage only yesterday."

"Ah! One more question, Mr. Wells. You say 'her last will.' Had Mrs. Inglethorp, then, made several former wills?"

"On an average, she made a new will at least once a year," said Mr. Wells imperturbably. "She was given to changing her mind as to her testamentary dispositions,[19] now benefiting one, now another member of her family."

"Suppose," suggested Poirot, "that, unknown to you, she had made a new will in favour of some one who was not, in any sense of the word, a member of the family—we will say Miss Howard, for instance—would you be surprised?"

"Not in the least."

"Ah!" Poirot seemed to have exhausted his questions.

I drew close to him, while John and the lawyer were debating the question of going through Mrs. Inglethorp's papers.

"Do you think Mrs. Inglethorp made a will leaving all her

---

[18] What?

[19] How she intended to disperse her worldly goods in her will, sometimes labeled a "Last Will and Testament." A testament means a covenant, or agreement, between God and the human race. This is why the early Christians organized their Bible by gathering the story of God's covenant with the Jews into the Old Testament and the story of Jesus' covenant into the New Testament.

money to Miss Howard?" I asked in a low voice, with some curiosity.

Poirot smiled.

"No."

"Then why did you ask?"

"Hush!"

John Cavendish had turned to Poirot.

"Will you come with us, Monsieur Poirot? We are going through my mother's papers. Mr. Inglethorp is quite willing to leave it entirely to Mr. Wells and myself."

"Which simplifies matters very much," murmured the lawyer. "As technically, of course, he was entitled—" He did not finish the sentence.

"We will look through the desk in the boudoir first," explained John, "and go up to her bedroom afterwards. She kept her most important papers in a purple despatch-case, which we must look through carefully."

"Yes," said the lawyer, "it is quite possible that there may be a later will than the one in my possession."

"There *is* a later will." It was Poirot who spoke.

"What?" John and the lawyer looked at him startled.

"Or, rather," pursued my friend imperturbably,[20] "there *was* one."

"What do you mean—there was one? Where is it now?"

"Burnt!"

"Burnt?"

"Yes. See here." He took out the charred fragment we had found in the grate in Mrs. Inglethorp's room, and handed it to the lawyer with a brief explanation of when and where he had found it.

"But possibly this is an old will?"

"I do not think so. In fact I am almost certain that it was made no earlier than yesterday afternoon."

"What?" "Impossible!" broke simultaneously from both

---

[20] Calmly.

men.

Poirot turned to John.

"If you will allow me to send for your gardener, I will prove it to you."

"Oh, of course—but I don't see—"

Poirot raised his hand.

"Do as I ask you. Afterwards you shall question as much as you please."

"Very well." He rang the bell.

Dorcas answered it in due course.

"Dorcas, will you tell Manning to come round and speak to me here."

"Yes, sir."

Dorcas withdrew.

We waited in a tense silence. Poirot alone seemed perfectly at his ease, and dusted a forgotten corner of the bookcase.

The clumping of hobnailed boots[21] on the gravel outside proclaimed the approach of Manning. John looked questioningly at Poirot. The latter nodded.

"Come inside, Manning," said John, "I want to speak to you."

Manning came slowly and hesitatingly through the French window, and stood as near it as he could. He held his cap in his hands, twisting it very carefully round and round. His back was much bent, though he was probably not as old as he looked, but his eyes were sharp and intelligent, and belied his slow and rather cautious speech.[22]

"Manning," said John, "this gentleman will put some ques-

---

[21] Boots whose soles are attached with short, large-headed nails. Hobnails provide traction on muddy, icy or snowy ground, but can slide on and mar smooth surfaces.

[22] Britain's class divide is at work here. Manning's hobnail boots and cap mark him as working class, and he displays knowledge of his place by his nervous behavior with his cap, his politeness ("Yes, sir"), the finger-to-the-forehead salute he'll perform before leaving and his determination not to slip into his working-class accent when talking with his betters.

tions to you which I want you to answer."

"Yessir," mumbled Manning.

Poirot stepped forward briskly. Manning's eye swept over him with a faint contempt.

"You were planting a bed of begonias round by the south side of the house yesterday afternoon, were you not, Manning?"

"Yes, sir, me and Willum."

"And Mrs. Inglethorp came to the window and called you, did she not?"

"Yes, sir, she did."

"Tell me in your own words exactly what happened after that."

"Well, sir, nothing much. She just told Willum to go on his bicycle down to the village, and bring back a form of will, or such-like—I don't know what exactly—she wrote it down for him."

"Well?"

"Well, he did, sir."

"And what happened next?"

"We went on with the begonias, sir."

"Did not Mrs. Inglethorp call you again?"

"Yes, sir, both me and Willum, she called."

"And then?"

"She made us come right in, and sign our names at the bottom of a long paper—under where she'd signed."

"Did you see anything of what was written above her signature?" asked Poirot sharply.

"No, sir, there was a bit of blotting paper over that part."

"And you signed where she told you?"

"Yes, sir, first me and then Willum."

"What did she do with it afterwards?"

"Well, sir, she slipped it into a long envelope, and put it inside a sort of purple box that was standing on the desk."

"What time was it when she first called you?"

"About four, I should say, sir."

"Not earlier? Couldn't it have been about half-past three?"

77

"No, I shouldn't say so, sir. It would be more likely to be a bit after four—not before it."

"Thank you, Manning, that will do," said Poirot pleasantly.

The gardener glanced at his master, who nodded, whereupon Manning lifted a finger to his forehead with a low mumble, and backed cautiously out of the window.

We all looked at each other.

"Good heavens!" murmured John. "What an extraordinary coincidence."

"How—a coincidence?"

"That my mother should have made a will on the very day of her death!"

Mr. Wells cleared his throat and remarked drily:

"Are you so sure it is a coincidence, Cavendish?"

"What do you mean?"

"Your mother, you tell me, had a violent quarrel with—some one yesterday afternoon—"

"What do you mean?" cried John again. There was a tremor in his voice, and he had gone very pale.

"In consequence of that quarrel, your mother very suddenly and hurriedly makes a new will. The contents of that will we shall never know. She told no one of its provisions. This morning, no doubt, she would have consulted me on the subject—but she had no chance. The will disappears, and she takes its secret with her to her grave. Cavendish, I much fear there is no coincidence there. Monsieur Poirot, I am sure you agree with me that the facts are very suggestive."

"Suggestive, or not," interrupted John, "we are most grateful to Monsieur Poirot for elucidating[23] the matter. But for him, we should never have known of this will. I suppose, I may not ask you, monsieur, what first led you to suspect the fact?"

Poirot smiled and answered:

"A scribbled over old envelope, and a freshly planted bed of begonias."

---

[23] To explain, analyze or clarify.

John, I think, would have pressed his questions further, but at that moment the loud purr of a motor was audible, and we all turned to the window as it swept past.

"Evie!" cried John. "Excuse me, Wells." He went hurriedly out into the hall.

Poirot looked inquiringly at me.

"Miss Howard," I explained.

"Ah, I am glad she has come. There is a woman with a head and a heart too, Hastings. Though the good God gave her no beauty!"

I followed John's example, and went out into the hall, where Miss Howard was endeavouring to extricate[24] herself from the voluminous mass of veils that enveloped her head.[25] As her eyes fell on me, a sudden pang of guilt shot through me. This was the woman who had warned me so earnestly, and to whose warning I had, alas, paid no heed! How soon, and how contemptuously, I had dismissed it from my mind. Now that she had been proved justified in so tragic a manner, I felt ashamed. She had known Alfred Inglethorp only too well. I wondered whether, if she had remained at Styles, the tragedy would have taken place, or would the man have feared her watchful eyes?

I was relieved when she shook me by the hand, with her well remembered painful grip. The eyes that met mine were sad, but not reproachful; that she had been crying bitterly, I could tell by the redness of her eyelids, but her manner was unchanged from its old gruffness.

"Started the moment I got the wire. Just come off night duty. Hired car. Quickest way to get here."[26]

---

[24] To unravel.

[25] Cars at the time did not have wraparound glass windows, but a windshield with canvas and plastic side curtains that can be attached to the frame for inclement weather. The result was a ride that could ruin a woman's styled hair, so many would resort to a hat and scarves for protection.

[26] A rented car. At a time when cars were beyond the reach of most incomes and public transport plentiful, renting was a practical solution when travel-

"Have you had anything to eat this morning, Evie?" asked John.

"No."

"I thought not. Come along, breakfast's not cleared away yet, and they'll make you some fresh tea." He turned to me. "Look after her, Hastings, will you? Wells is waiting for me. Oh, here's Monsieur Poirot. He's helping us, you know, Evie."

Miss Howard shook hands with Poirot, but glanced suspiciously over her shoulder at John.

"What do you mean—helping us?"

"Helping us to investigate."

"Nothing to investigate. Have they taken him to prison yet?"

"Taken who to prison?"

"Who? Alfred Inglethorp, of course!"

"My dear Evie, do be careful. Lawrence is of the opinion that my mother died from heart seizure."

"More fool, Lawrence!" retorted Miss Howard. "Of course Alfred Inglethorp murdered poor Emily—as I always told you he would."

"My dear Evie, don't shout so. Whatever we may think or suspect, it is better to say as little as possible for the present. The inquest isn't until Friday."

"Not until fiddlesticks!" The snort Miss Howard gave was truly magnificent. "You're all off your heads. The man will be out of the country by then. If he's any sense, he won't stay here tamely and wait to be hanged."

John Cavendish looked at her helplessly.

"I know what it is," she accused him, "you've been listening to the doctors. Never should. What do they know? Nothing at all—or just enough to make them dangerous. I ought to know—

---

ing beyond the reach of trains and buses, or, in the case of Miss Howard, when speed is of the essence.

my own father was a doctor. That little Wilkins is about the greatest fool that even I have ever seen. Heart seizure! Sort of thing he would say. Anyone with any sense could see at once that her husband had poisoned her. I always said he'd murder her in her bed, poor soul. Now he's done it. And all you can do is to murmur silly things about 'heart seizure' and 'inquest on Friday.' You ought to be ashamed of yourself, John Cavendish."

"What do you want me to do?" asked John, unable to help a faint smile. "Dash it all, Evie, I can't haul him down to the local police station by the scruff of his neck."

"Well, you might do something. Find out how he did it. He's a crafty beggar. Dare say he soaked fly papers.[27] Ask Cook if she's missed any."

It occurred to me very forcibly at that moment that to harbour Miss Howard and Alfred Inglethorp under the same roof, and keep the peace between them, was likely to prove a Herculean task,[28] and I did not envy John. I could see by the expression on his face that he fully appreciated the difficulty of the position. For the moment, he sought refuge in retreat, and left the room precipitately.[29]

Dorcas brought in fresh tea. As she left the room, Poirot came over from the window where he had been standing, and sat down facing Miss Howard.

"Mademoiselle," he said gravely, "I want to ask you something."

"Ask away," said the lady, eyeing him with some disfavour.

---

[27] Fly paper impregnated with arsenic was commonly sold. The sheets would be soaked in plates of water, and the flies would die from drinking the poison-laced water. The technique also worked on humans as proved by notorious poisoners such as Frederick Seddon and Florence Maybrick.

[28] Hercules is the Roman name for the Greek demigod Heracles. The son of Zeus and the human Alcmene, he was enormously strong and many stories were told of his adventures throughout the ancient world. One major cycle of tales told of the twelve labors he had to perform to atone for slaughtering his six sons while insane. Christie would use these as the inspiration for *The Labors of Hercules*, a short-story collection starring Poirot.

[29] Abruptly.

"I want to be able to count upon your help."

"I'll help you to hang Alfred with pleasure," she replied gruffly. "Hanging's too good for him. Ought to be drawn and quartered, like in good old times."[30]

"We are at one then," said Poirot, "for I, too, want to hang the criminal."

"Alfred Inglethorp?"

"Him, or another."

"No question of another. Poor Emily was never murdered until *he* came along. I don't say she wasn't surrounded by sharks—she was. But it was only her purse they were after. Her life was safe enough. But along comes Mr. Alfred Inglethorp—and within two months—hey presto!"[31]

"Believe me, Miss Howard," said Poirot very earnestly, "if Mr. Inglethorp is the man, he shall not escape me. On my honour, I will hang him as high as Haman!"[32]

"That's better," said Miss Howard more enthusiastically.

"But I must ask you to trust me. Now your help may be very valuable to me. I will tell you why. Because, in all this house of mourning, yours are the only eyes that have wept."

Miss Howard blinked, and a new note crept into the gruffness of her voice.

---

[30] In medieval times, men convicted of high treason in England were tortured to death. The victim was dragged to the execution site on a sledge or by a horse — the "drawn" part — hung nearly to death, then disemboweled and his entrails burned before his eyes. Finally, the body would be quartered into four pieces.

[31] Miss Howard is mimicking a magician revealing the climax of a trick.

[32] A story from the book of Esther. Haman was vizier to Persian King Artaxerxes II, who issued an edict to execute his adviser, Mordecai, and the kingdom's Jews after he refused to prostrate himself before Haman. Queen Esther, Mordecai's cousin, visited the king, revealed her Jewish heritage and told him that Mordecai had foiled a plot to assassinate the king. Artaxerxes couldn't withdraw the edict without losing status, but issued a new one allowing Jews to kill preemptively in self-defense. Esther armed the Jews and they attacked Haman's militia. Haman was hanged on the gallows he had built for Mordecai. This deliverance is celebrated at the feast of Purim.

"If you mean that I was fond of her—yes, I was. You know, Emily was a selfish old woman in her way. She was very generous, but she always wanted a return. She never let people forget what she had done for them—and, that way she missed love. Don't think she ever realized it, though, or felt the lack of it. Hope not, anyway. I was on a different footing. I took my stand from the first. 'So many pounds a year I'm worth to you. Well and good. But not a penny piece besides—not a pair of gloves, nor a theatre ticket.' She didn't understand—was very offended sometimes. Said I was foolishly proud. It wasn't that—but I couldn't explain. Anyway, I kept my self-respect. And so, out of the whole bunch, I was the only one who could allow myself to be fond of her. I watched over her. I guarded her from the lot of them, and then a glib-tongued scoundrel comes along, and pooh! all my years of devotion go for nothing."

Poirot nodded sympathetically.

"I understand, mademoiselle, I understand all you feel. It is most natural. You think that we are lukewarm—that we lack fire and energy—but trust me, it is not so."

John stuck his head in at this juncture, and invited us both to come up to Mrs. Inglethorp's room, as he and Mr. Wells had finished looking through the desk in the boudoir.

As we went up the stairs, John looked back to the dining-room door, and lowered his voice confidentially:

"Look here, what's going to happen when these two meet?"

I shook my head helplessly.

"I've told Mary to keep them apart if she can."

"Will she be able to do so?"

"The Lord only knows. There's one thing, Inglethorp himself won't be too keen on meeting her."

"You've got the keys still, haven't you, Poirot?" I asked, as we reached the door of the locked room.

Taking the keys from Poirot, John unlocked it, and we all passed in. The lawyer went straight to the desk, and John followed him.

"My mother kept most of her important papers in this despatch-case, I believe," he said.

Poirot drew out the small bunch of keys.

"Permit me. I locked it, out of precaution, this morning."

"But it's not locked now."

"Impossible!"

"See." And John lifted the lid as he spoke.

"*Milles tonnerres!*"[33] cried Poirot, dumbfounded. "And I—who have both the keys in my pocket!" He flung himself upon the case. Suddenly he stiffened. "*En voila une affaire!*[34] This lock has been forced."

"What?"

Poirot laid down the case again.

"But who forced it? Why should they? When? But the door was locked?" These exclamations burst from us disjointedly.

Poirot answered them categorically—almost mechanically.

"Who? That is the question. Why? Ah, if I only knew. When? Since I was here an hour ago. As to the door being locked, it is a very ordinary lock. Probably any other of the doorkeys in this passage would fit it."

We stared at one another blankly. Poirot had walked over to the mantel-piece. He was outwardly calm, but I noticed his hands, which from long force of habit were mechanically straightening the spill vases on the mantel-piece, were shaking violently.[35]

"See here, it was like this," he said at last. "There was something in that case—some piece of evidence, slight in itself perhaps, but still enough of a clue to connect the murderer with the crime. It was vital to him that it should be destroyed before it was discovered and its significance appreciated. Therefore, he took the risk, the great risk, of coming in here. Finding the case locked, he was obliged to force it, thus betraying his presence.

---

[33] A thousand thunders! Expressed as a curse.

[34] What an affair!

[35] A vase used to hold strips of curled paper or wood, called spills, that were used to light gas lamps, oil lamps, candles or cigarettes from the flames in a fireplace. The word comes from the Old English *spillan* for "waste" or "shed" as in blood.

For him to take that risk, it must have been something of great importance."

"But what was it?"

"Ah!" cried Poirot, with a gesture of anger. "That, I do not know! A document of some kind, without doubt, possibly the scrap of paper Dorcas saw in her hand yesterday afternoon. And I—" his anger burst forth freely—"miserable animal that I am! I guessed nothing! I have behaved like an imbecile! I should never have left that case here. I should have carried it away with me. Ah, triple pig![36] And now it is gone. It is destroyed—but is it destroyed? Is there not yet a chance—we must leave no stone unturned—"

He rushed like a madman from the room, and I followed him as soon as I had sufficiently recovered my wits. But, by the time I had reached the top of the stairs, he was out of sight.

Mary Cavendish was standing where the staircase branched, staring down into the hall in the direction in which he had disappeared.

"What has happened to your extraordinary little friend, Mr. Hastings? He has just rushed past me like a mad bull."

"He's rather upset about something," I remarked feebly. I really did not know how much Poirot would wish me to disclose. As I saw a faint smile gather on Mrs. Cavendish's expressive mouth, I endeavoured to try and turn the conversation by saying: "They haven't met yet, have they?"

"Who?"

"Mr. Inglethorp and Miss Howard."

She looked at me in rather a disconcerting[37] manner.

"Do you think it would be such a disaster if they did meet?"

"Well, don't you?" I said, rather taken aback.

"No." She was smiling in her quiet way. "I should like to see a good flare up. It would clear the air. At present we are all

---

[36] In France, to act like a pig is the mark of a despicable character. Tripling his curse acts as an intensifier, such as "three times a pig!"

[37] A look that causes confusion or to lose one's composure.

thinking so much, and saying so little."

"John doesn't think so," I remarked. "He's anxious to keep them apart."

"Oh, John!"

Something in her tone fired me, and I blurted out:

"Old John's an awfully good sort."

She studied me curiously for a minute or two, and then said, to my great surprise:

"You are loyal to your friend. I like you for that."

"Aren't you my friend too?"

"I am a very bad friend."

"Why do you say that?"

"Because it is true. I am charming to my friends one day, and forget all about them the next."

I don't know what impelled me, but I was nettled, and I said foolishly and not in the best of taste:

"Yet you seem to be invariably charming to Dr. Bauerstein!"

Instantly I regretted my words. Her face stiffened. I had the impression of a steel curtain coming down and blotting out the real woman. Without a word, she turned and went swiftly up the stairs, whilst I stood like an idiot gaping after her.

I was recalled to other matters by a frightful row going on below. I could hear Poirot shouting and expounding. I was vexed to think that my diplomacy had been in vain. The little man appeared to be taking the whole house into his confidence, a proceeding of which I, for one, doubted the wisdom. Once again I could not help regretting that my friend was so prone to lose his head in moments of excitement. I stepped briskly down the stairs. The sight of me calmed Poirot almost immediately. I drew him aside.

"My dear fellow," I said, "is this wise? Surely you don't want the whole house to know of this occurrence? You are actually playing into the criminal's hands."

"You think so, Hastings?"

"I am sure of it."

"Well, well, my friend, I will be guided by you."

"Good. Although, unfortunately, it is a little too late now."

"Sure."

He looked so crestfallen and abashed that I felt quite sorry, though I still thought my rebuke a just and wise one.[38]

"Well," he said at last, "let us go, *mon ami.*"

"You have finished here?"

"For the moment, yes. You will walk back with me to the village?"

"Willingly."

He picked up his little suit-case, and we went out through the open window in the drawing-room. Cynthia Murdoch was just coming in, and Poirot stood aside to let her pass.

"Excuse me, mademoiselle, one minute."

"Yes?" she turned inquiringly.

"Did you ever make up Mrs. Inglethorp's medicines?"

A slight flush rose in her face, as she answered rather constrainedly:

"No."

"Only her powders?"

The flush deepened as Cynthia replied:

"Oh, yes, I did make up some sleeping powders for her once."

"These?"

Poirot produced the empty box which had contained powders.

She nodded.

"Can you tell me what they were? Sulphonal? Veronal?"

"No, they were bromide powders."[39]

---

[38] *Crestfallen*: Sad and disappointed. *Abashed*: Embarrassed or ill at ease. *Rebuke*: To criticize sharply.

[39] *Sulphonal* is a sedative that induces sleep. It also was used in hypnosis and to treat insanity. It could not be taken for more than a few days at a time, and its side-effects include giddiness, an unsteady gait, skin eruptions and even paralysis. *Veronal* is a barbiturate that depresses the central nervous system. It was also used as a sleeping aid but had fewer side effects. Prolonged usage, however, required higher doses to reach the same effect, and

"Ah! Thank you, mademoiselle; good morning."

As we walked briskly away from the house, I glanced at him more than once. I had often before noticed that, if anything excited him, his eyes turned green like a cat's. They were shining like emeralds now.

"My friend," he broke out at last, "I have a little idea, a very strange, and probably utterly impossible idea. And yet—it fits in."

I shrugged my shoulders. I privately thought that Poirot was rather too much given to these fantastic ideas. In this case, surely, the truth was only too plain and apparent.

"So that is the explanation of the blank label on the box," I remarked. "Very simple, as you said. I really wonder that I did not think of it myself."

Poirot did not appear to be listening to me.

"They have made one more discovery, *la-bas*,"[40] he observed, jerking his thumb over his shoulder in the direction of Styles. "Mr. Wells told me as we were going upstairs."

"What was it?"

"Locked up in the desk in the boudoir, they found a will of Mrs. Inglethorp's, dated before her marriage, leaving her fortune to Alfred Inglethorp. It must have been made just at the time they were engaged. It came quite as a surprise to Wells— and to John Cavendish also. It was written on one of those printed will forms, and witnessed by two of the servants—not Dorcas."

---

overdoses were common. *Bromide powders:* A chemical compound used as a sleeping aid in the 19th and early 20th centuries. It was used as a headache remedy in products such as Bromo-Seltzer. Bromide stays in the system a long time and at toxic levels causes bromism, with skin rashes, psychosis, seizures and delirium. At one point, bromism was responsible for 5-10% of psychiatric hospital admissions. Bromide was banned in 1975. Bromide also describes a cliché, as in "he spoke in bromides."
[40] There.

"Did Mr. Inglethorp know of it?"

"He says not."

"One might take that with a grain of salt," I remarked sceptically. "All these wills are very confusing. Tell me, how did those scribbled words on the envelope help you to discover that a will was made yesterday afternoon?"

Poirot smiled.

"*Mon ami*, have you ever, when writing a letter, been arrested[41] by the fact that you did not know how to spell a certain word?"

"Yes, often. I suppose every one has."

"Exactly. And have you not, in such a case, tried the word once or twice on the edge of the blotting-paper, or a spare scrap of paper, to see if it looked right? Well, that is what Mrs. Inglethorp did. You will notice that the word 'possessed' is spelt first with one 's' and subsequently with two—correctly. To make sure, she had further tried it in a sentence, thus: 'I am possessed.' Now, what did that tell me? It told me that Mrs. Inglethorp had been writing the word 'possessed' that afternoon, and, having the fragment of paper found in the grate fresh in my mind, the possibility of a will—(a document almost certain to contain that word)[42]—occurred to me at once. This possibility was confirmed by a further circumstance. In the general confusion, the boudoir had not been swept that morning, and near the desk were several traces of brown mould and earth.[43] The weather had been perfectly fine for some days, and no ordinary boots would have left such a heavy deposit.

"I strolled to the window, and saw at once that the begonia beds had been newly planted. The mould in the beds was exactly similar to that on the floor of the boudoir, and also I learnt

---

[41] To be checked or slowed by an unexpected event.

[42] A standard text in wills affirms that the author is mentally able to dispose of his or her estate, usually with a phrase such as "I am possessed of a sound mind and body."

[43] *Mould:* Soil containing organic material, such as rotted leaf mold, that's suited for plant growth. *Earth:* Material from the subsoil.

from you that they had been planted yesterday afternoon. I was now sure that one, or possibly both of the gardeners—for there were two sets of footprints in the bed—had entered the boudoir, for if Mrs. Inglethorp had merely wished to speak to them she would in all probability have stood at the window, and they would not have come into the room at all. I was now quite convinced that she had made a fresh will, and had called the two gardeners in to witness her signature. Events proved that I was right in my supposition."

"That was very ingenious," I could not help admitting. "I must confess that the conclusions I drew from those few scribbled words were quite erroneous."

He smiled.

"You gave too much rein to your imagination. Imagination is a good servant, and a bad master. The simplest explanation is always the most likely."[44]

"Another point—how did you know that the key of the despatch-case had been lost?"

"I did not know it. It was a guess that turned out to be correct. You observed that it had a piece of twisted wire through the handle. That suggested to me at once that it had possibly been wrenched off a flimsy key-ring. Now, if it had been lost and recovered, Mrs. Inglethorp would at once have replaced it on her bunch; but on her bunch I found what was obviously the duplicate key, very new and bright, which led me to the hypothesis that somebody else had inserted the original key in the

[44] *Bad master:* The "good servant/bad master" comparison has been in print since at least 1800, when it was applied to money, imagination, anger, and philosophy. *Most likely:* Poirot is expressing the principle of Occam's Razor, which states that among several possibilities, the one making the fewest assumptions is the likeliest. Scottish metaphysician Sir William Hamilton (1788-1856) named the principle after Franciscan friar and philosopher William of Ockham, then known as Occam (c.1288-c.1348), who used a variation of this argument frequently. An earlier version was expressed by Greek mathematician and astronomer Ptolemy (c.90-c.168) who wrote, "we consider it a good principle to explain the phenomena by the simplest hypothesis possible."

lock of the despatch-case."

"Yes," I said, "Alfred Inglethorp, without doubt."

Poirot looked at me curiously.

"You are very sure of his guilt?"

"Well, naturally. Every fresh circumstance seems to establish it more clearly."

"On the contrary," said Poirot quietly, "there are several points in his favour."

"Oh, come now!"

"Yes."

"I see only one."

"And that?"

"That he was not in the house last night."

"'Bad shot!'[45] as you English say! You have chosen the one point that to my mind tells against him."

"How is that?"

"Because if Mr. Inglethorp knew that his wife would be poisoned last night, he would certainly have arranged to be away from the house. His excuse was an obviously trumped up one. That leaves us two possibilities: either he knew what was going to happen or he had a reason of his own for his absence."

"And that reason?" I asked sceptically.

Poirot shrugged his shoulders.

"How should I know? Discreditable, without doubt. This Mr. Inglethorp, I should say, is somewhat of a scoundrel—but that does not of necessity make him a murderer."

I shook my head, unconvinced.

"We do not agree, eh?" said Poirot. "Well, let us leave it. Time will show which of us is right. Now let us turn to other aspects of the case. What do you make of the fact that all the doors of the bedroom were bolted on the inside?"

"Well—" I considered. "One must look at it logically."

"True."

---

[45] A poor guess. Drawn from the reaction when a hunter misses his prey.

"I should put it this way. The doors *were* bolted—our own eyes have told us that—yet the presence of the candle grease on the floor, and the destruction of the will, prove that during the night some one entered the room. You agree so far?"

"Perfectly. Put with admirable clearness. Proceed."

"Well," I said, encouraged, "as the person who entered did not do so by the window, nor by miraculous means, it follows that the door must have been opened from inside by Mrs. Inglethorp herself. That strengthens the conviction that the person in question was her husband. She would naturally open the door to her own husband."

Poirot shook his head.

"Why should she? She had bolted the door leading into his room—a most unusual proceeding on her part—she had had a most violent quarrel with him that very afternoon. No, he was the last person she would admit."

"But you agree with me that the door must have been opened by Mrs. Inglethorp herself?"

"There is another possibility. She may have forgotten to bolt the door into the passage when she went to bed, and have got up later, towards morning, and bolted it then."

"Poirot, is that seriously your opinion?"

"No, I do not say it is so, but it might be. Now, to turn to another feature, what do you make of the scrap of conversation you overheard between Mrs. Cavendish and her mother-in-law?"

"I had forgotten that," I said thoughtfully. "That is as enigmatical as ever. It seems incredible that a woman like Mrs. Cavendish, proud and reticent[46] to the last degree, should interfere so violently in what was certainly not her affair."

"Precisely. It was an astonishing thing for a woman of her breeding to do."

"It is certainly curious," I agreed. "Still, it is unimportant, and need not be taken into account."

---

[46] Inclined toward silence and self-restraint.

A groan burst from Poirot.

"What have I always told you? Everything must be taken into account. If the fact will not fit the theory—let the theory go."

"Well, we shall see," I said, nettled.

"Yes, we shall see."

We had reached Leastways Cottage, and Poirot ushered me upstairs to his own room. He offered me one of the tiny Russian cigarettes he himself occasionally smoked.[47] I was amused to notice that he stowed away the used matches most carefully in a little china pot. My momentary annoyance vanished.

Poirot had placed our two chairs in front of the open window which commanded a view of the village street. The fresh air blew in warm and pleasant. It was going to be a hot day.

Suddenly my attention was arrested by a weedy looking young man rushing down the street at a great pace. It was the expression on his face that was extraordinary—a curious mingling of terror and agitation.

"Look, Poirot!" I said.

He leant forward.

"*Tiens!*"[48] he said. "It is Mr. Mace, from the chemist's shop.[49] He is coming here."

The young man came to a halt before Leastways Cottage, and, after hesitating a moment, pounded vigorously at the door.

"A little minute," cried Poirot from the window. "I come."

Motioning to me to follow him, he ran swiftly down the stairs and opened the door. Mr. Mace began at once.

"Oh, Mr. Poirot, I'm sorry for the inconvenience, but I heard that you'd just come back from the Hall?"

---

[47] Short cigarettes consisting of a cardboard tube at one end that acts as a holder and a tobacco-filled "warhead" at the other. The cigarette can be as short as two inches. Russian cigarettes were popular for their excellent tobacco.

[48] Wait. The word translates to "Hold!" but in this context "Wait!" is more accurate.

[49] A pharmacy that compounds and sells drugs.

"Yes, we have."

The young man moistened his dry lips. His face was working curiously.

"It's all over the village about old Mrs. Inglethorp dying so suddenly. They do say—" he lowered his voice cautiously— "that it's poison?"

Poirot's face remained quite impassive.

"Only the doctors can tell us that, Mr. Mace."

"Yes, exactly—of course—" The young man hesitated, and then his agitation was too much for him. He clutched Poirot by the arm, and sank his voice to a whisper: "Just tell me this, Mr. Poirot, it isn't—it isn't strychnine, is it?"

I hardly heard what Poirot replied. Something evidently of a non-committal nature. The young man departed, and as he closed the door Poirot's eyes met mine.

"Yes," he said, nodding gravely. "He will have evidence to give at the inquest."

We went slowly upstairs again. I was opening my lips, when Poirot stopped me with a gesture of his hand.

"Not now, not now, *mon ami*. I have need of reflection. My mind is in some disorder—which is not well."

For about ten minutes he sat in dead silence, perfectly still, except for several expressive motions of his eyebrows, and all the time his eyes grew steadily greener. At last he heaved a deep sigh.

"It is well. The bad moment has passed. Now all is arranged and classified. One must never permit confusion. The case is not clear yet—no. For it is of the most complicated! It puzzles *me*. *Me*, Hercule Poirot! There are two facts of significance."

"And what are they?"

"The first is the state of the weather yesterday. That is very important."

"But it was a glorious day!" I interrupted. "Poirot, you're pulling my leg!"

"Not at all. The thermometer registered 80 degrees in the shade. Do not forget that, my friend. It is the key to the whole riddle!"

"And the second point?" I asked.

"The important fact that Monsieur Inglethorp wears very peculiar clothes, has a black beard, and uses glasses."

"Poirot, I cannot believe you are serious."

"I am absolutely serious, my friend."

"But this is childish!"

"No, it is very momentous."

"And supposing the Coroner's jury returns a verdict of Wilful Murder[50] against Alfred Inglethorp. What becomes of your theories, then?"

"They would not be shaken because twelve stupid men had happened to make a mistake! But that will not occur. For one thing, a country jury is not anxious to take responsibility upon itself, and Mr. Inglethorp stands practically in the position of local squire. Also," he added placidly, "I should not allow it!"

"*You* would not allow it?"

"No."

I looked at the extraordinary little man, divided between annoyance and amusement. He was so tremendously sure of himself. As though he read my thoughts, he nodded gently.

"Oh, yes, *mon ami*, I would do what I say." He got up and laid his hand on my shoulder. His physiognomy[51] underwent a complete change. Tears came into his eyes. "In all this, you see, I think of that poor Mrs. Inglethorp who is dead. She was not extravagantly loved—no. But she was very good to us Belgians—I owe her a debt."

I endeavoured to interrupt, but Poirot swept on.

"Let me tell you this, Hastings. She would never forgive me if I let Alfred Inglethorp, her husband, be arrested now—when a word from me could save him!"

---

[50] The legal term for the killing of a human without justification or excuse. In the U.S., he would be charged with first-degree murder.
[51] Expression.

CHAPTER VI

THE INQUEST

IN THE INTERVAL BEFORE THE INQUEST, Poirot was unfailing in his activity. Twice he was closeted with Mr. Wells. He also took long walks into the country. I rather resented his not taking me into his confidence, the more so as I could not in the least guess what he was driving at.

It occurred to me that he might have been making inquiries at Raikes's farm; so, finding him out when I called at Leastways Cottage on Wednesday evening, I walked over there by the fields, hoping to meet him. But there was no sign of him, and I hesitated to go right up to the farm itself. As I walked away, I met an aged rustic,[1] who leered at me cunningly.

"You'm from the Hall, bain't you?" he asked.

"Yes. I'm looking for a friend of mine whom I thought might have walked this way."

"A little chap? As waves his hands when he talks? One of them Belgies from the village?"

"Yes," I said eagerly. "He has been here, then?"

"Oh, ay, he's been here, right enough. More'n once too. Friend of yours, is he? Ah, you gentlemen from the Hall—you'n a pretty lot!" And he leered more jocosely[2] than ever.

"Why, do the gentlemen from the Hall come here often?" I asked, as carelessly as I could.

He winked at me knowingly.

"*One* does, mister. Naming no names, mind. And a very lib-

---

[1] Simple and rough in appearance. It can be a condescending or derogatory term when applied to people.
[2] Characterized by joking.

eral gentleman too! Oh, thank you, sir, I'm sure."[3]

I walked on sharply. Evelyn Howard had been right then, and I experienced a sharp twinge of disgust, as I thought of Alfred Inglethorp's liberality with another woman's money. Had that piquant gipsy face been at the bottom of the crime, or was it the baser mainspring[4] of money? Probably a judicious mixture of both.

On one point, Poirot seemed to have a curious obsession. He once or twice observed to me that he thought Dorcas must have made an error in fixing the time of the quarrel. He suggested to her repeatedly that it was 4.30, and not 4 o'clock when she had heard the voices.

But Dorcas was unshaken. Quite an hour, or even more, had elapsed between the time when she had heard the voices and 5 o'clock, when she had taken tea to her mistress.

The inquest was held on Friday at the Stylites Arms[5] in the village. Poirot and I sat together, not being required to give evidence.

The preliminaries were gone through. The jury viewed the body, and John Cavendish gave evidence of identification.

Further questioned, he described his awakening in the early hours of the morning, and the circumstances of his mother's death.

The medical evidence was next taken. There was a breathless hush, and every eye was fixed on the famous London specialist, who was known to be one of the greatest authorities of the day on the subject of toxicology.

In a few brief words, he summed up the result of the postmortem. Shorn of its medical phraseology and technicalities, it

---

[3] *Liberal:* Generous, in this case with money. The old man's subsequent remark — "Oh, thank you, sir, I'm sure." — suggests that Hastings paid him for his information.

[4] Motive. The word is derived from the mechanism that drives an old-fashioned wind-up watch or clock.

[5] A pub in the village. At a time when bodies could not be refrigerated, inquests had to be held quickly. In villages lacking government buildings, inquests were held in public houses. Pub inquests when alternatives were available were banned in 1902, but they were still held well into the 20th century.

amounted to the fact that Mrs. Inglethorp had met her death as the result of strychnine poisoning. Judging from the quantity recovered, she must have taken not less than three-quarters of a grain of strychnine, but probably one grain or slightly over.[6]

"Is it possible that she could have swallowed the poison by accident?" asked the Coroner.

"I should consider it very unlikely. Strychnine is not used for domestic purposes, as some poisons are, and there are restrictions placed on its sale."

"Does anything in your examination lead you to determine how the poison was administered?"

"No."

"You arrived at Styles before Dr. Wilkins, I believe?"

"That is so. The motor met me just outside the lodge gates, and I hurried there as fast as I could."

"Will you relate to us exactly what happened next?"

"I entered Mrs. Inglethorp's room. She was at that moment in a typical tetanic convulsion. She turned towards me, and gasped out: 'Alfred—Alfred—'"

"Could the strychnine have been administered in Mrs. Inglethorp's after-dinner coffee which was taken to her by her husband?"

"Possibly, but strychnine is a fairly rapid drug in its action. The symptoms appear from one to two hours after it has been swallowed. It is retarded under certain conditions, none of which, however, appear to have been present in this case. I presume Mrs. Inglethorp took the coffee after dinner about eight o'clock, whereas the symptoms did not manifest themselves until the early hours of the morning, which, on the face of it, points to the drug having been taken much later in the evening."

"Mrs. Inglethorp was in the habit of drinking a cup of coco in the middle of the night. Could the strychnine have been ad-

---

[6] A obsolete unit of weight based on the size of a cereal seed. Since a standard aspirin tablet of 325 milligrams is five grains, the equivalent of one-fifth of a tablet was enough to kill Mrs. Inglethorp.

ministered in that?"

"No, I myself took a sample of the coco remaining in the saucepan and had it analysed. There was no strychnine present."

I heard Poirot chuckle softly beside me.

"How did you know?" I whispered.

"Listen."

"I should say"—the doctor was continuing—"that I would have been considerably surprised at any other result."

"Why?"

"Simply because strychnine has an unusually bitter taste. It can be detected in a solution of 1 in 70,000, and can only be disguised by some strongly flavoured substance. Coco would be quite powerless to mask it."

One of the jury wanted to know if the same objection applied to coffee.

"No. Coffee has a bitter taste of its own which would probably cover the taste of strychnine."

"Then you consider it more likely that the drug was administered in the coffee, but that for some unknown reason its action was delayed."

"Yes, but, the cup being completely smashed, there is no possibility of analyzing its contents."

This concluded Dr. Bauerstein's evidence. Dr. Wilkins corroborated[7] it on all points. Sounded as to the possibility of suicide, he repudiated[8] it utterly. The deceased, he said, suffered from a weak heart, but otherwise enjoyed perfect health, and was of a cheerful and well-balanced disposition. She would be one of the last people to take her own life.

Lawrence Cavendish was next called. His evidence was quite unimportant, being a mere repetition of that of his brother. Just as he was about to step down, he paused, and said rather hesitatingly:

"I should like to make a suggestion if I may?"

---

[7] To support with evidence or authority.
[8] To reject as untrue or unjust.

He glanced deprecatingly[9] at the Coroner, who replied
briskly:

"Certainly, Mr. Cavendish, we are here to arrive at the truth
of this matter, and welcome anything that may lead to further
elucidation."[10]

"It is just an idea of mine," explained Lawrence. "Of course
I may be quite wrong, but it still seems to me that my mother's
death might be accounted for by natural means."

"How do you make that out, Mr. Cavendish?"

"My mother, at the time of her death, and for some time
before it, was taking a tonic containing strychnine."[11]

"Ah!" said the Coroner.

The jury looked up, interested.

"I believe," continued Lawrence, "that there have been cases where the cumulative effect of a drug, administered for some
time, has ended by causing death. Also, is it not possible that
she may have taken an overdose of her medicine by accident?"

"This is the first we have heard of the deceased taking
strychnine at the time of her death. We are much obliged to
you, Mr. Cavendish."

Dr. Wilkins was recalled and ridiculed the idea.

"What Mr. Cavendish suggests is quite impossible. Any
doctor would tell you the same. Strychnine is, in a certain sense,
a cumulative poison, but it would be quite impossible for it to
result in sudden death in this way. There would have to be a
long period of chronic symptoms which would at once have
attracted my attention. The whole thing is absurd."

"And the second suggestion? That Mrs. Inglethorp may
have inadvertently taken an overdose?"

"Three, or even four doses, would not have resulted in
death. Mrs. Inglethorp always had an extra large amount of

---

[9] To play down, in this case the importance of his suggestion.

[10] A clearer explanation.

[11] Although a poison, strychnine in low doses has an effect similar to caffeine and was used at the time in tonics. For more information, see the
"Poison Nuts and Quaker Buttons" essay in the appendix.

medicine made up at a time, as she dealt with Coot's, the Cash Chemists in Tadminster.[12] She would have had to take very nearly the whole bottle to account for the amount of strychnine found at the post-mortem."

"Then you consider that we may dismiss the tonic as not being in any way instrumental[13] in causing her death?"

"Certainly. The supposition[14] is ridiculous."

The same juryman who had interrupted before here suggested that the chemist who made up the medicine might have committed an error.

"That, of course, is always possible," replied the doctor.

But Dorcas, who was the next witness called, dispelled even that possibility. The medicine had not been newly made up. On the contrary, Mrs. Inglethorp had taken the last dose on the day of her death.

So the question of the tonic was finally abandoned, and the Coroner proceeded with his task. Having elicited from Dorcas how she had been awakened by the violent ringing of her mistress's bell, and had subsequently roused the household, he passed to the subject of the quarrel on the preceding afternoon.

Dorcas's evidence on this point was substantially what Poirot and I had already heard, so I will not repeat it here.

The next witness was Mary Cavendish. She stood very upright, and spoke in a low, clear, and perfectly composed voice. In answer to the Coroner's question, she told how, her alarm clock having aroused her at 4.30 as usual, she was dressing, when she was startled by the sound of something heavy falling.

"That would have been the table by the bed?" commented the Coroner.

---

[12] Christie is disguising the name of Boots Cash Chemists — now Boots UK Ltd. — a pharmacy chain founded in 1849. The "Cash Chemists" name came from the company's practice of operating on a cash-only basi.

[13] Serving as a means to achieve a goal, in this case the extinction of Mrs. Inglethorp.

[14] A belief held without proof or certain knowledge.

"I opened my door," continued Mary, "and listened. In a few minutes a bell rang violently. Dorcas came running down and woke my husband, and we all went to my mother-in-law's room, but it was locked—"

The Coroner interrupted her.

"I really do not think we need trouble you further on that point. We know all that can be known of the subsequent happenings. But I should be obliged if you would tell us all you overheard of the quarrel the day before."

"I?"

There was a faint insolence[15] in her voice. She raised her hand and adjusted the ruffle of lace at her neck, turning her head a little as she did so. And quite spontaneously the thought flashed across my mind: "She is gaining time!"

"Yes. I understand," continued the Coroner deliberately, "that you were sitting reading on the bench just outside the long window of the boudoir. That is so, is it not?"

This was news to me and glancing sideways at Poirot, I fancied that it was news to him as well.

There was the faintest pause, the mere hesitation of a moment, before she answered:

"Yes, that is so."

"And the boudoir window was open, was it not?"

Surely her face grew a little paler as she answered:

"Yes."

"Then you cannot have failed to hear the voices inside, especially as they were raised in anger. In fact, they would be more audible where you were than in the hall."

"Possibly."

"Will you repeat to us what you overheard of the quarrel?"

"I really do not remember hearing anything."

"Do you mean to say you did not hear voices?"

"Oh, yes, I heard the voices, but I did not hear what they said." A faint spot of colour came into her cheek. "I am not in

---

[15] Contemptuous in speech or conduct.

the habit of listening to private conversations."

The Coroner persisted.

"And you remember nothing at all? *Nothing*, Mrs. Cavendish? Not one stray word or phrase to make you realize that it *was* a private conversation?"

She paused, and seemed to reflect, still outwardly as calm as ever.

"Yes; I remember. Mrs. Inglethorp said something—I do not remember exactly what—about causing scandal between husband and wife."

"Ah!" the Coroner leant back satisfied. "That corresponds with what Dorcas heard. But excuse me, Mrs. Cavendish, although you realized it was a private conversation, you did not move away? You remained where you were?"

I caught the momentary gleam of her tawny eyes as she raised them. I felt certain that at that moment she would willingly have torn the little lawyer, with his insinuations,[16] into pieces, but she replied quietly enough:

"No. I was very comfortable where I was. I fixed my mind on my book."

"And that is all you can tell us?"

"That is all."

The examination was over, though I doubted if the Coroner was entirely satisfied with it. I think he suspected that Mary Cavendish could tell more if she chose.

Amy Hill, shop assistant, was next called, and deposed to having sold a will form on the afternoon of the 17th to William Earl, under-gardener at Styles.

William Earl and Manning succeeded her, and testified to witnessing a document. Manning fixed the time at about 4.30, William was of the opinion that it was rather earlier.

Cynthia Murdoch came next. She had, however, little to tell. She had known nothing of the tragedy, until awakened by Mrs. Cavendish.

---

[16] An unpleasant, evil or immoral suggestion.

"You did not hear the table fall?"

"No. I was fast asleep."

The Coroner smiled.

"A good conscience makes a sound sleeper," he observed. "Thank you, Miss Murdoch, that is all."

"Miss Howard."

Miss Howard produced the letter written to her by Mrs. Inglethorp on the evening of the 17th. Poirot and I had, of course already seen it. It added nothing to our knowledge of the tragedy. The following is a facsimile:

> July 17th
>
> Styles Court
> Essex
>
> My dear Evelyn
>   Can we not bury the hatchet? I have found it hard to forgive the things you said against my dear husband but I am an old woman & very fond of you
>   yours affectionately
>   Emily Inglethorp

It was handed to the jury who scrutinized it attentively.

"I fear it does not help us much," said the Coroner, with a

sigh. "There is no mention of any of the events of that afternoon."

"Plain as a pikestaff[17] to me," said Miss Howard shortly. "It shows clearly enough that my poor old friend had just found out she'd been made a fool of!"

"It says nothing of the kind in the letter," the Coroner pointed out.

"No, because Emily never could bear to put herself in the wrong. But I know her. She wanted me back. But she wasn't going to own that I'd been right. She went round about. Most people do. Don't believe in it myself."

Mr. Wells smiled faintly. So, I noticed, did several of the jury. Miss Howard was obviously quite a public character.

"Anyway, all this tomfoolery[18] is a great waste of time," continued the lady, glancing up and down the jury disparagingly. "Talk—talk—talk! When all the time we know perfectly well—"

The Coroner interrupted her in an agony of apprehension:

"Thank you, Miss Howard, that is all."[19]

I fancy he breathed a sigh of relief when she complied.

Then came the sensation of the day. The Coroner called Albert Mace, chemist's assistant.

It was our agitated young man of the pale face. In answer to the Coroner's questions, he explained that he was a qualified pharmacist, but had only recently come to this particular shop, as the assistant formerly there had just been called up for the army.

---

[17] Very obvious or plain-looking. A pikestaff is a thrusting spear of between 10 and 25 feet long, reinforced with a metal spearhead. It was used by medieval infantry units who would form a square against a cavalry charge.
[18] Engaging in playful or silly behavior. It is derived from "tomfool" to describe a clumsy, witless idiot.
[19] A fear that something unpleasant is going to happen. Considering that Evie Howard had said in Chapter 1 that she could "spot the murderer right off," she could have been on the verge of saying Alfred Inglethorp poisoned his wife, a serious accusation that could have exposed her to a slander suit.

These preliminaries completed, the Coroner proceeded to business.

"Mr. Mace, have you lately sold strychnine to any unauthorized person?"

"Yes, sir."

"When was this?"

"Last Monday night."

"Monday? Not Tuesday?"

"No, sir, Monday, the 16th."

"Will you tell us to whom you sold it?"

You could have heard a pin drop.

"Yes, sir. It was to Mr. Inglethorp."

Every eye turned simultaneously to where Alfred Inglethorp was sitting, impassive and wooden. He started slightly, as the damning words fell from the young man's lips. I half thought he was going to rise from his chair, but he remained seated, although a remarkably well acted expression of astonishment rose on his face.

"You are sure of what you say?" asked the Coroner sternly.

"Quite sure, sir."

"Are you in the habit of selling strychnine indiscriminately over the counter?"

The wretched young man wilted visibly under the Coroner's frown.

"Oh, no, sir—of course not. But, seeing it was Mr. Inglethorp of the Hall, I thought there was no harm in it. He said it was to poison a dog."[20]

Inwardly I sympathized. It was only human nature to endeavour to please "The Hall"—especially when it might result in custom being transferred from Coot's to the local establishment.

---

[20] In the William Palmer poisoning case of 1846, the Rugeley doctor had asked a chemist about the proper dose of strychnine to kill a dog and the appearance of its stomach after death. Several events in *Styles* are so similar to the notorious case that one wonders if Christie was inspired by it. See the essay "The Case of the Doctoring Doctor" in the appendix.

"Is it not customary for anyone purchasing poison to sign a book?"

"Yes, sir, Mr. Inglethorp did so."

"Have you got the book here?"

"Yes, sir."

It was produced; and, with a few words of stern censure, the Coroner dismissed the wretched Mr. Mace.

Then, amidst a breathless silence, Alfred Inglethorp was called. Did he realize, I wondered, how closely the halter was being drawn around his neck?[21]

The Coroner went straight to the point.

"On Monday evening last, did you purchase strychnine for the purpose of poisoning a dog?"

Inglethorp replied with perfect calmness:

"No, I did not. There is no dog at Styles, except an outdoor sheepdog, which is in perfect health."

"You deny absolutely having purchased strychnine from Albert Mace on Monday last?"

"I do."

"Do you also deny *this*?"

The Coroner handed him the register in which his signature was inscribed.

"Certainly I do. The hand-writing is quite different from mine. I will show you."

He took an old envelope out of his pocket, and wrote his name on it, handing it to the jury. It was certainly utterly dissimilar.

"Then what is your explanation of Mr. Mace's statement?"

Alfred Inglethorp replied imperturbably:

"Mr. Mace must have been mistaken."

The Coroner hesitated for a moment, and then said:

"Mr. Inglethorp, as a mere matter of form, would you mind

---

[21] A reference to the noose used to execute convicted murderers in Britain. The halter is also a rope or strap that is tied around an animal's head in order to lead it.

telling us where you were on the evening of Monday, July 16th?"

"Really—I can't remember."

"That is absurd, Mr. Inglethorp," said the Coroner sharply. "Think again."

Inglethorp shook his head.

"I cannot tell you. I have an idea that I was out walking."

"In what direction?"

"I really can't remember."

The Coroner's face grew graver.

"Were you in company with anyone?"

"No."

"Did you meet anyone on your walk?"

"No."

"That is a pity," said the Coroner dryly. "I am to take it then that you decline to say where you were at the time that Mr. Mace positively recognized you as entering the shop to purchase strychnine?"

"If you like to take it that way, yes."

"Be careful, Mr. Inglethorp."

Poirot was fidgeting nervously.

"*Sacre!*" he murmured. "Does this imbecile of a man *want* to be arrested?"

Inglethorp was indeed creating a bad impression. His futile denials would not have convinced a child. The Coroner, however, passed briskly to the next point, and Poirot drew a deep breath of relief.

"You had a discussion with your wife on Tuesday afternoon?"

"Pardon me," interrupted Alfred Inglethorp, "you have been misinformed. I had no quarrel with my dear wife. The whole story is absolutely untrue. I was absent from the house the entire afternoon."

"Have you anyone who can testify to that?"

"You have my word," said Inglethorp haughtily.

The Coroner did not trouble to reply.

"There are two witnesses who will swear to having heard

your disagreement with Mrs. Inglethorp."

"Those witnesses were mistaken."

I was puzzled. The man spoke with such quiet assurance that I was staggered. I looked at Poirot. There was an expression of exultation on his face which I could not understand. Was he at last convinced of Alfred Inglethorp's guilt?

"Mr. Inglethorp," said the Coroner, "you have heard your wife's dying words repeated here. Can you explain them in any way?"

"Certainly I can."

"You can?"

"It seems to me very simple. The room was dimly lighted. Dr. Bauerstein is much of my height and build, and, like me, wears a beard. In the dim light, and suffering as she was, my poor wife mistook him for me."

"Ah!" murmured Poirot to himself. "But it is an idea, that!"

"You think it is true?" I whispered.

"I do not say that. But it is truly an ingenious supposition."[22]

"You read my wife's last words as an accusation"—Inglethorp was continuing—"they were, on the contrary, an appeal to me."

The Coroner reflected a moment, then he said:

"I believe, Mr. Inglethorp, that you yourself poured out the coffee, and took it to your wife that evening?"

"I poured it out, yes. But I did not take it to her. I meant to do so, but I was told that a friend was at the hall door, so I laid down the coffee on the hall table. When I came through the hall again a few minutes later, it was gone."

This statement might, or might not, be true, but it did not seem to me to improve matters much for Inglethorp. In any case, he had had ample time to introduce the poison.

At that point, Poirot nudged me gently, indicating two men

---

[22] Poirot is saying that Mr. Inglethorp's suggestion is clever and inventive but not provable.

who were sitting together near the door. One was a little, sharp, dark, ferret-faced man, the other was tall and fair.

I questioned Poirot mutely. He put his lips to my ear.

"Do you know who that little man is?"

I shook my head.

"That is Detective Inspector James Japp of Scotland Yard —Jimmy Japp. The other man is from Scotland Yard too. Things are moving quickly, my friend."

I stared at the two men intently. There was certainly nothing of the policeman about them. I should never have suspected them of being official personages.

I was still staring, when I was startled and recalled by the verdict being given:

"Wilful Murder against some person or persons unknown."[23]

---

[23] The jury concluded that a charge of wilful murder should be lodged, but it could not decide against whom.

CHAPTER VII

POIROT PAYS HIS DEBTS

A S WE CAME OUT OF THE Stylites Arms, Poirot drew me
aside by a gentle pressure of the arm. I understood his object. He was waiting for the Scotland Yard men.

In a few moments, they emerged, and Poirot at once
stepped forward, and accosted the shorter of the two.

"I fear you do not remember me, Inspector Japp."

"Why, if it isn't Mr. Poirot!" cried the Inspector. He turned
to the other man. "You've heard me speak of Mr. Poirot? It
was in 1904 he and I worked together—the Abercrombie for-
gery case—you remember, he was run down in Brussels. Ah,
those were great days, moosier.[1] Then, do you remember 'Bar-
on' Altara? There was a pretty rogue for you! He eluded the
clutches of half the police in Europe. But we nailed him in
Antwerp—thanks to Mr. Poirot here."

As these friendly reminiscences were being indulged in, I
drew nearer, and was introduced to Detective-Inspector Japp,
who, in his turn, introduced us both to his companion, Superintendent Summerhaye.[2]

"I need hardly ask what you are doing here, gentlemen,"
remarked Poirot.

Japp closed one eye knowingly.

"No, indeed. Pretty clear case I should say."

---

[1] Inspector Japp was attempting to use the French courtesy title "monsieur,"
but mispronounced it.

[2] A superintendent outranks an inspector. Inspectors are uniformed police
officers who oversee day-to-day policing or work in specialized roles. Plain-
clothes officers such as Japp are investigators called detective-inspectors.

But Poirot answered gravely:

"There I differ from you."

"Oh, come!" said Summerhaye, opening his lips for the first time. "Surely the whole thing is clear as daylight. The man's caught red-handed. How he could be such a fool beats me!"

But Japp was looking attentively at Poirot.

"Hold your fire, Summerhaye," he remarked jocularly. "Me and Moosier here have met before—and there's no man's judgment I'd sooner take than his. If I'm not greatly mistaken, he's got something up his sleeve. Isn't that so, moosier?"

Poirot smiled.

"I have drawn certain conclusions—yes."

Summerhaye was still looking rather sceptical, but Japp continued his scrutiny of Poirot.

"It's this way," he said, "so far, we've only seen the case from the outside. That's where the Yard's at a disadvantage in a case of this kind, where the murder's only out, so to speak, after the inquest. A lot depends on being on the spot first thing, and that's where Mr. Poirot's had the start of us. We shouldn't have been here as soon as this even, if it hadn't been for the fact that there was a smart doctor on the spot, who gave us the tip through the Coroner. But you've been on the spot from the first, and you may have picked up some little hints. From the evidence at the inquest, Mr. Inglethorp murdered his wife as sure as I stand here, and if anyone but you hinted the contrary I'd laugh in his face. I must say I was surprised the jury didn't bring it in Wilful Murder against him right off. I think they would have, if it hadn't been for the Coroner—he seemed to be holding them back."

"Perhaps, though, you have a warrant for his arrest in your pocket now," suggested Poirot.

A kind of wooden shutter of officialdom came down from Japp's expressive countenance.

"Perhaps I have, and perhaps I haven't," he remarked dryly.

Poirot looked at him thoughtfully.

"I am very anxious, Messieurs, that he should not be arrested."

"I dare say," observed Summerhaye sarcastically.

Japp was regarding Poirot with comical perplexity.

"Can't you go a little further, Mr. Poirot? A wink's as good as a nod—from you. You've been on the spot—and the Yard doesn't want to make any mistakes, you know."

Poirot nodded gravely.

"That is exactly what I thought. Well, I will tell you this. Use your warrant: Arrest Mr. Inglethorp. But it will bring you no kudos—the case against him will be dismissed at once! *Comme ça!*[3] And he snapped his fingers expressively.

Japp's face grew grave, though Summerhaye gave an incredulous snort.

As for me, I was literally dumb with astonishment. I could only conclude that Poirot was mad.

Japp had taken out a handkerchief, and was gently dabbing his brow.

"I daren't do it, Mr. Poirot. I'd take your word, but there's others over me who'll be asking what the devil I mean by it. Can't you give me a little more to go on?"

Poirot reflected a moment.

"It can be done," he said at last. "I admit I do not wish it. It forces my hand. I would have preferred to work in the dark just for the present, but what you say is very just—the word of a Belgian policeman, whose day is past, is not enough! And Alfred Inglethorp must not be arrested. That I have sworn, as my friend Hastings here knows. See, then, my good Japp, you go at once to Styles?"

"Well, in about half an hour. We're seeing the Coroner and the doctor first."

"Good. Call for me in passing—the last house in the village. I will go with you. At Styles, Mr. Inglethorp will give you, or if he refuses—as is probable—I will give you such proofs that shall satisfy you that the case against him could not possibly be sustained. Is that a bargain?"

---

[3] Like that.

"That's a bargain," said Japp heartily. "And, on behalf of the Yard, I'm much obliged to you, though I'm bound to confess I can't at present see the faintest possible loop-hole in the evidence, but you always were a marvel! So long, then, moosier."

The two detectives strode away, Summerhaye with an incredulous grin on his face.

"Well, my friend," cried Poirot, before I could get in a word, "what do you think? *Mon Dieu!*[4] I had some warm moments in that court; I did not figure to myself that the man would be so pig-headed as to refuse to say anything at all. Decidedly, it was the policy of an imbecile."

"H'm! There are other explanations besides that of imbecility," I remarked. "For, if the case against him is true, how could he defend himself except by silence?"

"Why, in a thousand ingenious ways," cried Poirot. "See; say that it is I who have committed this murder, I can think of seven most plausible stories! Far more convincing than Mr. Inglethorp's stony denials!"

I could not help laughing.

"My dear Poirot, I am sure you are capable of thinking of seventy! But, seriously, in spite of what I heard you say to the detectives, you surely cannot still believe in the possibility of Alfred Inglethorp's innocence?"

"Why not now as much as before? Nothing has changed."

"But the evidence is so conclusive."

"Yes, too conclusive."

We turned in at the gate of Leastways Cottage, and proceeded up the now familiar stairs.

"Yes, yes, too conclusive," continued Poirot, almost to himself. "Real evidence is usually vague and unsatisfactory. It has to be examined—sifted. But here the whole thing is cut and dried. No, my friend, this evidence has been very cleverly manufactured—so cleverly that it has defeated its own ends."

---

[4] My God.

"How do you make that out?"

"Because, so long as the evidence against him was vague and intangible, it was very hard to disprove. But, in his anxiety, the criminal has drawn the net so closely that one cut will set Inglethorp free."

I was silent. And in a minute or two, Poirot continued:

"Let us look at the matter like this. Here is a man, let us say, who sets out to poison his wife. He has lived by his wits as the saying goes.[5] Presumably, therefore, he has some wits. He is not altogether a fool. Well, how does he set about it? He goes boldly to the village chemist's and purchases strychnine under his own name, with a trumped up story about a dog which is bound to be proved absurd. He does not employ the poison that night. No, he waits until he has had a violent quarrel with her, of which the whole household is cognisant,[6] and which naturally directs their suspicions upon him. He prepares no defence—no shadow of an alibi,[7] yet he knows the chemist's assistant must necessarily come forward with the facts. Bah! do not ask me to believe that any man could be so idiotic! Only a lunatic, who wished to commit suicide by causing himself to be hanged, would act so!"

"Still—I do not see—" I began.

"Neither do I see. I tell you, *mon ami*, it puzzles me. Me—Hercule Poirot!"

"But if you believe him innocent, how do you explain his buying the strychnine?"

"Very simply. He did *not* buy it."

"But Mace recognized him!"

"I beg your pardon, he saw a man with a black beard like Mr. Inglethorp's, and wearing glasses like Mr. Inglethorp, and dressed in Mr. Inglethorp's rather noticeable clothes. He could

---

[5] Meaning that he took advantage of opportunities set before him, regardless of ethics, rather than succeeding through hard work.

[6] Knew about, especially through personal experience.

[7] A statement that a person, usually a suspect in a crime, was elsewhere when it was committed. From the Latin meaning "somewhere else."

not recognize a man whom he had probably only seen in the distance, since, you remember, he himself had only been in the village a fortnight, and Mrs. Inglethorp dealt principally with Coot's in Tadminster."

"Then you think—"

"*Mon ami*, do you remember the two points I laid stress upon? Leave the first one for the moment, what was the second?"

"The important fact that Alfred Inglethorp wears peculiar clothes, has a black beard, and uses glasses," I quoted.

"Exactly. Now suppose anyone wished to pass himself off as John or Lawrence Cavendish. Would it be easy?"

"No," I said thoughtfully. "Of course an actor—"

But Poirot cut me short ruthlessly.

"And why would it not be easy? I will tell you, my friend: Because they are both clean-shaven men. To make up successfully as one of these two in broad daylight, it would need an actor of genius, and a certain initial facial resemblance. But in the case of Alfred Inglethorp, all that is changed. His clothes, his beard, the glasses which hide his eyes—those are the salient points about his personal appearance. Now, what is the first instinct of the criminal? To divert suspicion from himself, is it not so? And how can he best do that? By throwing it on some one else. In this instance, there was a man ready to his hand. Everybody was predisposed to believe in Mr. Inglethorp's guilt. It was a foregone conclusion that he would be suspected; but, to make it a sure thing there must be tangible proof—such as the actual buying of the poison, and that, with a man of the peculiar appearance of Mr. Inglethorp, was not difficult. Remember, this young Mace had never actually spoken to Mr. Inglethorp. How should he doubt that the man in his clothes, with his beard and his glasses, was not Alfred Inglethorp?"

"It may be so," I said, fascinated by Poirot's eloquence. "But, if that was the case, why does he not say where he was at six o'clock on Monday evening?"

"Ah, why indeed?" said Poirot, calming down. "If he were arrested, he probably would speak, but I do not want it to come to that. I must make him see the gravity of his position. There is, of course, something discreditable behind his silence. If he did not murder his wife, he is, nevertheless, a scoundrel, and has something of his own to conceal, quite apart from the murder."

"What can it be?" I mused, won over to Poirot's views for the moment, although still retaining a faint conviction that the obvious deduction was the correct one.

"Can you not guess?" asked Poirot, smiling.

"No, can you?"

"Oh, yes, I had a little idea sometime ago—and it has turned out to be correct."

"You never told me," I said reproachfully.

Poirot spread out his hands apologetically.

"Pardon me, *mon ami*, you were not precisely *sympathique*."[8] He turned to me earnestly. "Tell me—you see now that he must not be arrested?"

"Perhaps," I said doubtfully, for I was really quite indifferent to the fate of Alfred Inglethorp, and thought that a good fright would do him no harm.

Poirot, who was watching me intently, gave a sigh.

"Come, my friend," he said, changing the subject, "apart from Mr. Inglethorp, how did the evidence at the inquest strike you?"

"Oh, pretty much what I expected."

"Did nothing strike you as peculiar about it?"

My thoughts flew to Mary Cavendish, and I hedged:

"In what way?"

"Well, Mr. Lawrence Cavendish's evidence for instance?"

I was relieved.

"Oh, Lawrence! No, I don't think so. He's always a nervous chap."

"His suggestion that his mother might have been poisoned accidentally by means of the tonic she was taking, that did not

---

[8] Sympathetic, understanding or empathetic.

strike you as strange—*hein?*"[9]

"No, I can't say it did. The doctors ridiculed it of course. But it was quite a natural suggestion for a layman[10] to make."

"But Monsieur Lawrence is not a layman. You told me yourself that he had started by studying medicine, and that he had taken his degree."

"Yes, that's true. I never thought of that." I was rather startled. "It *is* odd."

Poirot nodded.

"From the first, his behaviour has been peculiar. Of all the household, he alone would be likely to recognize the symptoms of strychnine poisoning, and yet we find him the only member of the family to uphold strenuously the theory of death from natural causes. If it had been Monsieur John, I could have understood it. He has no technical knowledge, and is by nature unimaginative. But Monsieur Lawrence—no! And now, to-day, he puts forward a suggestion that he himself must have known was ridiculous. There is food for thought in this, *mon ami.*"

"It's very confusing," I agreed.

"Then there is Mrs. Cavendish," continued Poirot. "That's another who is not telling all she knows! What do you make of her attitude?"

"I don't know what to make of it. It seems inconceivable that she should be shielding Alfred Inglethorp. Yet that is what it looks like."

Poirot nodded reflectively.

"Yes, it is queer. One thing is certain, she overheard a good deal more of that 'private conversation' than she was willing to admit."

"And yet she is the last person one would accuse of stooping to eavesdrop!"

---

[9] Strictly speaking, "What?" but also implying "Do you agree?"

[10] A person who does not belong to the profession in question, in this case the medical field.

"Exactly. One thing her evidence *has* shown me. I made a mistake. Dorcas was quite right. The quarrel did take place earlier in the afternoon, about four o'clock, as she said."

I looked at him curiously. I had never understood his insistence on that point.

"Yes, a good deal that was peculiar came out to-day," continued Poirot. "Dr. Bauerstein, now, what was *he* doing up and dressed at that hour in the morning? It is astonishing to me that no one commented on the fact."

"He has insomnia,[11] I believe," I said doubtfully.

"Which is a very good, or a very bad explanation," remarked Poirot. "It covers everything, and explains nothing. I shall keep my eye on our clever Dr. Bauerstein."

"Any more faults to find with the evidence?" I inquired satirically.

"*Mon ami*," replied Poirot gravely, "when you find that people are not telling you the truth—look out! Now, unless I am much mistaken, at the inquest to-day only one—at most, two persons were speaking the truth without reservation or subterfuge."[12]

"Oh, come now, Poirot! I won't cite Lawrence, or Mrs. Cavendish. But there's John—and Miss Howard, surely they were speaking the truth?"

"Both of them, my friend? One, I grant you, but both—!"

His words gave me an unpleasant shock. Miss Howard's evidence, unimportant as it was, had been given in such a downright straightforward manner that it had never occurred to me to doubt her sincerity. Still, I had a great respect for Poirot's sagacity[13]—except on the occasions when he was what I described to myself as "foolishly pig-headed."

"Do you really think so?" I asked. "Miss Howard had always seemed to me so essentially honest—almost uncomforta-

---

[11] An inability to sleep.

[12] *Reservation:* Without doubt or hesitation. *Subterfuge:* With the intention to deceive.

[13] Perceptive, able to tease conclusions from slender clues.

bly so."

Poirot gave me a curious look, which I could not quite fathom. He seemed to speak, and then checked himself.

"Miss Murdoch too," I continued, "there's nothing untruthful about *her*."

"No. But it was strange that she never heard a sound, sleeping next door; whereas Mrs. Cavendish, in the other wing of the building, distinctly heard the table fall."

"Well, she's young. And she sleeps soundly."

"Ah, yes, indeed! She must be a famous sleeper, that one!"

I did not quite like the tone of his voice, but at that moment a smart knock reached our ears, and looking out of the window we perceived the two detectives waiting for us below.

Poirot seized his hat, gave a ferocious twist to his moustache, and, carefully brushing an imaginary speck of dust from his sleeve, motioned me to precede him down the stairs; there we joined the detectives and set out for Styles.

I think the appearance of the two Scotland Yard men was rather a shock—especially to John, though of course after the verdict, he had realized that it was only a matter of time. Still, the presence of the detectives brought the truth home to him more than anything else could have done.

Poirot had conferred with Japp in a low tone on the way up, and it was the latter functionary who requested that the household, with the exception of the servants, should be assembled together in the drawing-room. I realized the significance of this. It was up to Poirot to make his boast good.

Personally, I was not sanguine.[14] Poirot might have excellent reasons for his belief in Inglethorp's innocence, but a man of the type of Summerhaye would require tangible proofs, and these I doubted if Poirot could supply.

---

[14] Optimistic. The word is derived from medieval medicine. Sanguine, from the Latin word for "blood," is one of the four temperaments — along with phlegmatic, choleric and melancholic — that affects personality traits and behaviors. Characteristics of sanguine people include sturdiness, a ruddy skin and cheerfulness.

Before very long we had all trooped into the drawing-room, the door of which Japp closed. Poirot politely set chairs for every one. The Scotland Yard men were the cynosure[15] of all eyes. I think that for the first time we realized that the thing was not a bad dream, but a tangible reality. We had read of such things—now we ourselves were actors in the drama. To-morrow the daily papers, all over England, would blazon out the news in staring headlines:

MYSTERIOUS TRAGEDY IN ESSEX
WEALTHY LADY POISONED

There would be pictures of Styles, snap-shots of "The family leaving the Inquest"—the village photographer[16] had not been idle! All the things that one had read a hundred times— things that happen to other people, not to oneself. And now, in this house, a murder had been committed. In front of us were "the detectives in charge of the case." The well-known glib[17] phraseology passed rapidly through my mind in the interval before Poirot opened the proceedings.

I think every one was a little surprised that it should be he and not one of the official detectives who took the initiative.

"*Mesdames* and *messieurs*," said Poirot, bowing as though he were a celebrity about to deliver a lecture, "I have asked you to

---

[15] Being at the center of attention or admiration. The word is derived from Cynosura, the ancient Greek name for the North Star, around which stars appear to rotate in the Northern Hemisphere.
[16] A local photographer who owned his own studio and photographed people and special events. Beginning in 1900, a technological revolution was launched with the introduction of cameras that anyone could use. Many village photographers turned to taking panoramic group photos, photo postcards, and, as we see in *Styles,* freelancing for newspapers. "The family leaving the Inquest" would be a typical newspaper caption.
[17] Superficial, lacking depth or substance.

come here all together, for a certain object. That object, it concerns Mr. Alfred Inglethorp."

Inglethorp was sitting a little by himself—I think, unconsciously, every one had drawn his chair slightly away from him—and he gave a faint start as Poirot pronounced his name.

"Mr. Inglethorp," said Poirot, addressing him directly, "a very dark shadow is resting on this house—the shadow of murder."

Inglethorp shook his head sadly.

"My poor wife," he murmured. "Poor Emily! It is terrible."

"I do not think, monsieur," said Poirot pointedly, "that you quite realize how terrible it may be—for you." And as Inglethorp did not appear to understand, he added: "Mr. Inglethorp, you are standing in very grave danger."

The two detectives fidgeted. I saw the official caution "Anything you say will be used in evidence against you," actually hovering on Summerhaye's lips. Poirot went on.

"Do you understand now, *monsieur*?"

"No. What do you mean?"

"I mean," said Poirot deliberately, "that you are suspected of poisoning your wife."

A little gasp ran round the circle at this plain speaking.

"Good heavens!" cried Inglethorp, starting up. "What a monstrous idea! I—poison my dearest Emily!"

"I do not think"—Poirot watched him narrowly—"that you quite realize the unfavourable nature of your evidence at the inquest. Mr. Inglethorp, knowing what I have now told you, do you still refuse to say where you were at six o'clock on Monday afternoon?"

With a groan, Alfred Inglethorp sank down again and buried his face in his hands. Poirot approached and stood over him.

"Speak!" he cried menacingly.

With an effort, Inglethorp raised his face from his hands. Then, slowly and deliberately, he shook his head.

"You will not speak?"

"No. I do not believe that anyone could be so monstrous as

to accuse me of what you say."

Poirot nodded thoughtfully, like a man whose mind is made up.

"*Soit!*[18] he said. "Then I must speak for you."

Alfred Inglethorp sprang up again.

"You? How can you speak? You do not know—" he broke off abruptly.

Poirot turned to face us. "*Mesdames* and *messieurs*! I speak! Listen! I, Hercule Poirot, affirm that the man who entered the chemist's shop, and purchased strychnine at six o'clock on Monday last was not Mr. Inglethorp, for at six o'clock on that day Mr. Inglethorp was escorting Mrs. Raikes back to her home from a neighbouring farm. I can produce no less than five witnesses to swear to having seen them together, either at six or just after and, as you may know, the Abbey Farm, Mrs. Raikes's home, is at least two and a half miles distant from the village. There is absolutely no question as to the alibi!"

[18] Very well.

CHAPTER VIII

FRESH SUSPICIONS

THERE WAS A MOMENT'S STUPEFIED[1] silence. Japp, who was the least surprised of any of us, was the first to speak.

"My word," he cried, "you're the goods![2] And no mistake, Mr. Poirot! These witnesses of yours are all right, I suppose?"

"*Voila*! I have prepared a list of them—names and addresses. You must see them, of course. But you will find it all right."

"I'm sure of that." Japp lowered his voice. "I'm much obliged to you. A pretty mare's nest arresting him would have been." He turned to Inglethorp. "But, if you'll excuse me, sir, why couldn't you say all this at the inquest?"

"I will tell you why," interrupted Poirot. "There was a certain rumour—"

"A most malicious and utterly untrue one," interrupted Alfred Inglethorp in an agitated voice.

"And Mr. Inglethorp was anxious to have no scandal revived just at present. Am I right?"

"Quite right." Inglethorp nodded. "With my poor Emily not yet buried, can you wonder I was anxious that no more lying rumours should be started."

"Between you and me, sir," remarked Japp, "I'd sooner have any amount of rumours than be arrested for murder. And I venture to think your poor lady would have felt the same. And, if it hadn't been for Mr. Poirot here, arrested you would

---

[1] To make someone unable to think properly.
[2] The real thing, a reference to his detecting ability.

have been, as sure as eggs is eggs!"[3]

"I was foolish, no doubt," murmured Inglethorp. "But you do not know, inspector, how I have been persecuted and maligned." And he shot a baleful glance at Evelyn Howard.[4]

"Now, sir," said Japp, turning briskly to John, "I should like to see the lady's bedroom, please, and after that I'll have a little chat with the servants. Don't you bother about anything. Mr. Poirot, here, will show me the way."

As they all went out of the room, Poirot turned and made me a sign to follow him upstairs. There he caught me by the arm, and drew me aside.

"Quick, go to the other wing. Stand there—just this side of the baize door.[5] Do not move till I come." Then, turning rapidly, he rejoined the two detectives.

I followed his instructions, taking up my position by the baize door, and wondering what on earth lay behind the request. Why was I to stand in this particular spot on guard? I looked thoughtfully down the corridor in front of me. An idea struck me. With the exception of Cynthia Murdoch's, every one's room was in this left wing. Had that anything to do with it? Was I to report who came or went? I stood faithfully at my post. The minutes passed. Nobody came. Nothing happened.

It must have been quite twenty minutes before Poirot rejoined me.

"You have not stirred?"

"No, I've stuck here like a rock. Nothing's happened."

"Ah!" Was he pleased, or disappointed? "You've seen nothing at all?"

"No."

"But you have probably heard something? A big bump—

---

[3] An idiom meaning absolutely certain. The phrase was recorded as early as 1680 and is thought to originate as a corruption of the mathematical statement "X is X."

[4] *Maligned:* Spoken of in a critical fashion. *Baleful:* Threatening or menacing.

[5] A door covered with a coarse woolen cloth to deaden noise. It is traditionally used to separate the servants' quarters from the family's living quarters.

eh, *mon ami?*"

"No."

"Is it possible? Ah, but I am vexed[6] with myself! I am not usually clumsy. I made but a slight gesture"—I know Poirot's gestures—"with the left hand, and over went the table by the bed!"

He looked so childishly vexed and crest-fallen that I hastened to console him.

"Never mind, old chap. What does it matter? Your triumph downstairs excited you. I can tell you, that was a surprise to us all. There must be more in this affair of Inglethorp's with Mrs. Raikes than we thought, to make him hold his tongue so persistently. What are you going to do now? Where are the Scotland Yard fellows?"

"Gone down to interview the servants. I showed them all our exhibits. I am disappointed in Japp. He has no method!"

"Hullo!" I said, looking out of the window. "Here's Dr. Bauerstein. I believe you're right about that man, Poirot. I don't like him."

"He is clever," observed Poirot meditatively.

"Oh, clever as the devil! I must say I was overjoyed to see him in the plight he was in on Tuesday. You never saw such a spectacle!" And I described the doctor's adventure. "He looked a regular scarecrow! Plastered with mud from head to foot."

"You saw him, then?"

"Yes. Of course, he didn't want to come in—it was just after dinner—but Mr. Inglethorp insisted."

"What?" Poirot caught me violently by the shoulders. "Was Dr. Bauerstein here on Tuesday evening? Here? And you never told me? Why did you not tell me? Why? Why?"

He appeared to be in an absolute frenzy.

"My dear Poirot," I expostulated,[7] "I never thought it would interest you. I didn't know it was of any importance."

---

[6] Distressed or annoyed by a petty provocation.

[7] To express disagreement.

"Importance? It is of the first importance! So Dr. Bauerstein was here on Tuesday night—the night of the murder. Hastings, do you not see? That alters everything—everything!"

I had never seen him so upset. Loosening his hold of me, he mechanically straightened a pair of candlesticks, still murmuring to himself: "Yes, that alters everything—everything."

Suddenly he seemed to come to a decision.

"*Allons!*[8] he said. "We must act at once. Where is Mr. Cavendish?"

John was in the smoking-room. Poirot went straight to him.

"Mr. Cavendish, I have some important business in Tadminster. A new clue. May I take your motor?"

"Why, of course. Do you mean at once?"

"If you please."

John rang the bell, and ordered round the car. In another ten minutes, we were racing down the park and along the high road[9] to Tadminster.

"Now, Poirot," I remarked resignedly, "perhaps you will tell me what all this is about?"

"Well, *mon ami*, a good deal you can guess for yourself. Of course you realize that, now Mr. Inglethorp is out of it, the whole position is greatly changed. We are face to face with an entirely new problem. We know now that there is one person who did not buy the poison. We have cleared away the manufactured clues. Now for the real ones. I have ascertained that anyone in the household, with the exception of Mrs. Cavendish, who was playing tennis with you, could have personated[10] Mr. Inglethorp on Monday evening. In the same way, we have his statement that he put the coffee down in the hall. No one took much notice of that at the inquest—but now it has a very

_____

[8] Let's go! Fans of *Doctor Who* will recognize this as part of a catchphrase ("Allons-y!") of the Tenth Doctor.

[9] A road that crosses a ridge or hill between two valleys or settlements.

[10] A variation of impersonate, or to assume a disguise.

different significance. We must find out who did take that coffee to Mrs. Inglethorp eventually, or who passed through the hall whilst it was standing there. From your account, there are only two people whom we can positively say did not go near the coffee—Mrs. Cavendish, and Mademoiselle Cynthia."

"Yes, that is so." I felt an inexpressible lightening of the heart. Mary Cavendish could certainly not rest under suspicion.

"In clearing Alfred Inglethorp," continued Poirot, "I have been obliged to show my hand sooner than I intended. As long as I might be thought to be pursuing him, the criminal would be off his guard. Now, he will be doubly careful. Yes—doubly careful." He turned to me abruptly. "Tell me, Hastings, you yourself—have you no suspicions of anybody?"

I hesitated. To tell the truth, an idea, wild and extravagant in itself, had once or twice that morning flashed through my brain. I had rejected it as absurd, nevertheless it persisted.

"You couldn't call it a suspicion," I murmured. "It's so utterly foolish."

"Come now," urged Poirot encouragingly. "Do not fear. Speak your mind. You should always pay attention to your instincts."

"Well then," I blurted out, "it's absurd—but I suspect Miss Howard of not telling all she knows!"

"Miss Howard?"

"Yes—you'll laugh at me—"

"Not at all. Why should I?"

"I can't help feeling," I continued blunderingly; "that we've rather left her out of the possible suspects, simply on the strength of her having been away from the place. But, after all, she was only fifteen miles away. A car would do it in half an hour. Can we say positively that she was away from Styles on the night of the murder?"

"Yes, my friend," said Poirot unexpectedly, "we can. One of my first actions was to ring up the hospital where she was working."

"Well?"

"Well, I learnt that Miss Howard had been on afternoon

duty on Tuesday, and that—a convoy[11] coming in unexpected-ly—she had kindly offered to remain on night duty, which offer was gratefully accepted. That disposes of that."

"Oh!" I said, rather nonplussed.[12] "Really," I continued, "it's her extraordinary vehemence against Inglethorp that start-ed me off suspecting her. I can't help feeling she'd do anything against him. And I had an idea she might know something about the destroying of the will. She might have burnt the new one, mistaking it for the earlier one in his favour. She is so ter-ribly bitter against him."

"You consider her vehemence[13] unnatural?"

"Y—es. She is so very violent. I wondered really whether she is quite sane on that point."

Poirot shook his head energetically.

"No, no, you are on a wrong tack there. There is nothing weak-minded or degenerate about Miss Howard. She is an ex-cellent specimen of well-balanced English beef and brawn. She is sanity itself."[14]

"Yet her hatred of Inglethorp seems almost a mania. My idea was—a very ridiculous one, no doubt—that she had in-tended to poison him—and that, in some way, Mrs. Inglethorp got hold of it by mistake. But I don't at all see how it could have been done. The whole thing is absurd and ridiculous to the last degree."

---

[11] A group of vehicles or ships traveling together.

[12] So surprised that he didn't know how to react.

[13] Intense emotion.

[14] Brawn is meat from a boar. Poirot is expressing the commonly held belief that English men and women were products of their wholesome country environment. Some believed that the purity of the English race was threat-ened by immigrants and native citizens who were not raised properly. In a 1905 article about a holiday weekend on London's Hampstead Heath, the reporter watching poor boys playing cricket observed "there is little of the traditional sturdiness of English blood and build in these weak-chinned, pimply-faced, undersized young Cockneys from the East End. They come of a stunted slum race which fills the London streets with human refuse that shames the fame of English beef and brawn."

"Still you are right in one thing. It is always wise to suspect everybody until you can prove logically, and to your own satisfaction, that they are innocent. Now, what reasons are there against Miss Howard's having deliberately poisoned Mrs. Inglethorp?"

"Why, she was devoted to her!" I exclaimed.

"Tcha! Tcha!" cried Poirot irritably. "You argue like a child. If Miss Howard were capable of poisoning the old lady, she would be quite equally capable of simulating devotion. No, we must look elsewhere. You are perfectly correct in your assumption that her vehemence against Alfred Inglethorp is too violent to be natural; but you are quite wrong in the deduction you draw from it. I have drawn my own deductions, which I believe to be correct, but I will not speak of them at present." He paused a minute, then went on. "Now, to my way of thinking, there is one insuperable[15] objection to Miss Howard's being the murderess."

"And that is?"

"That in no possible way could Mrs. Inglethorp's death benefit Miss Howard. Now there is no murder without a motive."

I reflected.

"Could not Mrs. Inglethorp have made a will in her favour?" Poirot shook his head.

"But you yourself suggested that possibility to Mr. Wells?"

Poirot smiled.

"That was for a reason. I did not want to mention the name of the person who was actually in my mind. Miss Howard occupied very much the same position, so I used her name instead."

"Still, Mrs. Inglethorp might have done so. Why, that will, made on the afternoon of her death may—"

But Poirot's shake of the head was so energetic that I stopped.

---

[15] Impossible to overcome.

"No, my friend. I have certain little ideas of my own about that will. But I can tell you this much—it was not in Miss Howard's favour."

I accepted his assurance, though I did not really see how he could be so positive about the matter.

"Well," I said, with a sigh, "we will acquit Miss Howard, then. It is partly your fault that I ever came to suspect her. It was what you said about her evidence at the inquest that set me off."

Poirot looked puzzled.

"What did I say about her evidence at the inquest?"

"Don't you remember? When I cited her and John Cavendish as being above suspicion?"

"Oh—ah—yes." He seemed a little confused, but recovered himself. "By the way, Hastings, there is something I want you to do for me."

"Certainly. What is it?"

"Next time you happen to be alone with Lawrence Cavendish, I want you to say this to him. 'I have a message for you, from Poirot. He says: "Find the extra coffee-cup, and you can rest in peace!"' Nothing more. Nothing less."

"'Find the extra coffee-cup, and you can rest in peace.' Is that right?" I asked, much mystified.

"Excellent."

"But what does it mean?"

"Ah, that I will leave you to find out. You have access to the facts. Just say that to him, and see what he says."

"Very well—but it's all extremely mysterious."

We were running into Tadminster now, and Poirot directed the car to the "Analytical Chemist."

Poirot hopped down briskly, and went inside. In a few minutes he was back again.

"There," he said. "That is all my business."

"What were you doing there?" I asked, in lively curiosity.

"I left something to be analysed."

"Yes, but what?"

"The sample of coco I took from the saucepan in the bedroom."

"But that has already been tested!" I cried, stupefied. "Dr. Bauerstein had it tested, and you yourself laughed at the possibility of there being strychnine in it."

"I know Dr. Bauerstein had it tested," replied Poirot quietly.

"Well, then?"

"Well, I have a fancy for having it analysed again, that is all."

And not another word on the subject could I drag out of him.

This proceeding of Poirot's, in respect of the coco, puzzled me intensely. I could see neither rhyme nor reason in it. However, my confidence in him, which at one time had rather waned, was fully restored since his belief in Alfred Inglethorp's innocence had been so triumphantly vindicated.

The funeral of Mrs. Inglethorp took place the following day, and on Monday, as I came down to a late breakfast, John drew me aside, and informed me that Mr. Inglethorp was leaving that morning, to take up his quarters at the Stylites Arms until he should have completed his plans.

"And really it's a great relief to think he's going, Hastings," continued my honest friend. "It was bad enough before, when we thought he'd done it, but I'm hanged if it isn't worse now, when we all feel guilty for having been so down on the fellow. The fact is, we've treated him abominably.[16] Of course, things did look black against him. I don't see how anyone could blame us for jumping to the conclusions we did. Still, there it is, we were in the wrong, and now there's a beastly feeling that one ought to make amends; which is difficult, when one doesn't like the fellow a bit better than one did before. The whole thing's damned awkward! And I'm thankful he's had the tact to take himself off. It's a good thing Styles wasn't the mater's to leave to him. Couldn't bear to think of the fellow lording it here. He's welcome to her money."

---

[16] Very unpleasantly or unfairly.

"You'll be able to keep up the place all right?" I asked.

"Oh, yes. There are the death duties,[17] of course, but half my father's money goes with the place, and Lawrence will stay with us for the present, so there is his share as well. We shall be pinched at first, of course, because, as I once told you, I am in a bit of a hole financially myself. Still, the Johnnies will wait now."

In the general relief at Inglethorp's approaching departure, we had the most genial breakfast we had experienced since the tragedy. Cynthia, whose young spirits were naturally buoyant, was looking quite her pretty self again, and we all, with the exception of Lawrence, who seemed unalterably gloomy and nervous, were quietly cheerful, at the opening of a new and hopeful future.

The papers, of course, had been full of the tragedy. Glaring headlines, sandwiched biographies of every member of the household, subtle innuendoes, the usual familiar tag about the police having a clue. Nothing was spared us. It was a slack time. The war was momentarily inactive, and the newspapers seized with avidity[18] on this crime in fashionable life: "The Mysterious Affair at Styles" was the topic of the moment.[19]

Naturally it was very annoying for the Cavendishes. The house was constantly besieged by reporters, who were consistently de-

---

[17] A tax on inheritance introduced in 1796 and increased in subsequent reforms. The imposition of death duties, helped by rising income taxes, the decline in the importance of agriculture, the loss of political power among the aristocracy with the spread of the right to vote, and population losses from two world wars, accelerated the breakup of large aristocratic estates and the crumbling of the old order. As a result, many owners abandoned or demolished their buildings, sold the land for business purposes or donated it to the National Trust. Those who yearn nostalgically for those times without having lived through them should listen to The Clash's "Something About England" for a contrary view.

[18] Keen interest or enthusiasm.

[19] When she imagined the swarm of newspaper coverage, Christie was still a decade away from experiencing this herself. In 1926, she disappeared for 11 days after her husband announced he was seeking a divorce. The events of that time would deeply scar her and create a lifelong aversion to publicity.

nied admission, but who continued to haunt the village and the grounds, where they lay in wait with cameras, for any unwary members of the household. We all lived in a blast of publicity. The Scotland Yard men came and went, examining, questioning, lynx-eyed[20] and reserved of tongue. Towards what end they were working, we did not know. Had they any clue, or would the whole thing remain in the category of unsolved crimes?

After breakfast, Dorcas came up to me rather mysteriously, and asked if she might have a few words with me.

"Certainly. What is it, Dorcas?"

"Well, it's just this, sir. You'll be seeing the Belgian gentleman to-day perhaps?" I nodded. "Well, sir, you know how he asked me so particular if the mistress, or anyone else, had a green dress?"

"Yes, yes. You have found one?" My interest was aroused.

"No, not that, sir. But since then I've remembered what the young gentlemen"—John and Lawrence were still the "young gentlemen" to Dorcas—"call the 'dressing-up box.' It's up in the front attic, sir. A great chest, full of old clothes and fancy dresses, and what not. And it came to me sudden like that there might be a green dress amongst them. So, if you'd tell the Belgian gentleman—"

"I will tell him, Dorcas," I promised.

"Thank you very much, sir. A very nice gentleman he is, sir. And quite a different class from them two detectives from London, what goes prying about, and asking questions. I don't hold with foreigners as a rule, but from what the newspapers say I make out as how these brave Belgies isn't the ordinary run of foreigners, and certainly he's a most polite spoken gentleman."

Dear old Dorcas! As she stood there, with her honest face upturned to mine, I thought what a fine specimen she was of

---

[20] Not looking like a lynx's eye, but having keen vision. Synonymous with eagle-eyed.

the old-fashioned servant that is so fast dying out.[21]

I thought I might as well go down to the village at once, and look up Poirot; but I met him half-way, coming up to the house, and at once gave him Dorcas's message.

"Ah, the brave Dorcas! We will look at the chest, although—but no matter—we will examine it all the same."

We entered the house by one of the windows.[22] There was no one in the hall, and we went straight up to the attic.

Sure enough, there was the chest, a fine old piece, all studded with brass nails, and full to overflowing with every imaginable type of garment.

Poirot bundled everything out on the floor with scant ceremony. There were one or two green fabrics of varying shades; but Poirot shook his head over them all. He seemed somewhat apathetic in the search, as though he expected no great results from it. Suddenly he gave an exclamation.

"What is it?"

"Look!"

The chest was nearly empty, and there, reposing right at the bottom, was a magnificent black beard.

"Oho!" said Poirot. "Oho!" He turned it over in his hands, examining it closely. "New," he remarked. "Yes, quite new."

After a moment's hesitation, he replaced it in the chest,

---

[21] Christie saw the servant class — once a necessity in middle-class households — slowly vanish over the course of her long life. "When I reread those first books," Christie told a reporter in 1966, "I'm amazed at the number of servants drifting about." (*Styles*, for example, mentions 4 servants and 3 gardeners — parlourmaid Dorcas, housemaid Elizabeth Wells, housemaid Annie, male servant Baily, and gardeners Manning, William Earl, and an unnamed female. Add the cook and there's 8 people taking care of 7 residents.) In the 19th century, nearly 10 percent of Britons were in service, the majority of them women. The servant population had been declining since the 1890s, and accelerated after World War I when young women rejected service to work as shop girls, waitresses, beauticians and in other professions that offered regular hours and the freedom to come and go as they pleased.

[22] They passed through French doors, essentially an outside door with one or more panes of glass set in it.

heaped all the other things on top of it as before, and made his way briskly downstairs. He went straight to the pantry, where we found Dorcas busily polishing her silver.

Poirot wished her good morning with Gallic politeness, and went on:

"We have been looking through that chest, Dorcas. I am much obliged to you for mentioning it. There is, indeed, a fine collection there. Are they often used, may I ask?"

"Well, sir, not very often nowadays, though from time to time we do have what the young gentlemen call 'a dress-up night.' And very funny it is sometimes, sir. Mr. Lawrence, he's wonderful. Most comic! I shall never forget the night he came down as the Char of Persia,[23] I think he called it—a sort of Eastern King it was. He had the big paper knife[24] in his hand, and 'Mind, Dorcas,' he says, 'you'll have to be very respectful. This is my specially sharpened scimitar, and it's off with your head if I'm at all displeased with you!' Miss Cynthia, she was what they call an Apache, or some such name—a Frenchified sort of cut-throat, I take it to be. A real sight she looked. You'd never have believed a pretty young lady like that could have made herself into such a ruffian. Nobody would have known her."[25]

"These evenings must have been great fun," said Poirot genially. "I suppose Mr. Lawrence wore that fine black beard in the chest upstairs, when he was Shah of Persia?"

"He did have a beard, sir," replied Dorcas, smiling. "And well I know it, for he borrowed two skeins of my black wool to

---

[23] Dorcas means shah, a title similar to emperor that was used in India and Persia, now Iran. In modern times, Mohammad Pahlavi was Shah of Iran until he was deposed in the Islamic Revolution of 1979.
[24] Another word for a letter opener, a knife-like object used to open mail.
[25] Not the Native American tribe, but members of a criminal subculture in Paris during the period called the Belle Époque ("Beautiful Era," 1871-1914). Apaches, pronounced "a-PASH," were given that name because their violent robbery tactics, including garroting, head butts, sudden kicks and sucker punches, reminded Parisians of the tribe's fierce warriors. Apaches developed a distinctive argot, look and dance that set them apart from mainstream society in their time much like rappers and hip-hop artists do in ours.

make it with! And I'm sure it looked wonderfully natural at a distance. I didn't know as there was a beard up there at all. It must have been got quite lately, I think. There was a red wig, I know, but nothing else in the way of hair. Burnt corks they use mostly—though 'tis messy getting it off again. Miss Cynthia was a nigger once, and, oh, the trouble she had."[26]

"So Dorcas knows nothing about that black beard," said Poirot thoughtfully, as we walked out into the hall again.

"Do you think it is *the* one?" I whispered eagerly.

Poirot nodded.

"I do. You notice it had been trimmed?"

"No."

"Yes. It was cut exactly the shape of Mr. Inglethorp's, and I found one or two snipped hairs. Hastings, this affair is very deep."

"Who put it in the chest, I wonder?"

"Some one with a good deal of intelligence," remarked Poirot dryly. "You realize that he chose the one place in the house to hide it where its presence would not be remarked? Yes, he is intelligent. But we must be more intelligent. We must be so intelligent that he does not suspect us of being intelligent at all."

I acquiesced.

"There, *mon ami*, you will be of great assistance to me."

I was pleased with the compliment. There had been times when I hardly thought that Poirot appreciated me at my true worth.

"Yes," he continued, staring at me thoughtfully, "you will be invaluable."

This was naturally gratifying, but Poirot's next words were not so welcome.

"I must have an ally in the house," he observed reflectively.

"You have me," I protested.

---

[26] A reference to the difficulty she must have had cleaning burnt cork off her face. It is implied later that she was impersonating a performer in a minstrel show.

"True, but you are not sufficient."

I was hurt, and showed it. Poirot hurried to explain himself.

"You do not quite take my meaning. You are known to be working with me. I want somebody who is not associated with us in any way."

"Oh, I see. How about John?"

"No, I think not."

"The dear fellow isn't perhaps very bright," I said thoughtfully.

"Here comes Miss Howard," said Poirot suddenly. "She is the very person. But I am in her black books,[27] since I cleared Mr. Inglethorp. Still, we can but try."

With a nod that was barely civil, Miss Howard assented to Poirot's request for a few minutes' conversation.

We went into the little morning-room,[28] and Poirot closed the door.

"Well, Monsieur Poirot," said Miss Howard impatiently, "what is it? Out with it. I'm busy."

"Do you remember, mademoiselle, that I once asked you to help me?"

"Yes, I do." The lady nodded. "And I told you I'd help you with pleasure—to hang Alfred Inglethorp."

"Ah!" Poirot studied her seriously. "Miss Howard, I will ask you one question. I beg of you to reply to it truthfully."

"Never tell lies," replied Miss Howard.

"It is this. Do you still believe that Mrs. Inglethorp was poisoned by her husband?"

"What do you mean?" she asked sharply. "You needn't think your pretty explanations influence me in the slightest. I'll admit that it wasn't he who bought strychnine at the chemist's shop. What of that? I dare say he soaked fly paper, as I told you at the beginning."

---

[27] To be in disgrace or out of favor. In medieval times, to be in one's book meant to be esteemed, so to be out of someone's book meant the opposite.

[28] A sitting room used in the morning when the sun shines brightest into it.

"That is arsenic—not strychnine," said Poirot mildly.

"What does that matter? Arsenic would put poor Emily out of the way just as well as strychnine. If I'm convinced he did it, it doesn't matter a jot to me *how* he did it."

"Exactly. *If* you are convinced he did it," said Poirot quietly. "I will put my question in another form. Did you ever in your heart of hearts believe that Mrs. Inglethorp was poisoned by her husband?"

"Good heavens!" cried Miss Howard. "Haven't I always told you the man is a villain? Haven't I always told you he would murder her in her bed? Haven't I always hated him like poison?"

"Exactly," said Poirot. "That bears out my little idea entirely."

"What little idea?"

"Miss Howard, do you remember a conversation that took place on the day of my friend's arrival here? He repeated it to me, and there is a sentence of yours that has impressed me very much. Do you remember affirming that if a crime had been committed, and anyone you loved had been murdered, you felt certain that you would know by instinct who the criminal was, even if you were quite unable to prove it?"

"Yes, I remember saying that. I believe it too. I suppose you think it nonsense?"

"Not at all."

"And yet you will pay no attention to my instinct against Alfred Inglethorp."

"No," said Poirot curtly. "Because your instinct is not against Mr. Inglethorp."

"What?"

"No. You wish to believe he committed the crime. You believe him capable of committing it. But your instinct tells you he did not commit it. It tells you more—shall I go on?"

She was staring at him, fascinated, and made a slight affirmative movement of the hand.

"Shall I tell you why you have been so vehement against Mr. Inglethorp? It is because you have been trying to believe what you wish to believe. It is because you are trying to drown and stifle your instinct, which tells you another name—"

"No, no, no!" cried Miss Howard wildly, flinging up her hands. "Don't say it! Oh, don't say it! It isn't true! It can't be true. I don't know what put such a wild—such a dreadful—idea into my head!"

"I am right, am I not?" asked Poirot.

"Yes, yes; you must be a wizard to have guessed. But it can't be so—it's too monstrous, too impossible. It must be Alfred Inglethorp."

Poirot shook his head gravely.

"Don't ask me about it," continued Miss Howard, "because I shan't tell you. I won't admit it, even to myself. I must be mad to think of such a thing."

Poirot nodded, as if satisfied.

"I will ask you nothing. It is enough for me that it is as I thought. And I—I, too, have an instinct. We are working together towards a common end."

"Don't ask me to help you, because I won't. I wouldn't lift a finger to—to—" She faltered.

"You will help me in spite of yourself. I ask you nothing—but you will be my ally. You will not be able to help yourself. You will do the only thing that I want of you."

"And that is?"

"You will watch!"

Evelyn Howard bowed her head.

"Yes, I can't help doing that. I am always watching—always hoping I shall be proved wrong."

"If we are wrong, well and good," said Poirot. "No one will be more pleased than I shall. But, if we are right? If we are right, Miss Howard, on whose side are you then?"

"I don't know, I don't know—"

"Come now."

"It could be hushed up."

"There must be no hushing up."

"But Emily herself—" She broke off.

"Miss Howard," said Poirot gravely, "this is unworthy of you."

Suddenly she took her face from her hands.

"Yes," she said quietly, "that was not Evelyn Howard who spoke!" She flung her head up proudly. "*This* is Evelyn Howard! And she is on the side of Justice! Let the cost be what it may." And with these words, she walked firmly out of the room.

"There," said Poirot, looking after her, "goes a very valuable ally. That woman, Hastings, has got brains as well as a heart."

I did not reply.

"Instinct is a marvellous thing," mused Poirot. "It can neither be explained nor ignored."

"You and Miss Howard seem to know what you are talking about," I observed coldly. "Perhaps you don't realize that I am still in the dark."

"Really? Is that so, *mon ami?*"

"Yes. Enlighten me, will you?"

Poirot studied me attentively for a moment or two. Then, to my intense surprise, he shook his head decidedly.

"No, my friend."

"Oh, look here, why not?"

"Two is enough for a secret."

"Well, I think it is very unfair to keep back facts from me."

"I am not keeping back facts. Every fact that I know is in your possession. You can draw your own deductions from them. This time it is a question of ideas."

"Still, it would be interesting to know."

Poirot looked at me very earnestly, and again shook his head.

"You see," he said sadly, "*you* have no instincts."

"It was intelligence you were requiring just now," I pointed out.

"The two often go together," said Poirot enigmatically.

The remark seemed so utterly irrelevant that I did not even take the trouble to answer it. But I decided that if I made any interesting and important discoveries—as no doubt I should—I would keep them to myself, and surprise Poirot with the ultimate result.

There are times when it is one's duty to assert oneself.

CHAPTER IX

DR. BAUERSTEIN

I HAD HAD NO OPPORTUNITY as yet of passing on Poirot's message to Lawrence. But now, as I strolled out on the lawn, still nursing a grudge against my friend's high-handedness, I saw Lawrence on the croquet lawn, aimlessly knocking a couple of very ancient balls about, with a still more ancient mallet.[1]

It struck me that it would be a good opportunity to deliver my message. Otherwise, Poirot himself might relieve me of it. It was true that I did not quite gather its purport, but I flattered myself that by Lawrence's reply, and perhaps a little skillful cross-examination on my part, I should soon perceive its significance. Accordingly I accosted him.

"I've been looking for you," I remarked untruthfully.

"Have you?"

"Yes. The truth is, I've got a message for you—from Poirot."

"Yes?"

"He told me to wait until I was alone with you," I said, dropping my voice significantly, and watching him intently out of the corner of my eye. I have always been rather good at what is called, I believe, creating an atmosphere.

"Well?"

There was no change of expression in the dark melancholic face. Had he any idea of what I was about to say?

"This is the message." I dropped my voice still lower. "'Find the extra coffee-cup, and you can rest in peace.'"

"What on earth does he mean?" Lawrence stared at me in

---

[1] An estate can have areas set aside for games, such as lawn bowls, tennis, and croquet, with equipment available for use by the guests.

quite unaffected astonishment.

"Don't you know?"

"Not in the least. Do you?"

I was compelled to shake my head.

"What extra coffee-cup?"

"I don't know."

"He'd better ask Dorcas, or one of the maids, if he wants to know about coffee-cups. It's their business, not mine. I don't know anything about the coffee-cups, except that we've got some that are never used, which are a perfect dream! Old Worcester.[2] You're not a connoisseur, are you, Hastings?"[3]

I shook my head.

"You miss a lot. A really perfect bit of old china—it's pure delight to handle it, or even to look at it."

"Well, what am I to tell Poirot?"

"Tell him I don't know what he's talking about. It's double Dutch to me."[4]

"All right."

I was moving off towards the house again when he suddenly called me back.

"I say, what was the end of that message? Say it over again, will you?"

"'Find the extra coffee-cup, and you can rest in peace.' Are you sure you don't know what it means?" I asked him earnestly.

He shook his head.

"No," he said musingly, "I don't. I—I wish I did."

The boom of the gong[5] sounded from the house, and we

---

[2] Royal Worcester, pronounced "wooster," is one of the oldest porcelain brands in England. It was founded in 1751 and given a royal warrant by King George III in 1788.

[3] An expert in areas that rely on taste instead of technical knowledge, such as wine and art.

[4] Incomprehensible gibberish.

[5] At a country house, lunch and dinner were served at regular times and announced with the ringing of a gong or bell to give guests time to dress for dinner.

went in together. Poirot had been asked by John to remain to lunch, and was already seated at the table.

By tacit[6] consent, all mention of the tragedy was barred. We conversed on the war, and other outside topics. But after the cheese and biscuits[7] had been handed round, and Dorcas had left the room, Poirot suddenly leant forward to Mrs. Cavendish.

"Pardon me, madame, for recalling unpleasant memories, but I have a little idea"—Poirot's "little ideas" were becoming a perfect byword—"and would like to ask one or two questions."

"Of me? Certainly."

"You are too amiable, madame. What I want to ask is this: the door leading into Mrs. Inglethorp's room from that of Mademoiselle Cynthia, it was bolted, you say?"

"Certainly it was bolted," replied Mary Cavendish, rather surprised. "I said so at the inquest."

"Bolted?"

"Yes." She looked perplexed.

"I mean," explained Poirot, "you are sure it was bolted, and not merely locked?"

"Oh, I see what you mean. No, I don't know. I said bolted, meaning that it was fastened, and I could not open it, but I believe all the doors were found bolted on the inside."

"Still, as far as you are concerned, the door might equally well have been locked?"

"Oh, yes."

"You yourself did not happen to notice, madame, when you entered Mrs. Inglethorp's room, whether that door was bolted or not?"

"I—I believe it was."

"But you did not see it?"

"No. I—never looked."

"But I did," interrupted Lawrence suddenly. "I happened to notice that it *was* bolted."

---

[6] An unspoken response that is implied by a person's behavior.
[7] A small baked unleavened cake, typically crisp, flat, and sweet.

"Ah, that settles it." And Poirot looked crestfallen.

I could not help rejoicing that, for once, one of his "little ideas" had come to naught.

After lunch Poirot begged me to accompany him home. I consented rather stiffly.

"You are annoyed, is it not so?" he asked anxiously, as we walked through the park.

"Not at all," I said coldly.

"That is well. That lifts a great load from my mind."

This was not quite what I had intended. I had hoped that he would have observed the stiffness of my manner. Still, the fervour of his words went towards the appeasing of my just displeasure. I thawed.

"I gave Lawrence your message," I said.

"And what did he say? He was entirely puzzled?"

"Yes. I am quite sure he had no idea of what you meant."

I had expected Poirot to be disappointed; but, to my surprise, he replied that that was as he had thought, and that he was very glad. My pride forbade me to ask any questions.

Poirot switched off on another tack.

"Mademoiselle Cynthia was not at lunch to-day? How was that?"

"She is at the hospital again. She resumed work to-day."

"Ah, she is an industrious little *demoiselle*.[8] And pretty too. She is like pictures I have seen in Italy. I would rather like to see that dispensary of hers. Do you think she would show it to me?"

"I am sure she would be delighted. It's an interesting little place."

"Does she go there every day?"

"She has all Wednesdays off, and comes back to lunch on Saturdays. Those are her only times off."

"I will remember. Women are doing great work nowadays, and Mademoiselle Cynthia is clever—oh, yes, she has brains,

---

[8] Damsel, a young, unmarried woman, from the Latin *domina* for "mistress."

that little one."

"Yes. I believe she has passed quite a stiff exam."[9]

"Without doubt. After all, it is very responsible work. I suppose they have very strong poisons there?"

"Yes, she showed them to us. They are kept locked up in a little cupboard. I believe they have to be very careful. They always take out the key before leaving the room."

"Indeed. It is near the window, this cupboard?"

"No, right the other side of the room. Why?"

Poirot shrugged his shoulders.

"I wondered. That is all. Will you come in?"

We had reached the cottage.

"No. I think I'll be getting back. I shall go round the long way through the woods."

The woods round Styles were very beautiful. After the walk across the open park, it was pleasant to saunter lazily through the cool glades.[10] There was hardly a breath of wind, the very chirp of the birds was faint and subdued. I strolled on a little way, and finally flung myself down at the foot of a grand old beech-tree. My thoughts of mankind were kindly and charitable. I even forgave Poirot for his absurd secrecy. In fact, I was at peace with the world. Then I yawned.

I thought about the crime, and it struck me as being very unreal and far off.

I yawned again.

Probably, I thought, it really never happened. Of course, it was all a bad dream. The truth of the matter was that it was Lawrence who had murdered Alfred Inglethorp with a croquet mallet. But it was absurd of John to make such a fuss about it, and to go shouting out: "I tell you I won't have it!"

I woke up with a start.

At once I realized that I was in a very awkward predica-

---

[9] Christie is speaking from experience. In 1917, she passed the Society of Apothecaries' exam on her second attempt to qualify as an assistant.

[10] An open space in a forest.

ment. For, about twelve feet away from me, John and Mary Cavendish were standing facing each other, and they were evidently quarrelling. And, quite as evidently, they were unaware of my vicinity, for before I could move or speak John repeated the words which had aroused me from my dream.

"I tell you, Mary, I won't have it."

Mary's voice came, cool and liquid:

"Have *you* any right to criticize my actions?"

"It will be the talk of the village! My mother was only buried on Saturday, and here you are gadding about with the fellow."

"Oh," she shrugged her shoulders, "if it is only village gossip that you mind!"

"But it isn't. I've had enough of the fellow hanging about. He's a Polish Jew, anyway."

"A tinge of Jewish blood is not a bad thing. It leavens the"—she looked at him—"stolid stupidity of the ordinary Englishman."[11]

Fire in her eyes, ice in her voice. I did not wonder that the blood rose to John's face in a crimson tide.

"Mary!"

"Well?" Her tone did not change.

The pleading died out of his voice.

"Am I to understand that you will continue to see Bauerstein against my express wishes?"

"If I choose."

"You defy me?"

"No, but I deny your right to criticize my actions. Have *you* no friends of whom I should disapprove?"

John fell back a pace. The colour ebbed slowly from his face.

---

[11] This would be the first of many references to Jews in Christie's books that would distress some of her readers. While she mirrored what cultural historian Jacques Barzun called "the usual tedious British anti-Semitism," she was also appalled when she encountered a Nazi's fanatical anti-Semitism. For more information, see "Fat Ikey and Noisy Negroes" in the appendix.

"What do you mean?" he said, in an unsteady voice.

"You see!" said Mary quietly. "You *do* see, don't you, that *you* have no right to dictate to *me* as to the choice of my friends?"

John glanced at her pleadingly, a stricken look on his face.

"No right? Have I *no* right, Mary?" he said unsteadily. He stretched out his hands. "Mary—"

For a moment, I thought she wavered. A softer expression came over her face, then suddenly she turned almost fiercely away.

"None!"

She was walking away when John sprang after her, and caught her by the arm.

"Mary"—his voice was very quiet now—"are you in love with this fellow Bauerstein?"

She hesitated, and suddenly there swept across her face a strange expression, old as the hills, yet with something eternally young about it. So might some Egyptian sphinx have smiled.

She freed herself quietly from his arm, and spoke over her shoulder.

"Perhaps," she said; and then swiftly passed out of the little glade, leaving John standing there as though he had been turned to stone.

Rather ostentatiously,[12] I stepped forward, crackling some dead branches with my feet as I did so. John turned. Luckily, he took it for granted that I had only just come upon the scene.

"Hullo, Hastings. Have you seen the little fellow safely back to his cottage? Quaint little chap! Is he any good, though, really?"

"He was considered one of the finest detectives of his day."

"Oh, well, I suppose there must be something in it, then. What a rotten world it is, though!"

"You find it so?" I asked.

"Good Lord, yes! There's this terrible business to start

---

[12] Obvious or conspicuous behavior exhibited in an attempt to be noticed. Sometimes seen as pretentious.

with. Scotland Yard men in and out of the house like a jack-in-the-box! Never know where they won't turn up next. Screaming headlines in every paper in the country—damn all journalists, I say! Do you know there was a whole crowd staring in at the lodge gates this morning. Sort of Madame Tussauds chamber of horrors business[13] that can be seen for nothing. Pretty thick,[14] isn't it?"

"Cheer up, John!" I said soothingly. "It can't last for ever."

"Can't it, though? It can last long enough for us never to be able to hold up our heads again."

"No, no, you're getting morbid on the subject."

"Enough to make a man morbid, to be stalked by beastly journalists and stared at by gaping moon-faced idiots, wherever he goes! But there's worse than that."

"What?"

John lowered his voice:

"Have you ever thought, Hastings—it's a nightmare to me—who did it? I can't help feeling sometimes it must have been an accident. Because—because—who could have done it? Now Inglethorp's out of the way, there's no one else; no one, I mean, except—one of us."

Yes, indeed, that was nightmare enough for any man! One of us? Yes, surely it must be so, unless—

A new idea suggested itself to my mind. Rapidly, I considered it. The light increased. Poirot's mysterious doings, his hints—they all fitted in. Fool that I was not to have thought of this possibility before, and what a relief for us all.

---

[13] Born Anna Maria Grosholtz (1761-1850), Marie Tussaud was a French woman who learned the art of modeling heads in wax under the tutelage of a Swiss doctor. She inherited his Paris waxworks at his death, and during the French Revolution cast the death masks of notable victims of the guillotine, including Marie Antoinette and Maximilien Robespierre. In 1806, she moved to London and founded a wax museum which exists today. One notable aspect of the museum is its display of infamous murderers. Late in life, Christie allowed her head to be measured for a display.

[14] Indecent.

"No, John," I said, "it isn't one of us. How could it be?"

"I know, but, still, who else is there?"

"Can't you guess?"

"No."

I looked cautiously round, and lowered my voice.

"Dr. Bauerstein!" I whispered.

"Impossible!"

"Not at all."

"But what earthly interest could he have in my mother's death?"

"That I don't see," I confessed, "but I'll tell you this: Poirot thinks so."

"Poirot? Does he? How do you know?"

I told him of Poirot's intense excitement on hearing that Dr. Bauerstein had been at Styles on the fatal night, and added:

"He said twice: 'That alters everything.' And I've been thinking. You know Inglethorp said he had put down the coffee in the hall? Well, it was just then that Bauerstein arrived. Isn't it possible that, as Inglethorp brought him through the hall, the doctor dropped something into the coffee in passing?"

"H'm," said John. "It would have been very risky."

"Yes, but it was possible."

"And then, how could he know it was her coffee? No, old fellow, I don't think that will wash."

But I had remembered something else.

"You're quite right. That wasn't how it was done. Listen." And I then told him of the coco sample which Poirot had taken to be analysed.

John interrupted just as I had done.

"But, look here, Bauerstein had had it analysed already?"

"Yes, yes, that's the point. I didn't see it either until now. Don't you understand? Bauerstein had it analysed—that's just it! If Bauerstein's the murderer, nothing could be simpler than for him to substitute some ordinary coco for his sample, and send that to be tested. And of course they would find no strychnine! But no one would dream of suspecting Bauerstein, or think of taking another sample—except Poirot," I added, with belated recognition.

"Yes, but what about the bitter taste that coco won't disguise?"

"Well, we've only his word for that. And there are other possibilities. He's admittedly one of the world's greatest toxicologists—"

"One of the world's greatest what? Say it again."

"He knows more about poisons than almost anybody," I explained. "Well, my idea is, that perhaps he's found some way of making strychnine tasteless. Or it may not have been strychnine at all, but some obscure drug no one has ever heard of, which produces much the same symptoms."

"H'm, yes, that might be," said John. "But look here, how could he have got at the coco? That wasn't downstairs?"

"No, it wasn't," I admitted reluctantly.

And then, suddenly, a dreadful possibility flashed through my mind. I hoped and prayed it would not occur to John also. I glanced sideways at him. He was frowning perplexedly, and I drew a deep breath of relief, for the terrible thought that had flashed across my mind was this: that Dr. Bauerstein might have had an accomplice.

Yet surely it could not be! Surely no woman as beautiful as Mary Cavendish could be a murderess. Yet beautiful women had been known to poison.

And suddenly I remembered that first conversation at tea on the day of my arrival, and the gleam in her eyes as she had said that poison was a woman's weapon. How agitated she had been on that fatal Tuesday evening! Had Mrs. Inglethorp discovered something between her and Bauerstein, and threatened to tell her husband? Was it to stop that denunciation that the crime had been committed?

Then I remembered that enigmatical conversation between Poirot and Evelyn Howard. Was this what they had meant? Was this the monstrous possibility that Evelyn had tried not to believe?

Yes, it all fitted in.

No wonder Miss Howard had suggested "hushing it up."

Now I understood that unfinished sentence of hers: "Emily herself—" And in my heart I agreed with her. Would not Mrs. Inglethorp have preferred to go unavenged rather than have such terrible dishonour fall upon the name of Cavendish?

"There's another thing," said John suddenly, and the unexpected sound of his voice made me start guiltily. "Something which makes me doubt if what you say can be true."

"What's that?" I asked, thankful that he had gone away from the subject of how the poison could have been introduced into the coco.

"Why, the fact that Bauerstein demanded a post-mortem. He needn't have done so. Little Wilkins would have been quite content to let it go at heart disease."

"Yes," I said doubtfully. "But we don't know. Perhaps he thought it safer in the long run. Some one might have talked afterwards. Then the Home Office might have ordered exhumation.[15] The whole thing would have come out, then, and he would have been in an awkward position, for no one would have believed that a man of his reputation could have been deceived into calling it heart disease."

"Yes, that's possible," admitted John. "Still," he added, "I'm blest if I can see what his motive could have been."

I trembled.

"Look here," I said, "I may be altogether wrong. And, remember, all this is in confidence."

"Oh, of course—that goes without saying."

We had walked, as we talked, and now we passed through the little gate into the garden. Voices rose near at hand, for tea was spread out under the sycamore-tree, as it had been on the day of my arrival.

Cynthia was back from the hospital, and I placed my chair beside her, and told her of Poirot's wish to visit the dispensary.

"Of course! I'd love him to see it. He'd better come to tea there one day. I must fix it up with him. He's such a dear little

---

[15] The act of digging up something buried.

man! But he *is* funny. He made me take the brooch out of my tie the other day, and put it in again, because he said it wasn't straight."

I laughed.

"It's quite a mania with him."

"Yes, isn't it?"

We were silent for a minute or two, and then, glancing in the direction of Mary Cavendish, and dropping her voice, Cynthia said:

"Mr. Hastings."

"Yes?"

"After tea, I want to talk to you."

Her glance at Mary had set me thinking. I fancied that between these two there existed very little sympathy. For the first time, it occurred to me to wonder about the girl's future. Mrs. Inglethorp had made no provisions of any kind for her, but I imagined that John and Mary would probably insist on her making her home with them—at any rate until the end of the war. John, I knew, was very fond of her, and would be sorry to let her go.

John, who had gone into the house, now reappeared. His good-natured face wore an unaccustomed frown of anger.

"Confound those detectives! I can't think what they're after! They've been in every room in the house—turning things inside out, and upside down. It really is too bad! I suppose they took advantage of our all being out. I shall go for that fellow Japp, when I next see him!"

"Lot of Paul Prys,"[16] grunted Miss Howard.

Lawrence opined that they had to make a show of doing something.

Mary Cavendish said nothing.

After tea, I invited Cynthia to come for a walk, and we

---

[16] Someone who meddles in other people's business. Inspired by the hero of the 1825 play of the same name by John Poole (1785-1872).

sauntered[17] off into the woods together.

"Well?" I inquired, as soon as we were protected from prying eyes by the leafy screen.

With a sigh, Cynthia flung herself down, and tossed off her hat. The sunlight, piercing through the branches, turned the auburn of her hair to quivering gold.

"Mr. Hastings—you are always so kind, and you know such a lot."

It struck me at this moment that Cynthia was really a very charming girl! Much more charming than Mary, who never said things of that kind.

"Well?" I asked benignantly,[18] as she hesitated.

"I want to ask your advice. What shall I do?"

"Do?"

"Yes. You see, Aunt Emily always told me I should be provided for. I suppose she forgot, or didn't think she was likely to die—anyway, I am *not* provided for![19] And I don't know what to do. Do you think I ought to go away from here at once?"

"Good heavens, no! They don't want to part with you, I'm sure."

Cynthia hesitated a moment, plucking up the grass with her tiny hands. Then she said: "Mrs. Cavendish does. She hates me."

"Hates you?" I cried, astonished.

Cynthia nodded.

"Yes. I don't know why, but she can't bear me; and *he* can't, either."

"There I know you're wrong," I said warmly. "On the contrary, John is very fond of you."

"Oh, yes—*John*. I meant Lawrence. Not, of course, that I care whether Lawrence hates me or not. Still, it's rather horrid when no one loves you, isn't it?"

---

[17] To walk about in a leisurely manner.

[18] Mild and kindly.

[19] That she would receive a portion of the estate, perhaps as a small annuity.

"But they do, Cynthia dear," I said earnestly. "I'm sure you are mistaken. Look, there is John—and Miss Howard—"

Cynthia nodded rather gloomily. "Yes, John likes me, I think, and of course Evie, for all her gruff ways, wouldn't be unkind to a fly. But Lawrence never speaks to me if he can help it, and Mary can hardly bring herself to be civil to me. She wants Evie to stay on, is begging her to, but she doesn't want me, and—and—I don't know what to do." Suddenly the poor child burst out crying.

I don't know what possessed me. Her beauty, perhaps, as she sat there, with the sunlight glinting down on her head; perhaps the sense of relief at encountering someone who so obviously could have no connection with the tragedy; perhaps honest pity for her youth and loneliness. Anyway, I leant forward, and taking her little hand, I said awkwardly:

"Marry me, Cynthia."

Unwittingly, I had hit upon a sovereign[20] remedy for her tears. She sat up at once, drew her hand away, and said, with some asperity:[21]

"Don't be silly!"

I was a little annoyed.

"I'm not being silly. I am asking you to do me the honour of becoming my wife."

To my intense surprise, Cynthia burst out laughing, and called me a "funny dear."

"It's perfectly sweet of you," she said, "but you know you don't want to!"

"Yes, I do. I've got—"

"Never mind what you've got. You don't really want to—and I don't either."

"Well, of course, that settles it," I said stiffly. "But I don't see anything to laugh at. There's nothing funny about a proposal."

[20] Extremely successful.
[21] Speaking severely.

"No, indeed," said Cynthia. "Somebody might accept you next time. Good-bye, you've cheered me up *very* much."

And, with a final uncontrollable burst of merriment, she vanished through the trees.

Thinking over the interview, it struck me as being profoundly unsatisfactory.

It occurred to me suddenly that I would go down to the village, and look up Bauerstein. Somebody ought to be keeping an eye on the fellow. At the same time, it would be wise to allay any suspicions he might have as to his being suspected. I remembered how Poirot had relied on my diplomacy. Accordingly, I went to the little house with the "Apartments" card inserted in the window, where I knew he lodged, and tapped on the door.

An old woman came and opened it.

"Good afternoon," I said pleasantly. "Is Dr. Bauerstein in?"

She stared at me.

"Haven't you heard?"

"Heard what?"

"About him."

"What about him?"

"He's took."

"Took? Dead?"

"No, took by the perlice."

"By the police!" I gasped. "Do you mean they've arrested him?"

"Yes, that's it, and—"

I waited to hear no more, but tore up the village to find Poirot.

CHAPTER X

THE ARREST

TO MY EXTREME ANNOYANCE, Poirot was not in, and the old Belgian who answered my knock informed me that he believed he had gone to London.

I was dumbfounded. What on earth could Poirot be doing in London! Was it a sudden decision on his part, or had he already made up his mind when he parted from me a few hours earlier?

I retraced my steps to Styles in some annoyance. With Poirot away, I was uncertain how to act. Had he foreseen this arrest? Had he not, in all probability, been the cause of it? Those questions I could not resolve. But in the meantime what was I to do? Should I announce the arrest openly at Styles, or not? Though I did not acknowledge it to myself, the thought of Mary Cavendish was weighing on me. Would it not be a terrible shock to her? For the moment, I set aside utterly any suspicions of her. She could not be implicated—otherwise I should have heard some hint of it.

Of course, there was no possibility of being able permanently to conceal Dr. Bauerstein's arrest from her. It would be announced in every newspaper on the morrow. Still, I shrank from blurting it out. If only Poirot had been accessible, I could have asked his advice. What possessed him to go posting off to London in this unaccountable way?

In spite of myself, my opinion of his sagacity[1] was immeasurably heightened. I would never have dreamt of suspecting the doctor, had not Poirot put it into my head. Yes, decidedly, the

---

[1] Wise judgment.

little man was clever.

After some reflecting, I decided to take John into my confidence, and leave him to make the matter public or not, as he thought fit.

He gave vent to a prodigious whistle, as I imparted the news.

"Great Scot![2] You *were* right, then. I couldn't believe it at the time."

"No, it is astonishing until you get used to the idea, and see how it makes everything fit in. Now, what are we to do? Of course, it will be generally known to-morrow."

John reflected.

"Never mind," he said at last, "we won't say anything at present. There is no need. As you say, it will be known soon enough."

But to my intense surprise, on getting down early the next morning, and eagerly opening the newspapers, there was not a word about the arrest! There was a column of mere padding about "The Styles Poisoning Case," but nothing further. It was rather inexplicable, but I supposed that, for some reason or other, Japp wished to keep it out of the papers. It worried me just a little, for it suggested the possibility that there might be further arrests to come.

After breakfast, I decided to go down to the village, and see if Poirot had returned yet; but, before I could start, a well-known face blocked one of the windows, and the well-known voice said:

"*Bon jour, mon ami!*"

"Poirot," I exclaimed, with relief, and seizing him by both hands, I dragged him into the room. "I was never so glad to see

---

[2] Great Scot: Who was Scot and what made him so wonderful? One theory contends the phrase was inspired by U.S. Gen. Winfield Scott (1786-1866), who rose to popularity after successfully leading the campaign against Mexico in 1847. Known as "Old Fuss and Feathers," he was lieutenant-general of the U.S. Army at the beginning of the Civil War in 1861, when a New York Times story welcomed "these gathering hosts of loyal freemen, under the command of the great SCOTT."

anyone. Listen, I have said nothing to anybody but John. Is that right?"

"My friend," replied Poirot, "I do not know what you are talking about."

"Dr. Bauerstein's arrest, of course," I answered impatiently.

"Is Bauerstein arrested, then?"

"Did you not know it?"

"Not the least in the world." But, pausing a moment, he added: "Still, it does not surprise me. After all, we are only four miles from the coast."

"The coast?" I asked, puzzled. "What has that got to do with it?"

Poirot shrugged his shoulders.

"Surely, it is obvious!"

"Not to me. No doubt I am very dense, but I cannot see what the proximity of the coast has got to do with the murder of Mrs. Inglethorp."

"Nothing at all, of course," replied Poirot, smiling. "But we were speaking of the arrest of Dr. Bauerstein."

"Well, he is arrested for the murder of Mrs. Inglethorp —"

"What?" cried Poirot, in apparently lively astonishment. "Dr. Bauerstein arrested for the murder of Mrs. Inglethorp?"

"Yes."

"Impossible! That would be too good a farce![3] Who told you that, my friend?"

"Well, no one exactly told me," I confessed. "But he is arrested."

"Oh, yes, very likely. But for espionage, *mon ami*."

"Espionage?" I gasped.

"Precisely."

"Not for poisoning Mrs. Inglethorp?"

"Not unless our friend Japp has taken leave of his senses," replied Poirot placidly.

---

[3] An absurd situation.

"But—but I thought you thought so too?"

Poirot gave me one look, which conveyed a wondering pity, and his full sense of the utter absurdity of such an idea.

"Do you mean to say," I asked, slowly adapting myself to the new idea, "that Dr. Bauerstein is a spy?"

Poirot nodded.

"Have you never suspected it?"

"It never entered my head."

"It did not strike you as peculiar that a famous London doctor should bury himself in a little village like this, and should be in the habit of walking about at all hours of the night, fully dressed?"

"No," I confessed, "I never thought of such a thing."

"He is, of course, a German by birth," said Poirot thought-fully, "though he has practiced so long in this country that no-body thinks of him as anything but an Englishman. He was naturalized about fifteen years ago. A very clever man—a Jew, of course."

"The blackguard!"[4] I cried indignantly.

"Not at all. He is, on the contrary, a patriot. Think what he stands to lose. I admire the man myself."

But I could not look at it in Poirot's philosophical way.

"And this is the man with whom Mrs. Cavendish has been wandering about all over the country!" I cried indignantly.

"Yes. I should fancy he had found her very useful," re-marked Poirot. "So long as gossip busied itself in coupling their names together, any other vagaries of the doctor's passed un-observed."

"Then you think he never really cared for her?" I asked ea-gerly—rather too eagerly, perhaps, under the circumstances.

"That, of course, I cannot say, but—shall I tell you my own private opinion, Hastings?"

---

[4] Pronounced "blaggard," it means a dishonest or immoral man. Seen in print as early as 1532, it is believed that the epithet was inspired by the Black Guard, a notorious company of soldiers at London's Westminster Palace.

"Yes."

"Well, it is this: that Mrs. Cavendish does not care, and never has cared one little jot[5] about Dr. Bauerstein!"

"Do you really think so?" I could not disguise my pleasure.

"I am quite sure of it. And I will tell you why."

"Yes?"

"Because she cares for some one else, *mon ami.*"

"Oh!" What did he mean? In spite of myself, an agreeable warmth spread over me. I am not a vain man where women are concerned, but I remembered certain evidences, too lightly thought of at the time, perhaps, but which certainly seemed to indicate—

My pleasing thoughts were interrupted by the sudden entrance of Miss Howard. She glanced round hastily to make sure there was no one else in the room, and quickly produced an old sheet of brown paper. This she handed to Poirot, murmuring as she did so the cryptic words:

"On top of the wardrobe."[6] Then she hurriedly left the room.

Poirot unfolded the sheet of paper eagerly, and uttered an exclamation of satisfaction. He spread it out on the table.

"Come here, Hastings. Now tell me, what is that initial—J. or L.?"

It was a medium sized sheet of paper, rather dusty, as though it had lain by for some time. But it was the label that was attracting Poirot's attention. At the top, it bore the printed stamp of Messrs. Parkson's, the well-known theatrical costumiers, and it was addressed to "—(the debatable initial) Cavendish, Esq., Styles Court, Styles St. Mary, Essex."

"It might be T., or it might be L.," I said, after studying the thing for a minute or two. "It certainly isn't a J."

"Good," replied Poirot, folding up the paper again. "I, also,

---

[5] A very small amount. Derived from *iōta*, the smallest letter in the Greek alphabet.

[6] A large freestanding cabinet in which clothes are stored, especially useful in homes built without closets.

am of your way of thinking. It is an L., depend upon it!"

"Where did it come from?" I asked curiously. "Is it important?"

"Moderately so. It confirms a surmise of mine. Having deduced its existence, I set Miss Howard to search for it, and, as you see, she has been successful."

"What did she mean by 'On the top of the wardrobe'?"

"She meant," replied Poirot promptly, "that she found it on top of a wardrobe."

"A funny place for a piece of brown paper," I mused.

"Not at all. The top of a wardrobe is an excellent place for brown paper and cardboard boxes. I have kept them there myself. Neatly arranged, there is nothing to offend the eye."

"Poirot," I asked earnestly, "have you made up your mind about this crime?"

"Yes—that is to say, I believe I know how it was committed."

"Ah!"

"Unfortunately, I have no proof beyond my surmise, unless—" With sudden energy, he caught me by the arm, and whirled me down the hall, calling out in French in his excitement: "Mademoiselle Dorcas, Mademoiselle Dorcas, *un moment, s'il vous plaît*."[7]

Dorcas, quite flurried by the noise, came hurrying out of the pantry.

"My good Dorcas, I have an idea—a little idea—if it should prove justified, what magnificent chance! Tell me, on Monday, not Tuesday, Dorcas, but Monday, the day before the tragedy, did anything go wrong with Mrs. Inglethorp's bell?"

Dorcas looked very surprised.

"Yes, sir, now you mention it, it did; though I don't know how you came to hear of it. A mouse, or some such, must have nibbled the wire through. The man came and put it right on Tuesday morning."

---

[7] One moment, if you please.

With a long drawn exclamation of ecstasy, Poirot led the way back to the morning-room.

"See you, one should not ask for outside proof—no, reason should be enough. But the flesh is weak, it is consolation to find that one is on the right track. Ah, my friend, I am like a giant refreshed. I run! I leap!"

And, in very truth, run and leap he did, gambolling[8] wildly down the stretch of lawn outside the long window.

"What is your remarkable little friend doing?" asked a voice behind me, and I turned to find Mary Cavendish at my elbow. She smiled, and so did I. "What is it all about?"

"Really, I can't tell you. He asked Dorcas some question about a bell, and appeared so delighted with her answer that he is capering[9] about as you see!"

Mary laughed.

"How ridiculous! He's going out of the gate. Isn't he coming back to-day?"

"I don't know. I've given up trying to guess what he'll do next."

"Is he quite mad, Mr. Hastings?"

"I honestly don't know. Sometimes, I feel sure he is as mad as a hatter; and then, just as he is at his maddest, I find there is method in his madness."

"I see."

In spite of her laugh, Mary was looking thoughtful this morning. She seemed grave, almost sad.

It occurred to me that it would be a good opportunity to tackle her on the subject of Cynthia. I began rather tactfully, I thought, but I had not gone far before she stopped me authoritatively.

"You are an excellent advocate, I have no doubt, Mr. Hastings, but in this case your talents are quite thrown away. Cynthia will run no risk of encountering any unkindness from me."

---

[8] To run or jump about in a playful way.
[9] To skip or dance in a happy and energetic fashion.

I began to stammer feebly that I hoped she hadn't thought—But again she stopped me, and her words were so unexpected that they quite drove Cynthia, and her troubles, out of my mind.

"Mr. Hastings," she said, "do you think I and my husband are happy together?"

I was considerably taken aback, and murmured something about it's not being my business to think anything of the sort.

"Well," she said quietly, "whether it is your business or not, I will tell you that we are *not* happy."

I said nothing, for I saw that she had not finished.

She began slowly, walking up and down the room, her head a little bent, and that slim, supple figure of hers swaying gently as she walked. She stopped suddenly, and looked up at me.

"You don't know anything about me, do you?" she asked. "Where I come from, who I was before I married John—anything, in fact? Well, I will tell you. I will make a father confessor[10] of you. You are kind, I think—yes, I am sure you are kind."

Somehow, I was not quite as elated as I might have been. I remembered that Cynthia had begun her confidences in much the same way. Besides, a father confessor should be elderly, it is not at all the role for a young man.

"My father was English," said Mrs. Cavendish, "but my mother was a Russian."

"Ah," I said, "now I understand—"

"Understand what?"

"A hint of something foreign—different—that there has always been about you."

"My mother was very beautiful, I believe. I don't know, because I never saw her. She died when I was quite a little child. I believe there was some tragedy connected with her death—she took an overdose of some sleeping draught[11] by mistake. How-

---

[10] A Roman Catholic priest who hears confessions.

[11] A British variant of draft, for the act of drinking, in this case a dose of medicine.

ever that may be, my father was broken-hearted. Shortly afterwards, he went into the Consular Service.[12] Everywhere he went, I went with him. When I was twenty-three, I had been nearly all over the world. It was a splendid life—I loved it."

There was a smile on her face, and her head was thrown back. She seemed to be living in the memory of those old glad days.

"Then my father died. He left me very badly off. I had to go and live with some old aunts in Yorkshire."[13] She shuddered. "You will understand me when I say that it was a deadly life for a girl brought up as I had been. The narrowness, the deadly monotony of it, almost drove me mad." She paused a minute, and added in a different tone: "And then I met John Cavendish."

"Yes?"

"You can imagine that, from my aunts' point of view, it was a very good match for me. But I can honestly say it was not this fact which weighed with me. No, he was simply a way of escape from the insufferable monotony of my life."

I said nothing, and after a moment, she went on:

"Don't misunderstand me. I was quite honest with him. I told him, what was true, that I liked him very much, that I hoped to come to like him more, but that I was not in any way what the world calls 'in love' with him. He declared that that satisfied him, and so—we were married."

She waited a long time, a little frown had gathered on her forehead. She seemed to be looking back earnestly into those past days.

"I think—I am sure—he cared for me at first. But I suppose we were not well matched. Almost at once, we drifted apart. He—it is not a pleasing thing for my pride, but it is the truth—tired of me very soon." I must have made some murmur of dissent, for she went on quickly: "Oh, yes, he did! Not that it mat-

---

[12] The government department responsible for helping to protect British citizens and their trade interests in foreign countries.

[13] A largely rural county in the northeastern part of England. Its inhabitants have a reputation for being insular and tight with money and conversation.

ters now—now that we've come to the parting of the ways."

"What do you mean?"

She answered quietly:

"I mean that I am not going to remain at Styles."

"You and John are not going to live here?"

"John may live here, but I shall not."

"You are going to leave him?"

"Yes."

"But why?"

She paused a long time, and said at last:

"Perhaps—because I want to be—free!"

And, as she spoke, I had a sudden vision of broad spaces, virgin tracts of forests, untrodden lands—and a realization of what freedom would mean to such a nature as Mary Cavendish. I seemed to see her for a moment as she was, a proud wild creature, as untamed by civilization as some shy bird of the hills. A little cry broke from her lips:

"You don't know, you don't know, how this hateful place has been prison to me!"

"I understand," I said, "but—but don't do anything rash."[14]

"Oh, rash!" Her voice mocked at my prudence.[15]

Then suddenly I said a thing I could have bitten out my tongue for:

"You know that Dr. Bauerstein has been arrested?"

An instant coldness passed like a mask over her face, blotting out all expression.

"John was so kind as to break that to me this morning."

"Well, what do you think?" I asked feebly.

"Of what?"

"Of the arrest?"

"What should I think? Apparently he is a German spy; so the gardener had told John."

Her face and voice were absolutely cold and expressionless.

---

[14] Acting without consideration of the consequences.
[15] Exhibiting caution or self-discipline.

Did she care, or did she not?

She moved away a step or two, and fingered one of the flower vases.

"These are quite dead. I must do them again. Would you mind moving—thank you, Mr. Hastings." And she walked quietly past me out of the window, with a cool little nod of dismissal.

No, surely she could not care for Bauerstein. No woman could act her part with that icy unconcern.

Poirot did not make his appearance the following morning, and there was no sign of the Scotland Yard men.

But, at lunch-time, there arrived a new piece of evidence— or rather lack of evidence. We had vainly tried to trace the fourth letter, which Mrs. Inglethorp had written on the evening preceding her death. Our efforts having been in vain, we had abandoned the matter, hoping that it might turn up of itself one day. And this is just what did happen, in the shape of a communication, which arrived by the second post from a firm of French music publishers, acknowledging Mrs. Inglethorp's cheque,[16] and regretting they had been unable to trace a certain series of Russian folksongs. So the last hope of solving the mystery, by means of Mrs. Inglethorp's correspondence on the fatal evening, had to be abandoned.

Just before tea, I strolled down to tell Poirot of the new disappointment, but found, to my annoyance, that he was once more out.

"Gone to London again?"

"Oh, no, *monsieur*, he has but taken the train to Tadminster. 'To see a young lady's dispensary,' he said."

"Silly ass!" I ejaculated. "I told him Wednesday was the one day she wasn't there! Well, tell him to look us up to-morrow morning, will you?"

"Certainly, monsieur."

But, on the following day, no sign of Poirot. I was getting

---

[16] The British spelling of check, for the printed form used to make payments from a bank account.

angry. He was really treating us in the most cavalier[17] fashion.

After lunch, Lawrence drew me aside, and asked if I was going down to see him.

"No, I don't think I shall. He can come up here if he wants to see us."

"Oh!" Lawrence looked indeterminate.[18] Something unusually nervous and excited in his manner roused my curiosity.

"What is it?" I asked. "I could go if there's anything special."

"It's nothing much, but—well, if you are going, will you tell him—" he dropped his voice to a whisper—"I think I've found the extra coffee-cup!"

I had almost forgotten that enigmatical[19] message of Poirot's, but now my curiosity was aroused afresh.

Lawrence would say no more, so I decided that I would descend from my high horse,[20] and once more seek out Poirot at Leastways Cottage.

This time I was received with a smile. Monsieur Poirot was within. Would I mount? I mounted accordingly.

Poirot was sitting by the table, his head buried in his hands. He sprang up at my entrance.

"What is it?" I asked solicitously. "You are not ill, I trust?"

"No, no, not ill. But I decide an affair of great moment."

"Whether to catch the criminal or not?" I asked facetiously.[21]

But, to my great surprise, Poirot nodded gravely.

"'To speak or not to speak,' as your so great Shakespeare says, 'that is the question.'"[22]

---

[17] Acting thoughtlessly and without regard for other people's feelings.

[18] Vague, uncertain what to say or do next.

[19] Something difficult to explain, obscure.

[20] To act in a haughty or self-righteous manner. Inspired by the sight of kings and their habit of dominating their subjects by riding on great war horses.

[21] Joking.

[22] A reference to Hamlet's soliloquy, which begins:

I did not trouble to correct the quotation.

"You are not serious, Poirot?"

"I am of the most serious. For the most serious of all things hangs in the balance."

"And that is?"

"A woman's happiness, *mon ami*," he said gravely.

I did not quite know what to say.

"The moment has come," said Poirot thoughtfully, "and I do not know what to do. For, see you, it is a big stake for which I play. No one but I, Hercule Poirot, would attempt it!" And he tapped himself proudly on the breast.

After pausing a few minutes respectfully, so as not to spoil his effect, I gave him Lawrence's message.

"Aha!" he cried. "So he has found the extra coffee-cup. That is good. He has more intelligence than would appear, this long-faced[23] Monsieur Lawrence of yours!"

I did not myself think very highly of Lawrence's intelligence; but I forebore to contradict Poirot, and gently took him to task for forgetting my instructions as to which were Cynthia's days off.

"It is true. I have the head of a sieve.[24] However, the other young lady was most kind. She was sorry for my disappointment, and showed me everything in the kindest way."

"Oh, well, that's all right, then, and you must go to tea with Cynthia another day."

I told him about the letter.

"To be or not to be, that is the question
Whether 'tis nobler in the mind to suffer
The slings and arrows of outrageous fortune.
Or to take arms against a sea of troubles.
And by opposing end them."

[23] Unhappy or disappointed.

[24] A tool consisting of a frame with a net attached. Used to separate solids from a liquid.

"I am sorry for that," he said. "I always had hopes of that letter. But no, it was not to be. This affair must all be unravelled from within." He tapped his forehead. "These little grey cells.[25] It is 'up to them'—as you say over here." Then, suddenly, he asked: "Are you a judge of finger-marks, my friend?"

"No," I said, rather surprised, "I know that there are no two finger-marks alike, but that's as far as my science goes."

"Exactly."

He unlocked a little drawer, and took out some photographs which he laid on the table.

"I have numbered them, 1, 2, 3. Will you describe them to me?"

I studied the proofs attentively.

"All greatly magnified, I see. No. 1, I should say, are a man's finger-prints; thumb and first finger. No. 2 are a lady's; they are much smaller, and quite different in every way. No. 3"—I paused for some time—"there seem to be a lot of confused finger-marks, but here, very distinctly, are No. 1's."

"Overlapping the others?"

"Yes."

"You recognize them beyond fail?"

"Oh, yes; they are identical."

Poirot nodded, and gently taking the photographs from me locked them up again.

"I suppose," I said, "that as usual, you are not going to explain?"

"On the contrary. No. 1 were the finger-prints of Monsieur Lawrence. No. 2 were those of Mademoiselle Cynthia. They are not important. I merely obtained them for comparison. No. 3 is a little more complicated."

---

[25] This is the first mention of Poirot's catch-phrase. Although he confidently informs Hastings — and the reader — that "every fact that I know is in your possession. You can draw your own deductions from them," he proves time and again that only he can draw the correct conclusion and identify the murderer. It is this promise of a battle of wits, fairly played, between Christie and the reader that draws us back to her books.

"Yes?"

"It is, as you see, highly magnified. You may have noticed a sort of blur extending all across the picture. I will not describe to you the special apparatus, dusting powder,[26] etc., which I used. It is a well-known process to the police, and by means of it you can obtain a photograph of the finger-prints of any object in a very short space of time. Well, my friend, you have seen the finger-marks[27]—it remains to tell you the particular object on which they had been left."

"Go on—I am really excited."

"*Eh bien!* Photo No. 3 represents the highly magnified surface of a tiny bottle in the top poison cupboard of the dispensary in the Red Cross Hospital at Tadminster—which sounds like the house that Jack built!"[28]

"Good heavens!" I exclaimed. "But what were Lawrence Cavendish's finger-marks doing on it? He never went near the poison cupboard the day we were there!"

"Oh, yes, he did!"

---

[26] Fine powder that adheres to the residue left by the skin on a surface and can be preserved and photographed.

[27] It has been known since 1880 that the ridges on the fingertips are unique to each person, but it wasn't until 1901 that the United Kingdom Fingerprint Bureau was founded at Scotland Yard. Two years later, French police officer Alphonse Bertillon invented the method of lifting fingerprints off smooth surfaces.

[28] A reference to the popular nursery rhyme which adds another detail with each iteration — similar to *The Twelve Days of Christmas* — until the poem's final 10-line stanza:

> "This is the horse and the hound and the horn
> That belonged to the farmer sowing his corn
> That kept the cock that crowed in the morn
> That woke the priest all shaven and shorn
> That married the man all tattered and torn
> That kissed the maiden all forlorn
> That milked the cow with the crumpled horn
> That tossed the dog that worried the cat
> That killed the rat that ate the malt
> That lay in the house that Jack built."

"Impossible! We were all together the whole time."

Poirot shook his head.

"No, my friend, there was a moment when you were not all together. There was a moment when you could not have been all together, or it would not have been necessary to call to Monsieur Lawrence to come and join you on the balcony."

"I'd forgotten that," I admitted. "But it was only for a moment."

"Long enough."

"Long enough for what?"

Poirot's smile became rather enigmatical.

"Long enough for a gentleman who had once studied medicine to gratify a very natural interest and curiosity."

Our eyes met. Poirot's were pleasantly vague. He got up and hummed a little tune. I watched him suspiciously.

"Poirot," I said, "what was in this particular little bottle?"

Poirot looked out of the window.

"Hydro-chloride of strychnine,"[29] he said, over his shoulder, continuing to hum.

"Good heavens!" I said it quite quietly. I was not surprised. I had expected that answer.

"They use the pure hydro-chloride of strychnine very little—only occasionally for pills. It is the official solution, Liq. Strychnine Hydro-clor. that is used in most medicines. That is why the finger-marks have remained undisturbed since then."

"How did you manage to take this photograph?"

"I dropped my hat from the balcony," explained Poirot simply. "Visitors were not permitted below at that hour, so, in spite of my many apologies, Mademoiselle Cynthia's colleague had to go down and fetch it for me."

"Then you knew what you were going to find?"

"No, not at all. I merely realized that it was possible, from

---

[29] A compound resulting from the reaction of hydrochloric acid with an organic base. Performed on strychnine, the process makes it water soluble and able to be absorbed into the body.

your story, for Monsieur Lawrence to go to the poison cupboard. The possibility had to be confirmed, or eliminated."

"Poirot," I said, "your gaiety[30] does not deceive me. This is a very important discovery."

"I do not know," said Poirot. "But one thing does strike me. No doubt it has struck you too."

"What is that?"

"Why, that there is altogether too much strychnine about this case. This is the third time we run up against it. There was strychnine in Mrs. Inglethorp's tonic. There is the strychnine sold across the counter at Styles St. Mary by Mace. Now we have more strychnine, handled by one of the household. It is confusing; and, as you know, I do not like confusion."

Before I could reply, one of the other Belgians opened the door and stuck his head in.

"There is a lady below, asking for Mr. Hastings."

"A lady?"

I jumped up. Poirot followed me down the narrow stairs. Mary Cavendish was standing in the doorway.

"I have been visiting an old woman in the village," she explained, "and as Lawrence told me you were with Monsieur Poirot I thought I would call for you."

"Alas, madame," said Poirot, "I thought you had come to honour me with a visit!"

"I will some day, if you ask me," she promised him, smiling.

"That is well. If you should need a father confessor, madame" —she started ever so slightly—"remember, Papa Poirot is always at your service."

She stared at him for a few minutes, as though seeking to read some deeper meaning into his words. Then she turned abruptly away.

"Come, will you not walk back with us too, Monsieur Poirot?"

"Enchanted, madame."

All the way to Styles, Mary talked fast and feverishly. It

[30] High spirits.

struck me that in some way she was nervous of Poirot's eyes.

The weather had broken, and the sharp wind was almost autumnal in its shrewishness.[31] Mary shivered a little, and buttoned her black sports coat closer. The wind through the trees made a mournful noise, like some great giant sighing.

We walked up to the great door of Styles, and at once the knowledge came to us that something was wrong.

Dorcas came running out to meet us. She was crying and wringing her hands. I was aware of other servants huddled together in the background, all eyes and ears.

"Oh, m'am! Oh, m'am! I don't know how to tell you—"

"What is it, Dorcas?" I asked impatiently. "Tell us at once."

"It's those wicked detectives. They've arrested him—they've arrested Mr. Cavendish!"

"Arrested Lawrence?" I gasped.

I saw a strange look come into Dorcas's eyes.

"No, sir. Not Mr. Lawrence—Mr. John."

Behind me, with a wild cry, Mary Cavendish fell heavily against me, and as I turned to catch her I met the quiet triumph in Poirot's eyes.

---

[31] *Autumnal:* Typical of the fall season. *Shrewishness:* Ill-nature.

CHAPTER XI

THE CASE
FOR THE PROSECUTION

T HE TRIAL OF JOHN CAVENDISH for the murder of his
stepmother took place two months later.

Of the intervening weeks I will say little, but my admiration
and sympathy went out unfeignedly to Mary Cavendish. She
ranged[1] herself passionately on her husband's side, scorning the
mere idea of his guilt, and fought for him tooth and nail.

I expressed my admiration to Poirot, and he nodded
thoughtfully.

"Yes, she is of those women who show at their best in ad-
versity. It brings out all that is sweetest and truest in them. Her
pride and her jealousy have—"

"Jealousy?" I queried.

"Yes. Have you not realized that she is an unusually jealous
woman? As I was saying, her pride and jealousy have been laid
aside. She thinks of nothing but her husband, and the terrible
fate that is hanging over him."

He spoke very feelingly, and I looked at him earnestly, remembering that last afternoon, when he had been deliberating
whether or not to speak. With his tenderness for "a woman's
happiness," I felt glad that the decision had been taken out of
his hands.

"Even now," I said, "I can hardly believe it. You see, up to
the very last minute, I thought it was Lawrence!"

---

[1] Place herself in opposition to a person or group.

Poirot grinned.

"I know you did."

"But John! My old friend John!"

"Every murderer is probably somebody's old friend," observed Poirot philosophically. "You cannot mix up sentiment and reason."

"I must say I think you might have given me a hint."

"Perhaps, *mon ami*, I did not do so, just because he *was* your old friend."

I was rather disconcerted[2] by this, remembering how I had busily passed on to John what I believed to be Poirot's views concerning Bauerstein. He, by the way, had been acquitted of the charge brought against him. Nevertheless, although he had been too clever for them this time, and the charge of espionage could not be brought home to him, his wings were pretty well clipped[3] for the future.

I asked Poirot whether he thought John would be condemned. To my intense surprise, he replied that, on the contrary, he was extremely likely to be acquitted.

"But, Poirot—" I protested.

"Oh, my friend, have I not said to you all along that I have no proofs? It is one thing to know that a man is guilty, it is quite another matter to prove him so. And, in this case, there is terribly little evidence. That is the whole trouble. I, Hercule Poirot, know, but I lack the last link in my chain. And unless I can find that missing link—" He shook his head gravely.

"When did you first suspect John Cavendish?" I asked, after a minute or two.

"Did you not suspect him at all?"

"No, indeed."

"Not after that fragment of conversation you overheard between Mrs. Cavendish and her mother-in-law, and her subse-

---

[2] Thrown into confusion.

[3] Restrained. From the practice of clipping the wings of birds, such as ducks and chickens, to keep them from flying away.

quent lack of frankness at the inquest?"

"No."

"Did you not put two and two together, and reflect that if it was not Alfred Inglethorp who was quarrelling with his wife—and you remember, he strenuously denied it at the inquest—it must be either Lawrence or John. Now, if it was Lawrence, Mary Cavendish's conduct was just as inexplicable. But if, on the other hand, it was John, the whole thing was explained quite naturally."

"So," I cried, a light breaking in upon me, "it was John who quarrelled with his mother that afternoon?"

"Exactly."

"And you have known this all along?"

"Certainly. Mrs. Cavendish's behaviour could only be explained that way."

"And yet you say he may be acquitted?"

Poirot shrugged his shoulders.

"Certainly I do. At the police court proceedings, we shall hear the case for the prosecution, but in all probability his solicitors will advise him to reserve his defence.[4] That will be sprung upon us at the trial. And—ah, by the way, I have a word of caution to give you, my friend. I must not appear in the case."

"What?"

"No. Officially, I have nothing to do with it. Until I have found that last link in my chain, I must remain behind the scenes. Mrs. Cavendish must think I am working for her husband, not against him."

"I say, that's playing it a bit low down," I protested.

"Not at all. We have to deal with a most clever and unscrupulous man, and we must use any means in our power—otherwise he will slip through our fingers. That is why I have been careful to remain in the background. All the discoveries have been made by Japp, and Japp will take all the credit. If I

---

[4] Declines to contest the charge until his trial. This keeps the prosecution from learning how the defendant will answer the accusation.

am called upon to give evidence at all"—he smiled broadly—"it will probably be as a witness for the defence."

I could hardly believe my ears.

"It is quite *en regle*,"[5] continued Poirot. "Strangely enough, I can give evidence that will demolish one contention of the prosecution."

"Which one?"

"The one that relates to the destruction of the will. John Cavendish did not destroy that will."

Poirot was a true prophet. I will not go into the details of the police court proceedings, as it involves many tiresome repetitions. I will merely state baldly that John Cavendish reserved his defence, and was duly committed for trial.

September found us all in London. Mary took a house in Kensington,[6] Poirot being included in the family party.

I myself had been given a job at the War Office,[7] so was able to see them continually.

As the weeks went by, the state of Poirot's nerves grew worse and worse. That "last link" he talked about was still lacking. Privately, I hoped it might remain so, for what happiness could there be for Mary, if John were not acquitted?

On September 15th John Cavendish appeared in the dock at the Old Bailey,[8] charged with "The Wilful Murder of Emily Agnes Inglethorp," and pleaded "Not Guilty."

Sir Ernest Heavywether, the famous K. C.,[9] had been engaged to defend him.

Mr. Philips, K. C., opened the case for the Crown.

---

[5] The rule

[6] A wealthy district in west-central London.

[7] The government agency that oversees administration of the British Army.

[8] The Central Criminal Court building in London, named for the street on which it is located.

[9] King's Counsel, a status granted by the king — so during Elizabeth II's reign they're known as Q.C.s — in which lawyers are allowed to wear silk gowns indicating they're a senior member of the profession. This award is known as "taking silk."

The murder, he said, was a most premeditated[10] and cold-blooded one. It was neither more nor less than the deliberate poisoning of a fond and trusting woman by the stepson to whom she had been more than a mother. Ever since his boyhood, she had supported him. He and his wife had lived at Styles Court in every luxury, surrounded by her care and attention. She had been their kind and generous benefactress.[11]

He proposed to call witnesses to show how the prisoner, a profligate and spendthrift,[12] had been at the end of his financial tether, and had also been carrying on an intrigue[13] with a certain Mrs. Raikes, a neighbouring farmer's wife. This having come to his stepmother's ears, she taxed him with it on the afternoon before her death, and a quarrel ensued, part of which was overheard. On the previous day, the prisoner had purchased strychnine at the village chemist's shop, wearing a disguise by means of which he hoped to throw the onus[14] of the crime upon another man—to wit, Mrs. Inglethorp's husband, of whom he had been bitterly jealous. Luckily for Mr. Inglethorp, he had been able to produce an unimpeachable[15] alibi.

On the afternoon of July 17th, continued Counsel, immediately after the quarrel with her son, Mrs. Inglethorp made a new will. This will was found destroyed in the grate of her bedroom the following morning, but evidence had come to light which showed that it had been drawn up in favour of her husband. Deceased had already made a will in his favour before her marriage, but—and Mr. Philips wagged an expressive forefinger—the prisoner was not aware of that. What had induced the deceased to make a fresh will, with the old one still extant,[16] he

---

[10] A legal term indicating the crime had been planned.

[11] A female benefactor who gives money to help a person or a cause.

[12] *Profligate:* Extravagant in behavior, particularly with money. *Spendthrift:* A person who spends a lot of money.

[13] A secret love affair.

[14] Responsibility or duty. From the Latin for "burden."

[15] Something that is completely trustworthy and should not be doubted.

[16] Still existing.

could not say. She was an old lady, and might possibly have forgotten the former one; or—this seemed to him more likely—she may have had an idea that it was revoked by her marriage, as there had been some conversation on the subject. Ladies were not always very well versed in legal knowledge. She had, about a year before, executed a will in favour of the prisoner. He would call evidence to show that it was the prisoner who ultimately handed his stepmother her coffee on the fatal night. Later in the evening, he had sought admission to her room, on which occasion, no doubt, he found an opportunity of destroying the will which, as far as he knew, would render the one in his favour valid.

The prisoner had been arrested in consequence of the discovery, in his room, by Detective Inspector Japp—a most brilliant officer—of the identical phial[17] of strychnine which had been sold at the village chemist's to the supposed Mr. Inglethorp on the day before the murder. It would be for the jury to decide whether or not these damning facts constituted an overwhelming proof of the prisoner's guilt.

And, subtly implying that a jury which did not so decide, was quite unthinkable, Mr. Philips sat down and wiped his forehead.

The first witnesses for the prosecution were mostly those who had been called at the inquest, the medical evidence being again taken first.

Sir Ernest Heavywether, who was famous all over England for the unscrupulous manner[18] in which he bullied witnesses, only asked two questions.

"I take it, Dr. Bauerstein, that strychnine, as a drug, acts quickly?"

"Yes."

"And that you are unable to account for the delay in this case?"

---

[17] A small cylindrical glass bottle used for holding medicines.
[18] The behavior of a person without principles, who will do anything to achieve his goals.

"Yes."

"Thank you."

Mr. Mace identified the phial handed him by Counsel as that sold by him to "Mr. Inglethorp." Pressed, he admitted that he only knew Mr. Inglethorp by sight. He had never spoken to him. The witness was not cross-examined.

Alfred Inglethorp was called, and denied having purchased the poison. He also denied having quarrelled with his wife. Various witnesses testified to the accuracy of these statements.

The gardeners' evidence, as to the witnessing of the will was taken, and then Dorcas was called.

Dorcas, faithful to her "young gentlemen," denied strenuously that it could have been John's voice she heard, and resolutely declared, in the teeth of everything, that it was Mr. Inglethorp who had been in the boudoir with her mistress. A rather wistful smile passed across the face of the prisoner in the dock. He knew only too well how useless her gallant defiance was, since it was not the object of the defence to deny this point. Mrs. Cavendish, of course, could not be called upon to give evidence against her husband.

After various questions on other matters, Mr. Philips asked:

"In the month of June last, do you remember a parcel arriving for Mr. Lawrence Cavendish from Parkson's?"

Dorcas shook her head.

"I don't remember, sir. It may have done, but Mr. Lawrence was away from home part of June."

"In the event of a parcel arriving for him whilst he was away, what would be done with it?"

"It would either be put in his room or sent on after him."

"By you?"

"No, sir, I should leave it on the hall table. It would be Miss Howard who would attend to anything like that."

Evelyn Howard was called and, after being examined on other points, was questioned as to the parcel.

"Don't remember. Lots of parcels come. Can't remember one special one."

"You do not know if it was sent after Mr. Lawrence Cavendish to Wales,[19] or whether it was put in his room?"

"Don't think it was sent after him. Should have remembered it if it was."

"Supposing a parcel arrived addressed to Mr. Lawrence Cavendish, and afterwards it disappeared, should you remark its absence?"

"No, don't think so. I should think some one had taken charge of it."

"I believe, Miss Howard, that it was you who found this sheet of brown paper?" He held up the same dusty piece which Poirot and I had examined in the morning-room at Styles.

"Yes, I did."

"How did you come to look for it?"

"The Belgian detective who was employed on the case asked me to search for it."

"Where did you eventually discover it?"

"On the top of—of—a wardrobe."

"On top of the prisoner's wardrobe?"

"I—I believe so."

"Did you not find it yourself?"

"Yes."

"Then you must know where you found it?"

"Yes, it was on the prisoner's wardrobe."

"That is better."

An assistant from Parkson's, Theatrical Costumiers, testified that on June 29th, they had supplied a black beard to Mr. L. Cavendish, as requested. It was ordered by letter, and a postal order[20] was enclosed. No, they had not kept the letter. All transactions were entered in their books. They had sent the beard, as directed, to "L. Cavendish, Esq.,[21] Styles Court."

[19] A country on the west side of Britain that is part of the United Kingdom.
[20] British word for a money order, a check issued by a post office, bank or telegraph office for payment of a specified sum of money.
[21] The abbreviation for esquire. Once a title awarded for a number of purposes — for example, to the eldest sons of knights, as a title for certain of-

Sir Ernest Heavywether rose ponderously.[22]

"Where was the letter written from?"

"From Styles Court."

"The same address to which you sent the parcel?"

"Yes."

"And the letter came from there?"

"Yes."

Like a beast of prey, Heavywether fell upon him:

"How do you know?"

"I—I don't understand."

"How do you know that letter came from Styles? Did you notice the postmark?"

"No—but—"

"Ah, you did *not* notice the postmark! And yet you affirm so confidently that it came from Styles. It might, in fact, have been any postmark?"

"Y—es."

"In fact, the letter, though written on stamped notepaper, might have been posted from anywhere? From Wales, for instance?"

The witness admitted that such might be the case, and Sir Ernest signified that he was satisfied.

Elizabeth Wells, second housemaid at Styles, stated that after she had gone to bed she remembered that she had bolted the front door, instead of leaving it on the latch as Mr. Inglethorp had requested. She had accordingly gone downstairs again to rectify[23] her error. Hearing a slight noise in the West wing, she had peeped along the passage, and had seen Mr. John Cavendish knocking at Mrs. Inglethorp's door.

Sir Ernest Heavywether made short work of her, and under

---

fices, or bestowed by the monarch — it has devolved into a courtesy title. In the U.S., however, it is used by men and women licensed to practice law.

[22] Awkward due to his heavy weight.

[23] To correct, especially by removing errors.

his unmerciful bullying she contradicted herself hopelessly, and
Sir Ernest sat down again with a satisfied smile on his face.

With the evidence of Annie, as to the candle grease on the
floor, and as to seeing the prisoner take the coffee into the boudoir, the proceedings were adjourned until the following day.

As we went home, Mary Cavendish spoke bitterly against
the prosecuting counsel.

"That hateful man! What a net he has drawn around my
poor John! How he twisted every little fact until he made it
seem what it wasn't!"

"Well," I said consolingly, "it will be the other way about
to-morrow."

"Yes," she said meditatively;[24] then suddenly dropped her
voice. "Mr. Hastings, you do not think—surely it could not
have been Lawrence—Oh, no, that could not be!"

But I myself was puzzled, and as soon as I was alone with
Poirot I asked him what he thought Sir Ernest was driving at.

"Ah!" said Poirot appreciatively. "He is a clever man, that
Sir Ernest."

"Do you think he believes Lawrence guilty?"

"I do not think he believes or cares anything! No, what he
is trying for is to create such confusion in the minds of the jury
that they are divided in their opinion as to which brother did it.
He is endeavouring to make out that there is quite as much evidence against Lawrence as against John—and I am not at all
sure that he will not succeed."

Detective-inspector Japp was the first witness called when
the trial was reopened, and gave his evidence succinctly[25] and
briefly. After relating the earlier events, he proceeded:

"Acting on information received, Superintendent
Summerhaye and myself searched the prisoner's room, during
his temporary absence from the house. In his chest of drawers,
hidden beneath some underclothing, we found: first, a pair of

---

[24] The act of giving serious thought to an issue.
[25] Briefly and clearly expressed.

gold-rimmed pince-nez similar to those worn by Mr. Inglethorp"—these were exhibited—"secondly, this phial."

The phial was that already recognized by the chemist's assistant, a tiny bottle of blue glass, containing a few grains of a white crystalline powder, and labelled: "Strychnine Hydrochloride. POISON."

A fresh piece of evidence discovered by the detectives since the police court proceedings was a long, almost new piece of blotting-paper. It had been found in Mrs. Inglethorp's cheque book, and on being reversed at a mirror, showed clearly the words: ". . . erything of which I die possessed I leave to my beloved husband Alfred Ing..." This placed beyond question the fact that the destroyed will had been in favour of the deceased lady's husband. Japp then produced the charred fragment of paper recovered from the grate, and this, with the discovery of the beard in the attic, completed his evidence.

But Sir Ernest's cross-examination was yet to come.

"What day was it when you searched the prisoner's room?"

"Tuesday, the 24th of July."

"Exactly a week after the tragedy?"

"Yes."

"You found these two objects, you say, in the chest of drawers. Was the drawer unlocked?"

"Yes."

"Does it not strike you as unlikely that a man who had committed a crime should keep the evidence of it in an unlocked drawer for anyone to find?"

"He might have stowed them there in a hurry."

"But you have just said it was a whole week since the crime. He would have had ample time to remove them and destroy them."

"Perhaps."

"There is no perhaps about it. Would he, or would he not have had plenty of time to remove and destroy them?"

"Yes."

"Was the pile of underclothes under which the things were hidden heavy or light?"

"Heavyish."

"In other words, it was winter underclothing. Obviously, the prisoner would not be likely to go to that drawer?"

"Perhaps not."

"Kindly answer my question. Would the prisoner, in the hottest week of a hot summer, be likely to go to a drawer containing winter underclothing. Yes, or no?"

"No."

"In that case, is it not possible that the articles in question might have been put there by a third person, and that the prisoner was quite unaware of their presence?"

"I should not think it likely."

"But it is possible?"

"Yes."

"That is all."[26]

More evidence followed. Evidence as to the financial difficulties in which the prisoner had found himself at the end of July. Evidence as to his intrigue with Mrs. Raikes—poor Mary, that must have been bitter hearing for a woman of her pride. Evelyn Howard had been right in her facts, though her animosity[27] against Alfred Inglethorp had caused her to jump to the conclusion that he was the person concerned.

Lawrence Cavendish was then put into the box. In a low voice, in answer to Mr. Philips' questions, he denied having ordered anything from Parkson's in June. In fact, on June 29th, he had been staying away, in Wales.

Instantly, Sir Ernest's chin was shooting pugnaciously[28] forward.

"You deny having ordered a black beard from Parkson's on

[26] Christie's inexperience with the legal system shows here. Sir Ernest's examination is full of leading questions and attempts to intuit what the prisoner was thinking. Even a half-competent prosecutor would have objected to this line of questioning.

[27] Strong dislike.

[28] Quarrelsome or combative, leading one to wonder how a chin could be itching for a fight.

June 29th?"

"I do."

"Ah! In the event of anything happening to your brother, who will inherit Styles Court?"

The brutality of the question called a flush to Lawrence's pale face. The judge gave vent to a faint murmur of disapprobation,[29] and the prisoner in the dock leant forward angrily.

Heavywether cared nothing for his client's anger.

"Answer my question, if you please."

"I suppose," said Lawrence quietly, "that I should."

"What do you mean by you 'suppose'? Your brother has no children. You *would* inherit it, wouldn't you?"

"Yes."

"Ah, that's better," said Heavywether, with ferocious geniality.[30] "And you'd inherit a good slice of money too, wouldn't you?"

"Really, Sir Ernest," protested the judge, "these questions are not relevant."

Sir Ernest bowed, and having shot his arrow proceeded.

"On Tuesday, the 17th July, you went, I believe, with another guest, to visit the dispensary at the Red Cross Hospital in Tadminster?"

"Yes."

"Did you—while you happened to be alone for a few seconds—unlock the poison cupboard, and examine some of the bottles?"

"I—I—may have done so."

"I put it to you that you did do so?"

"Yes."

Sir Ernest fairly shot the next question at him.

"Did you examine one bottle in particular?"

"No, I do not think so."

"Be careful, Mr. Cavendish. I am referring to a little bottle

---

[29] Strong disapproval, particularly on moral grounds.
[30] Exhibiting friendliness or sympathy.

of hydro-chloride of strychnine."

Lawrence was turning a sickly greenish colour.

"N—o—I am sure I didn't."

"Then how do you account for the fact that you left the unmistakable impress of your finger-prints on it?"

The bullying manner was highly efficacious[31] with a nervous disposition.

"I—I suppose I must have taken up the bottle."

"I suppose so too! Did you abstract[32] any of the contents of the bottle?"

"Certainly not."

"Then why did you take it up?"

"I once studied to be a doctor. Such things naturally interest me."

"Ah! So poisons 'naturally interest' you, do they? Still, you waited to be alone before gratifying that 'interest' of yours?"

"That was pure chance. If the others had been there, I should have done just the same."

"Still, as it happens, the others were not there?"

"No, but—"

"In fact, during the whole afternoon, you were only alone for a couple of minutes, and it happened—I say, it happened—to be during those two minutes that you displayed your 'natural interest' in Hydro-chloride of Strychnine?"

Lawrence stammered pitiably.

"I—I—"

With a satisfied and expressive countenance, Sir Ernest observed:

"I have nothing more to ask you, Mr. Cavendish."

This bit of cross-examination had caused great excitement in court. The heads of the many fashionably attired women present were busily laid together, and their whispers became so loud that the judge angrily threatened to have the court cleared

---

[31] Effective.
[32] Remove.

if there was not immediate silence.

There was little more evidence. The hand-writing experts were called upon for their opinion of the signature of "Alfred Inglethorp" in the chemist's poison register. They all declared unanimously that it was certainly not his hand-writing, and gave it as their view that it might be that of the prisoner disguised. Cross-examined, they admitted that it might be the prisoner's hand-writing cleverly counterfeited.

Sir Ernest Heavywether's speech in opening the case for the defence was not a long one, but it was backed by the full force of his emphatic manner. Never, he said, in the course of his long experience, had he known a charge of murder rest on slighter evidence. Not only was it entirely circumstantial,[33] but the greater part of it was practically unproved. Let them take the testimony they had heard and sift it impartially. The strychnine had been found in a drawer in the prisoner's room. That drawer was an unlocked one, as he had pointed out, and he submitted that there was no evidence to prove that it was the prisoner who had concealed the poison there. It was, in fact, a wicked and malicious attempt on the part of some third person to fix the crime on the prisoner. The prosecution had been unable to produce a shred of evidence in support of their contention that it was the prisoner who ordered the black beard from Parkson's. The quarrel which had taken place between prisoner and his stepmother was freely admitted, but both it and his financial embarrassments had been grossly exaggerated.

His learned friend—Sir Ernest nodded carelessly at Mr. Philips—had stated that if the prisoner were an innocent man, he would have come forward at the inquest to explain that it was he, and not Mr. Inglethorp, who had been the participator in the quarrel. He thought the facts had been misrepresented. What had actually occurred was this. The prisoner, returning to the house on Tuesday evening, had been authoritatively told that there had been a violent quarrel between Mr. and Mrs.

---

[33] Evidence that indirectly points to someone's guilt.

Inglethorp. No suspicion had entered the prisoner's head that anyone could possibly have mistaken his voice for that of Mr. Inglethorp. He naturally concluded that his stepmother had had two quarrels.

The prosecution averred that on Monday, July 16th, the prisoner had entered the chemist's shop in the village, disguised as Mr. Inglethorp. The prisoner, on the contrary, was at that time at a lonely spot called Marston's Spinney, where he had been summoned by an anonymous note, couched[34] in blackmailing terms, and threatening to reveal certain matters to his wife unless he complied with its demands. The prisoner had, accordingly, gone to the appointed spot, and after waiting there vainly for half an hour had returned home. Unfortunately, he had met with no one on the way there or back who could vouch for the truth of his story, but luckily he had kept the note, and it would be produced as evidence.

As for the statement relating to the destruction of the will, the prisoner had formerly practiced at the Bar, and was perfectly well aware that the will made in his favour a year before was automatically revoked by his stepmother's remarriage. He would call evidence to show who did destroy the will, and it was possible that that might open up quite a new view of the case.

Finally, he would point out to the jury that there was evidence against other people besides John Cavendish. He would direct their attention to the fact that the evidence against Mr. Lawrence Cavendish was quite as strong, if not stronger than that against his brother.

He would now call the prisoner.

John acquitted himself well in the witness-box. Under Sir Ernest's skilful handling, he told his tale credibly and well. The anonymous note received by him was produced, and handed to the jury to examine. The readiness with which he admitted his financial difficulties, and the disagreement with his stepmother, lent value to his denials.

---

[34] Expressed in a specified style.

At the close of his examination, he paused, and said:

"I should like to make one thing clear. I utterly reject and disapprove of Sir Ernest Heavywether's insinuations[35] against my brother. My brother, I am convinced, had no more to do with the crime than I have."

Sir Ernest merely smiled, and noted with a sharp eye that John's protest had produced a very favourable impression on the jury.

Then the cross-examination began.

"I understand you to say that it never entered your head that the witnesses at the inquest could possibly have mistaken your voice for that of Mr. Inglethorp. Is not that very surprising?"

"No, I don't think so. I was told there had been a quarrel between my mother and Mr. Inglethorp, and it never occurred to me that such was not really the case."

"Not when the servant Dorcas repeated certain fragments of the conversation—fragments which you must have recognized?"

"I did not recognize them."

"Your memory must be unusually short!"

"No, but we were both angry, and, I think, said more than we meant. I paid very little attention to my mother's actual words."

Mr. Philips' incredulous sniff was a triumph of forensic[36] skill. He passed on to the subject of the note.

"You have produced this note very opportunely. Tell me, is there nothing familiar about the hand-writing of it?"

"Not that I know of."

"Do you not think that it bears a marked resemblance to your own hand-writing—carelessly disguised?"

"No, I do not think so."

"I put it to you that it is your own hand-writing!"

---

[35] An unpleasant hint or suggestion of something illegal.

[36] The application of scientific methods to investigate crimes.

"No."

"I put it to you that, anxious to prove an alibi, you conceived the idea of a fictitious and rather incredible appointment, and wrote this note yourself in order to bear out your statement!"

"No."

"Is it not a fact that, at the time you claim to have been waiting about at a solitary and unfrequented spot, you were really in the chemist's shop in Styles St. Mary, where you purchased strychnine in the name of Alfred Inglethorp?"

"No, that is a lie."

"I put it to you that, wearing a suit of Mr. Inglethorp's clothes, with a black beard trimmed to resemble his, you were there—and signed the register in his name!"

"That is absolutely untrue."

"Then I will leave the remarkable similarity of hand-writing between the note, the register, and your own, to the consideration of the jury," said Mr. Philips, and sat down with the air of a man who has done his duty, but who was nevertheless horrified by such deliberate perjury.[37]

After this, as it was growing late, the case was adjourned till Monday.

Poirot, I noticed, was looking profoundly discouraged. He had that little frown between the eyes that I knew so well.

"What is it, Poirot?" I inquired.

"Ah, *mon ami*, things are going badly, badly."

In spite of myself, my heart gave a leap of relief. Evidently there was a likelihood of John Cavendish being acquitted.

When we reached the house, my little friend waved aside Mary's offer of tea.

"No, I thank you, madame. I will mount[38] to my room."

I followed him. Still frowning, he went across to the desk

---

[37] The act of lying while under oath. Perjury is a crime which could result in a jail sentence.

[38] To climb up. Usually used when applied to riding horses, it can also refer to climbing stairs.

and took out a small pack of patience cards.[39] Then he drew up a chair to the table, and, to my utter amazement, began solemnly to build card houses!

My jaw dropped involuntarily, and he said at once:

"No, *mon ami*, I am not in my second childhood! I steady my nerves, that is all. This employment requires precision of the fingers. With precision of the fingers goes precision of the brain. And never have I needed that more than now!"

"What is the trouble?" I asked.

With a great thump on the table, Poirot demolished his carefully built up edifice.[40]

"It is this, *mon ami*! That I can build card houses seven stories high, but I cannot"—thump—"find"—thump—"that last link of which I spoke to you."

I could not quite tell what to say, so I held my peace, and he began slowly building up the cards again, speaking in jerks as he did so.

"It is done—so! By placing—one card—on another—with mathematical—precision!"

I watched the card house rising under his hands, story by story. He never hesitated or faltered. It was really almost like a conjuring trick.

"What a steady hand you've got," I remarked. "I believe I've only seen your hand shake once."

"On an occasion when I was enraged, without doubt," observed Poirot, with great placidity.

"Yes indeed! You were in a towering rage. Do you remember? It was when you discovered that the lock of the despatch-case in Mrs. Inglethorp's bedroom had been forced. You stood by the mantel-piece, twiddling the things on it in your usual fashion, and your hand shook like a leaf! I must say—"

---

[39] A genre of card games more commonly known as solitaire. While decks of cards were sold as "patience cards," they're no different from the standard 52-card deck.

[40] A complex system of beliefs.

But I stopped suddenly. For Poirot, uttering a hoarse and inarticulate cry, again annihilated his masterpiece of cards, and putting his hands over his eyes swayed backwards and forwards, apparently suffering the keenest agony.

"Good heavens, Poirot!" I cried. "What is the matter? Are you taken ill?"

"No, no," he gasped. "It is—it is—that I have an idea!"

"Oh!" I exclaimed, much relieved. "One of your 'little ideas'?"

"Ah, *ma foi*,[41] no!" replied Poirot frankly. "This time it is an idea gigantic! Stupendous! And you—*you*, my friend, have given it to me!"

Suddenly clasping me in his arms, he kissed me warmly on both cheeks, and before I had recovered from my surprise ran headlong from the room.

Mary Cavendish entered at that moment.

"What is the matter with Monsieur Poirot? He rushed past me crying out: 'A garage! For the love of Heaven, direct me to a garage, madame!' And, before I could answer, he had dashed out into the street."

I hurried to the window. True enough, there he was, tearing down the street, hatless, and gesticulating as he went. I turned to Mary with a gesture of despair.

"He'll be stopped by a policeman in another minute. There he goes, round the corner!"

Our eyes met, and we stared helplessly at one another.

"What can be the matter?"

I shook my head.

"I don't know. He was building card houses, when suddenly he said he had an idea, and rushed off as you saw."

"Well," said Mary, "I expect he will be back before dinner."

But night fell, and Poirot had not returned.

---

[41] My faith!

CHAPTER XII

THE LAST LINK

POIROT'S ABRUPT DEPARTURE HAD intrigued us all greatly. Sunday morning wore away, and still he did not reappear. But about three o'clock a ferocious and prolonged hooting outside drove us to the window, to see Poirot alighting from a car, accompanied by Japp and Summerhaye. The little man was transformed. He radiated an absurd complacency.[1] He bowed with exaggerated respect to Mary Cavendish.

"Madame, I have your permission to hold a little *reunion* in the *salon*?[2] It is necessary for every one to attend."

Mary smiled sadly.

"You know, Monsieur Poirot, that you have *carte blanche*[3] in every way."

"You are too amiable, madame."

Still beaming, Poirot marshalled us all into the drawing-room, bringing forward chairs as he did so.

"Miss Howard—here. Mademoiselle Cynthia. Monsieur Lawrence. The good Dorcas. And Annie. *Bien!* We must delay our proceedings a few minutes until Mr. Inglethorp arrives. I have sent him a note."

Miss Howard rose immediately from her seat.

"If that man comes into the house, I leave it!"

"No, no!" Poirot went up to her and pleaded in a low voice.

---

[1] A smug and uncritical satisfaction with one's abilities or achievements.

[2] An elegant living room. Note that both it and reunion are italicized to indicate they were foreign words at the time.

[3] A blank check. Figuratively, absolute power to use at his discretion.

Finally Miss Howard consented to return to her chair. A few minutes later Alfred Inglethorp entered the room.

The company once assembled, Poirot rose from his seat with the air of a popular lecturer, and bowed politely to his audience.

"*Messieurs, mesdames*, as you all know, I was called in by Monsieur John Cavendish to investigate this case. I at once examined the bedroom of the deceased which, by the advice of the doctors, had been kept locked, and was consequently exactly as it had been when the tragedy occurred. I found: first, a fragment of green material; second, a stain on the carpet near the window, still damp; thirdly, an empty box of bromide powders.

"To take the fragment of green material first, I found it caught in the bolt of the communicating door between that room and the adjoining one occupied by Mademoiselle Cynthia. I handed the fragment over to the police who did not consider it of much importance. Nor did they recognize it for what it was—a piece torn from a green land armlet."[4]

There was a little stir of excitement.

"Now there was only one person at Styles who worked on the land—Mrs. Cavendish. Therefore it must have been Mrs. Cavendish who entered the deceased's room through the door communicating with Mademoiselle Cynthia's room."

"But that door was bolted on the inside!" I cried.

"When I examined the room, yes. But in the first place we have only her word for it, since it was she who tried that particular door and reported it fastened. In the ensuing confusion she would have had ample opportunity to shoot the bolt across. I took an early opportunity of verifying my conjectures. To begin with, the fragment corresponds exactly with a tear in Mrs. Cav-

---

[4] During World War I, the Women's Land Army was formed to replace men in the fields who went off to war. Volunteers were called land girls and awarded green armbands after they had worked on a farm for 30 days. See the essay "An Army of Land Girls" in the appendix for more details.

endish's armlet. Also, at the inquest, Mrs. Cavendish declared that she had heard, from her own room, the fall of the table by the bed. I took an early opportunity of testing that statement by stationing my friend Monsieur Hastings in the left wing of the building, just outside Mrs. Cavendish's door. I myself, in company with the police, went to the deceased's room, and whilst there I, apparently accidentally, knocked over the table in question, but found that, as I had expected, Monsieur Hastings had heard no sound at all. This confirmed my belief that Mrs. Cavendish was not speaking the truth when she declared that she had been dressing in her room at the time of the tragedy. In fact, I was convinced that, far from having been in her own room, Mrs. Cavendish was actually in the deceased's room when the alarm was given."

I shot a quick glance at Mary. She was very pale, but smiling.

"I proceeded to reason on that assumption. Mrs. Cavendish is in her mother-in-law's room. We will say that she is seeking for something and has not yet found it. Suddenly Mrs. Inglethorp awakens and is seized with an alarming paroxysm.[5] She flings out her arm, overturning the bed table, and then pulls desperately at the bell. Mrs. Cavendish, startled, drops her candle, scattering the grease on the carpet. She picks it up, and retreats quickly to Mademoiselle Cynthia's room, closing the door behind her. She hurries out into the passage, for the servants must not find her where she is. But it is too late! Already footsteps are echoing along the gallery which connects the two wings. What can she do? Quick as thought, she hurries back to the young girl's room, and starts shaking her awake. The hastily aroused household come trooping down the passage. They are all busily battering at Mrs. Inglethorp's door. It occurs to nobody that Mrs. Cavendish has not arrived with the rest, but— and this is significant—I can find no one who saw her come from the other wing." He looked at Mary Cavendish. "Am I

---

[5] A sudden attack of emotion or activity.

right, madame?"

She bowed her head.

"Quite right, monsieur. You understand that, if I had thought I would do my husband any good by revealing these facts, I would have done so. But it did not seem to me to bear upon the question of his guilt or innocence."

"In a sense, that is correct, madame. But it cleared my mind of many misconceptions, and left me free to see other facts in their true significance."

"The will!" cried Lawrence. "Then it was you, Mary, who destroyed the will?"

She shook her head, and Poirot shook his also.

"No," he said quietly. "There is only one person who could possibly have destroyed that will—Mrs. Inglethorp herself!"

"Impossible!" I exclaimed. "She had only made it out that very afternoon!"

"Nevertheless, *mon ami*, it was Mrs. Inglethorp. Because, in no other way can you account for the fact that, on one of the hottest days of the year,[6] Mrs. Inglethorp ordered a fire to be lighted in her room."

I gave a gasp. What idiots we had been never to think of that fire as being incongruous![7] Poirot was continuing:

"The temperature on that day, *messieurs*, was 80 degrees in the shade. Yet Mrs. Inglethorp ordered a fire! Why? Because she wished to destroy something, and could think of no other way. You will remember that, in consequence of the War economics[8] practiced at Styles, no waste paper was thrown away. There was therefore no means of destroying a thick document such as a will. The moment I heard of a fire being lighted in

---

[6] Although Essex lies near the same latitude as notoriously cold cities such as Berlin, Warsaw and Calgary, the Gulf Stream's warm currents make its weather temperate, if very changeable. Summer temperatures rarely rise higher than 86 degrees.

[7] Different from what is happening or expected.

[8] The careful use of resources, such as saving paper for scrap drives and not wasting food and fuel.

Mrs. Inglethorp's room, I leaped to the conclusion that it was to destroy some important document—possibly a will. So the discovery of the charred fragment in the grate was no surprise to me. I did not, of course, know at the time that the will in question had only been made this afternoon, and I will admit that, when I learnt that fact, I fell into a grievous error. I came to the conclusion that Mrs. Inglethorp's determination to destroy her will arose as a direct consequence of the quarrel she had that afternoon, and that therefore the quarrel took place after, and not before the making of the will.

"Here, as we know, I was wrong, and I was forced to abandon that idea. I faced the problem from a new standpoint.[9] Now, at 4 o'clock, Dorcas overheard her mistress saying angrily: 'You need not think that any fear of publicity, or scandal between husband and wife will deter me." I conjectured,[10] and conjectured rightly, that these words were addressed, not to her husband, but to Mr. John Cavendish. At 5 o'clock, an hour later, she uses almost the same words, but the standpoint is different. She admits to Dorcas, 'I don't know what to do; scandal between husband and wife is a dreadful thing.' At 4 o'clock she has been angry, but completely mistress of herself. At 5 o'clock she is in violent distress, and speaks of having had a great shock.

"Looking at the matter psychologically, I drew one deduction which I was convinced was correct. The second 'scandal' she spoke of was not the same as the first—and it concerned herself!

"Let us reconstruct. At 4 o'clock, Mrs. Inglethorp quarrels with her son, and threatens to denounce him to his wife—who, by the way, overheard the greater part of the conversation. At 4.30, Mrs. Inglethorp, in consequence of a conversation on the validity of wills, makes a will in favour of her husband, which

---

[9] A different set of beliefs or assumptions.

[10] A guess based on the situation and not on proof.

the two gardeners witness. At 5 o'clock, Dorcas finds her mistress in a state of considerable agitation, with a slip of paper—'a letter,' Dorcas thinks—in her hand, and it is then that she orders the fire in her room to be lighted. Presumably, then, between 4.30 and 5 o'clock, something has occurred to occasion a complete revolution of feeling, since she is now as anxious to destroy the will, as she was before to make it. What was that something?

"As far as we know, she was quite alone during that half-hour. Nobody entered or left that boudoir. What then occasioned this sudden change of sentiment?

"One can only guess, but I believe my guess to be correct. Mrs. Inglethorp had no stamps in her desk. We know this, because later she asked Dorcas to bring her some. Now in the opposite corner of the room stood her husband's desk—locked. She was anxious to find some stamps, and, according to my theory, she tried her own keys in the desk. That one of them fitted I know. She therefore opened the desk, and in searching for the stamps she came across something else—that slip of paper which Dorcas saw in her hand, and which assuredly was never meant for Mrs. Inglethorp's eyes. On the other hand, Mrs. Cavendish believed that the slip of paper to which her mother-in-law clung so tenaciously[11] was a written proof of her own husband's infidelity. She demanded it from Mrs. Inglethorp who assured her, quite truly, that it had nothing to do with that matter. Mrs. Cavendish did not believe her. She thought that Mrs. Inglethorp was shielding her stepson. Now Mrs. Cavendish is a very resolute woman, and, behind her mask of reserve, she was madly jealous of her husband. She determined to get hold of that paper at all costs, and in this resolution chance came to her aid. She happened to pick up the key of Mrs. Inglethorp's despatch-case, which had been lost that morning. She knew that her mother-in-law invariably kept all important papers in this particular case.

---

[11] Determined to keep an opinion.

"Mrs. Cavendish, therefore, made her plans as only a woman driven desperate through jealousy could have done. Some time in the evening she unbolted the door leading into Mademoiselle Cynthia's room. Possibly she applied oil to the hinges, for I found that it opened quite noiselessly when I tried it. She put off her project until the early hours of the morning as being safer, since the servants were accustomed to hearing her move about her room at that time. She dressed completely in her land kit,[12] and made her way quietly through Mademoiselle Cynthia's room into that of Mrs. Inglethorp."

He paused a moment, and Cynthia interrupted:

"But I should have woken up if anyone had come through my room?"

"Not if you were drugged, mademoiselle."

"Drugged?"

"*Mais oui!*[13]

"You remember"—he addressed us collectively again—"that through all the tumult and noise next door Mademoiselle Cynthia slept. That admitted of two possibilities. Either her sleep was feigned—which I did not believe—or her unconsciousness was indeed by artificial means.

"With this latter idea in my mind, I examined all the coffee-cups most carefully, remembering that it was Mrs. Cavendish who had brought Mademoiselle Cynthia her coffee the night before. I took a sample from each cup, and had them analysed—with no result. I had counted the cups carefully, in the event of one having been removed. Six persons had taken coffee, and six cups were duly found. I had to confess myself mistaken.

"Then I discovered that I had been guilty of a very grave oversight. Coffee had been brought in for seven persons, not

---

[12] Her land girl uniform. Your kit can mean the clothing you wear for a particular activity. You put your kit in your kit-bag, as recommended in the popular WWI marching song "Pack Up Your Troubles in Your Old Kit-Bag and Smile, Smile, Smile."

[13] Of course!

six, for Dr. Bauerstein had been there that evening. This changed the face of the whole affair, for there was now one cup missing. The servants noticed nothing, since Annie, the housemaid, who took in the coffee, brought in seven cups, not knowing that Mr. Inglethorp never drank it, whereas Dorcas, who cleared them away the following morning, found six as usual—or strictly speaking she found five, the sixth being the one found broken in Mrs. Inglethorp's room.

"I was confident that the missing cup was that of Mademoiselle Cynthia. I had an additional reason for that belief in the fact that all the cups found contained sugar, which Mademoiselle Cynthia never took in her coffee. My attention was attracted by the story of Annie about some 'salt' on the tray of coco which she took every night to Mrs. Inglethorp's room. I accordingly secured a sample of that coco, and sent it to be analysed."

"But that had already been done by Dr. Bauerstein," said Lawrence quickly.

"Not exactly. The analyst was asked by him to report whether strychnine was, or was not, present. He did not have it tested, as I did, for a narcotic."

"For a narcotic?"

"Yes. Here is the analyst's report. Mrs. Cavendish administered a safe, but effectual, narcotic to both Mrs. Inglethorp and Mademoiselle Cynthia. And it is possible that she had a *mauvais quart d'heure*[14] in consequence! Imagine her feelings when her mother-in-law is suddenly taken ill and dies, and immediately after she hears the word 'Poison'! She has believed that the sleeping draught she administered was perfectly harmless, but there is no doubt that for one terrible moment she must have feared that Mrs. Inglethorp's death lay at her door. She is seized with panic, and under its influence she hurries downstairs, and quickly drops the coffee-cup and saucer used by Mademoiselle Cynthia into a large brass vase, where it is discovered later by

---

[14] An unpleasant experience. It means literally "a bad quarter of an hour."

Monsieur Lawrence. The remains of the coco she dare not touch. Too many eyes are upon her. Guess at her relief when strychnine is mentioned, and she discovers that after all the tragedy is not her doing.

"We are now able to account for the symptoms of strychnine poisoning being so long in making their appearance. A narcotic taken with strychnine will delay the action of the poison for some hours."

Poirot paused. Mary looked up at him, the colour slowly rising in her face.

"All you have said is quite true, Monsieur Poirot. It was the most awful hour of my life. I shall never forget it. But you are wonderful. I understand now—"

"What I meant when I told you that you could safely confess to Papa Poirot, eh? But you would not trust me."

"I see everything now," said Lawrence. "The drugged coco, taken on top of the poisoned coffee, amply accounts for the delay."

"Exactly. But was the coffee poisoned, or was it not? We come to a little difficulty here, since Mrs. Inglethorp never drank it."

"What?" The cry of surprise was universal.

"No. You will remember my speaking of a stain on the carpet in Mrs. Inglethorp's room? There were some peculiar points about that stain. It was still damp, it exhaled a strong odour of coffee, and imbedded in the nap of the carpet I found some little splinters of china. What had happened was plain to me, for not two minutes before I had placed my little case on the table near the window, and the table, tilting up, had deposited it upon the floor on precisely the identical spot. In exactly the same way, Mrs. Inglethorp had laid down her cup of coffee on reaching her room the night before, and the treacherous table had played her the same trick.

"What happened next is mere guess work on my part, but I should say that Mrs. Inglethorp picked up the broken cup and placed it on the table by the bed. Feeling in need of a stimulant of some kind, she heated up her coco, and drank it off then and there. Now we are faced with a new problem. We know the coco contained no strychnine. The coffee was never drunk. Yet the strychnine must have been administered between seven and nine o'clock that evening. What third medium was there—a medium so suitable for disguising the taste of strychnine that it is extraordinary no one has thought of it?" Poirot looked round the room, and then answered himself impressively. "Her medicine!"

"Do you mean that the murderer introduced the strychnine into her tonic?" I cried.

"There was no need to introduce it. It was already there—in the mixture. The strychnine that killed Mrs. Inglethorp was the identical strychnine prescribed by Dr. Wilkins. To make that clear to you, I will read you an extract from a book on dispensing which I found in the Dispensary of the Red Cross Hospital at Tadminster:

"The following prescription has become famous in text books:

Strychninae Sulph. . . . . . gr.I
Potass Bromide 3vi
Aqua ad. 3viii
Fiat Mistura

This solution deposits in a few hours the greater part of the strychnine salt as an insoluble bromide in transparent crystals. A lady in England lost her life by taking a similar mixture: the precipitated strychnine collected at the bottom, and in taking the last dose she swallowed nearly all of it!"[15]

---

[15] From *The Practice of Pharmacy* (1891) by Joseph Price Remington. The item is on the left and the quantity on the right. The practice of writing it in Latin dates from the 1400s. It reads: *Strychninae Sulph:* Strychnine sulfate, 1 grain; *Potass Bromide:* Potassium bromide, a salt used as a sedative and anticonvulsant, 6 drams (3/4 of a fluid ounce); *Aqua ad:* Add water up to 8 drams; *Fiat Mistura:* Let the mixture be made.

"Now there was, of course, no bromide in Dr. Wilkins' prescription, but you will remember that I mentioned an empty box of bromide powders. One or two of those powders introduced into the full bottle of medicine would effectually precipitate[16] the strychnine, as the book describes, and cause it to be taken in the last dose. You will learn later that the person who usually poured out Mrs. Inglethorp's medicine was always extremely careful not to shake the bottle, but to leave the sediment at the bottom of it undisturbed.

"Throughout the case, there have been evidences that the tragedy was intended to take place on Monday evening. On that day, Mrs. Inglethorp's bell wire was neatly cut, and on Monday evening Mademoiselle Cynthia was spending the night with friends, so that Mrs. Inglethorp would have been quite alone in the right wing, completely shut off from help of any kind, and would have died, in all probability, before medical aid could have been summoned. But in her hurry to be in time for the village entertainment Mrs. Inglethorp forgot to take her medicine, and the next day she lunched away from home, so that the last—and fatal—dose was actually taken twenty-four hours later than had been anticipated by the murderer; and it is owing to that delay that the final proof—the last link of the chain—is now in my hands."

Amid breathless excitement, he held out three thin strips of paper.

"A letter in the murderer's own hand-writing, *mes amis!*[17] Had it been a little clearer in its terms, it is possible that Mrs. Inglethorp, warned in time, would have escaped. As it was, she realized her danger, but not the manner of it."

In the deathly silence, Poirot pieced together the slips of paper and, clearing his throat, read:

---

[16] To separate from a solution.
[17] My friends.

"Dearest Evelyn:

You will be anxious at hearing nothing. It is all right—only it will be to-night instead of last night. You understand. There's a good time coming once the old woman is dead and out of the way. No one can possibly bring home the crime to me. That idea of yours about the bromides was a stroke of genius! But we must be very circumspect. A false step—'

"Here, my friends, the letter breaks off. Doubtless the writer was interrupted; but there can be no question as to his identity. We all know this hand-writing and—"

A howl that was almost a scream broke the silence.

"You devil! How did you get it?"

A chair was overturned. Poirot skipped nimbly aside. A quick movement on his part, and his assailant fell with a crash.

"*Messieurs, mesdames,*" said Poirot, with a flourish, "let me introduce you to the murderer, Mr. Alfred Inglethorp!"

CHAPTER XIII

POIROT EXPLAINS

"POIROT, YOU OLD VILLAIN," I said, "I've half a mind to strangle you! What do you mean by deceiving me as you have done?"

We were sitting in the library. Several hectic days lay behind us. In the room below, John and Mary were together once more, while Alfred Inglethorp and Miss Howard were in custody. Now at last, I had Poirot to myself, and could relieve my still burning curiosity.

Poirot did not answer me for a moment, but at last he said:

"I did not deceive you, *mon ami.* At most, I permitted you to deceive yourself."

"Yes, but why?"

"Well, it is difficult to explain. You see, my friend, you have a nature so honest, and a countenance[1] so transparent, that—*enfin,*[2] to conceal your feelings is impossible! If I had told you my ideas, the very first time you saw Mr. Alfred Inglethorp that astute gentleman would have—in your so expressive idiom—'smelt a rat'![3] And then, *bon jour*[4] to our chances of catching him!"

"I think that I have more diplomacy than you give me credit for."

"My friend," besought Poirot, "I implore you, do not en-

---

[1] Facial expression.
[2] Finally.
[3] Meaning something is not right. Used since the 16th century, the phrase was probably inspired by how a dog sniffs out rodents.
[4] Good bye.

rage yourself! Your help has been of the most invaluable. It is but the extremely beautiful nature that you have, which made me pause."

"Well," I grumbled, a little mollified. "I still think you might have given me a hint."

"But I did, my friend. Several hints. You would not take them. Think now, did I ever say to you that I believed John Cavendish guilty? Did I not, on the contrary, tell you that he would almost certainly be acquitted?"

"Yes, but—"

"And did I not immediately afterwards speak of the difficulty of bringing the murderer to justice? Was it not plain to you that I was speaking of two entirely different persons?"

"No," I said, "it was not plain to me!"

"Then again," continued Poirot, "at the beginning, did I not repeat to you several times that I didn't want Mr. Inglethorp arrested *now*? That should have conveyed something to you."

"Do you mean to say you suspected him as long ago as that?"

"Yes. To begin with, whoever else might benefit by Mrs. Inglethorp's death, her husband would benefit the most. There was no getting away from that. When I went up to Styles with you that first day, I had no idea as to how the crime had been committed, but from what I knew of Mr. Inglethorp I fancied that it would be very hard to find anything to connect him with it. When I arrived at the chateau, I realized at once that it was Mrs. Inglethorp who had burnt the will; and there, by the way, you cannot complain, my friend, for I tried my best to force on you the significance of that bedroom fire in midsummer."

"Yes, yes," I said impatiently. "Go on."

"Well, my friend, as I say, my views as to Mr. Inglethorp's guilt were very much shaken. There was, in fact, so much evidence against him that I was inclined to believe that he had not done it."

"When did you change your mind?"

"When I found that the more efforts I made to clear him,

the more efforts he made to get himself arrested. Then, when I discovered that Inglethorp had nothing to do with Mrs. Raikes and that in fact it was John Cavendish who was interested in that quarter, I was quite sure."

"But why?"

"Simply this. If it had been Inglethorp who was carrying on an intrigue with Mrs. Raikes, his silence was perfectly comprehensible. But, when I discovered that it was known all over the village that it was John who was attracted by the farmer's pretty wife, his silence bore quite a different interpretation. It was nonsense to pretend that he was afraid of the scandal, as no possible scandal could attach to him. This attitude of his gave me furiously to think, and I was slowly forced to the conclusion that Alfred Inglethorp wanted to be arrested. *Eh bien!* from that moment, I was equally determined that he should not be arrested."

"Wait a minute. I don't see why he wished to be arrested?"

"Because, *mon ami*, it is the law of your country that a man once acquitted can never be tried again for the same offence. Aha! but it was clever—his idea! Assuredly, he is a man of method. See here, he knew that in his position he was bound to be suspected, so he conceived the exceedingly clever idea of preparing a lot of manufactured evidence against himself. He wished to be arrested. He would then produce his irreproachable alibi—and, hey presto,[5] he was safe for life!"

"But I still don't see how he managed to prove his alibi, and yet go to the chemist's shop?"

Poirot stared at me in surprise.

"Is it possible? My poor friend! You have not yet realized that it was Miss Howard who went to the chemist's shop?"

"Miss Howard?"

"But, certainly. Who else? It was most easy for her. She is of a good height, her voice is deep and manly; moreover, remember, she and Inglethorp are cousins, and there is a distinct

---

[5] Poirot is mimicking a stage magician revealing the climax of a trick.

resemblance between them, especially in their gait[6] and bearing. It was simplicity itself. They are a clever pair!"

"I am still a little fogged as to how exactly the bromide business was done," I remarked.

"Bon! I will reconstruct for you as far as possible. I am inclined to think that Miss Howard was the master mind in that affair. You remember her once mentioning that her father was a doctor? Possibly she dispensed his medicines for him, or she may have taken the idea from one of the many books lying about when Mademoiselle Cynthia was studying for her exam. Anyway, she was familiar with the fact that the addition of a bromide to a mixture containing strychnine would cause the precipitation of the latter. Probably the idea came to her quite suddenly. Mrs. Inglethorp had a box of bromide powders, which she occasionally took at night. What could be easier than quietly to dissolve one or more of those powders in Mrs. Inglethorp's large sized bottle of medicine when it came from Coot's? The risk is practically nil. The tragedy will not take place until nearly a fortnight later. If anyone has seen either of them touching the medicine, they will have forgotten it by that time. Miss Howard will have engineered her quarrel, and departed from the house. The lapse of time, and her absence, will defeat all suspicion. Yes, it was a clever idea! If they had left it alone, it is possible the crime might never have been brought home to them. But they were not satisfied. They tried to be too clever—and that was their undoing."

Poirot puffed at his tiny cigarette, his eyes fixed on the ceiling.

"They arranged a plan to throw suspicion on John Cavendish, by buying strychnine at the village chemist's, and signing the register in his hand-writing.

"On Monday Mrs. Inglethorp will take the last dose of her medicine. On Monday, therefore, at six o'clock, Alfred Inglethorp arranges to be seen by a number of people at a spot

---

[6] A particular way of walking.

far removed from the village. Miss Howard has previously made up a cock and bull story[7] about him and Mrs. Raikes to account for his holding his tongue afterwards. At six o'clock, Miss Howard, disguised as Alfred Inglethorp, enters the chemist's shop, with her story about a dog, obtains the strychnine, and writes the name of Alfred Inglethorp in John's handwriting, which she had previously studied carefully.

"But, as it will never do if John, too, can prove an alibi, she writes him an anonymous note—still copying his handwriting—which takes him to a remote spot where it is exceedingly unlikely that anyone will see him.

"So far, all goes well. Miss Howard goes back to Middlingham. Alfred Inglethorp returns to Styles. There is nothing that can compromise him in any way, since it is Miss Howard who has the strychnine, which, after all, is only wanted as a blind to throw suspicion on John Cavendish.

"But now a hitch occurs. Mrs. Inglethorp does not take her medicine that night. The broken bell, Cynthia's absence—arranged by Inglethorp through his wife—all these are wasted. And then—he makes his slip.

"Mrs. Inglethorp is out, and he sits down to write to his accomplice, who, he fears, may be in a panic at the nonsuccess of their plan. It is probable that Mrs. Inglethorp returned earlier than he expected. Caught in the act, and somewhat flurried he hastily shuts and locks his desk. He fears that if he remains in the room he may have to open it again, and that Mrs. Inglethorp might catch sight of the letter before he could snatch it up. So he goes out and walks in the woods, little dreaming that Mrs. Inglethorp will open his desk, and discover

[7] A highly colorful or unbelievable story. There are several possible origins. The most common is derived from fables in which cocks (adult male chickens), bulls and other animals converse. At the end of Laurence Stern's *Tristam Shandy* (published 1759-67), when Yorick is asked what the story is about, he replies "A Cock and a Bull ... and one of the best of its kind, I ever heard."

the incriminating[8] document.

"But this, as we know, is what happened. Mrs. Inglethorp reads it, and becomes aware of the perfidy[9] of her husband and Evelyn Howard, though, unfortunately, the sentence about the bromides conveys no warning to her mind. She knows that she is in danger—but is ignorant of where the danger lies. She decides to say nothing to her husband, but sits down and writes to her solicitor, asking him to come on the morrow, and she also determines to destroy immediately the will which she has just made. She keeps the fatal letter."

"It was to discover that letter, then, that her husband forced the lock of the despatch-case?"

"Yes, and from the enormous risk he ran we can see how fully he realized its importance. That letter excepted, there was absolutely nothing to connect him with the crime."

"There's only one thing I can't make out, why didn't he destroy it at once when he got hold of it?"

"Because he did not dare take the biggest risk of all—that of keeping it on his own person."

"I don't understand."

"Look at it from his point of view. I have discovered that there were only five short minutes in which he could have taken it—the five minutes immediately before our own arrival on the scene, for before that time Annie was brushing the stairs, and would have seen anyone who passed going to the right wing. Figure to yourself the scene! He enters the room, unlocking the door by means of one of the other doorkeys—they were all much alike. He hurries to the despatch-case—it is locked, and the keys are nowhere to be seen. That is a terrible blow to him, for it means that his presence in the room cannot be concealed as he had hoped. But he sees clearly that everything must be risked for the sake of that damning piece of evidence. Quickly, he forces the lock with a penknife, and turns

---

[8] Evidence or proof that a person was involved in a crime.
[9] Being deceitful and untrustworthy.

over the papers until he finds what he is looking for.

"But now a fresh dilemma arises: he dare not keep that piece of paper on him. He may be seen leaving the room—he may be searched. If the paper is found on him, it is certain doom. Probably, at this minute, too, he hears the sounds below of Mr. Wells and John leaving the boudoir. He must act quickly. Where can he hide this terrible slip of paper? The contents of the waste-paper-basket are kept and in any case, are sure to be examined. There are no means of destroying it; and he dare not keep it. He looks round, and he sees—what do you think, *mon ami?*"

I shook my head.

"In a moment, he has torn the letter into long thin strips, and rolling them up into spills he thrusts them hurriedly in amongst the other spills in the vase on the mantle-piece."

I uttered an exclamation.

"No one would think of looking there," Poirot continued. "And he will be able, at his leisure, to come back and destroy this solitary piece of evidence against him."[10]

"Then, all the time, it was in the spill vase in Mrs. Inglethorp's bedroom, under our very noses?" I cried.

Poirot nodded.

"Yes, my friend. That is where I discovered my 'last link,' and I owe that very fortunate discovery to you."

"To me?"

"Yes. Do you remember telling me that my hand shook as I was straightening the ornaments on the mantel-piece?"

"Yes, but I don't see—"

"No, but I saw. Do you know, my friend, I remembered

---

[10] A spill vase is used to hold strips of curled paper or wood, called spills, that were used to light gas lamps, oil lamps, candles or cigarettes from the flames in a fireplace. The word comes from the Old English *spillan* for "waste" or "shed" as in blood. Christie might have been inspired by one of her favorite novels, Anne Katharine Green's *The Leavenworth Case* (1878), in which an incriminating letter is hidden in the same way, and Edgar Allan Poe's *The Purloined Letter* (1844) with its "hiding in plain sight" conclusion.

that earlier in the morning, when we had been there together, I had straightened all the objects on the mantel-piece. And, if they were already straightened, there would be no need to straighten them again, unless, in the meantime, some one else had touched them."[11]

"Dear me," I murmured, "so that is the explanation of your extraordinary behaviour. You rushed down to Styles, and found it still there?"

"Yes, and it was a race for time."

"But I still can't understand why Inglethorp was such a fool as to leave it there when he had plenty of opportunity to destroy it."

"Ah, but he had no opportunity. I saw to that."

"You?"

"Yes. Do you remember reproving[12] me for taking the household into my confidence on the subject?"

"Yes."

"Well, my friend, I saw there was just one chance. I was not sure then if Inglethorp was the criminal or not, but if he was I reasoned that he would not have the paper on him, but would have hidden it somewhere, and by enlisting the sympathy of the household I could effectually prevent his destroying it. He was already under suspicion, and by making the matter public I secured the services of about ten amateur detectives, who would be watching him unceasingly, and being himself aware of their watchfulness he would not dare seek further to destroy the document. He was therefore forced to depart from the house, leaving it in the spill vase."

"But surely Miss Howard had ample opportunities of aiding him."

"Yes, but Miss Howard did not know of the paper's exist-

---

[11] Christie biographer Laura Thompson suggests that Christie knew instinctively to link the discovery of a clue to Poirot's passion for order and symmetry. "At her very first attempt Agatha understood — or intuited — that a clue based upon character has double the value."

[12] Reprimanding.

ence. In accordance with their prearranged plan, she never spoke to Alfred Inglethorp. They were supposed to be deadly enemies, and until John Cavendish was safely convicted they neither of them dared risk a meeting. Of course I had a watch kept on Mr. Inglethorp, hoping that sooner or later he would lead me to the hiding-place. But he was too clever to take any chances. The paper was safe where it was; since no one had thought of looking there in the first week, it was not likely they would do so afterwards. But for your lucky remark, we might never have been able to bring him to justice."

"I understand that now; but when did you first begin to suspect Miss Howard?"

"When I discovered that she had told a lie at the inquest about the letter she had received from Mrs. Inglethorp."

"Why, what was there to lie about?"

"You saw that letter? Do you recall its general appearance?"

"Yes—more or less."

"You will recollect, then, that Mrs. Inglethorp wrote a very distinctive hand, and left large clear spaces between her words. But if you look at the date at the top of the letter you will notice that 'July 17th' is quite different in this respect. Do you see what I mean?"

"No," I confessed, "I don't."

"You do not see that that letter was not written on the 17th, but on the 7th—the day after Miss Howard's departure? The '1' was written in before the '7' to turn it into the '17th'."

"But why?"

"That is exactly what I asked myself. Why does Miss Howard suppress the letter written on the 17th, and produce this faked one instead? Because she did not wish to show the letter of the 17th. Why, again? And at once a suspicion dawned in my mind. You will remember my saying that it was wise to beware of people who were not telling you the truth."

"And yet," I cried indignantly, "after that, you gave me two reasons why Miss Howard could not have committed the crime!"

July 17th

Styles Court

Essex

My dear Evelyn

Can we not bury the hatchet? I have found it hard to forgive the things you said against my dear husband but I am an old woman & very fond of you

Yours affectionately

Emily Inglethorp

"And very good reasons too," replied Poirot. "For a long time they were a stumbling-block to me until I remembered a very significant fact: that she and Alfred Inglethorp were cousins. She could not have committed the crime single-handed, but the reasons against that did not debar her from being an accomplice. And, then, there was that rather over-vehement[13] hatred of hers! It concealed a very opposite emotion. There was, undoubtedly, a tie of passion between them long before he came to Styles. They had already arranged their infamous plot—that he should marry this rich, but rather foolish old lady,

---

[13] Expressing strong feelings.

induce her to make a will leaving her money to him, and then gain their ends by a very cleverly conceived crime. If all had gone as they planned, they would probably have left England, and lived together on their poor victim's money.

"They are a very astute[14] and unscrupulous pair. While suspicion was to be directed against him, she would be making quiet preparations for a very different denouement.[15] She arrives from Middlingham with all the compromising[16] items in her possession. No suspicion attaches to her. No notice is paid to her coming and going in the house. She hides the strychnine and glasses in John's room. She puts the beard in the attic. She will see to it that sooner or later they are duly discovered."

"I don't quite see why they tried to fix the blame on John," I remarked. "It would have been much easier for them to bring the crime home to Lawrence."

"Yes, but that was mere chance. All the evidence against him arose out of pure accident. It must, in fact, have been distinctly annoying to the pair of schemers."

"His manner was unfortunate," I observed thoughtfully.

"Yes. You realize, of course, what was at the back of that?"

"No."

"You did not understand that he believed Mademoiselle Cynthia guilty of the crime?"

"No," I exclaimed, astonished. "Impossible!"

"Not at all. I myself nearly had the same idea. It was in my mind when I asked Mr. Wells that first question about the will. Then there were the bromide powders which she had made up, and her clever male impersonations, as Dorcas recounted them to us. There was really more evidence against her than anyone else."

"You are joking, Poirot!"

"No. Shall I tell you what made Monsieur Lawrence turn so

---

[14] Quick to take advantage of a situation.
[15] The end of the situation.
[16] Information, particularly of a sexual nature, that would damage a person's reputation.

pale when he first entered his mother's room on the fatal night? It was because, whilst his mother lay there, obviously poisoned, he saw, over your shoulder, that the door into Mademoiselle Cynthia's room was unbolted."

"But he declared that he saw it bolted!" I cried.

"Exactly," said Poirot dryly. "And that was just what confirmed my suspicion that it was not. He was shielding Mademoiselle Cynthia."

"But why should he shield her?"

"Because he is in love with her."

I laughed.

"There, Poirot, you are quite wrong! I happen to know for a fact that, far from being in love with her, he positively dislikes her."

"Who told you that, *mon ami*?"

"Cynthia herself."

"*La pauvre petite!*[17] And she was concerned?"

"She said that she did not mind at all."

"Then she certainly did mind very much," remarked Poirot. "They are like that—*les femmes!*"[18]

"What you say about Lawrence is a great surprise to me," I said.

"But why? It was most obvious. Did not Monsieur Lawrence make the sour face every time Mademoiselle Cynthia spoke and laughed with his brother? He had taken it into his long head that Mademoiselle Cynthia was in love with Monsieur John. When he entered his mother's room, and saw her obviously poisoned, he jumped to the conclusion that Mademoiselle Cynthia knew something about the matter. He was nearly driven desperate. First he crushed the coffee-cup to powder under his feet, remembering that *she* had gone up with his mother the night before, and he determined that there should be no chance of testing its contents. Thenceforward, he

---

[17] Poor little woman.
[18] Women.

strenuously, and quite uselessly, upheld the theory of 'Death from natural causes'."

"And what about the 'extra coffee-cup'?"

"I was fairly certain that it was Mrs. Cavendish who had hidden it, but I had to make sure. Monsieur Lawrence did not know at all what I meant; but, on reflection, he came to the conclusion that if he could find an extra coffee-cup anywhere his lady love would be cleared of suspicion. And he was perfectly right."

"One thing more. What did Mrs. Inglethorp mean by her dying words?"

"They were, of course, an accusation against her husband."

"Dear me, Poirot," I said with a sigh, "I think you have explained everything. I am glad it has all ended so happily. Even John and his wife are reconciled."

"Thanks to me."

"How do you mean—thanks to you?"

"My dear friend, do you not realize that it was simply and solely the trial which has brought them together again? That John Cavendish still loved his wife, I was convinced. Also, that she was equally in love with him. But they had drifted very far apart. It all arose from a misunderstanding. She married him without love. He knew it. He is a sensitive man in his way, he would not force himself upon her if she did not want him. And, as he withdrew, her love awoke. But they are both unusually proud, and their pride held them inexorably[19] apart. He drifted into an entanglement with Mrs. Raikes, and she deliberately cultivated the friendship of Dr. Bauerstein. Do you remember the day of John Cavendish's arrest, when you found me deliberating over a big decision?"

"Yes, I quite understood your distress."

"Pardon me, *mon ami*, but you did not understand it in the least. I was trying to decide whether or not I would clear John Cavendish at once. I could have cleared him—though it might

---

[19] Unstoppable.

have meant a failure to convict the real criminals. They were entirely in the dark as to my real attitude up to the very last moment—which partly accounts for my success."

"Do you mean that you could have saved John Cavendish from being brought to trial?"

"Yes, my friend. But I eventually decided in favour of 'a woman's happiness'. Nothing but the great danger through which they have passed could have brought these two proud souls together again."

I looked at Poirot in silent amazement. The colossal cheek[20] of the little man! Who on earth but Poirot would have thought of a trial for murder as a restorer of conjugal[21] happiness!

"I perceive your thoughts, *mon ami*," said Poirot, smiling at me. "No one but Hercule Poirot would have attempted such a thing! And you are wrong in condemning it. The happiness of one man and one woman is the greatest thing in all the world."

His words took me back to earlier events. I remembered Mary as she lay white and exhausted on the sofa, listening, listening. There had come the sound of the bell below. She had started up. Poirot had opened the door, and meeting her agonized eyes had nodded gently. "Yes, madame," he said. "I have brought him back to you." He had stood aside, and as I went out I had seen the look in Mary's eyes, as John Cavendish had caught his wife in his arms.

"Perhaps you are right, Poirot," I said gently. "Yes, it is the greatest thing in the world."

Suddenly, there was a tap at the door, and Cynthia peeped in.

"I—I only—"

"Come in," I said, springing up.

She came in, but did not sit down.

"I—only wanted to tell you something—"

"Yes?"

---

[20] To speak in an insolent or imprudent manner.
[21] Relating to the state of marriage.

Cynthia fidgeted with a little tassel for some moments, then, suddenly exclaiming: "You dears!" kissed first me and then Poirot, and rushed out of the room again.

"What on earth does this mean?" I asked, surprised.

It was very nice to be kissed by Cynthia, but the publicity of the salute rather impaired the pleasure.

"It means that she has discovered Monsieur Lawrence does not dislike her as much as she thought," replied Poirot philosophically.

"But—"

"Here he is."

Lawrence at that moment passed the door.

"Eh! Monsieur Lawrence," called Poirot. "We must congratulate you, is it not so?"

Lawrence blushed, and then smiled awkwardly. A man in love is a sorry spectacle. Now Cynthia had looked charming.

I sighed.

"What is it, *mon ami?*"

"Nothing," I said sadly. "They are two delightful women!"

"And neither of them is for you?" finished Poirot. "Never mind. Console yourself, my friend. We may hunt together again, who knows? And then—"[22]

THE END

---

[22] At the end of the second Poirot novel, *Murder on the Links* (1923), Christie married Hastings off and shipped him to Argentina. "I think I was getting a little tired of him," she said in *An Autobiography* (1977). "I might be stuck with Poirot, but no need to be stuck with Hastings, too." He would return to narrate most of the 52 short stories but appear in only eight of the 33 Poirot novels, including Poirot's swan song, *Curtain*, which was also set at Styles.

The
World
of
Styles

Poison Nuts
& Quaker Buttons
A Brief History of Strychnine

"It still seems to me that my mother's death might be accounted for by natural means."

"How do you make that out, Mr. Cavendish?"

"My mother, at the time of her death, and for some time before it, was taking a tonic containing strychnine."

— The Mysterious Affair at Styles

It starts in your mind.

Something is not right. Your heart is hammering in your chest. You fidget and find it hard to focus. You consider going for a walk to burn off the excess energy. You begin to feel nauseous.

Your mouth tastes of pennies.

The first sign that something is seriously wrong is when the muscles in your arms and legs stiffen, then jerk like you're a marionette. Close your eyes, and you see lights sparkle in the darkness. You grab your belly and heave. The spasms cause your hands and feet to draw closer to you. Your face contorts, and the pressure grows behind your eyeballs, causing them to swell.

You vomit some more. Quite a lot, actually.

If you know what to do at this point, you still have a chance of surviving. Otherwise, the time between spasms grow shorter and shorter. You're losing control of your body. If you haven't pissed yourself by now, you do. You can't taste the saliva frothing down your chin because you're suffocating. Taking a breath feels like someone is sitting on your chest.

Your body stiffens.

As the lack of oxygen sinks you into unconsciousness, your back thrusts into an arch and your head and heels stay on the floor and your arms jerk spasmodically in slower and smaller motions.

The muscles in your face settle into a teeth-baring grimace. A doctor passing by could tell you that the Joker-like expression is called the *risus sardonicus*, from the Latin for "sardonic smile," but you are beyond caring. There's nothing left to do but call the undertaker and order the flowers.

Total time: under an hour, tops.

That's what it is like to die of strychnine poisoning.

EVERYTHING IS A POISON

Mystery fans in particular know that strychnine is a poison. So it's understandable that readers of *The Mysterious Affair at Styles* would wonder why Mrs. Inglethorp is being fed a daily dose of the stuff in a tonic. What could she be thinking?

The answer lies in understanding how physicians look at poisons and what strychnine does to the human body. Because despite the fact that strychnine can kill, for a long time it was used to cure.

Still is, in fact.

Our story starts with Paracelsus, the German physician who during the Renaissance developed new methods for treating illnesses. He started from the standpoint that, as he wrote, "everything is poison, there is poison in everything. Only the dose makes a thing not a poison."

He was not just talking about strychnine or arsenic. Too much of anything is dangerous to the human body. Clean water is safe to drink, but slug down several gallons quickly and you develop water intoxication in which your cells swell as they try to absorb the excess. Breathing pure oxygen for too long causes hyperoxia, damaging the cell membranes and causing brain and lung damage.

So if everything is a poison, the reasoning goes, it simply becomes a matter of finding a safe dosage and learning what good it can do for you.

Even strychnine.

FROM QUAKERS TO QUACKS

Some folks like water,
Some folks like wine,
But I like a taste,
Of straight strychnine,

— *Strychnine*, The Sonics (1964)

Strychnine is the distilled essence of nuts from the Strychnos nux-vomica tree, found in India, Sri Lanka, Australia, and north-central Africa. The name is derived from the Greek word *strukhnos* for a type of nightshade, but it is more commonly called the poison nut or Quaker button tree.

("Quaker buttons," by the way, comes from the Religious Society of Friends. Their nickname "Quakers" originated as an insult, a play either on their belief that one should "quake before the Lord," or from the habit of some members to tremble during services when touched by the Holy Ghost.)

Healers would grind the nuts and stem bark and use them to give the heart and respiratory systems a boost as well as to treat a laundry list of problems, including dyspepsia, dysentery, paralysis and sexual impotence.

Scientifically, strychnine works as a neurotoxin, binding itself to the neurons that control the muscles and interfering with the electrical signals used to control them. By taking the place of glycine, the organic compound that inhibits muscle action, it causes the poison's characteristic muscle spasms that can end in death by asphyxiation.

Terrible, right? Why would anyone take something that stimulates your body that way?

Ever drink coffee? Tea? Red Bull? Strychnine and caffeine have a similar molecular structure and both block the glycine receptors. There are crucial differences — caffeine doesn't kill you for one — but at low doses strychnine acts as a stimulant.

The modern history of strychnine begins in the early nineteenth century. The plant had been known in Europe since the 1540s, but it wasn't until 1818 that French chemists Joseph Bienaimé Caventou and Pierre-Joseph Pelletier isolated the nux-vomica essence and named it strychnine. They tested it on rabbits and attempted to develop an antidote. Some of their ideas, such as ingesting chlorine water, were as deadly as the drug.

In the meantime, physician Pierre Fouquier experimented with nux-vomica on patients at a Paris hospital. The results, at best, were mixed. One experiment left its victim paralyzed for eight hours, frightening the assistants as much as the other patients. Some who survived the convulsions claimed they were cured and checked out of the hospital before the treatment was completed, or at least before the doctor could stop them.

By 1828, reports of the drug had reached England, and soon British doctors were testing strychnine on all kinds of problems such as intestinal worms, headaches, lead poisoning, diabetes, catatonia and cholera. They injected it into the eyelids as a possible blindness cure, and up the urethra and into the bladder for urinary retention. Surgeons would give it to their patients before the anesthetic was given.

Doctors and quacks alike promoted it as a wonder drug, and by the late Victorian period, it slipped into tonics as a pick-me-up.

ACCIDENTS WILL HAPPEN

Given its lethality in small doses — the equivalent of one-fifth of a standard aspirin tablet was enough to kill Mrs. Inglethorp — it was amazing anyone survived. For example, in 1900, a Dr. C.F. Abraham of Ontario prescribed for "Baby Smith" a mixture of belladonna, strychnine, aromatic ammonium and syrup of tolu balsam, to be taken with a little water every two hours. It's not known how well "Baby Smith" responded to this treatment.

Even professionals ran the risk of near-fatal accidents. In 1896, a medical student wrote to a British medical journal describing what happened when he needed a boost while studying:

> Three years ago I was reading for an examination, and feeling 'run down' I took 10 minims [about 1/50th of a fluid ounce] of strychnia solution with the same quantity of dilute phosphoric acid well diluted twice a day. On the second day of taking it, towards the evening, I felt a tightness in the 'facial muscles' and a peculiar metallic taste in the mouth. There was great uneasiness and restlessness, and I felt a desire to walk about and do something rather than sit still and read. I lay on the bed and the calf muscles began to stiffen and jerk. My toes drew up under my feet, and as I moved or turned my head flashes of light kept darting across my eyes.
>
> I then knew something serious was developing, so I crawled off the bed and scrambled to a case in my room and got out (fortunately) the bromide of potassium and the chloral. I had no confidence or courage to weigh them, so I guessed the quantity — about 30 gr. bromide of potassium and 10 gr. chloral — put them in a tumbler with some water, and drank it off. My whole body was in a cold sweat, with anginous attacks in the precordial [heart] region, and a feeling of 'going off.'
>
> I did not call for medical aid, as I thought the symptoms declining. I felt better, but my lower limbs were as cold as ice and the calf muscles kept tense and jerking. There was no opisthotonos [the characteristic arching of the back], only a slight stiffness at the back of the neck. Half an hour later, as I could judge, I took the same quantity of bromide of potassium and chloral, and a little time after I lost consciousness and fell into a 'profound sleep,' awaking in the morning with no unpleasant symptoms, no headache, &c., but a desire 'to be on the move' and a slight feeling of stiffness in the jaw.
>
> These worked off during the day.

STRYCHNINE AT THE OLYMPICS

By the turn of the century, athletes were taking strychnine to enhance their performances. Runners and cyclists drank it to boost their endurance. Boxing managers kept a bottle of strychnine-laced ointment at hand to dull their fighters' pain. Football trainers stocked their bags with strychnine pills along with the smelling salts, brandy and other tonics.

In an era before drug testing, such use was not illegal, but it did spark rumors. The Welsh championship bicyclist Arthur Linton was rumored to have died from a drug cocktail administered by his trainer, the notorious "Choppy" Warburton, but the truth is that he died at age 24 from typhoid. However, Warburton did carry with him a black bottle, possibly containing strychnine, that he used to dose his charges during races.

The most notorious use of the drug occurred during the 1904 Summer Olympics marathon in St. Louis, Missouri.

The event was a debacle. Of the 32 runners who started, only 14 finished. One runner rode over part of the course in a vehicle, ran into the stadium and attempted to claim the gold medal before his cheating was discovered.

It was a surprise anyone finished. St. Louis is hellishly hot in the summer. Temperatures that August were in the 90s, with the humidity nearly as high. Thirsty runners could find water only at a tower and a well. They raced over unpaved roads that quickly became choked with dust from the horses and vehicles that paraded with them. Several runners who breathed in too much dust finished the race in the hospital.

The event's only bright spot was that it made Olympic history for being the first in which black athletes participated. It wasn't intentional. The founder of the games, Pierre de Coubertin, had planned the Olympics as "the means of bringing to perfection the strong and hopeful youth of our white race." But the World's Fair was in St. Louis at the time, and two members of South Africa's Boer War Exhibit, Tswana tribesmen named Len Tau and Jan Mashiani, decided to compete. Mashiani finished twelfth. Tau did better by finishing ninth, and he could have won if a wild dog hadn't chased him off the course for a time.

The race was won by Thomas Hicks, an Englishman running for the United States. After 19 miles, Hicks was in first place by more than a mile, but fading fast. When he stopped to rest, his manager leapt from a car and dosed him with brandy mixed with a bit of strychnine sulfate, a.k.a. rat poison. That got him running again, until he collapsed, his face ash-white. His supporters bathed him in warm water and forced down another dose of strychnine, brandy and egg whites. Delirious and staggering — at one point his trainers carried him — Hicks finished first and collapsed. It took more than an hour before he could stand and receive his gold medal.

Given strychnine's lethal nature, it's not surprising that it would show up in some of the Victorian era's most notorious crimes. In the 1850s, Dr. William Palmer used it to poison several people — his crimes are discussed in "The Case of the Doctoring Doctor" essay in this section — and Thomas Neill Cream killed several London prostitutes with strychnine in the 1890s.

Thankfully, strychnine no longer appears on the shelf in tonics. But if Mrs. Inglethorp were alive today and in need of a pick-me-up, she could turn to homeopathic remedies sold in pellet or liquid form. Although it would be nowhere near the same strength as her tonic, it would also be nowhere near as lethal.

The Case of the Doctoring Doctor

The Crime of the Century That Influenced Styles

Immortality is a mischievous spirit, evading those who pursue it, and choosing those who never seek it. Take the case of William Palmer, the doctor and gambler whose life ended on the gallows in 1856, but whose reputation as the "Rugeley Poisoner" survives more than 150 years later.

The Palmer case was one of the most popular during a Victorian era that was stuffed with thrilling, bloody scandals. It had the pitiable, lingering death by poison of his gambler friend, John Parsons Cook. There was Palmer's shady past, with apprenticeships that ended in financial and sexual misconduct and rumors he fathered — and killed — several illegitimate children. There was also the suspicion that Cook was not Palmer's only victim. Palmer's wife, brother, mother-in-law, children and fellow gamblers also died mysteriously.

Finally, Palmer moved among the gamblers, bettors, fixers, touts and nobility in the world of horse racing, where races were rigged and fortunes won and lost. Perhaps not coincidentally, poison also played a role there, with strychnine used to stimulate the laggard horses and arsenic to nobble the favorites.

But the popularity of the Palmer case was also driven by cultural and technological forces. In the first half of the 19th century, the rise of the postal service and the lowering of taxes on newspapers ignited a boom in circulation. Readers of all classes demanded flesh-creeping tales of murder, mayhem, scandal and gossip, and printers competed eagerly to fulfill their desires. Newspapers and broadsides followed each crime's bloody trail, from the discovery of the body to the criminal's final confession uttered in the shadow of the gallows. They published detailed accounts of the trial, visited and described for readers the scene of the tragedy, and spoke at length with people who claimed to know the victim and the accused. Newspapers and printers published accusations, speculation, sometimes outright falsehoods. Anything if it would keep readers coming back.

And as "the crime of the century," the Palmer case was ripe for exploitation. The presiding judge, Lord Chief Justice Campbell, described it in his diary as "the most memorable judicial proceedings for the last fifty years, engaging the attention not only of this country but of all Europe." It proved so popular that in the *Illustrated Times'* broadside announcing his execution, it added a 40-page pamphlet with a transcript of the trial, a memoir of the prisoner and 60 illustrations. It sold 400,000 copies. Even in America, his trial was reported in the New York and Baltimore newspapers.

And one authority on poisons suspects that Agatha Christie had her eye on the doctor while composing *The Mysterious Affair at Styles*.

A TRAIL OF BODIES

Palmer's life and crimes took place in Staffordshire in central-western England. Born in the small market town of Rugeley in 1824, the son of a wealthy timber merchant had developed a sinister reputation early. An apprenticeship at a Liverpool wholesale druggist ended in his discharge for embezzlement. A second attempt with a surgeon ended over sexual and financial irregularities.

Palmer moved to London where he studied medicine at St. Bartholomew's Hospital — the same "Barts" where Dr. Watson later met Sherlock Holmes. This time, he completed his studies successfully and was accepted in the Royal College of Surgeons.

By 1847, the 23-year-old doctor was back in Rugeley, where he married Annie Thornton, the daughter of the mistress of Colonel William Brooks. Judging from the historical record, her mother (called Ann in some accounts, Mary in others) was a handful, a steady drinker with anger-management issues. In 1834, when Annie was a child, the colonel blew his brains out, leaving several thousand pounds to his mistress and property for Annie that would bring in a yearly income.

After his marriage, Palmer developed a passion for horse racing, a popular pastime in Staffordshire. He became a regular at the race meets, some of which lasted several days. By 1852, he had abandoned his medical practice. He began buying horses — including one called The Chicken — whose abilities on the turf would have a tragic effect on the doctor.

His first horse, named Goldfinder, won him £2,770 at a race meet in Chester. But running a stable takes money, and Palmer's expenses and gambling losses quickly put him in the hole. First he borrowed from his mother-in-law and fellow gamblers. Then he turned to moneylenders, accepting their loans at high interest rates. Soon, he was borrowing new money just to cover his old debts. He developed a reputation for not paying his debts, and he was suspected of doping horses. Tattersall's, the respected London auction house for horses, denied his application for membership.

In the meantime, death clung like a shadow to the doctor.

1849

Two weeks after moving in with the Palmer family, his mother-in-law died. Despite her wealth, the 50-year-old Ann/Mary had been living alone without servants but with her numerous cats. Palmer had found her insensible from drink and insisted she come live with them. She hated Palmer, suspecting him of poisoning her cats, but she feared more what he would do to her daughter if she refused and so agreed to the move. If she was poisoned for her money, she had the last laugh on the doctor, because her will gave her property to another relative.

1850

Leonard Bladen, a gambler who had loaned Palmer money, died in agony at the doctor's house. A few days before, he had met Palmer at the Chester races where he had won a substantial amount. He wrote to his wife to say that he was going to stop in Rugeley and collect on the loan. There is some doubt over the cause of his death. Several months before, he had been hit in the chest by a cart, and he had ignored his doctor's advice to rest. His death certificate recorded that he died of those injuries and that Palmer had been present at the time. When his wife came to Rugeley, however, she discovered that his betting books containing evidence of the loan had vanished, along with most of his winnings.

1851-1854

Of Palmer's five children by his wife, all except his eldest son died in infancy. Each lived between 7 hours and 10 weeks before dying of "convulsions."

1854

In September, it was Annie Palmer's turn. She had attended a concert in Liverpool with her sister-in-law and returned home feeling unwell. Palmer nursed her and called in other doctors, but she died within a few days. The official cause was cholera, enabling her husband to collect on a £13,000 life insurance policy he had taken out on her five months before. After Palmer's arrest, her body would be exhumed and a small amount of antimony, a poison, would be found in her stomach.

1855

Palmer's younger brother Walter, a drunkard heavily in debt, died in August. Palmer had talked his brother into getting his life insured, promising him £400 if he agreed. After failing to get a group of companies to insure him for a total of £82,000, he hired a man to keep Walter sober long enough to fool a company's doctor and succeeded in getting a £14,000 policy. He then reneged on Walter's share, offering him £60 and unlimited alcohol from the local inn.

We don't know if Walter Palmer was poisoned. It could be that he drank himself to death, with a little encouragement from the doctor. In the end, it didn't matter to Palmer, because this time his reputation had caught up with him. The insurance company delayed paying on the policy and made noises about investigating the death.

Meanwhile, Palmer owed huge sums of money. He had mortgaged his house and possessions for £10,400. After his wife's death, he had forged his mother's name as co-signer on £13,500 in loans, and his creditors were seeking repayment.

With the insurance company refusing to pay on Walter's death, Palmer returned to the insurance scheme, this time attempting to insure Bates, his groom, for £10,000 by passing him off to the company as "a well-to-do gentleman." The scheme fell apart when two of the company's detectives visited Rugeley and saw Bates for themselves.

By November, the moneylenders were telling Palmer they would take legal action against his mother if he didn't pay up. Once the writs were served on her, she would learn of his forgeries. He would be exposed, certainly jailed. He fended them off with another promise of payment, but he needed to act fast before his house of debt collapsed.

That's when John Parsons Cook won at the track.

THE UNLUCKY WINNER

Cook followed a similar path to the track as Palmer. He, too, had abandoned his profession — he was a solicitor — for the sporting life. He, too, owed money, although not as much. They may not have been close friends, but they knew each other well enough to co-own horses, raise joint loans and gamble together. They shared the same sitting room on out-of-town racing junkets. Cook also suffered from the chronic infections many Victorians endured, including syphilis, and probably consulted with the former physician about his aches and pains. It was this closeness that would explain Cook's trust in Palmer in the days to come.

On Nov. 13, Palmer and Cook visited the two-day race-meeting at Shrewsbury. Palmer lost betting on The Chicken. Cook, however, cleared £2,000, enough to pay off his debts.

The next night, at the Raven Hotel in Shrewsbury, Cook celebrated his great fortune with Palmer and other gentlemen. He finished a glass of brandy, then complained of a burning sensation in his throat. Palmer made a great show of sampling the empty glass and denied there was any problem with it. Cook fled the room to vomit and complained afterward, "I believe that damn Palmer has been dosing me."

They returned to Rugeley on the 15th, where Cook booked a room at the Talbot Arms, across the street from Palmer's home. As Cook rested and recovered over the next few days, Palmer suffered a double whammy: he bet heavily on a horse race and lost, and he received another creditor's threat to pay up.

On Saturday the 17th, Palmer visited Cook in his room and ordered a chambermaid to serve him a cup of coffee. Cook threw up within the half hour. Palmer decided to try broth, which was procured from a nearby inn and warmed over the stove in Palmer's kitchen. Cook vomited that up as well. "Palmer was constantly in and out," as one account put it, "ministering to Cook a variety of things, and whenever he did administer anything to him, sickness invariably ensued."

During the weekend, Cook was seen by a local physician named Dr. Bamford. He was 82, ancient at a time when the average life expectancy was half that, and probably not very qualified as well. He had treated Palmer's family and had signed the death certificates for Annie and Walter Palmer and the four children, so he certainly wasn't suspicious of a local colleague. After a consultation, he prescribed pills containing morphia, rhubarb and calomel. The latter, also known as mercurous chloride, would treat Cook's syphilis and purge him as well. He arranged to have them sent over after they were prepared on Monday.

On Sunday, more broth was brought in for the patient's breakfast. The chambermaid sampled two tablespoons before taking it to Cook, who ate it and became violently sick. The chambermaid followed his example a half hour later, and spent the rest of the afternoon throwing up.[1]

On Monday, Dr. Bamford's pills arrived and the chambermaid placed the box on Cook's dressing table. Palmer visited Cook briefly that morning before hurrying off to London to settle his friend's bets from the Shrewsbury races. He returned around 10 that night, but before going to bed, he called on a surgeon by the name of Salt and bought three grains of strychnine.

Cook took his pills before going to bed. In the middle of the night, his screams rang through the inn. By the dim light of her flickering candle, the chambermaid found him in his bed, eyeballs bulging, beating his bedclothes with his arms stretched out. "I cannot lie down," he called out. "I shall suffocate if I do. Oh, fetch Mr. Palmer." His body went into spasms. He threw his head back against the pillow and rose again like a puppet on a string.

When Palmer entered the room, Cook cried out, "Oh, Palmer, I shall die." Palmer replied, "Oh, my lad, you won't," and left to fetch more pills. By the time he returned, Cook's facial muscles were so rigid that he could not swallow. The pills were forced down with a bit of toast and water on a teaspoon. Cook snapped at the spoon so hard that it was locked between his teeth. The mixture went down, and when he released the

---

[1] Servants were notorious for sneaking bits of their masters' food and drink, but this practice only becomes notable in murder cases. The servants of Scottish poisoner Edward Pritchard (1825-1865) also fell ill after surreptitiously sampling the food he wanted served, with fatal outcomes, to his wife and mother-in-law.

spoon, he swallowed a glass of dark liquid which smelled to the chambermaid like opium. He threw this up, but the pills stayed down. The spasms eased, Cook relaxed and then fell asleep.

The next day, a third doctor arrived. William Jones was Cook's friend, and the three medical men held a conference in the patient's room. Jones objected to giving the patient morphia, but after he left the room, Palmer and Bamford overrode the decision. They went to fetch more pills, but that evening, Palmer returned alone with them. At first, Cook refused to take them, but Palmer overcame his resistance.

The end was near. Cook tried to sleep but became nauseous. He threw up, but the pills stayed down. Ten minutes later, he complained of stiffness. About an hour later, he rang for the chambermaid, who found him in bed with Jones at his side. He asked for Palmer, and she crossed the road to fetch him. He arrived at the inn only minutes later, and said in Cook's room that he'd "never got dressed so quickly in his life." The suspicious nature of his remark was brought up at trial, as if to suggest that he knew what would happen.

After a brief examination, Palmer left the room. He encountered the chambermaid in the hall, who said that Cook looked as ill as he did the night before. Palmer said that was nonsense, Cook was not so ill by the fiftieth part.

He was right. Cook was much worse. Forty-five minutes later he died, with Palmer taking his pulse and his friend Jones listening at his chest for a heartbeat.

The matter could have ended there, except that Cook's stepfather, William Stevens, arrived in Rugeley two days later. He had seen Cook earlier that month and couldn't believe he'd fallen so sick so fast. What he found and heard made him suspicious.

Palmer's behavior didn't help matters. He had taken charge of the funeral arrangements and had ordered an expensive coffin, as if the sooner Cook was in the ground the better. He also contended that Cook's estate belonged to him because of the mortgage they had taken out on several race horses (it came out at the trial that this was another behind-the-back deal that

Palmer had executed by forging Cook's signature). As for Cook's betting book, Palmer said he didn't know where it was.

At Stevens' insistence, a post-mortem was held at the Talbot Arms. The objective was to collect a sample of the stomach contents and send it by wagon to Dr. Alfred Swaine Taylor in London. On behalf of his stepson, Stevens was calling in Britain's most eminent physician and author of the *Manual of Medical Jurisprudence*, a highly-respected treatise on poisons and medical forensics.

Palmer insisted on attending the autopsy, and, according to witnesses, tried to sabotage it. He bumped into an assistant carrying the stomach and its contents in a jar and succeeded in spilling some of it into Cook's body. The jar was then covered with two layers of animal skin and placed on a table against the wall. One of the doctors later noticed the jar had disappeared and asked who was responsible. Palmer admitted he had moved it to a more convenient location. An examination of the skins revealed two fresh slits, which no one admitted to making.

Later, Palmer sought out the postboy responsible for transporting the jar to London, and offered him £10 to upset the wagon and break it. The postboy refused. He did succeed in bribing the local postmaster to open letters to the doctors so he could keep an eye on the inquiry.

In the end, it would have been better if he had done nothing. Taylor found no evidence of poison, and said that the samples were so degraded that a second post-mortem was needed. The results again proved inconclusive, but Taylor concluded that Cook had been poisoned anyway. The jury at the inquest agreed and ruled that the "deceased died of poison wilfully administered to him by William Palmer." The doctor was headed for the dock.

With the newspapers publishing reams of fact and speculation about the case, public opinion was so strong against Palmer in Rugeley that Parliament passed a law moving the trial to London's Old Bailey. Without intending to, Palmer entered the history books, because it was the first time a case was moved as a result of pretrial publicity.

Not that it helped Palmer. His curious behavior during and after Cook's death and the state of the body — with its rigid muscles and *risus sardonicus* characteristic of strychnine poison — convicted him. After a half-hour's deliberation and a single vote, the jury found him guilty.

It can be argued whether Palmer received a fair trial. Nobody had ever been tried before for strychnine poisoning. There were no legal precedents to follow. There wasn't even a standard test for the poison.

The physical evidence against him was flimsy. Poison had not been discovered in Cook's body. The surgeon, Salt, testified that he had sold Palmer strychnine, believing it was for poisoning a dog, and neglected to record the sale as required by law. A second chemist who sold Palmer strychnine testified that he did the same thing. Taylor even admitted in court that he had never seen what strychnine did to the human body, "but I have written a book on the subject," he loftily concluded.

Without proof that Cook died from strychnine, the prosecution resorted to calling witnesses from another poisoning case. Eight years before, a pharmacist, Mr. Jones, filled a prescription for Mrs. Sergison Smith, a 35-year-old officer's wife recovering from a miscarriage. She had been prescribed willow bark mixed with orange peel, but the pharmacist had kept the willow bark next to the strychnine hydrochloride and had gotten them mixed up.

Mrs. Smith downed half a wine glass of the dose, winced and said it didn't taste like her usual medicine. Seventy-five minutes later, she died.

At the trial, witnesses described Smith's terrifying death, the contractions and spasms, the clenched teeth, her lucidity up until the end, all symptoms seen in Cook's death.

In response, the defense presented its expert witnesses, who testified that Cook had died of anything but poison. Tetanus, most likely. Possibly arachnitis. Maybe epilepsy. But there were too many deaths around the doctor.

Palmer died well. On June 14, 1856, nearly 30,000 spectators turned out to watch the execution at a portable gallows outside Stafford prison. Amid catcalls of "Murderer!" and "Poisoner!" the prison's governor asked him if he had poisoned Cook with strychnine.

"Cook did not die from strychnine."

"This is no time for quibbling — did you, or did you not, kill Cook?"

"The Lord Chief Justice summed up for poisoning by strychnine."

His last words were equally memorable. Before stepping on the trap door, he reported said, "Are you sure it's safe?"

As for Palmer's horses, six months before his date with the hangman, they were taken to Tattersall's where they were auctioned. His brood mare, Trickstress, was bought by Queen Victoria's husband, Prince Albert. The Chicken, the horse that failed him one too many times, was bought for 800 guineas and renamed Vengeance. It won the Cesarewitch Handicap that year.

As for the family's sole survivor, William Brookes Palmer grew up, became a solicitor, and lived in Surrey until his death in 1926 at age 76. According to his death certificate, he died of poisoning after the gas pipe had been left turned on in his room.

THE CHRISTIE CONNECTION

Agatha Christie drew her inspiration for her stories from everywhere — from the people she knew, the strangers she met, overheard snatches of conversation, the books she read — so it shouldn't be surprising that she would immerse herself in the true-crime literature.

Her many notebooks contain references to some of the most notorious murders of the past. The Constance Kent case, in which the governess was convicted of killing her younger half-brother and served 20 years, helped shaped *Nemesis* (1971) and *Elephants Can Remember* (1972), and ex-governess Vera Claythorne in *Ten Little Niggers/And Then There Were None* might have been based on her. The murders of Lizzie Borden's parents are mentioned in the notes for *Five Little Pigs* (1943), *They*

Do It With Mirrors (1952), and *Elephants*. The unsolved antimony poisoning of Charles Bravo helped inspire *Third Girl* (1966) and *By the Pricking of My Thumbs* (1968).

Christie's notes for *Styles* do not exist, if, in fact, they ever did. But in his history of strychnine, *Bitter Nemesis*, John Buckingham contends that there are similarities between the *Styles* and the Palmer case:

* The poisoning of Emily Inglethorp shares some similarities with the death of Cook. In both cases, a coffee pot was left unattended into which anyone could have slipped poison and both victims died in the middle of the night.

* Dr. Palmer and Dr. Bauerstein both raise suspicions by being found unexpectedly dressed in the middle of the night. Christie emphasizes this point by having Poirot note, "It is astonishing to me that no one commented on the fact."

* In both cases, a witness testifies that he sold strychnine to a person who said they needed it to kill a dog.

* Finally, in the Palmer case, a witness testifying about the death of Mrs. Sergison Smith said that the pharmacist who compounded the fatal dose raced to the house after he discovered his mistake. In *Styles,* Mr. Mace runs to Leastways Cottage when he learns that the strychnine he sold might have been used to poison Mrs. Inglethorp.

Without desiring to, William Palmer achieved an immortality that spread into some unusual directions. The publicity surrounding his trial popularized the idea of strychnine as a murder weapon. Charles Dickens dissected Palmer's character in an essay for his *Household Words,* becoming in essence the first criminal profiler. Golden Age mystery writer Francis Iles modeled the caddish husband on Palmer in his novel *Before the Fact* (1932), becoming what crime novelist Colin Dexter called "the father of the psychological suspense novel." And in what must be the greatest distance between inspiration and realization, Alfred Hitchcock turned Iles' novel into *Suspicion* and cast Cary Grant in the Palmer-inspired role.

The only people who didn't benefit from "the Rugeley Poisoner," it seems, were the inhabitants of Rugeley. The village

and Palmer were so strongly linked that a story arose, now de-
bunked, that a delegation from the town approached the prime
minister and asked for permission to change the name.

The prime minister considered their request and with a
smile replied that he would agree to the change if they named
the town after him.

The punch line is that the prime minister was Lord Palmer-
ston

Newsvendor -- 'Now, my man, what is it?'
Boy -- 'I vonts a nillustrated newspaper with a norrid murder and a likeness in it.'
(From *Punch*, 1845)

'Brave Little Belgium'

How a German General Inspired Hercule Poirot

"The word Belgium is considered to be the rudest word in the universe, and is completely banned in all parts of the Galaxy, except in one part, where they don't know what it means."
— Douglas Adams, *Hitchhiker's Guide to the Galaxy*

"Sprouts ... Phlegms ... Miserable Fat Belgian Bastards"
— Top three derogatory terms for Belgians,
Monty Python's Flying Circus

While Agatha Christie could not remember how she created Hercule Poirot, she knew why she made him Belgian. In her time, the little country played a far more noble role than the above punch lines would suggest. The former imperial power was a rallying cry whose suffering boosted British morale during the opening months of World War I.

The great chain of events began at Waterloo. After Napoleon was deposed for the second and final time in 1815, the European nations realigned themselves to take advantage of the power vacuum. For the next six decades or so, the Great Powers — Austria, Prussia, the Russian Empire, the United Kingdom, and, after it had finished its stint in the corner, France — would meet as needed to negotiate issues as a kind of forerunner to the United Nations. This system, the Concert of Europe, helped maintain the balance of power for awhile until growing political and economic rivalries caused it to fall apart. One of its achievements, the 1839 Treaty of London, would have serious consequences for Britain nearly 75 years later.

Once the Concert became less effective in maintaining the balance of power, Europe resumed killing each other. Russia battled France, Britain and the Ottoman Empire in the Crimea from 1853 to 1856. The Italian states successfully fought the Austrian Empire during several wars of independence from 1848 to 1866. For seven weeks in 1866, Austria and Prussia went to war, each backed by an array of German duchies, free cities, kingdoms, electorates and other small states. Austria lost, and in consequence Prussian Chancellor Otto von Bismarck founded the North German Federation.

These relatively short conflicts caused limited damage to the national economies and affirmed Carl von Clausewitz's definition of war as "merely the continuation of policy by other means." This same kind of thinking was followed in the run-up to World War I with disastrous consequences.

But to explain Belgium's role in World War I, we have to make one more brief side trip to visit the Franco-Prussian War. By 1870, Bismarck was leading the North German Federation and wanted to expand southward. France opposed Bismarck's move, making war inevitable. The result was a five-month campaign in which France was defeated and its government overthrown. Napoleon III fled to England — where he paused for awhile at Christie's hometown of Torquay — and the North German Federation expanded southward and rebranded itself as the German Empire under Kaiser Wilhelm I.

Not surprisingly, once this war was over, everyone began planning for a rematch. In 1873, Russia formed the League of Three Emperors with Germany and Austria-Hungary, but competition for influence over the Balkan states led to its dissolution four years later. Bismarck tried to keep Tsar Alexander

III from moving closer to France, but failed, and the Franco-Russian alliance was formed in 1894.

Germany found itself in a potential bind. If it went to war with France, it risked being attacked by Russia, and vice versa. While it had a powerful army, it wasn't large enough to take on both countries at the same time. A way had to be found to quickly defeat one army before the other could mobilize.

Count Alfred von Schlieffen, the chief of the German General Staff, devised in 1899 the plan that would bear his name. Seeing that the French army was focused on defending its border with Germany, he decided to invade through neutral Belgium, outflanking the French and threatening Paris. The French would be defeated quickly — as they had been in 1870 — and if Russia still decided to invade, the German army would have time to shift its forces eastward to counter the threat. Violating Belgian neutrality could draw the British into the war, but Germany didn't believe that they would sacrifice their men over a matter of principle. After all, Germany wouldn't.

By 1907, after numerous treaties and alliances, the balance of power was established between the Triple Alliance, consisting of Germany, Italy and Austria-Hungary; and the Triple Entente (from the French for "good will") of France, Russia and Great Britain. The rest of Europe, except for neutral Switzerland, sided with one group or the other. As for Belgium, the 1839 Treaty of London obliged it to remain neutral in return for being protected militarily by Britain, France, Prussia and other European nations.

THE BALLOON GOES UP

That was the situation in June 1914, when a fanatical Serbian youth assassinated the Austrian heir apparent, Archduke Franz Ferdinand, in Sarajevo. Seeing an opportunity to clip Serbian influence in the Balkans, the Austrians sought revenge. With the backing of Germany, Austria-Hungary sent a list of harsh demands to Serbia, which were rejected as intended. As Austria-Hungary prepared to invade Serbia, Russia mobilized, followed by Germany. While the diplomats continued to talk about peace, Europe prepared for war.

In late July, Germany informed Belgium that France would invade it and asked that it allow German forces to "intrude" on it first. Accusations and counter-accusations by each side that the other was going to invade flew for several days until Germany issued a final ultimatum to Belgium on Aug. 2, the same day its troops marched into Luxembourg.

Then England got involved, giving Germany an ultimatum of its own. This led to one of the key moments of the war. German Chancellor Theobald von Bethmann-Hollweg met with British ambassador Sir Edward Goschen in a last-ditch attempt to keep England neutral. Bethmann-Hollweg explained that it was a matter of life and death that Germany violate Belgium's neutrality. Sir Edward replied that it was a matter of life and death that Great Britain keep its promise to Belgium.

The argument grew heated as both sides kept returning to their original point. When Sir Edward reiterated that Britain could not abandon the London treaty, Bethmann-Hollweg exploded. "I ejaculated impatiently that, compared to the fearful fact of an Anglo-German war, the treaty of neutrality was only a scrap of paper," he wrote in his memoirs.

In a single stroke, Germany lost the moral high ground. Sir Edward leaked the "scrap of paper" remark, revealing the Germans as oathbreakers and sparking outrage in Britain and the United States.

On Aug. 4, Germany declared war on Belgium and France. The Belgian army fought heroically, but futilely. As each city fell, the looting began. Germany issued "war levies" of millions of francs on Belgian cities. Bank officials were forced to open their vaults for looting. Factories were dismantled and shipped home to Germany.

Violating neutrality earned the invasion the Rape of Belgium, but it was the reprisals against civilians, including mass executions, arson and theft that portrayed the Germans as bent on destroying European civilization. The Germans blamed the Belgians, saying that guerrilla fighters known as *francs-tireur*s ("free shooters") were shooting at their soldiers. The Belgians must be punished. When the German commander was killed at Aerschot, 400 buildings were torched and 156 civilians were shot, including the burgomaster and his son, who was accused of the killing. At Andenne and Seilles, German soldiers shot and axed to death 262 civilians and burned 200 buildings. At Tamines, 384 were killed. In Dinant, 674 were executed and 1,100 buildings burned.

The worst incident happened in Leuven. On the night of Aug. 25, a German detachment returning from the front lines came under fire. The Germans claimed it was guerrillas, but it was more likely nervous German sentries or a deliberate provocation.

Three nights of butchery followed. Soldiers shot civilians in the streets or sent them to the train station where they were executed or deported to work as forced laborers in Germany. Priests, suspected to be leading the revolt, were targeted. Buildings were set on fire, and families who took refuges in their cellars were roasted alive.

After three days, a quarter of the town was destroyed, and its population of 10,000 expelled. The university library was set on fire, destroying 300,000 volumes, including 800 medieval books and manuscripts.

In the west, particularly in neutral America, the image of cultured Germans, the heirs of Beethoven and Goethe, was transformed into villainous Huns bent on killing, looting and raping. While America would not enter the war until 1917, public sentiment began to sway against Germany.

UNITED BEHIND BELGIUM

In Britain, the issue of freeing Belgium united the nation. Even those who were suspicious of helping the French or getting involved in continental politics fell silent rather than appear to oppose helping "brave little Belgium." Charity organizations organized relief efforts, sending nurses and medical aid to help the wounded and refugees.

The image of Belgium as an oppressed victim carries a

hefty dose of irony. In the 1860s, Belgium joined Europe in the race to exploit Africa's resources by exploring the Congo. A European conference in 1884 resulted in the formation of the Congo Free State that would be privately owned by King Leopold II. Plundering the region's natural resources and brutal treatment of the natives followed. An estimated 10 million people died from war, disease and starvation under the king's rule. Outrage was worldwide. In 1908, Belgium took over control of the king's domain and renamed it the Belgian Congo.

The image of brutal imperial Belgium was swept away by the German invasion and the subsequent arrival of refugees into England. Nearly 250,000 of them entered England, an enormous influx second only to the Irish who fled the Great Famine (1845-1852). To give you an idea of the size of the exodus, an estimated 120,000 Jews entered England during the 19th century; 80,000 fled Nazi Germany during the 1930s, and about 70,000 more during World War II.

The government was ill-equipped to care for the deluge of refugees. The task fell to more than a thousand local committees that found food, shelter, clothing and employment for the refugees, assisted by the War Refugees Committee.

A WELCOME AT RHYL

Across the country, communities organized welcoming ceremonies for the refugees. One example of the "loving kindness and sympathy" for the Belgians that Christie mentioned in her memoirs took place in the Welsh coastal town of Rhyl. The local newspaper described "a memorable scene" of 200 people gathering at the railway station, with thousands more lining the streets, to await the arrival of the first train bearing the Belgians.

When the 22 refugees alighted from the Liverpool train, they were met with deafening cheers and fluttering Belgian flags. Speeches were made. The children were given bags of sweets. The group was escorted to a charabanc — a long coach with benches in the back — that would parade them through the streets to their lodgings. It must have been an overwhelming sight to people who, days before, had endured an invasion and the loss of their homes and country.

As Christie noted, the Belgians and Britons did not always get along. There were fears that the flood of able-bodied men would provide a pool of cheap labor. The reluctance of Belgian men to enlist, and as refugees they were not required to, led to resentment. By 1916, London's Metropolitan Police was keeping an eye on Belgian-owned cafes, suspecting them of encouraging immoral behavior and acting as meeting places for spies.

But unlike the anger directed toward, say, Eastern European Jews, the resentment toward Belgians was tempered by the knowledge that they did not intend to stay. The Belgians would return home as soon as the war was over, and by 1919, they did.

Belgium refugees welcomed at Rhyl.

An Army of Land Girls
Women Get a Taste of Freedom in Uniform

"My wife works regularly 'on the land'. She is up at five every morning to milk, and keeps at it steadily until lunchtime."
— John Cavendish, *Styles*

Dark green threads caught in a door bolt. A land armlet. A wife working "on the land."

The meaning of these phrases, which form a major subplot in *Styles*, are forgotten today. Yet they represent one of the many sea changes British society underwent during WWI, a time when women struggled with shifting gender roles, occupations and expectations.

In the late 19th century, the strictures that confined women to the roles of wife and mother began to loosen. Encouraged by changes in the culture, technology and medicine, women became freer to pursue the lives they wanted, the work they wanted, even the men — and sometimes the women — they wanted. Protesters sought the right to vote, access to contraception and to be allowed to enter the medical and other professions.

So what does this have to do with a few strands of green thread and a white land smock? It starts with a war, and what it takes to fight it.

Armies are expensive to form and supply. They require a lot of men. In peacetime, most nations relied on a core group of highly trained soldiers. When war was declared, they went through a process called mobilization, in which men were recruited, organized into units, trained, armed, equipped and sent to fight. In addition, additional soldiers were needed to provide support behind the lines.

When war was declared in 1914, Britain had less than a quarter-million men in the regular army, about half of them serving overseas to keep an eye on India, South Africa and the rest of the empire. Add to that the soldiers in reserve units, and you had, on paper at least, about 700,000 men. It sounds like a lot, but by the end of the war, more than five million men had served, one in four of all the adult males in Britain. Of that number, 886,000 were killed and 1.6 million were wounded.

So when you pull 5.3 million able-bodied men from their jobs and send them off to fight, you create an enormous strain on the economy. Businesses had to make do with fewer workers. Industries shifted to a war footing to supply the armies with munitions, food, uniforms and equipment. Families had to make do with fewer servants.

One woman wrote in 1916 that her chauffeur was called up and her butler fell ill: "I have a load of domestic worries but no doubt will weather the storm somehow! It is a gt. bore losing one's Butler, as somehow it is the last male servant one expected to be bereft of."

So who was going to do those millions of jobs? Britain turned to its women.

ENTER THE LAND GIRLS

Taking care of a farm requires performing a lot of tasks that have to be done without delay. A harvest has to be gathered when it's ready. A cow giving birth on Sunday can't be persuaded to wait until the office opens on Monday. And feeding the nation is literally a life-and-death matter.

As early as 1915, the farmers were feeling the effect of the war. Over 40,000 soldiers were sent into the fields to help bring in the harvest, but that was a temporary solution.

The following year, the Women's National Land Service Corps was formed to organize the training and assignment of volunteers. The rules were simple. The farms had to provide a cottage for the women to live in, but they had to be self-supporting since they would be paid little. This meant volunteers would be drawn from the middle and upper classes. Depending on their ability and knowledge, they could be sent directly to a family farm, or train for six weeks at a women's college or an agricultural college. Job boards were set up to match farmers with volunteers.

It soon became apparent that a more regularized scheme was needed, and in March 1917, the Women's Land Army was formed. During the war, it had recruited 30,000 volunteers, known as "Wiffs," and placed more than 11,000 women into farm jobs.

The WLA had to struggle for each recruit. The young, mostly sheltered volunteers learned quickly that farm life could be isolating and exhausting.

It wasn't just dealing with suspicious farmers and their wives, shocked at seeing women in uniforms that included jodhpurs and breeches. Propaganda novels such as *The Land Girl's Love Story* (1918), in which a London typist finds love amid romantic pastoral scenes, could not hide the reality of farming as a hard, backbreaking job that did not pay as well as factory work and was not as exciting as nursing.

In many ways, farming had not changed since medieval times. Nothing was mechanized. Animals had to be fed by hand. Fields were tilled by animals pulling plows. Fertilizing the fields with manure was a disgusting job, even if it did inspire English writer Rose Macaulay, who worked on a farm outside Cambridge, to flights of poetry:

SPREADING MANURE

There are fifty steaming heaps in the One Tree field,
Lying in five rows of ten.

They must all be spread out ere the earth will yield
As it should (and it won't, even then).

Drive the great fork in, and fling it out wide;
Jerk it with a shoulder throw.
The stuff must be even, ten feet on each side,
Not in patches, but level—so.

When the heap is thrown, you must go all round
And flatten it out with the spade.
It must lie quite close and trim, till the ground
Is like bread spread with marmalade.

The north-east wind cuts and stabs our breath;
The soaked clay numbs our feet.
We are palsied, like people gripped by death.
In the beating of the frozen sleet.

I think no soldier is so cold as we,
Sitting in the Flanders mud.
I wish I was out there, for it must be
A shell would burst, to heat my blood,

I wish I was out there, for I should creep
In my dug-out, and bide my bead.
I should feel no cold when they laid me deep
To sleep in a six-foot bed.

I wish I was out there, and off the open land:
A deep trench I could just endure.
But, things being other, I needs must stand
Frozen and spread wet manure.

Volunteer Mary Hillyer's experiences were representative of
many land girls. She joined the corps as an alternative to staying
at home with her parents in Somerset. She knew little about
agriculture, so she was sent to Sealham College. Her inexperi-

ence showed when she was asked to take the sow to the boar (to be impregnated). Tying a rope around the sow's neck, she walked her down to the Boar Hotel and left her in the stable. "I thought I'd done my job rather well," she recalled years later, "but when I came back, of course, there was an almighty row."

After graduation, Hillyer was assigned to an isolated farm in the southwest English county of Devon. She worked from five in the morning to nine at night, milking cows, feeding the cattle and harvesting mangel beets. She lasted six months.

Farm work was not only messy and mucky, it was dangerous. The April 1919 issue of *Landswoman* magazine noted the death of Marjorie Keye. "A pretty girl and only 19, she had been working on the land since early in 1916. On January 14th last, while in charge of a load of fodder, the horse she was riding bolted and she was thrown off, the wheel of the cart passing over her chest, killing her instantly, the whole terrible accident being witnessed by her brother, who happened to be passing at the time. She was laid to rest in the beautiful churchyard of her native village of Moulsoe, Bucks."

For those who served, the rewards were meager. Those who performed 240 hours of service could wear on their sleeve a green armlet with a red crown. But for many women, putting on the uniform created unique experiences and opportunities, and society noticed.

'IMMUNE FROM JEER OR SNEER'

"Quite half the feminine world must be in uniform now," the *Daily Express* described in 1918, "in offices, shops, railway companies, banks, acting, writing, driving taxis, ploughing the land, taming vicious horses, felling trees ... [dressed] in khaki, blue, brown, or grey, with slouch hat, round hat, or no hat at all, in skirts as short as ballet girls' or in masculine breeches."

Whether they worked for groups such as the Women's Land Army, the Volunteer Aid Detachment — the group Christie joined — or the female auxiliary units supporting the army, navy and air force — women experienced an unaccustomed response: respect. "A war-related uniform was an immediately recognizable emblem of patriotic engagement, of dedication to the nation's cause," historian Angela Woollacott writes. "To wear such a uniform was a statement at once political and moral."

For some women, the experience of wearing something other than Edwardian-era fashions, with its constraining corsets and long skirts that made walking difficult, was liberating. Writer Vita Sackville-West discovered putting on clothes "like the women-on-the-land were wearing" awakened her masculinity:

"In the unaccustomed freedom of breeches and gaiters I went into wild spirits; I ran, I shouted, I jumped, I climbed, I vaulted over gates. I felt like a schoolboy let out on a holiday." The experience of "that wild irresponsible day" inspired her that evening to begin an affair with her childhood friend, Violet Trefusis.

But each woman's experience in uniform was different. The Marchioness of Londonderry found that "some people were always rude to a woman in uniform … they were incredulous or laughed outright." But the writer Mary Agnes Hamilton found that "women wore trousers or knickers and puttees in perfect immunity from the guffaws that once greeted the brave spirits who had clambered upon bicycles in divided skirts; the lift-girl in smart boots, the driver of official car and public taxi in neat breeches and leggings, the munition girl and the land girl in trousers and overall were not so much remarked upon by anybody. They were in uniform: uniform was immune from jeer or sneer."

There was even room for patriotic jokes, such as this one printed in the *Daily Mail*: "The guard of the train by which the 'Wiffs' travelled Londonwards asked what particular kind of land work they did. 'We are fellers,' replied one of the party. 'And I thought you were young ladies,' said the guard with a chuckle."

But once the war was over and the men returned from battle, a woman in uniform was no longer tolerated. With millions of men returning to civilian life and looking for work — a situation Archie Christie experienced, and Agatha used in her second novel, *The Secret Adversary* (1922) — a woman in men's clothes sparked fears of gender-bending, or at least a challenge to masculine authority.

But for awhile, women played a critical role in keeping the agricultural economy running, and when Britain and Germany returned to war in 1939, the lessons learned from the Women's Land Army were not forgotten.

An Era Preserved

in Melancholy

'The Mysterious Affair at Styles' on Film

There is only one film adaptation of *The Mysterious Affair at Styles*. Fortunately, it was from the excellent *Agatha Christie's Poirot* series starring David Suchet as the Belgian detective.

The British TV show is noted for remaining faithful to the stories and taking pains to use authentic props and locations. This fidelity to Christie rewards viewers unfamiliar with how people lived in Britain at that time. To Americans used to large houses, fluorescent lights and central heat, seeing Styles Court with its crowded rooms and quiet, expansive lawns where its residents take tea and play tennis can feel as exotic as visiting Middle-Earth.

Screenwriter Clive Exton conveyed the high points of the novel while paring away unnecessary scenes and adding new ones. In a London hospital, Hastings passes the time recovering from his war wounds by watching newsreel footage of the fighting. The movie is silent. Only the sound of a projector being cranked by an orderly can be heard. There is no dialog. There is no need. The look on Hastings' face, the thousand-yard stare of a suffering man, says it all.

Exton also added moments to emphasize Poirot's characteristic self-confidence and habitual desire for order. In one scene, British soldiers moving through a forest and firing their rifles are interrupted by Poirot as he leads his fellow refugees on a nature walk. His lecture on the scarlet pimpernel, observing "that when this flower is open, it is a sign of a prolonged spell of fine weather. It is seldom seen open in this country" is a droll joke worthy of Christie.

Because it is set during World War I, as Britain moves from the Edwardian Age to the Roaring Twenties, *Styles* feels far more atmospheric than other *Poirot* episodes. Almost everyone speaks slowly and softly. The furnishings look drab and the rooms feel small, almost claustrophobic. The quiet is almost palpable. The men dress in jackets, ties and shirts with stiff tab collars. Mrs. Inglethorp dresses as if Victoria was still on the throne. The curtain of dust hanging in the air gives the scenes a canvas texture, as if they were paintings momentarily coming to life.

While the mystery is engaging, it seems almost secondary. For a debut novel by a young woman — Christie was 25 — *Styles* is unusually perceptive about the changing world it inhabits. Characters lament the passing of old-fashioned servants such as Dorcas, and how one has to hire a woman to get the gardening done. Christie grew up in a world similar to Styles Court, and while she moved on with the world, she missed it, and preserved it in her stories.

It's wrongheaded to believe that times were better than today. There were enormous class inequalities, prejudice, and men fighting and dying on distant battlefields — not to mention worse dentistry and food and hard, backbreaking labor — but it took place in a society that seems more comfortable with itself: civilized, relaxed, gracious and personal. Christie recognized that as well. That's why *Styles* captures that time with affection and regret.

But the best reason to appreciate the *Agatha Christie's Poirot* series is that it has managed to film nearly all of the stories featuring the Belgian detective. Suchet's performance as Poirot is so spot-on that even Christie might approve. Purists may argue against some of the producers' decisions, such as shifting the chronology of some of the stories and how they were rewritten for television. But their choices were made with the intention of remaining faithful to Christie's works. And with the filming of the last five episodes — including *Curtain* — there will exist a library of 69 episodes covering a major portion of Christie's canon. Any writer would be proud to see their work preserved with such fidelity.

Cast: David Suchet (Hercule Poirot); Hugh Fraser (Captain Hastings); Philip Jackson (Chief Inspector Japp); Beatie Edney (Mary Cavendish); David Rintoul (John Cavendish); Gillian Barge (Mrs. Emily Inglethorp); Michael Cronin (Alfred Inglethorp); Joanna McCallum (Evelyn Howard); Anthony Calf (Lawrence Cavendish); Allie Byrne (Cynthia Murdoch); Lala Lloyd (Dorcas)

Writer: Clive Exton

Director: Ross Devenish

Producers: LWT Productions, ITV Productions, Agatha Christie Ltd.

Locations: Chavenage House, Tetbury, Gloucestershire, England; Easton Grey, Wiltshire, England.

David Suchet, right, as Poirot and Hugh Fraser as Hastings.

The Quotable Styles

A collection of quotes from the novel and TV show of particular interest, arranged by subject.

DECEPTION
"I did not deceive you, *mon ami*. At most, I permitted you to deceive yourself." *Poirot*

DETECTION
"Yes, he is intelligent. But we must be more intelligent. We must be so intelligent that he does not suspect us of being intelligent at all."

I acquiesced.

"There, *mon ami*, you will be of great assistance to me." *Poirot*

"What have I always told you? Everything must be taken into account. If the fact will not fit the theory — let the theory go." *Poirot*

"Every murderer is probably somebody's old friend." *Poirot*

"When you find that people are not telling you the truth—look out!" *Poirot*

"I am not keeping back facts. Every fact that I know is in your possession. You can draw your own deductions from them." *Poirot*

"This affair must all be unravelled from within." He tapped his forehead. "These little grey cells. It is 'up to them' — as you say over here." *Poirot*

FLOWERS

"Another example of the English bucolic belief — *anagallis arvensis* — the scarlet pimpernel. It is believed that when this flower is open, it is a sign of a prolonged spell of fine weather. It is seldom seen open in this country." *Poirot (TV show)*

IMAGINATION

"You gave too much rein to your imagination. Imagination is a good servant, and a bad master. The simplest explanation is always the most likely." *Poirot*

INSTINCT

"Instinct is a marvelous thing. It can neither be explained nor ignored." *Poirot*

JEWS

"A tinge of Jewish blood is not a bad thing. It leavens the stolid stupidity of the ordinary Englishman." *Mary Cavendish*

MISS HOWARD

"There is nothing weak-minded or degenerate about Miss Howard. She is an excellent specimen of well-balanced English beef and brawn. She is sanity itself." *Poirot*

POIROT

"Madame Dainty, has it ever occurred to you to organize the goods by the country of origin?" Poirot (*TV show*)

"A little chap? As waves his hands when he talks? One of them Belgies from the village?" *An old man*

"I don't hold with foreigners as a rule, but from what the newspapers say I make out as how these brave Belgies isn't the ordinary run of foreigners, and certainly he's a most polite spoken gentleman." *Dorcas*

Poirot was an extraordinary looking little man. He was hardly more than five feet, four inches, but carried himself with great dignity. His head was exactly the shape of an egg, and he always perched it a little on one side. His moustache was very stiff and military. The neatness of his attire was almost incredible. I believe a speck of dust would have caused him more pain than a bullet wound. *Captain Hastings*

POISON
"There is altogether too much strychnine about this case."
Poirot

WOMEN
Hastings: What a wonderful girl. I shall never understand women.

Hercule Poirot: Ah, console yourself *mon ami*. Perhaps one day when this terrible war is ended, we shall work again together, and Poirot will explain it all to you. *Poirot (TV show)*

The

World

of

Agatha Christie

The Construction of *Styles*
Ambition, Poison, and a Really Bad Contract

On a brisk winter's day in January of 1921, a debut novel by an unknown writer appeared in the windows of London's bookstores. The dust jacket depicted a dramatic scene in a bedroom. A man holds a candle, a stunned expression on his face. With him are two women, while a second man behind them bends over something on a table.

Less than a fortnight later, a review of *The Mysterious Affair at Styles* appeared in the *Times Literary Supplement*. Although it found the story "almost too ingenious," it approved of "little M. Poirot, a retired Belgian detective" and the book overall:

"In spite of its intricacy the story is very clearly and brightly told. There is a good deal of human interest in it apart from the crime, and it has a very happy ending. It is said to be the author's first book, and the result of a bet about the possibility of writing a detective story in which the reader would not be able to spot the criminal. Every reader must admit that the bet was won."

In the end, *Styles* sold 2,000 copies from its 2,500 first-edition run, a respectable return on investment that affirmed the decision of the publisher, John Lane at The Bodley Head, to sign its author to a six-book contract.

If anyone was disappointed, it should have been the author. Agatha Christie, a 30-year-old married mother with one daughter, had signed the contract without reading that she wouldn't earn royalties until after the first edition of 2,500 copies sold out. That year, she received £25 — worth roughly $1,000 or £625 today — her half-share from selling the serialization rights to a newspaper.

She would not make that mistake again, and she would go on to write more than 80 books with an estimated sales worldwide of more than four billion copies. She would also leave her publisher over their cavalier treatment of a naive author.

But that was in the future. For the moment, she was content. She was £25 the richer and a published writer working on her next book.

THE EVOLUTION OF A WRITER

Christie had been telling stories ever since she was a child. She grew up at Ashfield, her family's large home on a 2-acre parcel on the edge of Torquay, a seaside resort town in southwestern England. With her two siblings at least a decade older, she was a precocious child, self-taught to read by age four and used to playing by herself or with the servants. She would make up stories as she played and tell them to herself as she wandered the walled kitchen garden, the woods, and the nearby fields of rural Devon.

Like many children of her class and time, before television, radio, movies and other distractions, Christie was exposed to a wide variety of literature. Her family library was well-stocked. There was the Bible, of course, and books by Shakespeare and Tennyson, but there were also complete sets of Charles Dickens, Anthony Trollope, George Eliot, Lord Bryon and Rudyard Kipling; bound volumes of *Cornhill Magazine, The Nineteenth Century* and *The Lady's Magazine*; poems by Oscar Wilde and plays by Arthur Wing Pinero.

The late 1890s and early 1900s was also a golden era for children's writers such as Evelyn Nesbit and Frances Hodgson Burnett, whose boys and girls went on marvelous adventures.

Agatha was a curious reader, and new words and unfamiliar locations would send her to the dictionary or atlas. Plenty of unfettered time to read, write and dream makes an ideal training ground for writers.

But her family's finances were shaky, and she would grow anxious over the possibility of being abandoned. At the age of seven, she wrote in her family's "Album of Confessions" that misery was "Someone I love to go away from me."

Sometimes, her imagination could overwhelm her, such as when she dreamed of the "Gun Man." Sometimes, he'd look like a colonial Frenchman with a uniform, powdered hair in a queue and a tri-cornered hat. Other times, he'd appear as a specter with murderer's eyes and stumps in the place of hands. Writing as Mary Westmacott in *Unfinished Portrait* (1934), Christie described the awful moment when, in the middle of a happy dream about a party or picnic, the face of a trusted, loving person — sometimes her mother or father — would change into the Gun Man. This anxiety, seemingly about the destructive power of love, would surface again and again in her writing.

In 1901, at age 11, Agatha's childhood ended. Her beloved father, who suffered from years of heart problems, died from complications of double pneumonia. Her mother, Clara, was devastated. She, too, suffered from mild heart problems. Agatha assumed the roles of companion and nurse, prepared to revive her mother with doses of brandy or sal volatile when her attacks came on at night.

As she grew older, Agatha began transferring her imagination onto paper. The year of her father's death, she won a prize for a poem about electric trams. She would continue her education: at home, at a Torquay school for girls for 18 months, then finishing school in Paris. Turning 17, Agatha accompanied her mother on a three-month visit to Egypt, where she danced with potential suitors at parties and visited ancient sites.

Then came one of those turning points in her life that she would recall in her memoirs. The next year, while she was confined to her bed with influenza, her mother, Clara, suggested writing a story to pass the time. She wrote "The House of

Beauty," about dreams and madness, and submitted it to magazines. More stories followed, usually inspired by whatever she was reading at the time. She wrote a novel, *Snow Upon the Desert*, drawing on her memories of her trip to Egypt. The woman who told stories to entertain herself was developing an ambition to tell them to others.

At her mother's suggestion, Agatha showed her work to a neighbor, the novelist Eden Phillpotts. His letters were honest and encouraging. He recommended books such as Thomas De Quincey's *Confessions of an English Opium-Eater* (1821), praised her ability to write convincing dialog and warned against moralizing, instead letting her characters' actions carry the theme. When she showed him *Snow Upon the Desert*, he offered to introduce her to his agent, Hughes Massie. While the meeting did not come off well — she was terrified of this "large dark swarthy man" — she was inspired by his recommendation that she abandon the novel and try again.

A SISTER'S CHALLENGE

In her early twenties, Agatha fell into an engagement with a family friend, Reggie Lucy. But her lukewarm interest faded in 1912 when Archibald Christie, a soldier with ambitions to be a pilot, danced with her at a house party. A few weeks later, he unexpectedly rolled up at Ashfield on his motorcycle and was invited to stay for supper. They exchanged books and met for tea. It was a civilized courtship, but he wanted her and wasn't shy about saying so, and they were soon engaged.[1]

Agatha and Archie wanted to get married, but Clara held her daughter back until Archie could earn enough to support a wife. He joined the Royal Flying Corps and spent much of his time with his squadron. Adjusting to a long-distance courtship was not easy for either partner. For the next 18 months, the

---

[1] Christie coincidentally had motorcycles in common with her future rival on the mystery scene, Dorothy L. Sayers. Early in her writing career, Sayers had an affair with a man on a motorcycle. Both relationships came to a bad end: divorce and scandal in Christie's case, a baby out of wedlock in Sayers'.

couple alternated between engagement and estrangement.

It took a war to settle matters. The outbreak of hostilities sent Agatha and Archie to the altar on Christmas Eve 1914. While he was in France flying planes into battle, the newly minted Agatha Christie stayed at Ashfield with her mother and joined the Volunteer Aid Detachment. She worked as a nurse at a hospital in Torquay, taking care of wounded soldiers, then moved in 1916 to the dispensary, mixing drugs and beginning her education in poisons that would prove so useful throughout her life.

Dispensary work gave her plenty of time to think, and her thoughts turned to writing a novel, in particular a mystery. Edgar Allen Poe had kicked off the genre with short stories such as *The Murders in the Rue Morgue* (1841) and *The Purloined Letter* (1844). Wilkie Collins scored successes with his detective novels *The Woman in White* (1859) and *The Moonstone* (1868). But it was Arthur Conan Doyle's Sherlock Holmes stories that really captured the imagination of the reading public. Crime permeated the culture of the Victorian era. Newspapers attracted and entertained readers with crime stories. Murderers such as William Palmer, Madeline Kent, Thomas Neill Cream, Florence Maybrick and Jack the Ripper became as familiar to the public as politicians and entertainers.

By picking the mystery genre, Christie was also indulging in a bit of sibling rivalry. Christie's sister, Madge, was not only a writer herself, but had introduced Agatha to these stories as a child. She told Agatha the plot of Anna Katharine Green's *The Leavenworth Case* (1878), and the story became one of Agatha's favorites. They steeped themselves in the genre, at a time when it was still possible to do so. They would debate the merits of the stories.

During a discussion of Gaston Leroux's *The Mystery of the Yellow Room* (1908), Agatha said she could write a story just as good.

"I don't think you could do that," Madge said. "They are very difficult to do. I've thought about it."

"I should like to try."

"Well, I bet you couldn't."

It was an joshing remark, not seriously meant. But Christie remembered it as an important moment in her life. It fired in her a determination to prove her sister wrong.

THE ROAD TO STYLES COURT

Now, in the quiet of the dispensary, between filling prescriptions, Christie turned the idea over in her mind. Rather than wait for inspiration, she approached her story in a methodical fashion, asking herself questions and finding the answers.

First, how to kill? Poison was the obvious method. She devised an appropriately mysterious method of introducing it into the victim, then turned to her cast of characters. Her limited life experience dictated what she called "an *intime* murder," set within a family, and she imagined a country house similar to the one she grew up in and knew well. She picked the victim and the villain. Unlike Sayers' decision to create the aristocratic Lord Peter, Christie stayed firmly within her social class. The closest to the aristocracy she would get in her first book would be Mrs. Inglethorp's mention of writing "the Princess," Lady Tadminster, and the Duchess to invite them to her charity events.

Down the list she went, assembling the pieces of her story. The appearance in the neighborhood of a couple — the man obviously younger than his wealthy wife and sporting an impressively sinister black beard — inspired the creation of Emily and Alfred Inglethorp. She learned not to rely on one person for a character, but to assemble a mosaic of impressions. She began talking the story out to herself, just as she had done as a child.

When she was ready, she began handwriting each chapter. Then she dug out Madge's typewriter and typed a second draft. She liked dreaming up her story, less so getting it down properly on paper. Then, she encountered a rough patch by the middle of the book, as her story grew more complicated and with the end not in sight.

Her mother suggested a solution: go to a hotel for her two-week holiday where she could write without being disturbed. Christie agreed and settled in at the Moorland Hotel in Dartmoor. Her schedule was unvaried: she'd write in the morning, read a book by herself at lunchtime, then walk the moors talking out the next day's work. Clara's suggestion worked. By the time she returned to Torquay, she carried with her a draft of *The Mysterious Affair at Styles.* She continued working at it, she recalled decades later in *An Autobiography* (1977), until "It was roughly as I had intended it to be, but I didn't see just how *I* could make it better, so I had to leave it as it was."

For better or for worse, *Styles* was ready to face the publishers.

SELLING *STYLES*

Publishing is a game of winners and losers. Every editor has at least one story of The One That Got Away. Nearly every best-seller has been rejected at least once. Editors learn to shrug off the missed opportunities and look forward to the next winner.

Still, it must have pained the publishers at the houses that rejected *Styles* — including notable names such as Methuen and Hodder and Stoughton — to reflect on what they had passed up. It must be especially galling since the debut Christie did not change very much from the mature Christie at the height of her powers. Her first attempt was rough in places, and the solution was too complex. But her talent for plotting and characterization were on display from the start. It would only get better.

Christie finished *Styles* in 1916 and the manuscript began making its rounds. While she waited, her life grew intensely busy. The war ended in 1918. Archie was transferred to the Air Ministry in London, and for the first time in four years, Agatha was living with her husband.

While Archie endured the emotional fallout of the war — he had fought well and earned several decorations — he needed to adjust to civilian life with his wife. Agatha got pregnant, endured nine months of morning sickness, and gave birth to their daughter, Rosalind, at Ashfield in August 1919.

By this time, Christie saw herself more as a wife and mother than as a writer. Then her life changed again. Soon after Rosalind's birth, and nearly two years after receiving the manuscript, John Lane at The Bodley Head — the name a reference to the bust of Sir Thomas Bodley that was mounted above the publisher's door — wrote to Christie with an offer to publish *Styles.*

After signing the contract, she was asked to rewrite parts of the book. Lane made several minor suggestions, but what concerned him most was the ending, which had Poirot delivering the solution to the mystery while testifying in court. Christie had no experience with legal proceedings and it showed. She rewrote it so that Poirot gathered the suspects in a room and ran through the clues, building suspense as first one person is accused, then another, before — like a magician — he reveals the murderer. Without intending to, she had created an enduring mystery trope. It would not be her last.

With the publication of *Styles* in the U.S. in October 1920, Christie's journey to literary success had begun.

'An Extraordinary
Looking Little Man'

How Christie Assembled Hercule Poirot

Even today, nearly a century after he collided into Captain Hastings outside Styles St. Mary's post office, Hercule Poirot remains one of the world's more ridiculous detectives: a short Belgian with tiny feet, an egg-shaped head, a compulsive lover of order who mangles the English language and raves about the power of his "little grey cells." A man so obsessive about his appearance that even Hastings said "a speck of dust would have caused him more pain than a bullet wound."

If that weren't improbable enough, he was created, fully formed, by a tall, untidy, eccentrically educated Englishwoman in her mid-twenties.

Christie began writing *Styles* in 1916 when she was working as a Volunteer Aid Detachment nurse at a hospital dispensary in Torquay. The major decision Christie faced was what kind of detective she wanted, and she pursued the question in a methodical manner. He had to be different from Sherlock Holmes, but still intelligent and good at his job. He must be able to mingle with all classes and travel, so he should not be a policeman. Christie split the difference, giving Poirot the detecting skills he learned on the police force, then retiring him to give him the freedom to move about as needed. His enormous ego, his foreignness — which would excuse outrageous behavior — backed by his widespread reputation, opened doors everywhere.

Whereas Holmes and most other detectives were serious, Christie struck a difference by making hers comic, starting with his appearance. He was a caricature, with his short height — at five foot four inches, he was three inches below the average World War I soldier — his ovoid head and his tiny feet. As an older, retired policeman, he was denied a youthful sexiness and strength. Comically egocentric about his powers of deduction, he babbles excitedly in fractured English phrases such as "triple pig!"

As for his nationality, Christie was inspired by the mystery genre she knew intimately. A voracious reader since she childhood, she particularly favored mysteries, many of them featuring French detectives such as Edgar Allan Poe's C. Auguste Dupin and Gaston Leroux's Joseph Rouletabille. In fact, Leroux's *The Mystery of the Yellow Room* (1908) was one of her favorites, and Rouletabille's suspicion of the value of material clues was an attitude Christie gave to her detectives.

But Christie chose to make her detective Belgian out of respect for the thousands of refugees in Torquay who fled the German invasion of their country at the outbreak of World War I. The image of the tiny, gallant nation resisting the Huns inspired a wave of patriotism, and many English woman, including Christie's favorite novelist, May Sinclair, traveled to Belgium to help the wounded and refugees.

Christie's decision also gave her an advantage in plotting her stories. Given England's xenophobia about foreigners, making Poirot Belgian denied him the romanticism of the French and the threatening Teutonic authority of the German, but made him safe to associate with and even condescend to. Behind the mask of the comic foreigner, Poirot could safely observe the people around him and ask questions without raising suspicions, until the moment when he brought the suspects together and revealed who did it.

As for personal habits, Christie looked at her somewhat messy life and decided to make him pick up after himself. "I could see him as a tidy little man, always arranging things, liking things in pairs, liking things square instead of round," she wrote in *An Autobiography* (1977). In fact, it would be this habit of keeping everything around him in order that would help him discover the killer of Mrs. Inglethorp.

As for his name, Christie's choice of Hercule, a Gallicized form of Hercules, was not only amusing when applied to the diminutive detective, but also recalls Marie Belloc Lowndes and her French detective Hercules Popeau, and G.K. Chesterton's criminal-turned-detective Hercule Flambeau. The origins of Poirot's last name, however, have been forgotten. While Popeau is close to Poirot, one critic points out that the French-speaking Christie could have been inspired by *poireau*, for leek (as well as wart), or *poire*, for pear-shaped.

Throughout his career, Poirot would be revered by every-one who knew his true worth, such as Detective-Inspector Japp in *Styles*. Everyone, that is, except Christie. While one of her two official biographers said there is no "official evidence" for this belief, there's no doubt Christie took to insulting him to her agent and friends as "insufferable" and "a detestable, bom-bastic, tiresome, ego-centric little creep." In *An Autobiography*, she lamented bringing him in so late in her well-regarded coun-try-house mystery *The Hollow* (1946), saying it "ruined" the at-mosphere she had worked so hard to establish. She even paro-died Poirot. Her mystery-writing alter ego, Ariadne Oliver, writes books about a vegetarian Finnish detective, Sven Hjerson, whom she particularly dislikes but can't get rid of be-cause he was too popular. "If I met that bony gangling vegeta-ble-eating Finn in real life," Oliver says in *Mrs. McGinty's Dead* (1952), "I'd do a better murder than any I've ever invented."

Besides, what are we to make of the fates of Christie's two great detectives? At the end of *Sleeping Murder* (1976), Miss Marple lives, smiling and looking out over Torbay from the terrace of the Imperial Hotel. But in *Curtain* (1975), Poirot ended up where he began: at Styles Court. There, while investigating his last case, he died of natural causes. *The New York Times* reported it on its front page, the first and, still, only fictional character so honored.

Hercule Poirot Is Dead; Famed Belgian Detective

By THOMAS LASK

Hercule Poirot, a Belgian detective who became internationally famous, has died in England. His age was unknown.

Mr. Poirot achieved fame as a private investigator after he retired as a member of the Belgian police force in 1904. His career, as chronicled in the novels of Dame Agatha Christie, was one of was one of the most illustrious in fiction.

At the end of his life, he was arthritic and had a bad heart. He was in a wheelchair often, and was carried from his bedroom to the public lounge at Styles Court, a nursing home in Essex, wearing a wig and false mustaches to mask the signs of age that offended his vanity. In his active days, he was always impeccably dressed.

Mr. Poirot, who was just 5 feet 4 inches tall, went to England from Belgium during World War I as a refugee.

Continued on Page 16, Column 1

Illustrated London News and Sketch, Ltd.
Hercule Poirot, painted in the mid-1920's by W. Smithson Broadhead.

Murder on the English Riviera

Christie's Roots in Devon

"I begin to think of Devon, of red rocks and blue sea. It is lovely to be going home."

— *Come, Tell Me How You Live*

It was a plot twist worthy of a Christie story when her mother's decision to disobey her husband meant that she became Britain's Queen of Crime rather than America's.

Where she ended up was, as Wellington said about Waterloo, a near-run thing. Her father, Frederick Miller, was a native New Yorker who enjoyed, as Laura Thompson described in her biography of Christie, "a Swiss education, a Frenchman's worldliness [and] an English sense of protocol." After he married Clara Boehmer, they had their eldest daughter, Madge, in Torquay. The next year, they moved to America to be closer to his grandfather and to oversee the income from his inheritance and his partnership in a business. That's where they had their son, Monty.

Their return to Torquay, however, was intended to be a temporary move. They were only going to stay a year or so, while Frederick returned to America to oversee his investments. In the meantime, he asked Clara to rent a place while he was gone.

When he returned, he found himself the owner of Ashfield. After looking at a number of houses, Clara had decided on the large villa on the edge of town. But the owner wanted to sell Ashfield, not rent it, so Clara took her inheritance and bought it. Once he was over his surprise, the genial Frederick agreed to stay.

Part of the reason was that he had come to like Torquay. The port at the time was a refined watering spot that catered to the wealthy. Napoleon III, in exile after losing the Franco-Prussian War in 1870, had stayed at the Imperial Hotel, and poet Elizabeth Barrett Browning had taken the waters in an attempt to restore her health. Torquay was so genteel and re-fined that it infuriated the morally upright Rudyard Kipling, who described it as full of "villas, clipped hedges, fat old ladies with respirators and obese landaus" that made him want to dance through it "with nothing on but my spectacles."

The beauty of the resort port was matched by its surround-ings. In some respects, the Devon countryside resembles the south of France more than the rest of England. Located in the southwestern part of Britain, it enjoys clement weather from the effects of the warm waters from the North Atlantic Drift, with occasional hot spells and mild winters with snow in the higher elevations. Tropical plants grow there that are found nowhere else in Britain.

Then there was Ashfield. To Agatha, its 2-acre grounds was like Wonderland: vast, strange and welcoming to an imaginative child. It boasted a walled kitchen garden, a lawn with a variety of trees — beeches, cedars, firs and a strange, sticky resinous tree Agatha called "the Turpentine Tree" — and a small ash wood leading to the tennis court and croquet lawn. Beyond, the fields and lanes of rural Devon invited exploring. Later in life, she described Ashfield as "my background, my shelter, the place where I truly belong."

Because her much-older brother and sister were away at boarding school most of the time, she occupied herself playing with the servants, reading from her family's vast library and roaming happily in the gardens, making up stories for her private amusement.

As she grew up, Agatha became aware of the world outside her home. She developed a connection to the church, All Saints, after her father had contributed money in her name to its construction. Not only was Agatha baptized there, but she was listed as one of the church's founding members, which delighted her.

Torquay's status as a resort town provided plenty of opportunities for entertainment. There was the theater, which sparked her love of drama that would lead her to write her plays. Dances were held under the copper-colored domes of the Pavilion on the seafront. Cricketers in their white flannel uniforms played matches at the Torquay Cricket Club, where her father officiated matches. "I was extremely proud of being allowed to help my father with the scoring and took it very seriously," she recalled in her memoirs.

Then there was the annual Torquay Regatta. The Miller family would spend the day watching the boat races from Haldon Pier and enjoying the fireworks at night. At the regatta's fair, Agatha would ride the merry-go-rounds, watch her brother Monty shy coconuts at targets for prizes and collect small fluffy monkeys on long pins that she would stick in her coat. Her parents would throw house parties that Agatha couldn't attend, but she would watch the preparations from the periphery.

Then there were the garden parties where guests were served fruit-flavored ices, grapes, nectarines, peaches and cream cakes. The older people who could afford it would ride carriages, while the young people would walk as far as two miles, in their best clothes, in order to attend.

It was not a perfect life — her father's death in 1901, when Agatha was 11, devastated the family personally and financially — but Devon retained its hold on her imagination. As it changed through the years, her memories of it would grow even more magical.

Soon, Devon would show up in her books. The Imperial Hotel, where she attended tea dances, would be renamed the Majestic and show up in *Peril at End House* (1932) and *The Body in the Library* (1942). It would appear under its own name in *Sleeping Murder* (1976). One of her favorite bathing spots, Elberry Cove, became the scene of Sir Carmichael Clarke's death in *The ABC Murders* (1936).

Torquay under various names would be the setting for *Three Act Tragedy* (1934) (as Loomouth) and *Evil Under the Sun* (1941) (as St. Loo). The train that took her to and from London would be immortalized in *Mystery of the Blue Train* (1928) and *The ABC Murders*.

Christie also drew on Devon and its environs for character and place names: Narracott in *The Sittaford Mystery (1931), And Then There Were None* (1939) and *Sleeping Murder*); Dittisham in *Five Little Pigs* (1943); Luscombe Road in *At Bertram's Hotel* (1965); and Barton Road in *The Moving Finger* (1942) and *Sparkling Cyanide* (1945).

The year 1938 would mark a change in Christie's relationship with Devon. The area around Ashfield was becoming crowded with developments with the nearby larger homes knocked down or converted into nursing homes. Her husband, Max Mallowan, whom she married in 1930, didn't like the place, and her daughter, Rosalind, was no longer a child. She decided to sell Ashfield.

In the meantime, she had fallen in love with Greenway, an 18th century Georgian mansion with 30 acres of gardens, a battery with a pair of 18th-century cannons, and a boathouse on the River Dart. She rarely, if ever, wrote there. Instead, it was a place where she could be Mrs. Mallowan, walking the trails amid gardens and woods, playing host to family and friends, and visiting the shops as just another member of the community.

Inevitably, the new house began to appear in her fiction. *Five Little Pigs* would be set there. In *Dead Man's Folly* (1956), the strangled body of Marlene Tucker would be found in the boathouse.

But, as Thompson laments in her biography, the Torquay

of Agatha Christie's time no longer exists. Ashfield fell under the bulldozer in her lifetime, despite her attempts to buy it back. The Pavilion where dances and concerts were held, where Archie Christie proposed to her, is now a shopping mall. Girls in long skirts and voluminous hats no longer skate on the Princess Pier. The young Agatha who sought pleasure there, Thompson writes: "... would have doubted Miss Marple's creed — that 'the new world was the same as the old,' that 'human beings were the same as they had always been' — when she saw the holidaymakers and their urgency for sensation, their burgers belched into the sun and their bottles swung like lances."

So when Christie died, she chose to be buried at St. Mary's Church in Cholsey, near Winterbrook, her final home. Perhaps it was because the area reminded her of the Devon hills she roamed as a girl.

Not that Torquay minded. Despite being described in *Postern of Fate* (1973) as "a has-been if ever there was," it has capitalized on its connections. The Agatha Christie Mile shows visitors the places touched by her in person or in her books. Since 2006, the weeklong annual Agatha Christie Festival in September features tours, talks, plays, river cruises and other events.

And Greenway still stands, now owned by the National Trust. Visitors can stay in its cottages, even on the home's second floor, and experience life there as Christie lived it.

DEVON IN FICTION

Here are some of the stories that use Devon, Torquay, Greenway and other area locations:

Ashfield garden: *Postern of Fate*

Burgh Island: *And Then There Were None (1939), Evil Under the Sun* (1941)

Dartmoor: *The Big Four* (1927), *The Sittaford Mystery*

Devon: *Cards on the Table* (1936), *Double Sin* (1961)

Elberry Cove: *The ABC Murders*

Greenway: *Five Little Pigs, Dead Man's Folly*

Imperial Hotel: *Peril at End House* and *The Body in the Li-*

brary (as the Majestic), *Sleeping Murder*

    Kents Caverns: *The Man in the Brown Suit* (1924)

    Salcome and Kingsbridge Estuary: *Towards Zero* (1944; as Saltcreek village and Saltington)

    Torquay: *Peril at End House* (as St. Loo), *Three Act Tragedy* (as Loomouth, near Torquay), *Mrs. McGinty's Dead* (1952; as Cullenquay), *Ordeal by Innocence* (1958; as Redquay), *Postern of Fate* (as Hollowquay), *The Rose and Yew Tree* (1948) and *Evil Under the Sun* (as St. Loo), *Sleeping Murder.*

'Fat Ikey' and Noisy Negroes

The Mystery of Christie's Racial Attitudes

"A tinge of Jewish blood is not a bad thing. It leavens the stolid stupidity of the ordinary Englishman."
— Mary Cavendish, *The Mysterious Affair at Styles*

"I think people should be interested in books, *and not their authors!"*
— Agatha Christie

Was Agatha Christie racist and anti-Semitic?

It's an inescapable question. At some point in one of her books, she'll describe a Jew, Italian, Chinese, Arab or a member of some other race, ethnic group, or religion with words and descriptions that explode like landmines. Books where Chinese are referred to as "heathen" and Italians as "dagos." Passages that affirm cultural stereotypes, such as French people who go into hysterics over every little incident or that Jews are exceptionally sound with money.

Sometimes, the references will seem puzzling. Lord Catherham in *The Seven Dials Mystery* (1929) complains, "I don't get on with Canadians — never did. Especially those who have lived much in Africa." Who dislikes Canadians? Or when the young man in *The Body in the Library* (1942) chastises his girl-friend who "lets a disgusting Central European paw her about." Then there's *Death in the Clouds* (1935), with its jaw-dropping moment when the lovers bond over their mutual dislike of "loud voices, noisy restaurants and negroes."

Some of these can be written off as an observant author reflecting the way people talk in her day. Other passages imply much darker beliefs, like the respectable financier in *The Secret of Chimneys* (1925) — with a knighthood, no less — being described as having "a fat yellow face, black eyes, impenetrable as a cobra's, and a generous curve to the big nose" and referred to as "Noseystein" and "Fat Ikey."

Of all the races and religious groups in Christie's books, Jews hold a unique position. Jewish characters show up in 23 of her novels and stories, robed in their threadbare tropes and descriptions. If they have money, they're financiers, bankers, scholars and solicitors. If they're poor, they're peddlers, or agents of international conspiracies. They're sharp with money, have great artistic judgment and never forgive an enemy.

Over and over, they're described as having curved, hooked or fleshy noses, black eyes and shiny faces. Their hair is frequently greasy. If they're beautiful, it's of the exotic type. In the 1930s short story *The Gypsy*, Esther Lawes is described as "six foot one of Jewish perfection" with "the marble whiteness of her face with its delicate down-drooping nose and the black splendor of her eyes and hair."

What are we readers to make of this?

The answer is complicated. Christie never spoke publicly about her racial attitudes, and the clues found in her books is colored by the complicated motives that drive authors to create their stories. Apart from a few personal anecdotes, her words are all we have.

So let's review the evidence, look at the most common explanations her defenders have used, and, like Hercule Poirot, use our "little grey cells."

SHE WAS A PRODUCT OF HER TIMES

The argument: Christie grew up in the Edwardian period, when anti-Semitism was in the air. She absorbed the prejudices of her time unthinkingly, but never seriously believed it.

Britain's relationship with the Jews has swung widely over the years. King Edward I expelled them in 1290. Oliver Cromwell readmitted them in the 1650s. Except for occasional outbreaks of violence, they experienced nothing on the scale of the pogroms in the late 19th century in Eastern Europe that caused a wave of refugees to find themselves on the shores of warm beer and cold shoulders.

But beginning in the 1880s, Tsar Alexander III's anti-Semitic policies and massive pogroms encouraged millions of Jews to emigrate. More than 140,000 of them arrived in England and settled in the major cities, particularly London, Manchester, and Leeds. Their arrival sparked uneasiness in English hearts that grew into full-blown xenophobia. To the monocultural English, the Middle and Eastern Europeans were an alien race. They looked different, used an incomprehensible language, celebrated different holidays and, in general, did not act British.

At the time, emigrating to England was easy: Step off the boat, register with the nice man at the desk, maybe receive an Anglicized name and find a bit of floor space in the nearest tenement. But the flood of unwashed hordes yearning to breathe the free air of Britain led to growing support for immigration restrictions that resulted in 1905 with the passage of the Aliens Act, which for the first time imposed immigration controls — particularly for Jews.

The law received support from nearly every level of society. The Socialists favored it because they suspected Jews would work hard to become capitalists and leech off the working classes like the pure-blooded English businessmen. The working classes backed it because they thought Jews were taking their jobs. Even the Jewish establishment — which wasn't crazy about the law — wanted to show they could act just as English as anyone. They were even willing to make a deal to ship back

Jews fleeing the pogroms in Russia and Poland.

Paradoxically, even while under suspicion, Jews were gaining legal rights and growing successful. In 1874, Benjamin Disraeli became prime minister. London elected its first Jewish mayor in 1885. Jewish politicians were taking their seats in Parliament. By 1890, the legal barriers in public and professional life had fallen.

Only the prejudices stayed. Jews were loyal to their religion before their country and hence not to be trusted. Rich Jews were capitalists who controlled the press and major industries and started wars for profit. Poor Jews were either anarchists intent on blowing up society or working hard to become capitalists. If that reasoning seems contradictory, you're right: Cognitive dissonance is a hallmark of bigotry.

The resentment grew worse during World War I. By this time, there were tens of thousands of Russian Jews living in London, and they had no desire to fight on the same side as the Tsar. As resident aliens, they were not eligible for conscription, which spurred further resentment.

This was the society Agatha Christie grew up in, and her books reflected England's suspicion of the foreigner.

Whether this is true or not, her success came with a price. Her books did not just reflect anti-Semitic beliefs, they efficiently polished them as well. Christie's ability to write an entertaining mystery made the expression of her prejudices equally compelling and readable. Her success exposed more people to her unsavory characterizations. *The Seven Dials Mystery* (1929) described the "opulent Jewesses" who inhabit the sleazy nightclubs of Soho. *The Mystery of the Blue Train* (1928) featured Boris Ivanovitch Krassnine, the rat-faced son of a Polish Jew described as having "the least hint of a curve to the thin nose." In *Blue Train*, when Poirot comments to Demetrius Papopolous that "your race does not forget," this exchange takes place:

"A Greek?' murmured Papopolous, with an ironical smile.

"It was not as a Greek I meant," said Poirot.

There was a silence, and then the old man drew himself up proudly.

"You are right, M. Poirot," he said quietly. "I am a Jew. And, as you say, our race does not forget."

Christie's ignorance about Jews reaches its apogee in *The Secret of Chimneys* (1925) which one commentator said contains "more racist comments than any other book." with her creation of financier Sir Herman Isaacstein, a name designed to be so obviously Jewish that he might as well be called Sir Jewey McJewishstein. The name might have been inspired by the popular 1916 song "Sergeant Solomon Isaacstein," subtitled "the only Yiddish Scotsman in the Irish Fusiliers."

Even late in life, she continued to define people by their nationality. In her memoirs, she described Syrians as "simple people" who knew how to enjoy life, "who are idle and gay, and who have dignity, good manners, and a great sense of humor, and to whom death is not terrible." And when it came to a nanny for her daughter, she thought French women were "hopeless disciplinarians," Germans "good and methodical," and the Irish "gay and made trouble in the house." She preferred Scottish helpers.

But the picture of Christie as an anti-Semite — even of the less-poisonous type observed by Harold Abrams in the movie *Chariots of Fire* as always "on the edge of a remark" — should be tempered with how and why Christie created her characters. Then, in her defense, we should consider the portrait of the Levinne family she created as Mary Westmacott in *Giant's Bread* (1930).

But first, let's look at how Christie the writer used race.

CHRISTIE WROTE IN STEREOTYPES

The argument: Christie was not interested in creating characters with depth and distinction. The puzzle always came first: who is the killer, how did he or she do it, and how can Poirot, or Miss Marple, or Inspector Battle prove it? She worked with stereotypes that were instantly familiar to her readers such as reverent vicars, gregarious pub owners, bluff retired majors, vulgar businessmen, egotistical actors, ne'er-do-well young men, flighty maids and stolid butlers. To Christie, the characteristics attributed to Jews, Arabs, Italians, Chinese and other races and religions were simply cards in her deck of characters, to be reshuffled and dealt for each story. Relying on stereotypes made it easier to deceive readers by using their prejudices against them.

Christie wrote to entertain and to make money. She was not interested in advocating for a cause or creating high art. She admired literary writing, but she knew her limits. "If I could write like Elizabeth Bowen, Muriel Spark or Graham Greene," she wrote, "I would jump to high heaven with delight, but I know I can't."

From the beginning, with the sinister Dr. Bauerstein in *Styles,* Christie knew that Jewish characters made useful red herrings. They may be alien, they may act furtively, they may even be communists — such as Oliver Manders in *Murder in Three Acts* (1934) — but they weren't killers (Manders, in fact, turns out to be the romantic lead, and ends the book engaged to the aristocratic "Egg" Lytton Gore!). Even in her thrillers, she might have Jewish characters plotting to destroy civilization, but they act only as individuals, not as a group. She did not fall back on the typical Jewish-dominated conspiracies with communists or Freemasons, unlike other writers of her time.

We see the same sinister characterization in *A Murder is Announced* (1950) but with an odd twist. Christie creates Mitzi the cook, a woman from "Mittel Europa" who has seen her family killed during the war. Yet we're meant to laugh at her. Not only is she called a liar repeatedly, but no one takes seriously her fear of policemen, writing it off as a persecution mania (as a prank, one character even sends her a postcard saying the Gestapo is after her). When she complains during questioning "You come to torture me, yes. ... And you will send me away to a concentration camp," the policeman drolly replies that she'll be taken to the police station instead "as I haven't got my nail-pulling apparatus and the rest of the bag of tricks with me."

It seems that Christie establishes Mitzi as a funny foreigner and a liar to make the surprise ending more effective. Not only has Mitzi has told the truth — and should have been trusted — but she courageously risks her life to help trap the killer. What can appear as racism and insensitivity on the author's part can also be seen as a narrative strategy to deliver to readers the frisson of surprise they expect.

At the end, Mitzi overcomes her fear of authority figures and happily moves on to another household. But, in a way, the joke is still on her, when another character describes Mitzi's reaction with a comic imitation of her speech: "I go there and if they say to me you have to register with the Police — you are an alien, I say to them, 'Yes, I will register! The Police, they know me well. I assist the Police! Without me the Police never would they have made the arrest of a very dangerous criminal. I risked my life because I am brave — brave like a lion — I do not care about risks.'"

So the argument goes that Christie believes her books are fantasy worlds, the only one where her convoluted plots, with their conspiracies, disguises, dying messages and strange poisons are possible. She is not interested in how her characters are presented. "What really matters," she puts in the mouth of her self-caricature, Ariadne Oliver, in *Cards on the Table*," "is plenty of *bodies*. If the thing's getting a little dull, some more blood cheers it up." We're simply not meant to take her people seriously.

SHE DID NOT EXHIBIT ANTI-SEMITIC BEHAVIOR

The argument: She personally got along with Jews and was horrified the one time she encountered hatred for them.

In *An Autobiography*, she tells this story: Before World War II, she and her husband, Max Mallowan, visited Dr. Jordan, a German director of antiquities at a Baghdad museum. They spent the afternoon, drinking tea and listening to the good doctor's performance of Beethoven on the piano. Then, she writes, someone said something "quite casually" about Jews.

"His face changed," she wrote, "changed in an extraordinary way that I had never noticed on anyone's face before.

"He said, 'You do not understand. Our Jews are perhaps different from yours. They are a danger. They should be exterminated. Nothing else will really do but that.' I stared at him unbelievingly."

Otherwise, the record is silent about Christie's beliefs about Jews. Her letters remain unpublished, and few of her contemporaries have written about her.

Except one. There is an unsettling anecdote in journalist Christopher Hitchens' memoir, *Hitch-22*. As a young man invited to a dinner party at the Mallowans' home in Iraq, he wrote that "the anti-Jewish flavour of the talk was not to be ignored or overlooked, or put down to heavy humour or generational prejudice. It was vividly unpleasant and it was bottom-numbingly boring."

But we should tread carefully before finding Christie guilty of anti-Semitism. Hitchens did not say if Christie contributed to the conversation. Friends and family members have said she preferred to say little and listen attentively. But if Hitchens' account is accurate, at the very least, Christie continued to be immersed in a prejudicial stew.

WHAT ABOUT *GIANT'S BREAD*?

The argument: Hiding behind the penname Mary Westmacott, Christie felt free to write about events and feelings that interested her without exposing herself to the judgment of readers and critics. And in Giant's Bread *(1930), she wrote about a Jewish family and their struggle to assimilate into English society with sensitivity and compassion.*

Giant's Bread is the story of Vernon Deyre, the son of a once-wealthy English family, and his three lifelong desires: to keep his family home, to marry his love, Nell Vereker, and to fulfill his destiny as a composer. In tracing the course of Deyre's quest, Christie borrowed heavily from her life, including her idyllic, isolated upbringing and her early music training.

Giant's Bread is also a melodramatic tragedy. Deyre goes off to war and is reported killed in battle. His wife remarries. When he discovers this, he contemplates suicide and accidentally steps in front of a vehicle. He survives, but loses his memory. He recovers, and in the end, resurfaces under an assumed name and becomes a renowned Modernist composer.

A subplot of *Giant's Bread* concerns Deyre's friendship with Sebastian, the only child of the Levinne family. As wealthy Jews, they are at first regarded with suspicion by the neighbors when they buy the local estate, but they turn out to be "a very Christian brand of Jew." The family is decent and generous. They convert to Christianity and buy a pew at the church. Although never "admitted to intimacy," they become socially acceptable.

But even in her Westmacott novels, the stereotypes surface. Sebastian's father looks like a typical fictional Jew, with the sallow face, stout body and a lisp. He might be only a generation removed from the pogroms, but he's made enough money to buy a down-on-its-heels English country estate. His wife is equally unpleasant-looking. As they enter the church one Sunday: "First came Mr. Levinne — very round and stout, tightly frock-coated — an enormous nose and a shining face. Then Mrs. — an amazing sight! Colossal sleeves! Hour-glass figure! Chains of diamonds! An immense hat decorated with feathers and black tightly curling ringlets underneath it! With them was a boy with a long yellow face and protruding ears."

Christie also has her characters express attitudes that make one wonder if they came from her, or from people she met. Such as when Sebastian Levinne observes:

"Everyone hates us down here. ... But it doesn't matter. They won't be able to do without us because my father is so rich. You can buy everything with money. ... Jews are frightfully powerful. My father says people can't do without them. ..." A sudden chill came over Vernon. He felt ... that he was talking to a member of an enemy race."

But Christie is clearly on the Levinnes' side. Their drive and artistic ambitions contrast favorably with the Deyres, an ancient English family fallen on hard times. Captain Deyre's inability to recover the family fortune reflects Christie's father, who lost most of his inherited fortune before he died. In fact, Sebastian Levinne bookends the novel. He takes over his father's estate and uses his money to support Vernon's artistic ambitions, as well as keep his identity secret. *Giant's Bread* contains the most positive portrayal of Jews in the Christie corpus.

HER BIOGRAPHERS DEFEND HER

The argument: Biographers with access to her papers say she was a sheltered, apolitical woman who unquestioningly reflected the attitudes and beliefs of her class.

For her authorized account, Janet Morgan was given access to Christie's papers. She noted in the preface that Christie's daughter, Rosalind Hicks — a firm advocate for her mother — had read the manuscript several times, "without once insisting on a view of her character or work that might differ from my own."

Morgan agreed that Christie made in her books "blunt and often uncomplimentary references to her Jewish characters," that sparked criticism, particularly after World War II.

One incident over *The Hollow* (1946) resulted in an editorial decision that reveals how her publishers and agents cosseted their profitable writer. The Jewish Anti-Defamation League had sent a letter of protest to Christie's U.S. publisher complaining about a prejudicial passage in the Poirot mystery, the characterization of Madame Alfredge as "a vitriolic little Jewess," and the repeated jokes characters made about her lisp.

Generally, a writer would be told about the problem, if only to avoid such problems in future books. Morgan could not say if Christie's agent talked to her about it, but she tells us that her agents made two decisions. First, publishers were given the authority to remove offending remarks. Second, letters from the public would be sent to her agents who would decide what Christie would see.

Whether by her choice, or the blue pen wielded by her editors, the frequency of references to Jews in her novels and short-story collections fell after the war, from 15 in the 36 books before 1945 to six in the 30 after the war. Other references, such as the lovers' objections to Negroes in *Death in the Clouds*, were quietly excised in subsequent editions.

Christie "was neither cosmopolitan nor intellectually so-phisticated," Morgan concluded. "Her horizons were limited and her perspective that of an ordinary, upper-class Edwardian Englishwoman." While she was enormously interested in her surroundings — reflected in the title of her archaeological memoir *Come, Tell Me How You Live* (1946) — she exhibited lit-tle indication that she absorbed anything from the outside world beyond direct experience.

The other major biographer, Laura Thompson, concluded in *Agatha Christie: An English Mystery* that she wasn't a serious anti-Semite. She simply couldn't draw a connection between her views and that of Dr. Jordan in Baghdad.

To buttress her defense, Thompson also points to *Racial Musings,* a poem Christie wrote that observes:

> *Presumptive is Man to claim the right*
> *To arbitrate between God's creatures so*
> *And place a gulf between the Black and White*
> *Deeper than sea or ocean waters flow.*

"Agatha might have made crass remarks about Jews or blacks or servants," Thompson writes, "but it would never have occurred to her that conclusions about her own character might be drawn from this, any more than her relaxed and 'lib-eral' portrayal of a lesbian couple in *A Murder is Announced* (1950). To her, life was not so simple."

Other biographers were equally forgiving. In *Agatha Christie: The Woman and her Mysteries,* Gillian Gill identified Christie's "exceptionally sheltered childhood" as the source of her apolit-ical beliefs as well as her "jingoistic, knee-jerk anti-Semitism." She might have been "stupidly unthinking," Gill writes, but Christie was not "deliberately vicious."

Unlike several popular writers from mystery's golden age.

OTHER WRITERS WERE FAR WORSE

The argument: People who have read Christie have not compared her depictions with real anti-Semitic writers. In addition to describing Jews using stereotypical descriptions and occupations, these writers took more seriously, at least in their fiction, the notion of Jewish conspiracies to foment revolution in Russia or to take over the world.

Sometimes, the anti-Semitism can be nuanced, as in the case of John Buchan, the Scottish politician and author of thrillers such as *The Thirty-nine Steps* (1915). Like other authors, he was comfortable using Jewish tropes. In *The Half-Hearted* (1909), the doomed hero Lewis and his friend, George, discusses with the villainous Constantine Marker Russia's attempts to dislodge the British presence in Afghanistan:

> "We shall not fall just yet, though you think so badly of us."
>
> "You will not fall just yet," said Marker slowly, "but that is not your fault. You British have sold your souls for something less than the conventional mess of pottage. You are ruled in the first place by money-bags, and the faddists whom they support to blind your eyes. If I were a young man in your country with my future to make, do you know what I would do? I would slave in the Stock Exchange. I would spend my days and nights in the pursuit of fortune, and, by heaven, I would get it. Then I would rule the market and break, crush, quietly and ruthlessly, the whole gang of Jew speculators and vulgarians who would corrupt a great country. Money is power with you, and I should attain it, and use it to crush the leeches who suck our blood."
>
> "Good man," said George, laughing. "That's my way of thinking. Never heard it better put."
>
> "I have felt the same," said Lewis. "When I read of 'rings' and 'corners' and 'trusts' and the misery and vulgarity of it all, I have often wished to have a try myself, and see whether average brains and clean blood could not beat these fellows on their own ground."

Jews have their uses to Buchan. If they country ahead of their tribe, their financial acumen could be harnessed in service of the empire. In *Greenmantle* (1916), Richard Hannay observes that "in Germany only the Jew can get outside of himself, and that is why, if you look into the matter, you will find the Jew is at the back of most German enterprises." He also credited Jew-ish efforts in Palestine for creating "by far the cheapest of our Imperial commitments."

Buchan's supporters defend him as being, as his son Alastair Buchan described, "the prisoner of a genre and a set of charac-ters from whom he can depart only at the cost of failing to meet the demands of a clamouring public." Which seems to shift the responsibility for an author's choices on the reader, in the belief that Jewish characters must be shaken at the readers like bo-gymen or the books won't sell. Critic Richard Usborne called Buchan's characters "slightly anti-Semitic, but no more so than was polite in any author in the pre-Hitler period," which seems to recast prejudice as a civilized act. This is patent nonsense.

While Buchan, according to his biographer, Janet Adam Smith, used derogatory references to Jews in his letters and conversations, at least he publicly condemned the persecution of Russian Jews and supported Zionism, the quest for a Jewish homeland that led to the creation of Israel. Buchan was chair-man of the Parliamentary Palestine Committee in 1932 and be-friended the president of the World Zionist Organization, Chaim Weizmann.

But Buchan was a model of tolerance and brotherhood — even if he was motivated by the prospect of a *Judenfrei* England — compared to H.C. McNeile, the creator of Bulldog Drum-mond. In *The Final Count* (1926), Drummond strives to protect a scientist's lethal invention from falling into the hands of Rus-sia, "ruled by its clique of homicidal, alien Jews." *The Island of Terror* (1931) features Isaac Goldstein, a cowardly moneylender who charges 100% interest, and blackmailer and slave trader Emil Dressler. Jews and working-class revolutionaries conspire with a foreign agent in *The Black Gang* (1922) and are punished by being whipped by Drummond and his friends "to within an inch of their lives." This novel also features the spectacle of Drummond and his gang, dressed in masks and black shirts like proto-Oswald Mosleys, attacking the enemies of all right-thinking Britons, including lefties, revolutionaries and "Bol-shie" Jews, with the tacit consent of Scotland Yard.

But by the time Hitler rose to power in Germany in the early 1930s, the game was up. Whether it was revulsion at the violence and government repression of the Jews in Germany, or the feeling that racial stereotypes were unpopular with readers, authors were either abandoning the tropes or reversing them.

Even Buchan saw the light. *A Prince of the Captivity* (1933) offered a patriotic Jew fighting for his homeland as a member of the British secret service. And Dorothy L. Sayers — who wasn't above using Jewish stereotypes occasionally — parodied Jewish conspiracies in *Murder Must Advertise* (1933) and in *Strong Poison* (1930). She married off Lord Peter's cousin, Freddie Arbuthnot, to Rachel Levy, the daughter of a Jewish financier murdered in her debut novel, *Whose Body?* (1923).

SHOULD SHE BE FORGIVEN?

Judging by the evidence, Christie seems to fall into the unthinking anti-Semitic camp. A woman who built a high wall of privacy around her life — abetted by her literary agents who monitored her mail and scissor-wielding publishers — she never had to reflect, discuss or justify her attitudes toward Jews and other minority groups.

And, it should be noted with dismay, her depictions dovetailed exactly into the expectations of her readers. Writers cannot successfully use racial stereotypes if their readers fail to understand their import.

But some critics do not forgive. Dilys Winn, mystery bookseller and author of overviews of the mystery genre *Murder Ink* and *Murderess Ink* condemns the "deep, constant and pervasive" strain of anti-Semitism that run through English mysteries of the twenties and thirties: "It is a virulent, insidious attempt to verbally annihilate a race. ... Let us no longer blithely ignore the anti-Semitism Sayers and Christie and the bulk of the Golden Agers perpetrated. It is as much a part of their books as the corpse. And just as unlikable. And, in most cases, even more offensive."

Chronology

Undated events are placed at the top of each year. Christie wrote so much that details about her writing will be limited to her first novel, notable events and her plays.

Key:
  (Debut) Detective's debut novel
  (P) Features Hercule Poirot
  (M) Features Miss Marple
  (TT) Features Tommy and Tuppence Beresford
  (O) Features Ariadne Oliver
  (B) Features Superintendent Battle
  (SS) Short stories, with the number of stories featuring each detective

1890

Sept. 15: Born Agatha Mary Clarissa Miller, the second daughter and third child to Frederick Miller and Clarissa (Clara) Boehmer, in Torquay (pronounced Tor-KEE), Devon. Father's income is derived from investments, particularly in the U.S., which will become mismanaged over the years, causing much distress. Because sister Madge was 11 years older and brother Louis "Monty" 10, Agatha grows up as if she were an only child at Ashfield, a large house with extensive gardens and lawns.

1895

Self-taught to read against her mother's wishes.

1897

Lists her favorite authors as Shakespeare and Tennyson. Develops fantasy life through making up stories.

1901

Nov. 26: Suffering from heart problems and financial reversals, Frederick Miller dies of pneumonia at age 55. Christie would say this event marked the end of her childhood.

1902

Madge Miller marries James Watt and moves to his family home, Abney Hall, in Cheshire. Christie would visit frequently throughout her life.

1903

Attends Miss Guyer's Girls' School in Torquay two days a week for 18 months to learn algebra and grammar.

1905

Attends school in Paris, receiving lessons in singing and piano. Ends formal education at a finishing school. Hopes for an opera career dashed after her voice was judged too weak.

1907

Spends three months in Egypt with her mother during her "coming out" season. Visits ancient monuments. Attends more than 50 dances and other social functions and meets 30 men. Shyness inhibits attempt to find a husband. One suitor tells her mother: "She has learnt to dance. In fact, she dances beautifully. You had better try and teach her to talk now."

1908

To pass the time while bedridden with influenza, begins writing stories at her mother's suggestion. Writes "The House of Beauty," a 6,000-word story about dreams and madness. Revised version published in Sovereign Magazine in 1926 as "The House of Dreams." Continues writing stories.

1909

Feb. 6: Asks author and neighbor Eden Phillpotts for advice about her writing. He responds with several letters, including one on this day saying "I never prophesy; but I should judge that if you can write like this now you might go far."

1911

May: Exhibits an adventurous spirit by attending flying exhibition with Clara and going up in a biplane.

1912

Rejects two offers of marriage. Accepts offer from Reggie Lucy, a major in the Gunners and part of a large, boisterous family, with his proviso they wait a few years so she could be sure of her choice.

Oct. 12: Meets at a dance Archibald (Archie) Christie, an aviator with the Royal Flying Corps, who pursues her ardently.

1914

July 28: First World War breaks out when Austria-Hungary invades Serbia. Joins Voluntary Aid Detachment and works in Red Cross hospital in Torquay until December 1916 when she moves to the dispensary.

Aug. 5: Archie joins British Expeditionary Force in France. He participates in several battles and gets mentioned in dispatches for bravery several times.

Dec. 21: Meets Archie in London while he is home on leave. Objects to his gift of an expensive dressing-case, thinking it frivolous for wartime and symbolizes impermanence. They quarrel.

Dec. 24: While visiting his mother and stepfather in Clifton, Bristol, Archie proposes. They get married by a special license. During the next three years, they would spend only a few days together when he is on leave.

1915

July: Grounded by sinus trouble and now a captain in the Royal Field Artillery, Archie visits her in London on three days' leave. She follows him to Paris to learn that further leave had been postponed. Returns to England and succumbs to influenza and bronchitis.

Autumn: Begins studying for Society of Apothecaries examinations that would qualify her to dispense medicine.

1916

Jan. 27: Archie promoted to squadron commander and temporary major.

September: Archie posted to Britain as colonel in the Air Ministry.

December: Moves to the Red Cross dispensary at Castle Chambers, a large Victorian limestone building in Torquay, at £16 a year.

Begins work on *The Mysterious Affair at Styles*. When she has trouble finishing the first draft, takes Clara's suggestion and spends two weeks at the Moorland Hotel in Haytor, Dartmoor, working in the morning and walking the moors in the afternoon. Manuscript would be rejected by several publishers before being accepted by The Bodley Head in 1919.

1917

February: Archie promoted to depot commander and lieutenant colonel. Awarded the Russian Order of St. Stanislaus

Third Class with swords.

April 30: Qualifies as assistant for the Society of Apothecaries, passing the examination on her second attempt.

1918

Jan. 1: Archie awarded Distinguished Service Order medal for military service and made a Companion of St. Michael and St. George, an order of chivalry.

September: Leaves V.A.D. service, takes courses in shorthand and bookkeeping. Archie posted to London as colonel in the Air Ministry. The couple live together for the first time, in a flat at 5 Northwick Terrace, St. John's Wood, northwest London.

Nov. 11: World War I ends. Archie leaves Air Ministry to work in the financial district. Couple moves to unfurnished flat at Addison Mansions. Begins lifetime of owning multiple houses by acquiring a flat at Battersea as rental property.

1919

Signs six-book contract with John Lane at The Bodley Head for *The Mysterious Affair at Styles*. Contract would pay no advance and no royalties until 2,000 books are sold in Britain, 1,000 in U.S. Christie would make £25 from her share of serial rights. Begins her next book, *The Secret Adversary*.

Aug. 5: Rosalind Margaret Clarissa, the Christies' only child, born at Ashfield.

1920

Published: *The Mysterious Affair at Styles* (Debut P)

1922

Published: *The Secret Adversary* (Debut TT)

Jan. 20: Leaves Rosalind with her family and accompanies Archie on yearlong world tour to promote Empire Exhibition of 1924. Takes to traveling and its hardships with pleasure and enthusiasm, setting a pattern for a lifetime of movement.

1923

Published: *Murder on the Links* (P)

Dissatisfied with her treatment at The Bodley Head, meets with Edmund Cork, who becomes her lifelong literary agent and adviser.

1924

Published: *The Man in the Brown Suit, Poirot Investigates* (SS/P14), *The Road of Dreams* (self-published poetry)

Christies rent a flat at Scotswood in Sunningdale, 30 miles west of London. Later, they will buy a home in the area and rename it Styles after her first book. Archie will take up golf and the couple will grow apart.

January: Fulfills her contract with The Bodley Head by submitting *The Secret of Chimneys* and signs contract with Collins.

March 28: Lord Louis Mountbatten sends letter suggesting a plot similar to one she receives from brother-in-law James Watt that she will use in *The Murder of Roger Ackroyd.*

1925
Published: *The Secret of Chimneys* (Debut B)

1926
Published: *The Murder of Roger Ackroyd* (P)

April 5: Mother Clara Miller dies at 72. Receives £13,527 after paying death duties. Under enormous strain from settling the estate, clearing out Ashfield and her collapsing marriage.

August: Archie announces his intention to divorce Christie and marry Nancy Neele, a younger woman he had met through golfing friends, with whom he'd been having an affair for 18 months. After celebrating Rosalind's birthday at Ashfield, Archie returns to London. On her trip to Styles, Agatha is further traumatized from seeing her terrier knocked unconscious by a car and fearing he was killed.

A fortnight later, Archie agrees to try a reconciliation. Christie suggests a year, but Archie would only agree to three months.

October: Christies spend month in Guéthary, Spain. Relations still strained.

Dec. 3: Christies argue. Archie ends the reconciliation, refuses to accompany her to Yorkshire for the weekend and intends to spend it with his mistress. He leaves for work. Visits Archie's mother with Rosalind for tea, and returns to Styles in the evening. About 9:45 p.m., leaves Styles in her car and vanishes, setting off a police manhunt and sparking nationwide publicity.

Dec. 14: Found 11 days later at Swan Hydropathic Hotel in Harrogate, Yorkshire. Uses the alias Teresa Neele, taking the last name from her husband's mistress.

1927

Published: *The Big Four* (P)

Takes Rosalind to live in Chelsea. Seeks treatment for memory loss during disappearance.

Writes that she's slogging through "that rotten" *The Big Four* and will "force myself" to write *The Mystery of the Blue Train.*

1928

Published: *The Mystery of the Blue Train* (P)

Edmund Cork negotiates contract with Collins with higher advances and royalties.

Feb. 4: Spends month with Rosalind on Canary Islands to finish *The Mystery of the Blue Train.*

April 20: Attends hearing in divorce case. Divorce from Archie would be approved in October. Keeps his love letters and photographs, but never sees him again. Two weeks later, Archie marries Nancy Neele. They would stay together until her death in 1958.

Autumn: Travels alone to Baghdad, Iraq, via the Orient Express. Visits Leonard Woolley's excavations at the ancient city of Ur. Meets Woolley and his imperious wife, Katharine, who had liked *The Murder of Roger Ackroyd,* and receives a tour of the site.

1929

Published: *Partners in Crime* (SS/TT17), *The Seven Dials Mystery* (B)

January: Delivers manuscript of *Giant's Bread,* her first Mary Westmacott novel, to Collins.

Summer: Leonard and Katharine Woolley stay with Christie in London and invite her to visit the excavations next year.

Sept. 20: Brother Louis "Monty" Miller dies from a cerebral hemorrhage in France at 49.

Begins work on first play, *Black Coffee.*

Buys 22 Cresswell Place in Chelsea.

1930

Published: *The Murder at the Vicarage* (Debut M), *The Mysterious Mr. Quin, Giant's Bread* (as Mary Westmacott)

February: Revisits Woolley's excavations in Ur and is introduced to his assistant, Max Mallowan. She is 39, he is 25. At Katharine Woolley's orders, he escorts her to sites on their return to Baghdad. They arrive late, causing proprietorial behavior from Katharine. The party travels to Athens, where Christie learns her daughter is seriously ill. Sprains her ankle, and Max volunteers to escort her as far as Paris.

April: While visiting Christie and Rosalind in Torquay, Max proposes marriage.

June 21: Reads over BBC radio her episode of a six-part serial *Behind the Screen* written with Dorothy L. Sayers, Hugh Walpole, E.C. Bently, Ronald Knox and Anthony Berkeley.

Sept. 11: Christie and Max are married at St. Cuthbert's Church in Edinburgh, Scotland. Couple honeymoons in Venice and Greece, where Christie suffers food poisoning. Max leaves for Ur expedition while Christie returns home. Ordered to be on time to be instructed on finishing expedition buildings, Max discovers that Woolleys would not arrive for another week. Max takes revenge by finishing job to his specifications, giving Katharine a cramped bathroom that would have to be rebuilt. Mallowans buy a house at 47-48 Campden St., in west London's Campden Hill district.

1931

Published: *The Sittaford Mystery* (U.S.: *Murder at Hazelmoore*), *The Floating Admiral* (collaboration with Detection Club)

Suffers a miscarriage.

Jan. 17: Reads over BBC radio her episode of *The Scoop*, a second collaborative radio serial written with Dorothy L. Sayers and other mystery writers. She would also read the fourth episode on Jan. 31. Then-Assistant Producer J.R. Ackerley would recall later "with pain" that Christie was "extremely tiresome. She was always late sending in her stuff, very difficult to pin down to any engagements and invariably late for them."

Spring: Travels to Ur to join Max.

Autumn: Travels to the island of Rhodes, then to ancient city of Nineveh in Iraq to visit Max. Returns alone to London before Christmas via the Orient Express. The trip would be beset with delays and Christie would draw on this experience for *Murder on the Orient Express*.

1932

Published: *Peril at End House* (P), *The Thirteen Problems* (U.S.: *The Tuesday Club Murders*)(SS/M13)

1933

Published: *The Hound of Death and Other Stories* (U.K. only, SS), *Lord Edgware Dies* (U.S.: *Thirteen at Dinner*) (P)

Accompanies Max, commanding his first expedition, to Arpachiyah, Iraq. Writes, keeps records, and reassembles and sketches pottery fragments. This begins five years of regular travel: spring and autumn on Middle East expeditions, summers at Ashfield with Rosalind, Christmas at her brother-in-law's Abney Hall in Cheshire, and the rest of the time in London or, in later years, Wallingford.

1934

Published: *The Listerdale Mystery* (U.K. only, SS), *Murder on* *the Orient Express* (U.S.: *Murder in the Calais Coach*)(P), *Parker Pyne Investigates* (U.S.: *Mr. Parker Pyne, Detective*) (SS/O1), *Why Didn't They Ask Evans?* (U.S.: *The Boomerang Clue*), *Unfinished Portrait* (as Mary Westmacott), *Murder in Three Acts* (U.K.: *Three Act Tragedy*) (P)

Buys home at 58 Sheffield Terrace, Kensington, where they will live — renting it out occasionally — until 1941. Christie will write *Murder on the Orient Express* and *Death on the Nile* here.

November-December: Buys Winterbrook House at Wallingford, near Oxford. Accompanies Max to survey possible excavation sites in the Habur Valley, Syria.

1935

Published: *Death in the Clouds* (U.S.: *Death in the Air*) (P)

January-February: Mallowans conduct dig at Chagar Bazar, northeast Syria.

1936

Published: *The ABC Murders* (P), *Cards on the Table* (P/B/Debut O), *Murder in Mesopotamia* (P)

January-February: Mallowans return to dig at Chagar Bazar, northeast Syria.

1937

Published: *Death on the Nile* (P), *Dumb Witness* (U.S.: *Poirot Loses a Client*) (P), *Murder in the Mews and Other Stories* (U.S.: *Dead Man's Mirror and Other Stories*) (SS/P4)

January-February: Mallowans conduct dig at Tell Brak, 20 miles from Chagar Bazar in northeast Syria.

1938

Published: *Appointment With Death* (P), *Hercule Poirot's Christmas* (U.S.: *Murder for Christmas*) (P)

Summer: U.S. tax authorities open investigation of Christie's American royalties.

Autumn: Max finishes at Chagar Bazar and Tell Brak and the Mallowans move the expedition to Balikh Valley to avoid local sheiks attempting to get the workers to strike.

Oct. 28: Feeling crowded by development in Torquay, sells Ashfield and buys Greenway on the River Dart for £6,000. Orders half the house demolished and rebuilt to suit her needs.

1939

Published: *Ten Little Niggers* (U.S.: *And Then There Were None*), *Murder Is Easy* (U.S.: *Easy to Kill*) (B), *The Regatta Mystery and Other Stories* (U.S. only, SS/P5, M1)

Writes as Mary Westmacott a play, *A Daughter's a Daughter*, which she puts away and forgets until 1951.

Sept. 1: Germany invades Poland, beginning World War II. Max applies to join the services, but his age and his father's Austrian origins prove obstacles.

1940

Published: *One, Two, Buckle My Shoe* (U.S.: *The Patriotic Murders*, later as *An Overdose of Death*) (P), *Sad Cypress* (P)

Concerned about her ability to support her family, writes two "nest egg" novels to be held back and published when needed: *Curtain* (published in 1975) and *Cover Her Face* (published in 1976 as *Sleeping Murder*). In *Agatha Christie's Secret Notebooks*, John Curran upends previous dating of *Cover Her Face* by showing Christie working on it as late as 1948. Assigns *Curtain*'s copyright to Max; *Sleeping Murder*'s to Rosalind.

Fearing it would upset readers, American magazines decline to publish *N or M?* because of its anti-Nazi slant.

Rents Greenway to friends avoiding air raids on the coast, then later to evacuees. Takes flat in London to be with Max, first on Half Moon Street, then at Park Place near St. James's Street. Moves into her Sheffield Terrace home after tenants leave. Takes a course in air raid precautions and brings dispensing knowledge up to date.

Summer: Max becomes secretary of Anglo-Turkish Relief Committee to raise and distribute funds to aid earthquake victims.

June 11: Rosalind Christie marries Hubert Prichard, a soldier in the Royal Welch Fusiliers, with Christie in attendance.

August: U.S. court rules that British author Rafael Sabatini owes back taxes on American income despite paying taxes on them in the U.K. Based on that ruling, U.S. tax authorities freeze Christie's American royalties pending settlement of her case. Meanwhile, U.K. tax authorities seek tax payments on that same income. The case would drag on for years and cause much anxiety.

1941

Published: *Evil Under the Sun* (P), *N or M?* (TT)

Under financial pressure, Christie tries to sell Greenway.

Begins working at University College Hospital dispensary. When German bombs make their Sheffield Terrace flat inaccessible, the Mallowans move into Lawn Road Flats, a modernist building in Hampstead built in 1934 by architect Wells Coates.

February: Max sent to Cairo to establish a branch of the directorate.

1942

Published: *The Body in the Library* (M), *Five Little Pigs* (U.S.: *Murder in Retrospect*) (P), *The Moving Finger* (M)

Writes Westmacott novel *Absent in the Spring* in three days. Considers adapting an old play, *Moon on the Nile*, for the stage.

February: Max is transferred from Cairo to Tripolitania, the northern half of what is now Libya, to act as colonial administrator for the former Italian colony.

Aug. 31: Writes to Max informing him that the Admiralty will be taking over Greenway. It will house officers from the U.S. Coast Guard preparing for the D-Day invasion.

Sept. 21: Rosalind gives birth to her son, Mathew Prichard, at Abney Hall, Cheshire.

1943

November: *Moon on the Nile* opens in the West End to good reviews.

1944

Published: *Towards Zero* (B), *Absent in the Spring* (as Mary Westmacott), *Death Comes As the End*

Leaves dispensary work, worn out from overseeing her theater projects.

January: Attends rehearsals in Dundee, Scotland, for *Moon on the Nile*, renamed *Hidden Horizon*.

March: Adapts *Appointment with Death* for the stage.
August: Rosalind's husband, Hubert Prichard, killed in France.

1945

Published: *Sparkling Cyanide* (U.S.: *Remembered Death*)

February: Government returns Greenway to Christie. British Revenue reaches an agreement on the amount of tax she owes.

March: *Appointment With Death* opens in London to scathing reviews.

May: Max returns home unexpectedly, the first time they've seen each other since 1941. U.S. and United Kingdom reach agreement on double-taxation treaty, brightening hopes Christie would receive overseas royalties.

September: *Hidden Horizon* opens in Cambridge.

1946

Published: *The Hollow* (U.S.: *Murder after Hours*) (P), *Come, Tell Me How You Live* (memoir as Agatha Christie Mallowan)

March 19: *Hidden Horizon* opens in Wimbledon.

September: *Hidden Horizon*, renamed *Murder on the Nile*, opens in New York.

1947

Published: *The Labours of Hercules* (SS/P12)

The Jewish Anti-Defamation League sends a letter to Christie's U.S. publisher, Dodd, Mead, protesting references to Jews in her books, particularly in *The Hollow*. Agents give publisher permission to delete references in *The Hollow* and future books.

Spring: Mallowans visit Switzerland and the south of France.

May 26: Written at Queen Mary's request for her 70th birthday, Christie's play *Three Blind Mice* is broadcast on the BBC.

Autumn: Max appointed chair of Western Asiatic Archaeology at the Institute of Archaeology in the University of London.

1948

Published: *Taken at the Flood* (U.S.: *There Is a Tide*) (P), *Witness for the Prosecution and Other Stories* (U.S. only, SS/P1), *The Rose and the Yew Tree* (as Mary Westmacott)

Buys flat at 48 Swan Court where she works on *Witness for the Prosecution* and *The Crooked House*.

Mallowans spend five months in Baghdad, where Max negotiates for permission to conduct archaeological digs and Christie reads "thousands of American detective stories."

U.S. and British literary agents continue negotiating with tax authorities, settling with the U.S. first, then dealing with Inland Revenue wanting to tax same income. Fears bankruptcy and writes, "Oh, it is so beautiful, I shall go on enjoying myself and then have a slap-up bankruptcy!!!" Doesn't write a word all year.

1949

Published: *Crooked House*

Censors at the NBC radio network block serialization of *Crooked House* on Sunday nights as unsuitable. Harold Ober, Christie's U.S. agent, sarcastically remarks that "the public has been complaining in droves about the number of murders being committed over the air."

A *London Times* columnist reveals identity of Mary Westmacott, upsetting Christie.

After beating back an inquiry from Inland Revenue's Torquay office, receives an inquiry from the London office seeking more information, noting "Agatha Christie is to all intents and purposes a pen name, and it would appear that the tax district of the husband is the one that is required." Comments "I don't understand a word of it! Anyway, what the Hell is what I now feel about income tax."

January-February: Mallowans resume their annual expeditions, traveling to Nimrud, Iraq.

October: Adaptation of *The Murder at the Vicarage* opens in Northampton.

Rosalind remarries, this time to barrister Anthony Hicks.

December: Mallowans return to Nimrud excavations.

1950

Published: *A Murder is Announced* (M), *Three Blind Mice and Other Stories* (U.S. only, SS/P3, M4)

For the next decade, the Mallowans make yearly expeditions to Nimrud, leaving in December or January and returning in March. Continues photographing finds, cleaning pieces, taking an interest in domestic arrangements, and writing.

Begins dramatizing *The Hollow* and writing her memoirs.

Rediscovers Westmacott play, *A Daughter's a Daughter*, which she wrote in 1939. Permits it to be tried out in Bath. The play becomes a success once its true author is revealed but it is not brought to London. Turns the play into a novel.

August: Sister Madge Miller Watt dies.

September: Celebrates 60th birthday at Greenway. Attends public celebrations so long as she doesn't have to make a speech.

1951

Published: *They Came to Baghdad, The Under Dog and Other Stories* (U.S. only, SS/P9)

February: *The Hollow* opens successfully in Cambridge. The play will run for 11 months in London.

Summer: Finishes stage adaptation of *Three Blind Mice*, renamed *The Mousetrap*.

1952

Published: *Mrs. McGinty's Dead* (P/O), *They Do It With Mirrors* (U.S.: *Murder With Mirrors*) (M), *A Daughter's a Daughter* (as Mary Westmacott)

Adapts *Witness for the Prosecution* for the stage.

Finishes short radio play, *Personal Call*, in Nimrud.

Feb. 6: King George VI dies. Mallowans attend a memorial service in Baghdad.

Sept. 15: Falls and breaks the wrist on her writing hand on her 62nd birthday. She begins using a dictating machine.

Oct. 6: *The Mousetrap* opens in Nottingham. Christie predicts it will run for eight months.

Nov. 25: *The Mousetrap* opens in London

1953

Published: *After the Funeral* (U.S.: *Funerals Are Fatal*) (P), *A Pocket Full of* Rye (M)

Due to growing paperback sales, royalty is bumped up to a penny ha'penny per copy in Great Britain, a penny for export sales (about 38 and 25 pence, or 59 and 39 U.S. cents today).

September: Writes a play, *Spider's Web*, within a month for actress Margaret Lockwood.

Sept. 26: *Witness for the Prosecution* opens in Nottingham.

Oct. 28: *Witness for the Prosecution* opens in London to acclaim. Rights to the play are sought worldwide, and Hollywood movie studios bid for the movie rights.

1954

Published: *Destination Unknown* (U.S.: *So Many Steps to Death*)

Writes first short story in eight years, *Sanctuary*, with proceeds from its sale donated to a fund for restoring Westminster Abbey.

Dec. 13: *Spider's Web* opens in London, making Christie the first female playwright to have three plays — along with *The Mousetrap* and *Witness for the Prosecution* — running simultaneously in the West End.

Dec. 16: *Witness for the Prosecution* opens in New York. It would win the New York Drama Critics Circle award for best foreign play.

1955

Published: *Hickory Dickory Dock* (U.S.: *Hickory Dickory Death*) (P)

Agatha Christie Ltd. formed to shelter income from Britain's 90 percent surtax.

February: Turned down repeatedly for interviews, BBC radio profiles Christie on *Close-Up*, featuring contributions from her friends and colleagues. She is not amused.

April 22: *The Mousetrap* reaches 1,000-performance milestone.

September: Mallowans celebrate 25th wedding anniversary.

1956

Published: *Dead Man's Folly* (P/O), *The Burden* (as Mary Westmacott)

Writes screenplay for *Spider's Web* (not filmed).

January: Made a Commander of the Order of the British Empire, a "gong" awarded by Queen Elizabeth II. "One up to the Low-Brows!!" she writes to literary agent Edmund Cork.

March: Sends draft for *4.50 from Paddington* to Cork. She'll revise the time in the title several times, alternating among 4.15, 4.30, and 4.54 — and consider changing the station to London for American readers — before settling on 4.50.

May: Spends two weeks in America with Max as he receives medal from University of Pennsylvania in Philadelphia. Visits New York, Grand Canyon and Hollywood, where she visits set of *Witness for the Prosecution*.

1957

Published: *4.50 from Paddington* (U.S.: *What Mrs. McGillicuddy Saw!*) (M)

January: In another attempt to reduce her tax bill, Christie Copyrights Trust formed to hold copyrights to pre-1955 works.

Spring: Pays for stained-glass window at the church in Churston, Greenway's parish. Works with the designer to fulfill her wish for "a happy window … for a simple country church with a rural population."

May 22: *The Verdict* opens. It's savaged by critics.

Aug. 12: *The Unexpected Guest* opens in London and runs for 18 months, atoning in Christie's eyes for the failure of *The Verdict*.

Sept. 13: *The Mousetrap* celebrates becoming the longest-running non-musical play in the West End. Fellow playwright Noël Coward telegrams, "Much as it pains me I really must congratulate you …"

1958

Published: *Ordeal By Innocence*

April 12: At 2,239 performances, *The Mousetrap* passes the musical *Chu Chin Chow* (1916) to become the longest-running show in the West End.

Summer: Nancy Neele Christie dies. Agatha writes letter of condolence to Archie.

1959

Published: *Cat Among the Pigeons* (P)

Autumn: American agent, Harold Ober, dies of a heart attack at 78.

1960

Published: *The Adventure of the Christmas Pudding* (U.K. only:

SS/P5, M1)

Max made Commander of the Order of the British Empire.

January-February: Accompanied by grandson Mathew, Mallowans visit Ceylon, India, Pakistan and Persia. Pestered by photographers while swimming in Ceylon and in her hotel in Tehran. Fans seek her autograph during a train trip in Pakistan. Approaching 70, travels upcountry as far as the Khyber Pass.

March 23: Attends first night in London for *Go Back for Murder*, based on *Five Little Pigs*. Cork describes the reviews as "the most malicious press we have ever had, not even excepting *Verdict*."

Sept. 15: Celebrates 70th birthday by attending *Das Rheingold* at Covent Garden and eats lobster for dinner at Greenway: "Hardly felt my age!!"

1961

Published: *Double Sin and Other Stories* (U.S. only, SS/P4, M2), *The Pale Horse* (O), *Thirteen for Luck* (SS/P4, M3, T1)

Summer: Drafts parts of two plays: *The Patient* and *Afternoon at the Seaside*, later to be combined and mounted as *Rule of Three*. Attends Samuel Beckett plays and the opera.

1962

Published: *The Mirror Crack'd from Side to Side* (U.S.: *The Mirror Crack'd*) (M)

Works on screenplay of Dickens' *Bleak House* for MGM. Studio abandons project before she could finish. Other unfinished projects include adapting *Hickory, Dickory Dock* as a musical called *Death Beat* with Peter Sellers as Poirot, and *Ten Little Niggers 2*, a sequel to the play.

Summer: Max suffers a mild stroke.

August: Attends Bayreuth Festival in Germany. Agrees to sign books, privately, for an hour each day, and spends days studying scores with Mathew. Irritated by German magazine saying her dog ate a manuscript and that she drank alcohol.

Autumn: Mallowans visit Persia and Kashmir.

Rule of Three debuts to poor reviews.

Gives the second speech of her life at *The Mousetrap's* 10th anniversary.

December: Mathew Prichard arranges to meet his grandfather, Archie Christie, for the first time, but before they could so, Christie collapses on Dec. 20 and dies.

1963

Published: *The Clocks* (P)

Battles MGM over their adaptations of her books. She hates *Murder at the Gallop*, based on *After the Funeral*, with Poirot replaced by Miss Marple, and dreads what they would do to *Mrs. McGinty's Dead*, renamed *Murder Most Foul*: "Can you imagine a triter title?"

December: Max finishes his book *Nimrud and Its Remains*.

1964

Published: *A Caribbean Mystery* (M)

January: Visits Upper Egypt.

May: MGM's British unit releases *Murder Most Foul*, based on *Mrs. McGinty's Dead*, with Miss Marple again replacing

Poirot. Objects to proposed Miss Marple movie *Murder Ahoy!* set aboard a Royal Navy training ship and not based on her books, and *The Alphabet Murders,* based on *The ABC Murders,* fearing Poirot would be turned "into some sort of gorilla or private eye — and a lot of violence and brutality ... if people have liked Poirot for about forty years as an ego-centric creep they would probably prefer him to go on that way." For *The Alphabet Murders,* comedy film director Frank Tashlin casts American actor Tony Randall as Poirot. Later, MGM cancels the contract, much to everyone's relief.

Dec. 9: *The Mousetrap* gives its 5,000th performance.

1965

Published: *At Bertram's Hotel* (M), *Star Over Bethlehem* (children's poems, SS)

1966

Published: *Third Girl* (P/O), *Thirteen Clues for Miss Marple* (U.S. only, M:13)

January: Visits Paris.

June: During trip to Belgium, Mallowans visit museum named for Poirot.

August: Visits Switzerland.

Autumn: Accompanies Max on his lecture tour of America. Visits grandfather's grave in Green-Wood Cemetery, Brooklyn, N.Y. Finishes writing autobiography. It would be published after her death.

1967

Published: *Endless Night*

Offer to buy film rights brings spirited rejection: "It always makes my blood boil. My own feeling remains the same. I have suffered enough!"

Berates publisher over editing of *By the Pricking of My Thumbs*: "… make it clear not to change the spelling of the author unless it is actually misspelt. If I prefer phantasy to fantasy (both words are in dictionary) I want it left alone."

January: Mallowans travel to Persia.

May: Mathew Prichard marries Angela Maples. Mallowans visit Yugoslavia.

Autumn: Visits Spain. In October, Max suffers stroke during solo lecture trip to Persia and is flown home.

1968

Published: *By the Pricking of My Thumbs* (TT)

Agatha Christie Ltd. reorganized when Booker McConnell Co. buys 51% of the company.

Rosalind and her second husband, Anthony Hicks, move into Greenway.

January: Max knighted for his work in archaeology.

1969

Published: *Hallowe'en Party* (P/O)

1970

Published: *Passenger to Frankfurt*

January: Visits Cyprus.

Easter: Visits Austria and sees the Passion Play at Ober-ammergau.

Sept. 15: Spends summer celebrating her 80th birthday at parties in London and Greenway. Charmed at receiving a gold pen, her first: "Death to anyone who borrows it and doesn't give it back."

1971

Published: *The Golden Ball and Other Stories, Nemesis* (M)

January: Named Dame Commander of the British Empire, the equivalent of a knighthood (starting *Nemesis* this month, she'll write "DBE" above the title of her notebook). Mallowans visit Paris.

Finishes draft of play *This Mortal Coil*. The next year, she'll revise it and change the title to *Fiddlers Three*.

June: Operated on to repair a broken hip suffered in a fall.

August: Attends opening of *Fiddlers Three* in Guildford. It is not taken to London.

Christmas: Visits Madame Tussauds wax museum to have her head measured for an exhibit.

1972

Published: *Elephants Can Remember* (P/O)

1973

Published: *Postern of Fate* (TT) the last novel she wrote, *Poems*

1974

Published: *Poirot's Early Cases* (SS/P18)

October: Suffers heart attack.

November: Attends premiere of *Murder on the Orient Express*.

December: Falls into French window at Winterbrook and injures her head.

1975

Published: *Curtain* (P), Poirot's last case

Attends annual celebration for *The Mousetrap*, her last public appearance.

Aug. 6: New York Times publishes Poirot's obituary upon publication of *Curtain*.

1976

Published: *Sleeping Murder* (M), the last Miss Marple case

Jan. 12: Dies at age 85 at Wallingford, Oxfordshire. Buried at St. Mary's churchyard, Cholsey, 2 miles south of Wallingford.

May: Memorial service at St. Martin-in-the-Fields, London.

Dec. 17: *The Mousetrap* gives its 10,000th performance.

1977

Published: *An Autobiography* (memoir)

September: Max marries his longtime assistant, Barbara Parker.

1978

Aug. 19: Max dies at age 74 at Wallingford. He is buried next to Christie at Saint Mary's.

1979

Published: *Miss Marple's Final Cases and Two Other Stories* (SS/M6)

1991

Published: *Problem at Pollensa Bay and Other Stories* (SS/P2)

1993

Barbara Parker Mallowan dies at age 85 at Wallingford.

1997

Published: *The Harlequin Tea Set and Other Stories* (U.K.: *While the Light Lasts and Other Stories*) (SS/P1), *Black Coffee* (P, play novelization by Charles Osborne)

1999

Published: *The Unexpected Guest* (P, play novelization by Charles Osborne)

2000

Published: *Spider's Web* (play novelization by Charles Osborne)

National Trust takes over Greenway to open in 2009 as an historical site.

Dec. 16: *The Mousetrap* gives its 20,000th performance.

2004

Oct. 28: Rosalind Christie Hicks dies at 85.

2013

Christie's estate signs with talent agency William Morris Endeavor to develop adaptations for film, television, and digital media.

2014

The Monogram Murders by Sophie Hannah, the first author-ized original Hercule Poirot novel, published by HarperCollins.

2016

Closed Casket by Sophie Hannah, the second authorized Hercule Poirot novel published.

2018

The Mystery of Three Quarters by Sophie Hannah, the third authorized Hercule Poirot novel published.

2019

HarperCollins signs deal for exclusive English-language rights worldwide with Agatha Christie Ltd. to run until 2030.

Books Sorted by Detective

This section lists the books published during and after Christie's lifetime starring her major characters, followed by her stand-alone books and those she published under other names.

Untangling the Christie bibliography is challenging. Books were published only in the U.K. or the U.S. Titles were changed as they crossed the Atlantic. Short stories that appeared in a collection on one side of the Atlantic were reshuffled in editions on the other side.

Take the extreme example of *Three Blind Mice and Other Stories*. This short story collection was published in the U.S. in 1950, and all but one story were separated and reprinted in four books: *The Adventure of the Christmas Pudding* (1960), *Poirot's Early Cases* (1974), *Miss Marple's Final Cases and Two Other Stories* (1979), and *Problem at Pollensa Bay* (1992). The title story, an alternative version of her play *The Mousetrap*, will not be published in the U.K. at Christie's request until the run of *The Mousetrap* is finished. As the play has been running continuously since 1952, this might take awhile.

The short story collections are noted with an (SS) followed by the number of stories in that collection starring the main detective. For example, *The Regatta Mystery and Other Stories* (US: SS/P5, M1), initially published in the U.S., contains five stories featuring Poirot and one featuring Miss Marple. Novels with two or more detectives are noted with a (w/), e.g. 1936: *Cards On the Table* (w/O/B/R) for "with Ariadne Oliver, Superintendent Battle and Colonel Race."

Key:

(P) Hercule Poirot
(M) Miss Marple
(TT) Tommy and Tuppence Beresford
(O) Ariadne Oliver
(B) Superintendent Battle
(R) Colonel Race
(SS) Short stories

HERCULE POIROT

1920: *The Mysterious Affair at Styles*
1923: *Murder on the Links*
1924: *Poirot Investigates* (SS/P14)
1926: *The Murder of Roger Ackroyd*
1927: *The Big Four*
1928: *The Mystery of the Blue Train*
1932: *Peril at End House*
1933: *Lord Edgware Dies* (U.S.: *Thirteen at Dinner*)
1934: *Murder on the Orient Express* (U.S.: *Murder in the Calais Coach*)
1934: *Murder in Three Acts* (UK: *Three Act Tragedy*)
1935: *Death in the Clouds* (U.S.: *Death in the Air*)
1936: *The ABC Murders*
1936: *Cards On the Table* (w/O/B/R)
1936: *Murder in Mesopotamia*
1937: *Death on the Nile* (w/R)
1937: *Dumb Witness* (U.S.: *Poirot Loses a Client*)
1937: *Murder in the Mews and Other Stories* (U.S.: *Dead Man's Mirror and Other Stories*) (SS/P4)
1938: *Appointment With Death*
1938: *Hercule Poirot's Christmas* (U.S.: *Murder for Christmas*)
1939: *The Regatta Mystery and Other Stories* (U.S.: SS/P5, M1)
1940: *One, Two, Buckle My Shoe* (U.S.: *The Patriotic Murders*, later *An Overdose of Death*)
1940: *Sad Cypress*
1941: *Evil Under the Sun*
1942: *Five Little Pigs* (U.S.: *Murder in Retrospect*)
1946: *The Hollow* (U.S.: *Murder after Hours*)
1947: *The Labours of Hercules* (SS/P12)
1948: *Taken at the Flood* (U.S.: *There Is a Tide*)
1948: *Witness for the Prosecution and Other Stories* (US: P1)

1950: *Three Blind Mice and Other Stories* (U.S.: SS/P3, M4)

1951: *The Under Dog and Other Stories* (U.S.: SS/P9)

1952: *Mrs. McGinty's Dead* (w/O)

1953: *After the Funeral* (U.S.: *Funerals are Fatal*)

1955: *Hickory Dickory Dock* (U.S.: *Hickory Dickory Death*)

1956: *Dead Man's Folly* (w/O)

1959: *Cat Among the Pigeons*

1960: *The Adventure of the Christmas Pudding* (U.K.: SS/P5, M1)

1961: *Double Sin and Other Stories* (U.S.: SS/P4, M2)

1963: *The Clocks*

1966: *Third Girl* (w/O)

1969: *Hallowe'en Party* (w/O)

1972: *Elephants Can Remember* (w/O)

1974: *Poirot's Early Cases* (SS/P18)

1975: *Curtain*

1991: *Problem at Pollensa Bay and Other Stories* (SS/P2)

1997: *Black Coffee* (play novelization by Charles Osborne)

1997: *The Harlequin Tea Set and Other Stories* (U.K.: *While the Light Lasts and Other Stories*) (SS/P1)

2014: *The Monogram Murders* (by Sophie Hannah)

2016: *Closed Casket* (by Sophie Hannah)

2018: *The Mystery of Three Quarters* (by Sophie Hannah)

MISS MARPLE

1930: *The Murder at the Vicarage*

1932: *The Thirteen Problems* (U.S.: *The Tuesday Club Murders*) (SS/M13)

1939: *The Regatta Mystery and Other Stories* (US: SS/P5, M1)

1942: *The Body in the Library*

1942: *The Moving Finger*

1950: *A Murder is Announced*

1950: *Three Blind Mice and Other Stories* (U.S. only, SS/P3, M4)

1952: *They Do It With Mirrors* (U.S.: *Murder With Mirrors*)

1953: *A Pocket Full of Rye*

1957: *4.50 From Paddington* (U.S.: *What Mrs. McGillicuddy Saw!*)

1960: *The Adventure of the Christmas Pudding* (SS/P5, M1)

1961: *Double Sin and Other Stories* (U.S. only, SS/P4, M2)

1962: *The Mirror Crack'd from Side to Side* (U.S.: *The Mirror Crack'd*)

1964: *A Caribbean Mystery*

1965: *At Bertram's Hotel*

1971: *Nemesis*
1976: *Sleeping Murder*
1979: *Miss Marple's Final Cases and Two Other Stories* (SS/M6)

TOMMY AND TUPPENCE BERESFORD

1922: *The Secret Adversary*
1929: *Partners in Crime (SS/TT17)*
1941: *N or M?*
1968: *By the Pricking of My Thumbs*
1973: *Postern of Fate*

ARIADNE OLIVER

1934: *Parker Pyne Investigates* (U.S.: *Mr. Parker Pyne, Detective*) (SS/O1)
1936: *Cards on the Table* (w/P/B/R)
1952: *Mrs. McGinty's Dead* (w/P)
1956: *Dead Man's Folly* (w/P)
1961: *The Pale Horse*
1966: *Third Girl (w/P)*
1969: *Hallowe'en Party (w/P)*
1972: *Elephants Can Remember (w/P)*

SUPERINTENDENT BATTLE

1925: *The Secret of Chimneys*
1929: *The Seven Dials Mystery*
1936: *Cards On the Table* (w/P/O/R)
1939: *Murder Is Easy* (U.S.: *Easy to Kill*)
1944: *Towards Zero*

COLONEL RACE

1924: *The Man in the Brown Suit*
1936: *Cards On the Table* (w/P/O/B)
1937: *Death on the Nile* (w/P)
1945: *Sparkling Cyanide* (U.S.: *Remembered Death*)

OTHER BOOKS

1924: *The Road of Dreams* (poetry)
1930: *The Mysterious Mr. Quin*
1931: *The Sittaford Mystery* (U.S.: *Murder at Hazelmoore*)
1931: *The Floating Admiral* (collaboration)

1933: *The Hound of Death and Other Stories* (U.K. only)
1934: *The Listerdale Mystery* (U.K. only)
1934: *Why Didn't They Ask Evans?* (U.S.: *The Boomerang Clue*)
1939: *Ten Little Niggers* (U.S.: *And Then There Were None*)
1944: *Death Comes As the End*
1949: *Crooked House*
1951: *They Came to Baghdad*
1954: *Destination Unknown* (U.S.: *So Many Steps to Death*)
1958: *Ordeal by Innocence*
1967: *Endless Night*
1970: *Passenger to Frankfurt*
1971: *The Golden Ball and Other Stories*
1973: *Poems*
1977: *An Autobiography*

AS MARY WESTMACOTT
1930: *Giant's Bread*
1934: *Unfinished Portrait*
1944: *Absent in the Spring*
1948: *The Rose and the Yew Tree*
1952: *A Daughter's a Daughter*
1956: *The Burden*

AS AGATHA CHRISTIE MALLOWAN
1946: *Come, Tell Me How You Live* (memoir)
1965: *Star Over Bethlehem* (children's poems, SS)

Bibliography

Exceptionally noteworthy books for Christie fans are **highlighted in bold**.

Adams, Cecil. "What do 'drawn and quartered' and 'keelhauling' mean?" *The Straight Dope*, www.straightdope.com/columns/read/1049/what-do-drawn-and-quartered-and-keelhauling-mean, accessed Sept. 19, 2012.

Ager, Stanley and Fiona St. Aubyn. *The Butler's Guide*. New York: Clarkson Potter, 1980.

Anonymous. *The Illustrated Life and Career of William Palmer of Rugeley*. London: Ward and Lock, 1856.

Apperson, George Latimer and Martin H. Manser. *Dictionary of Proverbs*. Hertfordshire: Wordsworth Editions Ltd., 2006.

Barnard, Robert. *A Talent to Deceive: An Appreciation of Agatha Christie*. New York: Dodd, Mead & Co., 1980. Barnard draws on his experience as a mystery writer — whose books I highly recommend — to discuss aspects of Christie's life and works: her thrillers, her Miss Marple books, the way she surprises the reader and her disappearance. This takes up only 126 pages. The remaining 88 pages are devoted to a substantial Christie bibliography.

Benstock, Bernard, editor. *Essays on Detective Fiction*. London: The Macmillan Press, 1983.

Buckingham, John. *Bitter Nemesis: The Intimate History of Strychnine*. New York: CRC Press, 2008.

Bunson, Matthew. *The Complete Christie: An Agatha Christie Encyclopedia*. New York: Pocket Books, 2000. The best of several books that have gathered information about Christie's works, characters, movies, plays and TV shows. Also contains a long suggested reading list.

Cade, Jared. *Agatha Christie and the Eleven Missing Days*. London: Peter Owen, 1998. Christie's grandson Mathew Prichard understandably railed against the book and its author. Cade draws on the memories of a different branch of the Christie family. Its conclusion that Christie planned her disappearance as a way of getting back at her husband, Archie, deviates from the official history. Laura Thompson responds to this book in her biography.

Christie, Agatha. *An Autobiography*. New York: Bantam Books, 1977. The author's story in her own words. What she leaves out can be just as revealing as what she discusses.

—————————. Mathew Prichard, ed. ***The Grand Tour: Around the World With the Queen of Mystery*. New York: HarperCollins, 2012.** In 1922, Christie accompanied her husband, Archie, on a world tour as part of his job promoting the British Empire Exhibition. This collection of letters, photographs and memorabilia, expertly edited by her grandson, reveals Christie as a delightful traveling companion with a sharp eye for character.

—————————. ***Hercule Poirot's Casebook*. New York: Dodd, Mead & Co., 1989.** Although out of print, this compilation is an inexpensive way to collect all of the Poirot short stories.

—————————. ***Miss Marple: The Complete Short Stories*. New York: G.P. Putnam's Sons, 1985.** This volume is a worthy companion to *Hercule Poirot's Casebook*. Together, they make available 80 of Christie's short stories.

Cray, Ed. *The Erotic Muse: American Bawdy Songs*. Champaign, Ill.: University of Illinois Press, 1999.

Curran, John. *Agatha Christie's Secret Notebooks*. New York: Harper, 2009, and *Agatha Christie: Murder in the Making*. New York: Harper, 2011. Curran draws on Christie's notebooks in the family's archives to reveal insights into her working methods. Mystery writers in particular should find them fascinating as will fans who delight in peeking behind the scenes.

Devlin, Vivien. "Murder on the English Riviera." *TravelLady Magazine*. www.travellady.com/Issues/July07/ 4323MurderRiviera. html, accessed Feb. 1, 2013. A travel writer visits the Agatha Christie Festival in Torquay in 2007.

Framer, John Stephen and William Ernest Henley. *A Dictionary of Slang and Colloquial English: Abridged from the Seven-Volume Work*. London: G. Routledge & Sons, Ltd., 1905.

Fitzgibbon, Russell H. *The Agatha Christie Companion*. Bowling Green, Ky.: Bowling Green State University Popular Press, 1980.

Gill, Gillian. *Agatha Christie: The Woman and Her Mysteries*. New York: The Free Press, 1990. This unauthorized biography discusses the Christie as revealed through her writings, particularly as Mary Westmacott. An interesting alternative take.

Green, Jonathon. *Cassell's Dictionary of Slang, 2nd Edition*. London: Orion Publishing Group, 2005.

Hack, Richard. *Duchess of Death: The Unauthorized Biography of Agatha Christie*. Beverly Hills, Calif.: Phoenix Books, 2009. Included only as a warning. Covers the same ground as the more thorough official biographies, and the boast on the cover that the book was based on "over 5,000 unpublished letters, notes and documents" is a reference to the papers of Christie's agent, not the Christie archives.

Hurdle, Judith. *The Getaway Guide to Agatha Christie's England*. Oakland, Calif.: RDR Books, 1999.

International Program for Chemical Safety. "Strychnine." www.

inchem.org/documents/pims/chemical/pim507.htm. Accessed Nov. 13, 2012.

Iwu, Maurice M. *Handbook of African Medicinal Plants.* Boca Raton, Fla.: CRC Press, 1993.

Jackson, Graham and Geoffrey Diggle. "Strychnine-containing Tonics." *British Medical Journal,* April 21, 1973. www.ncbi.nlm.nih. gov/pmc/articles/PMC1589243/pdf/brmedj01553-0068c.pdf, accessed Nov. 13, 2012.

Lord K. "Soviet Tobacco Art." *Dieselpunks.* www.dieselpunks. org/profiles/blogs/soviet-tobacco-art, accessed Feb. 1, 2013.

Macaskill, Hilary. *Agatha Christie at Home.* London: Frances Lincoln Ltd., 2009. Coffee-table book about Greenway, Christie's home on the River Dart in her native Devon. It also looks at the settings — fields, farms, coastal towns, churches, etc. — she used in her books. Ideal for literary tourists.

McGarry, Ronald C. and Pamela McGarry. "Please Pass the Strychnine: The Art of Victorian Pharmacy." *CMAJ,* www.cmaj.ca/content/161/12/1556.full, accessed March 5, 2013.

Morgan, Janet. *Agatha Christie.* New York: Knopf, 1985. The standard biography, written with the family's cooperation.

Most, Glenn W. and William W. Stowe, eds. *The Poetics of Murder.* New York: Harcourt Brace Jovanovich, 1983.

Osborne, Charles. *The Life and Crimes of Agatha Christie.* New York: St. Martin's Press, 1999. A biography told through Christie's publications. Osborne would go on to novelize three Christie plays: *Black Coffee, The Unexpected Guest* and *Spider's Web.*

Panda, H. *Herbs Cultivation and Medicinal Uses.* Delhi, India: National Institute of Industrial Research, 2000.

Pendergast, Bruce. *Everyman's Guide to the Mysteries of Agatha Christie.* New York: Trafford Publishing, 2006.

Powell, Margaret. *Servants' Hall.* New York: St. Martin's Press, 1979.

Riley, Dick and Pam McAllister. *The New Bedside, Bathtub & Armchair Companion to Agatha Christie.* New York: Ungar Publishing Co., 1986.

Robb, George. *British Culture and the First World War.* New York: Palgrave, 2002.

Room, Adrian. *Brewer's Dictionary of Phrase and Fable.* 16th edition. New York: HarperResource, 1999.

Rosen, Daniel. *Dope: A History of Performance Enhancement in Sports from the Nineteenth Century to Today.* Westport, Conn.: Praeger Publishers, 2008.

Rowse, A.L. *Memories and Glimpses.* London: Metheun Publishing Ltd., 1986. Contains a chapter on the Oxford professor's friendship with Christie.

Sanders, Dennis and Len Lovallo. *The Agatha Christie Companion: The Complete Guide to Agatha Christie's Life and Work.* New York: Avenel, 1984.

Sova, Dawn B. *Agatha Christie A to Z.* New York: Facts on File, 1996.

Thompson, Laura. *Agatha Christie: An English Mystery.* London: Headline, 2007. Worthwhile companion to the Morgan biography. Written with the family's cooperation. Thompson uses fictional techniques to tell her story and weaves excerpts from Christie's books to buttress her suppositions. Also spends several pages rebutting Jared Cade's book. Highly recommended.

Toye, Randall. *The Agatha Christie Who's Who.* New York: Holt, Rinehart and Winston, 1980.

Turnbull, Malcolm J. *Victims or Villains: Jewish Images in Classic English Detective Fiction.* Bowling Green, Ky.: Bowling Green State University Popular Press, 1998.

Winn, Dilys. *Murder Ink / Murderess Ink.* New York: Workman Publishing, various editions. Idiosyncratic, opinionated, personal, and always enjoyable, these books discuss the mystery genre from its founding fathers (Poe, Collins, Conan Doyle), its nurturing mothers (Christie, Sayers, Allingham) and its later practitioners. There are three editions: the doorstop-sized *Murder Ink* (522 pages, 1977); the shorter revised version (398 pages, 1984) and *Murderess Ink*, which focuses on women in mysteries (304 pages, 1979). There is some overlap among the *Murder Inks*, but given the price of used books, who cares?

Wynne, Nancy Blue. *An Agatha Christie Chronology*. New York: Ace Books, 1976.

WEBSITES

Cambridge Dictionaries Online. www.dictionary.cambridge.org/

Lewis, Dave. Dr. William Palmer. www.williampalmer.co.uk/.

The Infamous Rugeley Poisoner William Palmer. www.palmer.staffscc.net/.

Evans, Phil. Old U.K. photos. www.oldukphotos.com/index.htm

Martin, Gary. The Phrase Finder. www.phrases.org.uk/index.html

Merriam-Webster Dictionary. www.merriam-webster.com/dictionary/text

Oxford Dictionaries. www.oxforddictionaries.com/english/

Watton, Cherish. The Women's Land Army. www.womenslandarmy.co.uk/Archives.html

Wikipedia. www.wikipedia.com

Acknowledgements

My trip to Styles Court could not have been accomplished without the help of many people.

* The staff at the Hershey Public Library, particularly Denise Phillips in the interlibrary loan department.

* My children, Lily and Matthew, whose questions about *Styles* guided my annotations.

* My wife, Teresa, who provided support, asked questions, and edited the manuscript several times without complaint (except about my mistakes).

* And, of course, Agatha Christie, without whom none of this would have been possible.

About the Authors

Over a long, prolific career, AGATHA CHRISTIE (1890-1976) created two iconic characters in the mystery genre — Hercule Poirot and Miss Jane Marple — and wrote eighty crime novels and collections of stories, nineteen plays, six novels written as Mary Westmacott, an autobiography and a memoir, *Come, Tell Me How You Live*. Her play, *The Mousetrap*, is the longest-running play in history.

BILL PESCHEL is a former journalist who shares a Pulitzer Prize with the staff of The Patriot-News in Harrisburg, Pa. He also is a mystery fan who has run the Wimsey Annotations at www.planetpeschel.com for nearly two decades. He is the author of *Writers Gone Wild* (Penguin). Through Peschel Press he publishes Sherlock parodies and pastiches in the 223B Casebook Series and annotated editions of novels by Dorothy L. Sayers and Agatha Christie. He lives with his family, dog and two cats in Hershey, where the air really smells like chocolate. Visit Bill at Peschel Press (www.peschelpress.com) and sign up for his newsletter. Email Bill at Peschel@peschelpress.com

The Complete, Annotated Series

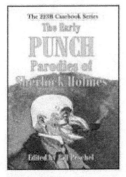

CPSIA information can be obtained
at www.ICGtesting.com
Printed in the USA
LVHW032340151220
674261LV00002B/138